Majuba House

The House of Majesty

Joyce Sidey Brogdon

Majuba House
by Joyce Sidey Brogdon

Printed in the United States of America

Library of Congress Control Number: 2002117692
ISBN 1-591604-73-7

Unless otherwise indicated, Bible quotations are taken from the King James Version.

Quotations from the Church of England Book of Common Prayer, 1622.

The stories related in this book are true, but some of the names have been changed to protect the privacy of the people mentioned.

Xulon Press
10640 Main Street
Suite 204
Fairfax, VA 22030
(703) 934-4411
XulonPress.com

To order additional copies, call 1-866-909-BOOK (2665).

Dedication

To my Heavenly Father, in whose house I shall dwell eternally

AND

To my life partner Bill, who daily makes our home on earth
a sanctuary filled with love and joy.

Acknowledgments

With special thanks

To Walter Wilson, a school chum who helped jog my faltering memory, and to Jean, his wife, who resurrected the old house so beautifully.

To Betty, Reggie, Eric, Phyllis, and Christopher, for providing forgotten photographs and encouragement. To June, Bob, John, Maureen, Frank, and Monica for cheering me on.

To the prayer warriors; my sisters in Christ, Marilyn DeVries, Pattie Eaton, Jean Blanchard, Carole Brown, Nancy Brammer, Jackie Luckenbill and Toni Wright, whose faithful prayers and love sustained me and kept the manuscript moving along.

To Alex Slaunwhite, for drawing the beautiful map.

To Ron Howard, for scanning and enhancing the photographs.

To Elizabeth Holt, Editor of Wenhaston Word, Richard Havard, and Peter Lewis for their timely contributions.

To all the people who have allowed me to use their names and their memories in this book. There are a few fictional names included, when such permission was unavailable.

To Jim and Karen Kochenburger and the Xulon Press crew for their excellent support.

To Bill, the one who has navigated the book through some dangerous shoals, my husband, best friend, long-suffering editor, prayer partner and encourager: God Bless Your House!

Table of Contents

Street Map of Wenhaston

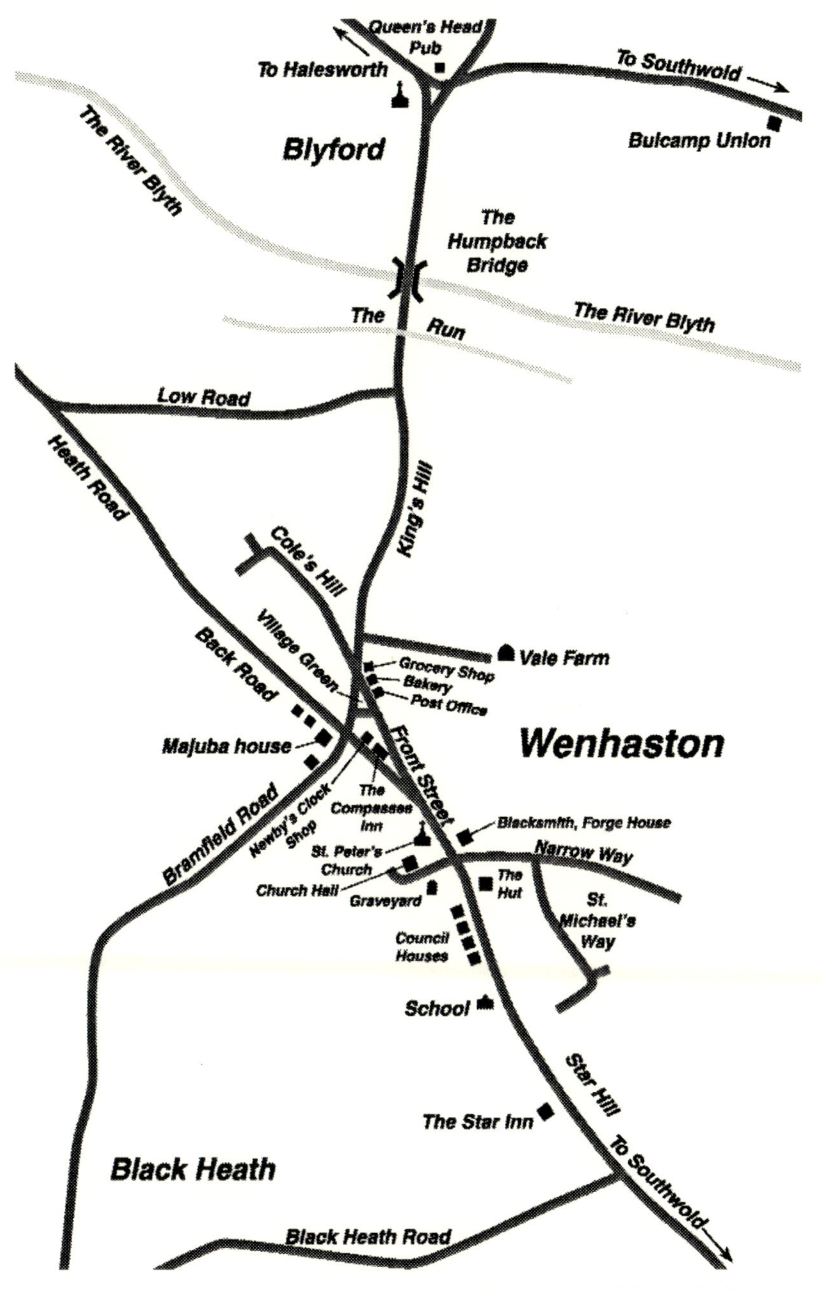

ALEX SLAUNWHITE,SIMPSONVILLE, S.C.

Village Emblem

Introduction

"Our birth is but a sleep and a forgetting;
The soul that rises with us, our life's star,
Hath had elsewhere its setting,
And cometh from afar;
Not in entire forgetfulness,
And not in utter nakedness,
But trailing clouds of glory do we come
From God, who is our home.

Wordsworth

The Wenhaston school bell rang at half past three, and at the sound of it we primary students drew a collective breath, shuffled our feet, cleared our throats and looked for a sign from Miss Danford at the front of the room. Each of us carefully avoided overdoing the stirring; to do so would mean being left behind with our teacher until the older classes were dismissed a half hour later. Once cautiously beyond the hallway, through the playground and onto the road, we were free to raise our voices, which we did with gusto. Our pent-up energy gave wings to our feet. We ran and skipped in bunches, calling to each other as first one and then another peeled off for home.

We stampeded down the pavement past the council houses and shouted goodbye to Barbara English and her brother Ivan, Ruth Napthine and Margaret Chapman. On we went, chattering, past the cemetery, the big brick wall and then the church. At the divide in the road that separated the Front and Back Roads of the village, the Front Road group swung right and departed noisily. The rest of us, a rag-tag group, turned left. Walter Wilson, Gladys Spencer, Connie Mayhew, Clara Block and I took the Back Road past the back of the Compass Inn and the Newbys' house and clock shop.

Sometimes, if we thought no one was watching, one of us would dare to knock on the Newbys' house door, and the rest would run like the dickens in case he caught us as we passed his shop. I was now within a few yards of my house. Walter peeled off to the right, skirting the Village Green to Ivy Cottage at the top of Coles

Hill. The others would travel further down Back Road, down a hill and past the windmill to their homes.

So I arrived at the garden gate, totally out of breath, waved cheerio to the others and scanned the windows, looking for the familiar face that watched for me. Goofie the dog had heard the noisy group coming long before we reached the Newbys' house. As I neared the gate, he jumped and wagged impatiently, waiting for me to undo the latch so he could greet me with his own brand of joy and exuberance, to welcome me home to Majuba House.

I was six years old when I first saw Majuba House, and for the next ten years it was my adoptive home. I was sent there as a foster child by Dr. Barnardo's orphanage, where I had been a ward since the age of two. I was born Joyce Muriel Florence Sidey, on 30 July 1928. When my father abandoned the family in 1929, my mother was left to cope with five small children with hardly any means of support. She eventually put three of us into Dr. Barnardo's Home For Children, a well-established and respected institution that took in orphaned children from all walks of life and under a variety of circumstances. At age two I was placed in one of the orphanage's many cottages in Barkingside in Essex, just outside London. At age three I was moved to another cottage at Syndal, Hove, moved back to Barkingside the next year, and from there, at age four, was boarded out to a foster home in the small Suffolk village of Peasenhall.

I lived in Peasenhall with a woman who must have been in her early thirties. According to the records, her name was Miss Howard. I've never been sure whether she was married to a man who was on an overseas assignment or whether she was simply engaged to be married. At any rate, she lived alone, and the postman was always bringing letters and strange little packets to our door. Interesting things, funny looking shoes, beads and oriental jewelry arrived by post at various intervals.

I have very few memories of the woman who cared for me during the year and a half I stayed with her. But certain incidents remain. I remember the school she took me to each day, and how she waited at the garden gate for me to return in the afternoon. We lived in a duplex house quite near the school. The lady next door was a frequent visitor. She "read" tea leaves, interpreting the patterns left in the bottom of the cup. She read people's palms too, and had many superstitious sayings for things that happened. If you dropped a knife it meant a man was either coming to visit or leaving, depending on which way the handle pointed. A fork was a woman and a spoon a child. Another lady used to come round and cut my hair and give me cod liver oil mixed with treacle, a ghastly concoction.

I was a fidget in school, always flailing about, and one day fell backward onto the huge steam radiator and gashed open the back of my scalp. I was taken to surgery to have stitches and some sort of packs and bandages applied. However, I must have healed quickly, and my hair grew back eventually. At least I had no more worries about it. My one and only problem from the accident seemed to be a bad memory or just plain disobedience; I don't know which.

There was a little ditch that ran along the street near the schoolhouse. Some of the children floated paper boats in it and pushed them along with sticks. Every day my guardian would tell me not to walk in the water, but every day I did. She was always waiting at the gate for me, and the moment I saw her I would remember that I wasn't supposed to get my shoes wet. She punished me by making me stay in my room without any tea, but still I couldn't remember the next day.

One day while I was being punished, and howling my head off, she came in to tell me that I was going to a new school and a new home. Perhaps she'd consulted with her tea-leaf reading neighbour and come to that conclusion. It turned out to be true, for shortly afterwards she packed a small suitcase for me and I was off with a strange lady I'd never met before. That was how I began the journey to Wenhaston to live with the Saunders family at Majuba House.

This book, then, is an account of that period of my life that began in the village of Wenhaston, in 1935. It begins there with a first impression of a unique house, continues through the happy, innocent years of childhood, through the short-lived tumultuous teens, and into an abrupt, too early adulthood that was thrust upon all of us who were children in Britain during World War II. It is a story that has begged my soul to be told since I was ten years old, and has nibbled at the edges of my brain for over half a century.

My prayer, first of all, is that this true story will bless those who read it. I pray that it will serve to give and preserve golden nuggets of enjoyment for many. I also pray that where there remains for any who know me a shred of bitter regret, it will be forever discarded, leaving for future generations a clean foundation on which to build.

Naturally, Majuba house represents more than just an era in my own life. It is a symbol of the way life should be, and indeed once was, before the world went mad. More than that, it exemplifies a certain dignity, grace and strength that has endured silently through both sunshine and shadow. Though the world has changed around it, the house has stood firm. It and the ideals its family stood for, have weathered joy, sickness, death, war and societal changes. Most of all, it has exposed for me a deeper footing whose elements go far beyond bricks and mortar.

By God's own design, I realized belatedly, I was placed at Majuba House. Finally, in these last years, I have come to grips with the fact that God has guided me my whole life long. None of the joy, laughter, struggles, pain, or shame were accidental. God prepared me in His own way for His own purposes. He made my fingerprints uniquely mine and designed a blueprint for every other aspect of my being.

In fashioning my life on earth, God has shown me the pathway to Heaven through Christ Jesus, our Saviour. His faithfulness blesses me and daily nourishes my soul. Jesus once said, "In my Father's house are many mansions." This implies multiple dwellings individually created for each of His children. He also said "I go to prepare a place for you." How wonderful it is to think on these statements and rest on His promises; to know that His plan for my future is secure. To know that the dwelling place He is preparing will last throughout eternity. To know that the wonderful dwelling that He prepared for me as a child was but a foretaste of my eternal dwelling. To know, too, that some day, with joy, He personally will welcome me to His original House of Majesty.

2002 Joyce Brogdon

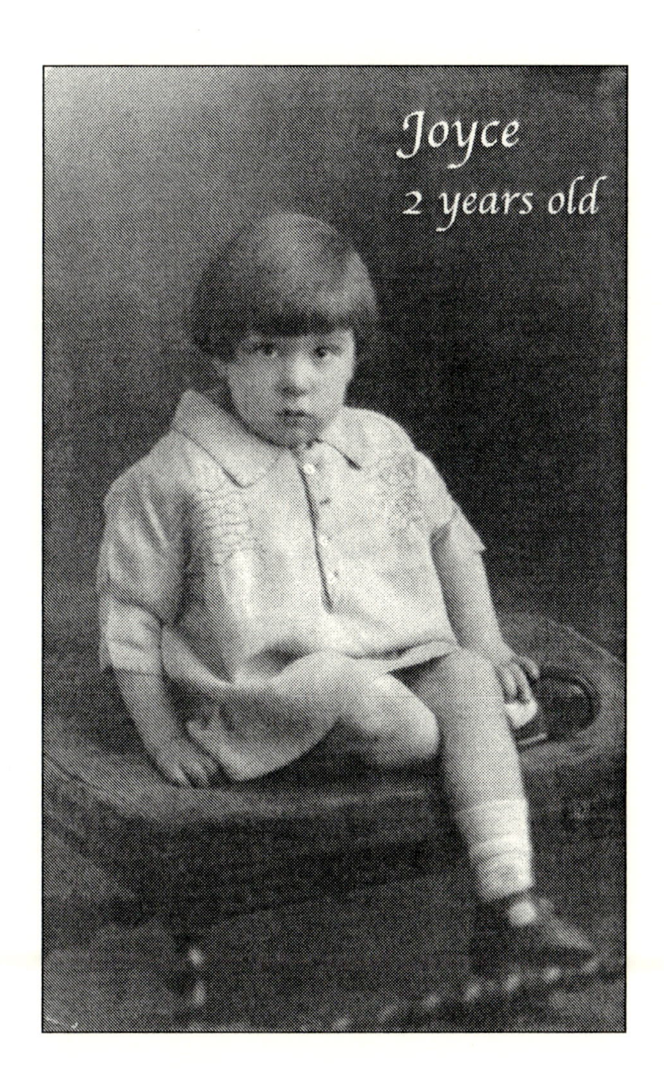
Joyce
2 years old

Chapter 1

Coming to Majuba, House of Majesty

And he who gives a child a treat
Makes joy-bells ring in Heaven's street,
And he who gives a child a home
Builds palaces in Kingdom come.

Masefield

There was always something mystically ambiguous about the old house. It exuded a certain ethereal charm that welcomed some, but repelled others. There was at once a radiant sense of staunch character and nobility that emanated from its well-bred lines, but yet a tinge of darkness, of shadows, that lay partially hidden behind its stately walls.

Majuba House, with its high windows, tiled roof, tall chimneys and dark facade, frequently seemed a rather forbidding structure. Truly, at times when it sat in gloomy shadow on a winter's day with no sunlight to warm it, there was a certain quiet melancholy that clung like moss to its swarthy rubineous frontage. I saw it many times over the years when the red brick looked gray and the windows seemed withdrawn and hooded. I saw it also in the rain when the windswept brick looked forlorn and lonely. I saw it enshrouded with fog when the mist gave it a tinge of foreboding and a touch of mystery. Indeed the house reflected the moods and shades of character that weather and outside circumstances frequently heaped upon it.

But the very first time I saw it, the sun winked on the windows and bounced off the polished brass fixtures invitingly. To my young and eager eyes, it looked as regal and majestic as its name implied. There were no dark surfaces or shadows. A bright radiance emanated from its walls and giddy splashes of yellow sunbeams shone on its warm and inviting expanse. The house, for all its dignity, had a strange and imposing brick front. Though all one piece, it was divided by totally different appearances that melded beautifully. One half of the house was living quarters, staid, solid, and gracious, while the other half was a shop: fanciful, lively and modern.

Distinguished from the house proper, the shop was an impressive one for a small Suffolk village. It was the largest of four similar shops in Wenhaston including the Post Office, not counting the watchmaker, the baker, the cobbler or the blacksmith. In my opinion there was not another village shop that could hold a candle to it in all of East Anglia, perhaps in all of England.

On the left hand, or "living side" of the house, there was a large imposing door with a heavy, ornate brass door-knocker, that was polished weekly to a fare-the-well. Below it, about in the middle of the door, was a gleaming brass letterbox, with the house name inscribed in block letters just above it: "MAJUBA HOUSE." This was the grand entrance to the house itself, seldom used by anyone except for the twice daily visits by the postman, the occasional Sunday afternoon guest, and those who tended the garden. A black iron boot scraper to the right of the doorstep and a wide doormat bespoke the importance of the entry hall within. No one dared enter without first wiping every speck of soil from his soles, as I learned on my arrival that first day.

I never learned her name, the lady from Dr. Barnardo's orphanage who brought me that day. She instructed me to call her "Miss," to hold her hand, to sit quietly, and to speak only when spoken to. It was a tall order for a noisy, squirmy chatter-box like me. This was my first train ride and was very exciting. And though I managed to obey most of the time, she scolded me roundly when I stuck my head out of the train window to feel the air on my face. I got a cinder in my eye as well, which hurt a lot and smarted for ages after we'd managed to remove it with the corner of my clean white hanky. We made the rest of the journey by train and then by bus in almost total silence.

As we walked away from the train at Halesworth, my escort suddenly became a bit more talkative. She instructed me on using the toilet at the train station by placing a penny in the slot and sliding the bolt. That was great fun, I thought. It was my first experience with an automatic toilet, so it took three attempts to get the desired "whoosh" when I pulled the chain. She then supervised my hand washing and drying process on the big roller towel.

"Grasp it firmly with both hands and pull until you find a dry spot," she said, her voice echoing hollowly against the white tiled walls.

We could hear the engine throbbing as we walked across the station yard to the big, red double-decker bus. As we climbed aboard, the conductor took my case and placed it with others in a little alcove beneath the staircase.

"There yer are youn' lady," he said with a smile, "It'll be safe fer yer thar," and he doffed his cap as he turned away to help a lady carrying a huge shopping basket. Others were hurrying with cases and shopping bags, chatting and laughing, and some clattered up the steps noisily. My "Miss" wouldn't let me sit on the upper deck, though I did pluck up the courage to ask. She said something about the swaying making me sick. But she did allow me to sit on the window side of the seat, where I pressed my nose flat against the glass.

The bus shuddered and roared noisily down the hill from the train station, past a row of tiny cottages on the main road and into the Blyford Road. I loved watching the countryside flash by: the thatched roofed cottages, the farmhouses, and the animals in the open meadows. I delighted to watch passengers as they alighted at every stop along the way, wondering who they were and where they were going with their shopping bags and satchels over their arms.

After drawing up outside the *Queens Head* pub at Blyford to discharge more passengers, the bus took a swing round the triangle of grass that had a multi-armed signpost in the middle. "Halesworth 2 1/2" and "Holton 2" it said, pointing in the direction from which we had just come. "Blythburgh 1/2" and "Southwold 6 1/2" it said, pointing further down the road we were traveling. "Wenhaston 1" pointed to the right. The bus made a sharp half-circle to the right, swaying and rattling down the narrow tree-lined road toward the river and Wenhaston. At the river, I experienced for the first of countless times to come, the stomach-turning thrill of riding over the "humpback bridge." Though surely our fellow passengers had made this journey dozens of times, I heard a collective whoop, loudest from the upper deck, as the bus crested the steep and narrow bridge, and teetered for a brief second before plunging awkwardly down the other side.

Sign Post
Blyford

After a few more stops, we alighted at the *Compasses Inn* in the village of Wenhaston. My escort picked up my suitcase from the alcove, and once outside, handed it to me to carry. Then she took my other hand firmly in hers, straightened her hat, and began giving me my final instructions. She told me as we walked that the name of my new family was Saunders. I was to begin to act ladylike and to "mind my Ps and Qs." I had not the slightest idea how to act ladylike, and wondered whether she meant I was to curtsy. I'd already learned how to do that; we practiced doing curtsies in our class at Peasenhall. I decided to wait and see what she did, then I could show off my own abilities.

As we approached the house, her last minute warnings were most explicit, particularly her instructions for wiping my feet, blowing my nose only on my handkerchief, and remembering to say "please" and "thank you." So it was with some trepidation and heady expectation that I was ushered in through the front door of Majuba House on that spring day in 1935.

The massive front door was hemmed in by a low wall that

enclosed a small garden with a cobbled walkway. The wrought iron gate was kept shut, but the hinges were well oiled and didn't squeak. Mrs. Saunders saw to things like that. Being a tidy sort, she quickly corrected things that rusted or showed signs of wear.

The little garden softened the austerity of the imposing frontage. Roses bloomed there in utter profusion, spilling over the wall, their petals often blowing across the path and through the gate. It was Mrs. Saunders' private garden that she tended herself. There was nearly always a bowl of roses on the dining table, and she saved the loose petals and dried them, to be put in jars and sachets throughout the house. Though I didn't have much to do with the care and arranging of the flowers, I did enjoy the gardening tasks that had any connection with their care.

My most important job was to run into the street to scoop up steaming manure from the dairy cart horse, on those days when we were fortunate enough to have a pile deposited for us. Every day we saved the tea leaves and the dishwater to nourish the "tea garden." It was often my job to get these items from the scullery, through the Front room and the hallway, and maneuver unlocking the front door to distribute them without spilling any on the way. The roses thrived on the exemplary care they received.

In contrast to the heavy house door, the door to the right was a glass paned shop entrance. It had a dark green window shade that was rolled up when the shop was open, and was pulled down promptly at six o'clock, just as the BBC time "pips" were sounding on the wireless for the daily news broadcast. It was pulled down on weekdays only for funeral processions passing by, and on Wednesday afternoons during "half closing."

A bell on a jiggly metal bar above the door tinkled merrily whenever customers came in or went out. The large glass display window to the right of the door had bolts of fabric that stood at rakish angles with little hand-lettered cards propped against them, listing their prices. There was a large sign above the window:

G. A. SAUNDERS
GROCER AND DRAPER

Between the shop entrance and the display window, in a narrow space, hung a green metal cigarette machine with a sign "Woodbines and Cadets, five for tuppence." This was a fascinating contraption that worked most of the time, but often swallowed coins in the middle of the night, causing much banging and swearing. Often Mrs. Saunders would put on a dressing gown and slip down the stairway into the shop to help put the matter right, if she recognized the voices. Mostly it would be some lads staggering home from the pub, whose pennies were a little bent.

The shop was also enclosed by a low wall, but without flowers or a gate. Customers kicked up a dust in dry weather as they came in and propped their bicycles against the wall. The women with their babies in prams shopped in the early morning hours. Later in the morning and early afternoon the older women came with their string bags and little purses clutched in their hands. Mrs. Saunders had two wooden chairs with round seats in the shop. In the winter she lighted a paraffin heater, and the older women would exchange bits of gossip while they warmed themselves and waited for their half-pound of flour, rice, or sugar to be weighed.

The children on their way home from school in the afternoon at four o'clock might stop for a ha'penny bag of sweets, an enormous treat. They would ponder their options with studied care—licorice allsorts, acid drops, toffees or a peppermint stick. For tuppence, we could buy a chocolate bar—a plain Cadbury's milk chocolate or one with nuts and raisins. There were Nestles Kit-Kat bars and Rollos with toffee centres, and there were packets of Ju-Jubes and sticks of black or red licorice. It was hard to choose.

Only a few motorcars came through the village in the 1930s, and I only knew three people who owned one when I arrived: the District Nurse, the Philbin sisters who were the Girl Guide leaders, and the headmaster of the village school, Mr. Sangster. The usual modes of transportation, outside of the daily Halesworth and Southwold bus service, were bicycles or our own two feet. People carried great loads of goods by bicycle and invented many systems for carrying bulky objects. Nearly everyone had large permanent saddlebags attached to their bicycle seats, and the women had additional carrier baskets on their handlebars. Those that didn't have saddlebags strapped their boxes and parcels to the carrier frame with leather belts or string, or simply carried large, awkward items under one arm.

It never seemed strange to see someone carrying a huge wash-basket, a bucket or even a window pane under one arm and steering the bike with the other. Sometimes people needed to carry objects with both hands. In those instances, one had to learn to balance and steer without using the handlebars, just well-placed knees to keep the front frame steady. I much admired this feat. I practiced and achieved it by my eighth birthday.

Sometimes men on their way home in the evenings would linger outside the Saunders shop to talk, leaning against the wall, knocking out the old tobacco from their wooden pipes, or sharing a "fag" while speculating on the weather or farming conditions. Agriculture and farming were the main occupations not only for Wenhaston, but for all of the surrounding Suffolk villages.

The men who worked the farms and tilled the fields were a tightly knit brotherhood in bib overalls and hobnailed boots. No matter the weather, the work had to be done. It was a common sight toward evening to see the men on their bicycles heading home with their tea flasks strapped across their chests, a cigarette drooping from one corner of their mouths, calling to a mate that pleasant and comforting Suffolk phrase: "Mind 'ow you go then, 'ol fella."

Majuba House stood on a corner where two roads came together to form a rather awkward triangle. The smaller road, simply called "Back Road" ran past the front of the shop, and the larger, more heavily traveled Bramfield Road ran past the side of the house. It created a busy junction, and was a dangerous corner for bicyclists and pedestrians alike. The low wall from the front of the house curved and continued round the corner and down to the small garden gate at the end of the property, causing some visibility problems.

To add to the difficulty, the Wenhaston Council had insisted a high restraining fence be attached above the wall to keep the Saunders' large Alsatian puppy from jumping over it and causing injury to unsuspecting bicyclists. To comply with the ordinance, the Saunders had built a framework six feet high on the inside and above the brick wall and covered it with wire netting. It worked well in keeping the dog in, but made the view round the corner even more limited.

The greatest hazard was that the young dog "Wolf" loved people, and especially people on bicycles who rang their bells as they whizzed round the corner and up the Bramfield Road. Whenever Wolf was outside, he thought it fair game to bark at every moving head and chase it excitedly all the way to the garden gate at the end of the property. Most of the natives, and especially the younger boys, weren't bothered by Wolf's exuberance, often exciting him further by running a stick over the wire netting as they rode by. But it was a shock to strangers to be greeted in this manner. Many a mishap occurred and fists were raised in anger over the Saunders' "bugger of a dog."

Wolf had almost outgrown his wild days by the time we met. Though he still threw himself at the wire netting occasionally, barking loudly, he was much more restrained most of the time. For me, six years old, it was love at first sight. His thick sandy fur had distinctive black markings down his back and across his handsome face. For his size, he was a remarkably gentle and affectionate dog. Without meaning to, he could overwhelm me with affection, licking my ears and bowling me over unceremoniously as we played.

It was at our first meeting that Wolf's name changed forever to "Goofie." It happened because of my slight speech impediment and because the Saunders, in their efforts to make me feel at home, adopted my name for him immediately. For the next few years, though he was always restricted to the house and its two yards, Goofie was my constant home companion and playmate. He went with me to the garden gate each school day morning to see me off, and watched, tail wagging and barking a greeting, upon my return. But though I became an important part of his daily routine, his first loyalty was always to Mr. Saunders, his true master. He was never far from his side.

On that first day, his ears pricked up and his brown eyes greeted me the moment I stepped in the room. I must have flinched as he came over to inspect me because Mr. Saunders called him to sit, which he did obediently. Then "Dadda," as I came to call him, guided my hand to stroke his ear in that special spot that Goofie liked best. The dog touched me with his black, wet nose and sniffed my hair and round my neck, licking me with his great long tongue, inviting me to scratch behind his ear some more. In fact, Goofie never tired of having his ears scratched, and it was always a toss-up which of us would give up first.

Goofie's special place was beside his master's chair in the kitchen. His private space was a small alcove to the left of the large black coal stove, where he squeezed in between Dadda's big chair and the bookcase. In the winter the flat square stove top was used for cooking as well as for warmth, and cakes, pies, and scones were baked in the oven underneath. Most of the year there was a huge kettle singing on the corner of the fireplace. It provided hot water not only for tea, but also for washing-up and incidental needs throughout the day. The stove was only cold through the month of July, when the weather was warm and the chimneys were swept. A small paraffin heater sat on top of the coal stove through the summer season. It was mainly to heat water for tea, but it was not unusual to have a cold and rainy summer day, when the heater was used to warm the room and drive the damp away.

Though this room at the back of the house was always called the kitchen, it could more properly have been called the dining, or secondary sitting room. The real kitchen, which we called the "copper shed" was across the bricked back yard. It had a large oven, a huge built-in laundry copper, galvanized rinsing tubs, a mangle (or wringer as it was sometimes called), ironing tables and flat irons. Most of the baking, all of the laundry and full-body bathing were done in this wonderful warm place. Like the house kitchen and paraffin shed, it too had split, or half doors, with the top half perpetually open during the daylight hours.

The French style split kitchen door led directly to the enclaved back yard. This yard was a bricked over, U-shaped enclosure of outbuildings, with tall, wooden door-like gates on either end of the house itself. Looking out from the kitchen door and starting at the right hand side was the "pump" door, outside of which was a cart-wide path leading past other back door gates and eventually to some fields. It was through this door and up this path that I traveled, sometimes twice daily, as did the surrounding neighbours, to bring a pail of clear cool drinking water from Miss Danford's community pump. Rainwater used for everything else was caught in cisterns from the roof gutters. This water, especially soft and desirable for washing clothes and acquiring shiny hair, was carefully screened of impurities by a contrivance on the end of the downspout, which had to be disassembled frequently and cleaned of twigs and leaves.

The copper house and paraffin shed made up the right hand buildings of the enclosure. Then came the enormous dustbin in the square of the "U." Next to that and in the left hand corner was the lavatory, which, by the standard of the era, was a posh commodity. To tell the truth and by comparison to many, it was done up rather nicely. It had two well-placed seats at different heights, with highly varnished lids. It even had a receptacle in the wall for toilet tissue: little slips of thin, rather stiff paper, which, as a shopkeeper, Mrs. Saunders purchased in quantity. One entered the lavatory through a mini maze of two high walls, possibly to give an occupant advance warning of someone approaching. More likely it was made that way to deflect the wind gusts and rain that often howled over the rooftops and through the yard.

Further around on the left side of the "U" was the bicycle shed that was used not only for bicycles, but for everything else as well. A workbench ran down two sides and in the back was a long bin that held the coal for the fires. Lenny, the Saunders' only son, kept all his bicycle tools, spare tyres and a marvelous accumulation of discarded children's paraphernalia stacked in corners and hung on the walls of this interesting shed.

The garden gate to the left of the kitchen door, beyond the bicycle shed, led out to the Bramfield side yard. This was the space where Goofie exercised and where several flower beds struggled to survive. There was a large open shed originally intended to store a carriage, but now unused except to store gardening tools, a wheelbarrow and assorted clay pots. Next to that was the most important building of all: Mr. Saunders' bird shed.

It was a dark brown, wooden, L-shaped building with white trim around the windows and doors. In the L-part that was the entrance, four large cages were fitted for pairing purposes. There was a small window facing the entrance that we had to pass to enter the main room to the right. This main room was a much larger room than the "L" part and much brighter, too. All the windows were along the side facing the garden gate. The cages took up the other three walls. They were fitted from about two feet off the floor to the ceiling. Two or three travelling bird cases were stored under the cages, along with several large seed bins and a specially designed watering can.

There was a long bench-like table with open cubbyholes across the top and shelves beneath under the large windows. Dadda's stool stood beside the bench. He would often sit on the stool, rest his "gimpy" arm on the bench, and brace himself with one foot on the bench foundation. In that position, Dadda could work most of the morning. Sometimes he would forget the time, so absorbed he would be in his work. He wouldn't bring his pipe into the bird shed, but carried instead a piece of licorice or a small tin of lemon drops to suck on.

Though Goofie obediently remained outside, usually sprawled across the lowest step, I was always welcome in the bird shed. Under Dadda's direction, I loved to help blend and measure out the seed into the containers attached to every cage and then clean and refill the water containers. As these were prize birds, being raised and crossbred for experimentation and showing, we had to make the mixtures precisely right for each individual canary, budgerigar, or finch. The floor to each cage had a moveable tray that we pulled out daily, cleaned thoroughly, and sprinkled with fresh sawdust before returning it to its place.

Dadda had several wounds from the First World War that limited his movements. Shrapnel that remained just above his right temple caused dizziness that made bending over particularly difficult. Another piece of shrapnel had been removed from his left leg, and though it left a very ugly scar, wasn't debilitating in any way. He used a cane occasionally mainly to steady himself because of his "wobbly" head. He was able to make his way round the house and through most of the garden by having special handholds and stopping places, but walking outside the garden gate was beyond his capabilities.

He also carried the effects of gas poisoning in his system that made him cautious about the things he could eat. His biggest handicap, though he never saw it that way, was the fact that his right arm had been blown off just below the elbow. He wore a prosthesis that was lifelike, but heavy. The metal fingers were always encased in a brown leather glove, that had to be replaced every so often when the fingers became worn. Many of the duties that became my exclusive privileges, like carrying in the new sacks of sawdust and carrying out the rubbish, I now see as jobs that would have been impossible for him without assistance.

There was always something going on at the bird shed. A bird of a new species would arrive and have to be fetched from the bus stop at the *Compasses Inn* or the railway station in Halesworth. Broken cages would have to be mended, or a perch replaced. A mother's eggs would hatch and the scrawny little chicks would immediately set about squawking for food. Dadda would see to it that there were special morsels for the new brood, and I would watch as the mother rolled seed in her bill, cracked and softened it before feeding it to her young.

The majority of the birds were canaries, but there were several budgerigars and chaffinches that Dadda also raised in this controlled environment. Part of his intent, I'm sure, was to simply study the normal habits of these birds. But beyond that he strove to raise hearty and healthy specimens for sale. There was great satisfaction of achievement in knowing his birds were top quality and were sought after for their clear song or unusual colouration. He noted the effects of every experiment with seeds and colouring, sometimes adding blue or red powder to the daily diet of certain birds.

All the birds were special, but some, for one reason or another, became favourites and they were given names. I remember a particular budgie whose colours were amazing: all lovely red, yellow, black and green. Very agile and noisy he was. We named him Sir Lancelot. He had all the qualities of a courageous Knight of the round table. He strutted about, whistling and calling to his Lady Guinevere, who was several cages removed from him. Finally Dadda put them together in one of the larger cages, tied bits of thready string to the bars, and left little pieces of straw lying about in the bottom of the cage. They, of course, immediately fell in love, and contrary to history, raised a small, but beautiful, family without starting a war.

Tiny Tim was another memorable bird, a scrawny runt hatched with a large brood of healthy canaries one spring. Dadda paid special attention when there were eggs ready to hatch. I knew I shouldn't make any sudden moves near the nesting cages, and never touch the eggs. But on those rare occasions when the mother was off the nest, I could get a good look at the eggs. Dadda had been giving me daily reports and keeping a sharp eye on "Penny," a lovely songstress, who was setting on five beautiful eggs in one of the three nesting cages. Dadda held up his good arm to quiet me as I came bounding in from school one afternoon.

"Have they...?" I began. Dadda pointed to the cage as he nodded yes and together in hushed silence we inspected the bits of shell lying about at the bottom of Penny's cage. We counted four scrawny heads, with open mouths that looked too big for their bodies. It was several days later that Dadda realized that "Tim" would not survive without special care. He was the runt of the family, hidden beneath his mother's feathers. Dadda had to remove Tim from the rest of his family so he wouldn't get trampled to death. While the others began to be lively, squawking for their mother to feed them constantly, Tiny Tim was too weak to move. Dadda put him in a special insulated container lined with straw and feathers to keep him warm. For feeding, Dadda would perch the homemade nest on his gloved prosthesis and with his good hand feed Tim special ground up food through a medicine dropper.

When Tim became a little stronger, I was able to hold him in my hand while Dadda fed him. It was a bit overwhelming for me to hold him the first time and feel his little heart beating. I was a bit awkward about it, and so afraid I would hurt him. But Dadda reassured me and together we weaned the little bird and watched him grow from a scrawny little reject into a fine fledgling who soon learned to fend for himself.

Each cage had a long list hanging beside it that gave the full breeding history, notes on past and present experimentation, what the bird was currently being fed and its reaction to it, and many other facts of this sort. At the lowest point on the list was a small notation of where and when that particular bird was destined to go when it left Dadda's care. They all did go eventually, and as new ones were bred, the cycle began again.

The Saunders' only son Lenny had planted sunflowers that grew very tall next to the bird shed. They faced the morning sun and seemed never to stop growing. In fact they grew higher than the windows of the bird shed and had to be cut down to harvest the seeds.

A few months after my arrival, on my seventh birthday, Mrs.

Saunders took a photograph of Lenny and me beside the giant sunflowers. Lenny, an affable and tall young man, stands hands in pockets, handsome and smiling broadly. I'm standing beside him enjoying the moment, with Goofie's tail swishing round my legs. Dadda, who never would come outside to have a photograph taken, stayed inside the bird shed and watched with amusement through the forest of sunflower stems. The day was filled with yellow sunlight and laughter.

Lenny Saunders
Outside the Birdshed
1936

Chapter 2

Eternity Now, My New Family

It is eternity now. I am in the midst of it.
It is about me in the sunshine.

Jefferies

Lenny was 18 years old when I first met him. He had been working at a trade for four years, as a skilled mechanic. Full of energy and bright ideas, he was the light of the Saunders' lives. He was a good son in the best sense of the word, thoughtful of them, yet moving in completely different directions from them. He had no interest in being a shopkeeper, preferring rather to work with his hands building and remodeling engines. His job often took him to places too far from home to return on a daily basis. On these times, he would board the train at Halesworth, loading his bicycle in the luggage car so that he would have transportation after he arrived at his destination.

He was seldom at home, but when he was there, he brought a new dimension into it. Full of exuberance and fun, he made the sedate and quiet house come alive with noisy talk and boisterous laughter. He was quite strong and thought nothing of picking me up bodily and swinging me over his head, or he would challenge me to race him, each of us carrying a pail for water from Mrs. Danford's pumphouse.

Some of his friends had motorbikes, and I know he longed to own one, but out of respect for his parents' wishes he never bought one. Though motorization was beginning to be popular in some places, motorbikes hadn't really caught on in the village. There was much fear attached to anything that was as noisy and went at the speeds they did. However, when he was at home there always seemed to be a disassembled motorbike in the back yard or in the

Joyce 1936

Mummy Saunders

bicycle shed. His best friend Jimmy Broom, who was a fearless terror on a motorbike, enlisted Lenny's help to build an entire bike from pieces of scrap. It was a remarkable challenge that the two enjoyed immensely. They spent hours poring over strange bits of metal and various wires.

My first bicycle was one of Lenny's old ones. He cleaned it all up for me, put new tubes in the tyres, and mended the loose carrier on the back. He replaced the rusty bell and put the seat all the way down to its lowest point, but I still couldn't reach the pedals. He taught me how to ride it with one foot stuck through under the crossbar. He held onto the back of the seat and ran up and down Bramfield Road with me until I was able to stay steady enough to manage fairly well on my own. While he was away, I was only allowed to ride around the pathway in the back garden, on the inside of the wire netting. Goofie was delighted with this arrangement and ran, tail-wagging, ears flying and yapping happily inches away from the rear mudguard, while I teetered in my ungainly position around and around, past the gate, the bird shed, the grassy patch and the flower beds, full speed ahead.

Lenny finally fitted blocks of wood to the pedals and Mummy gave me a pair of his old trousers, so I could get on and off by throwing one leg over the back of the seat, the way the boys did.

Though it was a bit decrepit, it was my first bike and I knew I was lucky to have it. Since not all my classmates were so lucky, we often doubled up, having one ride on the handlebars, one on the back carrier and taking turns being the one to pedal. Having a boy's bike made a big difference, because in emergencies one more small body could find room to ride on the crossbar.

School was a pleasure to me. I looked forward to it from the very beginning, knowing somehow that school in Wenhaston would be a far different experience than it had been in Peasenhall, the village from whence I had recently come. Though I couldn't put my finger on what would be different, I gained an anticipation of something through Dadda's proud looks as Mummy (Mrs. Saunders) fitted me out with new white blouses to go with the navy blue woolen "gym-slip" that was the standard uniform for all British schoolgirls of that era.

"My word," he said as I stood in the middle of the kitchen in my new finery, "You do look smart. We've got a beauty on our hands, May Lydia Louisa." I discovered that he called his wife "Mum," or by all her names, when he was pleased and happy. This was one of those special moments. When he was a bit upset about anything, Mummy became just plain "May."

Dadda's moods were easy to read. His pet name for me was "Beauty;" he seldom called me by my given name. Whenever he did, I knew Lettie, our house girl, or Mummy had reported some mischievous act that I'd been caught doing. Most of the time I knew I was the apple of his eye, and the admiration was mutual. He was a loving father: thoughtful, generous and kind in ways that heretofore I had never experienced. More than anything else, he was always at home, always available to listen to my joys and griefs, and to guide me to resolve thorny problems. I trusted him implicitly. There was no one in the world who meant more to me.

Dadda's armchair sagged a bit at the front, in the place where he leaned forward. He sat with one knee a bit higher than the other, with his left elbow propped on it to hold his pipe. He used his right arm, his "gimpy" one, to support the ever-present book or newspaper he was reading. I saw him most often in this familiar posture. Whenever I entered the kitchen, he would look up from his book, take his pipe out of his mouth and with a smile, welcome me to sit on his knee. I loved the smell of him. As I kissed his cheek in greeting, I always got a wonderful whiff of his pipe tobacco mingled with Pears soap and the shaving cologne he used.

He was not a tall man, not nearly as tall as Lenny, but taller than Mummy or Letty. He was not overly stout, but his slightly jowly cheeks, brown eyes and hair made him look a little bit like a thinner version of Winston Churchill. Dadda was fastidious about his attire and about his personal hygiene. He took at least an hour each morning to do, as Mummy called it, his daily "ablutions." He always wore three piece suits, fresh white shirts with detachable starched collars, and a tie knotted precisely. I never saw him dressed in any other way, except infrequently in his dressing gown early in the mornings.

Occasionally, before leaving for school, I was asked to take him his morning tea. Mummy or Letty always had the fire going and the tea made before I came downstairs. On those times when I was allowed to take his tea, I would carry the tea on a tray, the saucer with two biscuits on it covering the cup to keep the tea warm. I had to be most careful not to spill any going up the long staircase. At the top I had to transfer the tray to one hand so I could knock with the other. I was always glad when the door stood ajar, and I could just nudge it open with my shoulder.

When the door was closed, Dadda was still in his dressing robe. I had to wait for him to call to me, then I would set the tray on the round table by the fireplace, kiss his whiskery face, and leave the room. When the door was open, Dadda was dressed in shirt and trousers, and sometimes already in the middle of shaving. After I put the tray down, he let me sit on the edge of the bed and watch while he contorted his face and stripped away the creamy lather. It was many years later that I realized what a feat it was for him to manage to shave himself with one hand, his left hand at that. But at that time I felt lucky to have a dollop of shaving cream laughingly dabbed on my nose or cheek.

On weekdays he wore his second best suit, which was brown with an almost indefinable stripe. On Sundays he wore his newer "best" suit which was also brown, just not quite as worn. His suit jacket was seldom buttoned, but most often hung open. His waistcoat, with the two small pockets at the waistline, was always buttoned tightly. Every day he wore the same two pieces of jewelry: his watch and his signet ring. He wore his signet ring with his engraved initials on the little finger of his left hand. I never knew him to take it off. I have it now tucked away in a drawer. It is among my most treasured possessions.

His gold watch chain hung loosely across his waist, fastened with a device that attached through the centre buttonhole. A round gold watch fob with a set-in ruby hung from the centre fastener. The chain ended in the right hand pocket with a tiny replica of an old tinderbox. It was flat and about two inches square, its tiny hinges set in the smoothly worn silver of its lid. In the left hand pocket, the chain ended with his gold watch, with two hinged covers, one over the face and one that opened the back where the "works" could be inspected.

It was a most reliable watch that kept precise time. When I was very young, it was a big treat when Dadda held it to my ear to listen to its steady tick. He loved to check it nightly with the six o'clock "pips" to make sure it kept correct time. He would further check all the clocks in the house, to make sure they agreed. If one of them was off by a few seconds, he would grunt and huff and monitor the offending timepiece more closely for the next few days. Sometimes everything would be fine, but if a problem persisted, I would be enlisted to take the timepiece in question to Newby's repair shop just down the road.

It was something of an adventure to go to Mr. Newby's clock shop, to come face to face with the wizened figure bent over minute pieces of clock innards, with a magnifying device that seemed permanently attached at his eye. So intent was he that he'd hardly look up when you entered his shop. There would always be time to study the clocks of all shapes and sizes that lined the walls. When he finally did look up, he'd push his eye-glass up to his forehead and fix you with his watery grey eyes. He wasn't a very kindly man at any time, and his demeanor was not improved by the fact that my playmates and I loved to play pranks on him. We'd knock on his door and run away quickly, almost daily. Sometimes we'd hear him shout at us, but he seldom chased us.

His nickname around the village was "Conk," but none of us children dared to call him that to his face. When we did visit his shop, we politely called him "Mr. Newby." His appearance was unkempt. His straggly gray hair gave him a wild look, and his untidy gray mustache had a brown arc over one corner of his lip from his pipe. His uneven teeth were darkened from years of tea and tobacco stains, but he knew his trade and the villagers respected his talent for repairing clocks and watches of all shapes and sizes.

His wife, who was slightly daft, was another story. She was affectionately known as "Conkers." She was a funny but harmless soul, who flitted around the village with pounds of make-up on her face. In our small village, most of the ladies used cosmetics sparingly, if at all. A little powder, some rouge for the afternoon and imperceptible amounts of lip colour were acceptable and fashionable. But Conkers, in her sweet gentle way, dramatically overdid the mascara and eye shadow. She walked with a strange little twist on very high heels, sashaying her shoulders and mincing her hips in her overly tight skirts. Her filthy nails were long claw-like talons that she kept polished with garish red polish. She greeted everyone with a sweet smile, her painted lips parted to show gaps where some of her front teeth used to be. She was pathetically naive and vulnerable.

Though the children were cruel and openly made sport of her, the grown-ups were kinder and more patient with her. "Poor old soul," they'd whisper over afternoon tea. "She wants putting away before she does herself harm." They meant, of course, she needed to be put in Bulcamp Union, the institution in nearby Blythburgh that housed and cared for the homeless, the destitute and especially the mentally defective. When Mrs. Newby went shopping beyond our shop, which was within sight of her home, she often got lost. She had a problem of getting lost when she ventured any farther away.

It was not uncommon for her to lose her way and not know how to get home from the bakery or the Post Office on Front Street (or The Street). The poor woman would wander, grinning grotesquely, until some kind soul would set her back in the right direction for her front door. Some thought she wasn't quite as daft as she made out to be. They said she was trying to make friends in the only way she knew how. It was rumoured that her husband did his level best to keep her inside their house. But while he concentrated intently on his clock repairs, studying the little springs and wheels, she escaped and wandered blissfully through the village.

The Newbys lived differently than did most of the villagers. That the majority lived frugally was known and understood, even expected and admired. But "neat and clean" were revered attributes in every household, except the Newbys'. "It doesn't cost much for soap and elbow grease" was an oft repeated maxim. "Cleanliness is next to Godliness" was part of the Wenhaston catechism that was mostly directed at us children by matrons who wore lace collars for afternoon tea.

"Balmy" or "daft" were descriptions they used mainly for the lower classes to explain a simpleton whose behavior was strange, but moderately acceptable. A proper English expression for upper class bizarre behavior was "eccentric." Eccentricity was looked upon as the prerogative of the rich. It was sometimes excused even in the poorer classes if the eccentric was additionally a gifted conversationalist, could play a musical instrument, or accidentally won the penny football pool, a weekly gambling venture that relied on guessing the National football scores correctly.

Nearly every family had an eccentric or two that the relatives either touted or tucked away depending on the extent and bent of their eccentric's artistic abilities. But dirt was something else. It was taboo, forbidden, looked down upon, and openly abhorred. So while most of the ladies shunned the Newby home, not wanting any association except as an occasional benevolent street guide, we children would make up excuses to visit there.

Mrs. Newby looked forward to our visits. She invited us inside eagerly. It is obvious to me now that she was starved for attention. At the time, though, I was flattered by the attention she gave to my playmates and me. To our shame, we gloated over our ability to manipulate this strange and silly woman.

Most of my mates were game for anything. We fished out gobs of gooey frog larvae that we could watch turn into tadpoles. We climbed trees for fun or to get chestnuts or apples. We dammed up the water across the road at the Blyford run with mud and gunk to see what it would do. Most dangerous of all, we dared each other to run across the top of the wall of the humpback bridge. The boys were usually less squeamish than the girls, but not by much. We were an adventurous lot.

I once had a tea party in the open shed by the bird shed. Letty made us a pot of tea, and gave us a plate of sandwiches and some biscuits to eat. We set some boards across two barrels to make a table and covered it with an old piece of oilcloth. Someone brought some yellow cowslips to put on the table, to dress it up. But the stems were too short and too soft to stand up in the jar we had. They kept falling down inside the jar. None of us knew what to do. We needed something to put in the bottom of the jar to make the flowers stand up, preferably something soft.

Just at that precise moment, Goofie provided the perfect solution by depositing a big brown object on the grass a few feet away. It was exactly what we needed. We scooped it into the jam jar while it was still very fresh and plonked the flowers in on top. They sat nicely in there, their little heads just resting on the edge of the jar. It made a wonderful centrepiece, and I was quite pleased that we'd been so clever. Margie and Barbara didn't mind either, and Walter and Peter Elmy both giggled. The rest of us had no qualms about eating our sandwiches, but Gladys was a bit hesitant. She was, in many ways, a bit more refined than the rest of us.

It was an undisputed fact that I was a tomboy. Most of my friends were equally daring, the boys more so than the girls. No matter how sweetly Mummy dressed me, I never became "dainty" as did some of my blonde friends whose hair curled easily and always looked attractive. On occasion I thought about feminine things. Gladys and I were especially curious about forbidden things such as cosmetics. No one we knew wore make-up quite the way Mrs. Newby did. It was a mystery where she was able to purchase her seemingly vast supply. We were sure that she never ventured on the bus to Halesworth, and there were no shops in the village that stocked eye shadow or mascara. More than anything else, we wanted to be able to just "see" what make-up looked like, what form it took in the boxes, jars or bottles.

We went one day to take some bits of leftover sponge cake from a church social to Mrs. Newby. She invited us in as usual and fluttered over us, offering us a nice cup of tea. We could smell something putrid, and thinking it might be the tea, we both begged off. The smell was a combination of things, but the most powerful component was paraffin. I readily identified it because I often went to the paraffin shed to measure out a gallon for a shop customer. As we moved into the room, we could see the remains of fish that had been eaten sometime before. The bones were on the uppermost plates of a pile on the corner of the table. The smell of stale fish and paraffin was combined with the odor of something we had never smelled before: nail polish. It made a potent stench. Undaunted by the ghastly aroma, Gladys and I were ready for an adventure into unknown territory.

We had unwittingly and providentially stumbled into a manicure session. How delighted we were, and how fascinated. Mrs. Newby was pleased to show us the whole procedure. She was removing the old polish from her long, curved fingernails with a rag dipped in paraffin. Some of the dirt caked under the nails and in the cracks of her hands came off as well.

After she'd finished getting most of the polish off, she motioned for one of us to bring some hot water from the kettle and pour it into the round enamel bowl on the kitchen table. The water was too hot, so Gladys ran and got a dipper full of cold water from the pail by the door. Next she needed soap and indicated where it might be. I hunted around until I found a sliver of yellow carbolic soap. It was hard as a rock, but the warm water softened it enough to make it usable.

Mrs. Newby babbled to us as she did each step. We could see she was pleased as punch to have us hovering over her, watching and learning this important skill. We watched as she soaked her fingertips and worked with a teaspoon, pushing the cuticle back, "to make the moons show," she said. It looked painful to us, but Mrs. Newby worked diligently and did in fact get the "moons" to show.

Next she rolled some cotton wool round the end of a wooden stick, dipped it in a white, thick paste and rolled it under each fingernail and across each half moon. It looked suspiciously like whitewash, the kind we used on the copper shed walls each spring, only much thicker. She was quite adept at getting the white stuff in the right places and we were impressed. As it dried it made very white half circles that became a bit powdery to the touch. We helped her wipe the excess from around the fleshy part of her bony fingers before it hardened completely.

We were having such a good time and had just got to the "good" part, the actual painting with the red polish, when we thought we heard footsteps coming. At once we flew to the door and out into the street as though the devil himself were after us. Our lesson was incomplete, but we knew more than most of our contemporaries about doing our nails. It was left for another day for us to try our skills out on each other.

We were not caught that day, but we were always on guard. We were most careful to make sure Mr. Newby was ensconced in his shop before we entered. One of us would peep through the second window to the left of the door to make sure he was on his stool, hunched over his workbench. If that were the case, it was safe to enter.

The Newby house was a small one. The largest room at the front was a rather cramped sitting room. It had a door to the left that led to the shop. It was sparsely furnished, and rubbish took up any empty spaces. There was barely room enough for two decrepit lounge chairs by the unlit fireplace. The remaining decor was made up of a small table piled high with bits of everything; clothes to be sewn, some crockery, and lots of magazines that spilled over onto the floor.

The door at the back of the room led to a small, dark kitchen with a large cookstove as the centerpiece. To the right of the cookstove sat a rusty coal scuttle with a small bent shovel leaning against it. On one side, below the small-paned kitchen window, there was a wooden table and four chairs. Two of the chairs consistently were piled high with "outside" clothes: coats, macs, scarves and gloves. Tea towels and bits of rag were everywhere. Mrs. Newby always cleaned off a space on the chairs with a great show of hospitality, throwing anything from the seat to the chair back. Then she'd clean off a space on the table for us, strewing empty tins and other rubbish in an untidy pile. The bare tabletop revealed the places where the white paint was cracked and peeling. What would have been a total embarrassment to any housekeeper in our village, was a source of natural pride and enjoyment to our hostess.

Mrs. Newby took delight in her culinary skills. We were seldom able to identify what she was cooking, but there was usually something stewing in a big cookpot on the kitchen stove. For all her strange wanderings, she seemed conscientious about being hospitable. She occasionally invited us to sample her stew, but none of us were brave enough to risk having any. We once sampled her tea, which was black and very thick. Not even three spoonfuls of sugar could make it drinkable, and it was all we could do to swallow a mouthful. In time, we tried the different tack of selling our wares to her.

No one else in the village would deign to buy our homemade lemonade or the sweets we offered, complete with pocket lint. But Mrs. Newby could nearly always be persuaded to give us a penny for almost anything we had. Selling it to her was the easy part; finding a clean jug to empty lemonade into at her house was the greatest trick of all. We usually left her the jam jar we'd brought it in, and resorted to paper doilies to bring her our bits of sweets and cake.

From inside the house, we could hear the clocks chiming in the shop. A few of them chimed every fifteen minutes, but most of them on the half-hour and then the hour. Such a din it was to hear them all chiming the hour, some not quite in sync. with the rest of them, but all with melodies or clangings. It's a wonder poor old Conk wasn't driven out of his mind with it all.

Dadda didn't like it when I made fun of Mrs. Newby or took advantage of her hospitality. But she was such an easy target it was hard to resist the temptation to exploit her. He scolded me mildly when he caught me knocking on the Newby's door and running away, which was almost a daily occurrence. But the time I accidentally smashed the Newby's window, Dadda let me know I had overstepped the line.

I tried desperately at first to explain to him that I had banged on the windowpane instead of the door by mistake, and my fist went through the glass accidentally. I knew I was in trouble as soon as I heard the glass shatter. I outwardly pretended nonchalance, but inwardly I was shaken to the core. Though the breaking glass was truly an accident, I had boldly rapped on Conk Newby's shop window instead of the door, to show off for my friends. I was daring the old man to come out after us. The prank backfired.

Dadda was implacable. I tried reasoning; that was nearly always a good way to get round Dadda. When that didn't work, I tried whining and then cajoling him into seeing my point of view. I don't know why I thought he'd be sympathetic. But I finally realized that even with my bleeding hand pathetically extended, and floods of tears, he was in no mood to let me off lightly.

After Mummy had dressed my wound, scolding furiously the whole time, Dadda made me empty my tin savings bank that sat on the kitchen shelf. It was a replica of the round Post Office pillar boxes used to post letters. You had to use a dinner knife to get the money out through the same slot you put it in. It was tricky business, and painful too, since this was money I earned by delivering groceries and lovingly saved for special events such as our annual seaside outings in the summertime.

I counted out every penny and ha'penny it contained, folded it all in my handkerchief, and sniveling noisily, walked somberly with Goofie to the garden gate. At the gate I turned to look back with what I hoped was a piteous expression. I was still hoping for a reprieve, even at this late hour. But there was no sign of weakening from Dadda. He watched from the window while I took all my hard-earned savings up the road to Mr. Newby's shop.

Mr. Newby sensed my presence, met me at the shop door and stepped halfway outside. The force of his angry breathing almost bowled me over. His hair looked wilder than I'd ever seen it, and his bony arms were raised above his head threateningly. His normally watery eyes were fiery as he cursed me roundly. I stood in front of him, shaking, my usual bravado totally gone. Had it not been that I could feel Dadda's eyes on my back, I would have turned tail and run without a moment's hesitation.

My muffled apology was obviously difficult to hear. Mr. Newby took a step toward me, still swearing. I extended my trembling hand, and muttering something totally incoherent, dropped the money at his feet and fled. He stopped, looked genuinely startled as the coins rolled out of the hanky and onto the pavement. My last fleeting glance was of him bent to the ground picking up the money with one hand, and shaking his fist at me with the other.

Chapter 3

Of Many Things

The time has come, the Walrus said,
to talk of many things:
Of shoes,and ships, and sealing wax,
of cabbages and kings.

Lewis Carroll

There was a patch of wild violets just outside the garden gate, out of Goofie's reach and half hidden in the embankment. Whenever I remembered, I would stop and pick a handful and put them on the kitchen table. Dadda loved violets. Next to roses, they were his favourite flowers. It always seemed to please him when I was able to forage enough to make a decent bouquet, and I delighted to see his broad smile.

To my idealistic childish mind, Dadda was not just the bravest soldier who ever lived, but also the wisest, most knowledgeable, intelligent human being on earth. He taught me many things I couldn't learn in the most prestigious University. He taught me trivial things such as how to start the Primus stove and how to melt lead to make pellets for the air gun. He showed me how to sight that gun and hit a target from across the yard; he called it good training for the occasional rat that frequented the dustbin. He taught me how to make a kite that would fly, and watched me as I struggled with it in the field across the road from the bird shed. He showed me how to make a catapult out of a piece of old leather fastened to a knobbly forked hedgerow stick with rubber straps, a weapon that caused me and some of the villagers much unintentional grief a few years later.

He taught me life-lessons, too, that weren't so easy to recognize at the time, but have since become valuable. His lessons were about integrity, faithfulness, endurance and honour. He taught me daily, but I never realized how important those lessons were until much later in life. He loved poetry and often quoted it to make an indelible point, wanting me to remember. One of his many quotations was:

> *"When the One Great Scorer comes*
> *to write against your name,*
> *He marks—not that you won or lost—*
> *but how you played the game."*

His love of reading rubbed off on me. At a very young age he introduced me to the giants of poetry and literature. I learned from Tennyson's *Ulysses* that "I am a part of all that I have met," and was challenged: "to strive, to seek, to find, and not to yield." I learned from Browning's *Home-Thoughts* about an exquisite love and longing for the British country-side. From Chaucer's *Canterbury Tales*, I gained a sense of the ridiculous, and from Shelley's *To a Skylark* the pure joy that comes through hearing nature's free expression of praise.

Intermittently Dadda read and quoted from the old black Bible that stayed on the top shelf of the bookcase beside his kitchen chair. Often when I was learning to recite one of the Psalms or the Beatitudes at school, I would come in from school and begin the quote. Dadda would take down the Bible, and finding the right place, would coach me further. At school, none of us had a Bible to follow along with; we were taught by rote, repeating the verses after the teacher. Because of this teaching method that I now see constituted a surface religious exercise with very little depth, I learned the words without learning anything much about their relationship to me. At that time I gained the fallacious impression that recitation of scripture was on a par with reciting poetry, that it was mainly part of one's early training, and that, while the Bible had merit, it had the same quality as any other good literature. No more, no less.

In later years I became extremely grateful for the stored wealth of scripture that this early training afforded me. I would wish for every child on earth the blessing derived from a well-spring such as I was privileged to have. I realize now that God's Word, once planted, no matter the circumstances, cannot be easily erased. I came to understand God's purpose was to fill my vessel early, while

I was totally unaware of His guidance. What a glorious awakening it was, decades later, when I finally received this full and wonderful knowledge. Then I was able to embrace fully, without restraints, His love and grace.

But the process toward that knowledge was slow and often painful. I know I still have a long way to go. The journey, even now, is still not without its pitfalls. My ideas about the role of scripture that were formed in early childhood stayed with me a very long time. There have been moments in my life when I have looked back with much regret at the useless waste of time my early instruction seemed to be. But thankfully, I can now see the way God has used every part of it to fashion me into the person He purposed I should be.

It was many years before I actually owned a Bible and was bold enough to look up scripture for myself. I always knew the Bible was a sacred book to be revered, but hardly to be studied. I knew, too, that only the church leaders, the Vicars and Bishops, had total authority and correct interpretation of it. I had no knowledge then of the role that the Holy Spirit plays as Divine teacher and interpreter.

The Prayer Book, I was taught rightly, holds a place of great respect. As part of my training, I learned to follow the weekly routines as the church calendar ordered. The Collects, prescribed prayers for every situation and need, that were then merely habitual mouthings. I now view them in an entirely different light. I have come to appreciate these prayers more and more for their beautifully worded expressions of praise, thanksgiving, and worship. That I grew to love the familiar formulas was so very natural. To deviate from following what was ordained would have been unthinkable.

From Dadda and from my daily and Sunday school teachers I learned the Old Testament Bible stories of Noah and the ark, Abraham and Isaac, Jacob, Joseph and his coat of many colours, the baby Moses in the bullrushes, the adult Moses wandering in the desert with the children of Israel, David and Goliath, David as King of Israel and Daniel in the lions' den. From the New Testament I learned about the Virgin Mary who gave birth to the baby Jesus in a manger. I heard the story of his growing up, and how as a young lad, He stayed behind at the temple in Jerusalem to "be about His Father's business." I learned of Jesus' baptism and his ministry of healing and feeding thousands of people. I was well aware of the story of Christ's crucifixion and of His glorious resurrection and that He had gone through the process to save the world from sin.

But somehow I never made the connection that it was all done for ME, that I was born in sin that I could not get rid of by any means other than through His sacrificial blood shed on calvary. Though it is plainly written, and I had often repeated the words of the Way of salvation, the truth did not penetrate. For more years than I care to remember, the notion remained that my salvation rested not so much on what Christ had done, but what I needed to do to gain eternal forgiveness.

Despite Dadda's gift to me in introducing me to books and joining with me in exploring them, the Bible was a strangely remote entity. There were bookcases in almost every room, and a large cupboard in the Front room that was also packed with books. But the Bible sat alone on the kitchen shelf, in a class by itself.

I was at liberty to read any of the books in the house, provided I was careful not to spill anything on them. It never occurred to me to pay special attention to the Bible, nor was I encouraged to do so. I remember the huge set of Charles Dickens books that filled up a whole shelf in the glass-fronted bookcase, well-thumbed volumes of Spencer, Thackeray, Milton and Wordsworth, and dozens more. I could never have exhausted the supply of reading material. Dadda loved having me read to him from my own books. He, in turn, selected poems and stories to read to me. Our happiest hours were spent by the fire in the kitchen reading aloud, first one and then the other, while the kettle sang and Goofie snored.

Dadda showed that he held to the moral values of the Bible. He believed strongly in fair play and "gentleman's honour" which often meant sacrificing not only his own, but our benefits as well. Mummy was occasionally at cross purposes with him, especially about matters to do with the shop tradesmen.

"You're too easy, George," she'd say. "That one's crooked as a donkey's hind leg. He'll take the shop if you give it him." And so they'd have their disagreements, but usually Dadda would prevail. Mummy would shake her head, mutter, and give in to whatever Dadda suggested. Everything would be all right again.

The shop was busiest in the mornings when the women came in

to buy their daily supplies. Mummy minded the shop for the busy early shift while Letty made the beds, emptied the chambers, and cleaned the house. Letty took her turn in the shop later in the morning through the noon dinner hour. Dadda said you could almost set your watch by Mummy's well-oiled household routine, as astute and efficient as she was.

Mummy took her daily bath at eleven o'clock, brushed out her long hair and wound it in a braided bun on top of her head. She used Dadda's washstand, but her own lavender soap in the dish with the pink rosebuds on it. Her dressing table stood over by the window and contained an array of refined ladies' necessities. There was a flat dish that held rounded combs, a hairpin box and several crystal pots with silver tops. One of these particularly fascinated me because it had a hole in the middle of it and lettering in fancy script around the edge. For years I was convinced it had the name "Sidey" (my surname) on it. I later found out that the script actually was "Hair Tidy." Mummy wound her excess hair from the brush through the hole in the centre so as not to have unsightly globs on the table or floor.

There were other elegant pieces, all engraved with her initials, "MLLS." These included a silver handled brush, comb and hand held mirror. There was also a velvet lined jewelry box that held the gold brooch she wore. She only wore it when she put on her "afternoon" dress with the separate lace neckpiece. She would fasten the brooch right at her throat. The lettering on the brooch was only a few words. The largest lettering spelled out "Mizpah," and smaller letters that said, "Lord watch between." It came from the verse in Genesis 31 that says: "The Lord watch between me and thee while we are absent one from another." Dadda must have given it to her during the war.

I doubt that Mummy understood that the saying was an agreement between two men, Jacob and his father-in-law Laban, who mistrusted each other greatly. To her it was a symbol of Dadda's love and faithfulness and I suspect the Biblical origin mattered very little. She only wore it when she was suitably attired, for afternoons in the shop or for Sunday church. Each afternoon she tied on her clean starched apron over her dress, put on her "good" shoes, dusted her face with powder and squirted one drop of "attar of roses" from the scent bottle with the syphon attached. She then descended the stairs to serve the noon meal.

She was a hard worker, rising early in the day. As a rule she was the first one downstairs. Her first chore was to let Goofie out for his morning airing. I knew instantly when she let him out because he would run and bark in the side yard under my window. Lettie would be next up. She'd help Mummy get the ashes sifted from the kitchen stove, and haul them to the dustbin across the kitchen yard. Between them, they would rejuvenate the embers, and have the fire blazing in short order. By the time I got downstairs, the fire was lovely and hot and the kettle was boiling for tea.

I was excited when I got my first girl's bike. It was a second-hand, medium sized ladies' upright that was quite nice, but not exactly what I would have chosen. Lenny's old bike was now too small for me, and was part of the trade for the larger, more practical one. I was pleased to move up to a newer model, and to have some added features. This one had its own attached bicycle pump and a basket in front for carrying bags of groceries.

Best of all, I now got permission to ride to school, which meant I was able also to ride home for the lunch hour. This was a wonderful bonus, as time at home in the middle of the day for even one brief hour was a special privilege. Not many of my classmates were allowed to ride their bicycles to school, and few went home for lunch. It gave me a certain freedom that I found exhilarating.

Most of the time Dadda could be found tending to the birds at the noon hour. Goofie usually greeted me first, for either he was outside the bird shed "on guard" or Dadda let him out when he saw me peddling past the Newby's house. Though time was short, I managed to accomplish much in the lunchtime, and loved having certain small responsibilities that were mine alone. Any chores Mummy asked me to do connected with the shop were special duty. I was glad to help get orders ready to be delivered, and occasionally wait on customers while Mummy had a sandwich in the kitchen. I was very much a part of all that was going on at home, and that was important to me. I had purpose and I was a vital part of the daily routine.

The shop carried no dairy products, since there was daily farm delivery around the whole village. The one exception was the enormous wheels of cheese that came in two or three times a year. When the new cheese arrived, it was covered in an open-weave cotton fabric embedded so tightly as to form a kind of skin. As the cheese aged, the skin became a hardened rind. It took three of us to lift and hold the new wheel into position and to make the proper cuts.

We made the first cut right across the middle with a strong wire attached to two handles. Mummy, Letty, or I would hold the cheese in position while the other two drew the wire through the center, cutting it completely in half. We would divide the halves, wrap the large pieces in clean cloth, and place them in large storage tins where the mice couldn't get to them. We left one quarter piece on the round wooden table under a wire mesh cover, ready to be sliced and weighed on greaseproof paper on the brass scale.

The shop carried a wide variety of goods. The most popular everyday things like tea and biscuits were displayed on the shelves directly behind the counter. Things such as cinnamon, ginger, nutmeg and other spices in tiny jars or cellophane bags were neatly arranged in groups on the top shelf. We had a small ladder that could be folded into a stool for the things displayed there.

The tins of sardines, jars of jam and marmalade, *Bovril, Ovaltine, Marmite, Oxo* cubes, meat paste and bottles of *Camp Coffee* and *HP Sauce* were at eye level and within easy reach for Mummy and Letty. For several years they were out of my reach without the aid of the folding ladder. The tins of black and brown shoe polish were stacked near the floor polish, and *Brasso* and bars of laundry soap were just inside the door from the scullery.

The strong odor of the thick yellow bars of carbolic soap was the first scent to greet you when you stepped into the shop from the pantry. Farther down the counter on the back wall there were boxes of chocolate bars and wrapped sweets. On the lower shelves were packets of *Lyons* and *Typhoo* tea in colourful wrappings. Next to the tea was a large section where many varieties of biscuits in tins and different size packets were kept. Jars of licorice sticks and unwrapped lemon drops, peppermint balls and "gob-stoppers" stood on one side of the counter next to the beautifully polished scales.

Under the counter, beneath the scales, we kept the cigarettes: *Players, Capstans, Benson & Hedges* cost sixpence a box, while the smaller packets of *Woodbines* and *Cadets* were five for tuppence. We kept pipe tobacco in small packets in a drawer beneath the counter. The cigarettes and the loose tobacco gave off a pungent odor that blended with other scents in the shop to make a memorable aroma.

One small section to the right of the entrance was devoted to drapery and sewing items. We kept needles, thread, thimbles, buttons and button hooks in small drawers built into the wall. Wooden cases with open shelves to hold bolts of cloth and cards of lace sat opposite the drawers, with a narrow space between just wide enough to walk through. The top of the wooden cases provided space to roll out cloth and lace to be measured on the yardstick attached to the counter.

We kept no knitting supplies in our shop, nor did any other shops in Wenhaston. This was strange, considering the demand for them. In England in the 1930s, knitting was not simply a hobby, it was a way of life. Every female, and even some men, learned how to knit. We strove to learn the simple stitches first: to "cast on" correctly so the hem didn't sag. Then came knit one, purl one, moss stitch and cable, and the first "wearable" jumper. The more complicated socks and gloves came later. These required not only specialized wool, but also four double pointed needles and great concentration.

We learned how to take apart and re-use discarded garments by undoing the seams, catching the main thread, pulling out the stitches and rolling the yarn into a tight ball around our hands. The more experienced knitters, like Mummy and Letty, pulled miles of three-ply wool under a damp cloth and hot iron to make it look like new again. We were able to salvage much good yarn from old garments to make newer, more stylish jumpers and cardigans. If the wool garment was very old and worn, we had to make it do for smaller, less important items such as mittens, hats, multi-coloured scarves and pot-holders.

A strange little contraption called a "wool dolly" was my first introduction to the art of knitting. Wool dollies were made from empty thread spools by knocking four small nails into the top of the empty spool (the bigger the spool the better). We wound the yarn around them in such a way as to make the first round secure. It was then just a matter of pulling the thread round, and using a slim nail or crochet hook to loop the bottom strand over the new piece. The "knitting" grew like a long tube as it went through the hole in the center of the spool. In this fashion we wound up with long and colourful lengths that could be wound into hot plate holders, tea cozies, and earmuffs.

Whatever we children made out of the old wool had many knots and strange stitches, but we were proud of our accomplishments. It was a rare treat to be able to buy brand new wool for a project. When our work began to show promise, our reward was having the privilege of selecting first-hand goods from the wool shop. There was a wool shop on Main Street in Halesworth close to my friend Owen's house that had a marvelous display of all the newest knitting patterns, new-fangled needles, and a wide selection of wool. It was one of the places I liked to stop and browse, to see what was new, even if on that day I couldn't afford to buy anything.

People didn't come in the Saunders' shop to browse. It wasn't that kind of shop. Customers came in regularly with specific items in mind to buy. Though they might sometimes haggle a bit over the price, they seldom went away empty handed. We had to be especially careful about giving honest weight. When I was allowed to weigh out rice or sugar, I held my breath over the scale so as not to tip it one way or the other. The customers watched as carefully as I did.

Some, like old Mrs. Woolnough, would come right round the counter to my side to get a closer look. She'd chatter and point, giving me many directives. I learned quickly that it was always better to be a little on the heavy side in the customers favour than to be a hair short. It saved a lot of headaches for everyone.

Though there was the odd one who could be tedious, there were many more like Mrs. Elmy, Mrs. Ellis who lived next door, and Doreen Page's mother, who were friendly and trusting. They made it a pleasure for me to learn the ways of shopkeeping. I became adept at tallying items with paper and pencil that were beside the till, and in making correct change. A five or ten shilling note was a lot of money in those days and a pound note was an absolute fortune, so to be trusted with making change was a big responsibility. I learned to lay the note on the register and count the change into the customer's hand before putting the note away.

Mummy taught me that, and also how to measure rice and sugar to the fraction of an ounce by putting the brass weights on one side of the scale and watching until the scoop side was exactly level with the weighted side. The inspectors came once a year to examine the scales and weights to test their accuracy and to make necessary adjustments. It was a relief to Mummy and Dadda when they were finished with their testing and had put their stamp of approval on them once again.

The daily routine of the shop became an apprenticeship for me. Much of my practical education was learned behind the shop counter and in being part of the everyday jobs connected with it. But waiting on customers, as pleasant as that was, took second place to going to Wenhaston County Council School.

Though the school building and the playground were similar to the ones in Peasenhall, there was an indefinable difference in the atmosphere—almost of delight—that I had not known before. On the first day, each student was assigned a peg in one of the long hallways on either side of the largest of the three classrooms, which was used on occasion for general assembly. Boys used the hallway to the right and the girls used the left hallway. The assigned peg was our own space to hang our plimsolls for play, our mackintoshes for wet weather, and whenever needed, a small lunch bag that held a jam sandwich and a flask of milk.

At the end of each hallway there were two washbasins with a length of cotton toweling hanging on a wooden roller that you pulled round until you found a dry spot. Since there was only cold water to wash in, I don't believe any of us would have risked getting chilblains in winter except for our mentor, Miss Danford. The toilets were across the back playgrounds, four of them in a neat brick building. Always when we came back in the rear door, Miss Danford stepped out of her classroom to remind us to wash our hands. No one ever, to my memory, got past her room door without being directed to the washbasins, and no one dared defy her.

On the first day of school after my arrival, some of the children who lived further down Back Road came to call for me. This became a familiar pattern, though after the first day I joined them in the road. Some like Kathy and Walter Wilson came from just around the corner, but Gladys, Connie, and her cousins Tom and Clara Block came from farther afield. Others like Harold Hatcher and the two Dr. Barnardo's boys who lived at the Ablett's Farm, Bernie Mansfield, and George Sturgeon, frequently merged at the Saunders corner on our journey to school. Getting to and fro was half the fun in those days.

As we straggled, skipped, laughed, and walked toward the school, past the back entrance to the *Compass* and on up Back Road to the place where Back Street and Front Street met, other children joined us. There was Joy Youngs, the baker's daughter, George Durrant, Arthur and Dick Cannon, Julia Ethridge, and William Hammond, hurrying to school. To arrive early meant a precious few moments on the school playyard before Mr. Sangster blew the second whistle. We walked up past the church, always peeking in the blacksmith's door on the left as we went. We passed the Village Hut on the same side as the blacksmith's, then crossed over the road to pass the cemetery on the other side. Other children joined us from the lanes and from the Council Houses, Margaret Hazel, Morris Atmer, Barbara English, her brother Ivan and the Tibbenhams: Roy, Margie and Primrose, and Ann Leach, Ruth Napthine and Norman Battle. In all, it was a journey of about a mile from the shop to Wenhaston County Council School. A very short and interesting mile it seemed to me.

Another crowd came from the Black Heath in the opposite

direction, making a total of about forty to fifty children converging on the playground in front of the school to spend a delicious few minutes playing in groups until the whistle sounded to signal the beginning of the school day.

At the whistle, the teachers appeared at the doorway to help us form up into our special class groups and to march us inside. On rainy days we formed our groupings in the hallways, hanging our wet macs on our own pegs and changing out of our wellingtons into the plimsols that hung by their laces in readiness. In the classrooms, we were grouped by age. Gladys Spencer, Barbara English and I all shared birthdays in July of the same year, which gave us instantaneous common ground.

All of the twenty-odd children in Miss Danford's room were within a few months to a year's age spread. We moved through the school system, through the various forms and classrooms, through the years in friendly unison. We were inexorably bound together from the beginning. Our lives at school, at home, and at play were always intertwined, and we flowed and bumped together with mischievous exuberance. We knew we were lucky to be young and alive in our very own Suffolk village.

Miss Danford was everyone's first teacher. Old people in the Village would smile at the remembrance of having been taught by her when they were young and in the Primary class. "Aggie," as some of the grown-ups called her, was a spinster who had devoted her entire life to teaching. Though she was a strict disciplinarian, often cracking our knuckles with the ruler, she also coached her pupils into a love relationship with the whole education process. She taught us our sums, the multiplication tables, writing, and especially reading. Miss Danford introduced us to the magic world of fairy tales, such as *Aladdin and his Magic Lamp, Sinbad the Sailor, Snow White and the Seven Dwarfs, Cinderella, Little Red Riding Hood, Aesop's Fables,* and dozens more.

We eventually learned to recite many poems written for children, including the long ones such as Robert Louis Stevenson's *The Land of Counterpane*. Best of all, on rainy days when we couldn't go out on the playground for our usual mid-morning and mid-afternoon play periods, Miss Danford read to us. These were wonderful long and imaginative stories that had to be continued on another day. One of my favourites was *The Water Babies* and another was *Treasure Island*. They went on for ages and we didn't want them to ever end.

I savored those stories and waited impatiently for every new installment. At home, Dadda listened while I repeated whatever new story I had learned that day. He would clamp his old pipe between his teeth, and fix me with total attention while the kettle whistled and Goofie slept peacefully on the hearth.

Just before we were ready to leave Miss Danford's class, she coached us in the art of composing poetry. She explained that we were to use rhyme and verse to construct a meaningful statement about something that was of great interest to us. We could chose any subject, but it had to make sense and rhyme properly. It was a hard task. It was one thing to memorize a well-written poem, but quite another to compose a poem of one's own. Though our attempts must have caused her great consternation, we were proud of our work. Because he was the most important person in my life, I wrote about Dadda, and after many corrections, ran home one afternoon gleefully brandishing my graded paper.

When he'd lighted his pipe and smoothed out the crumpled paper, he held it out to catch the light from the window. I was hoping desperately that he wouldn't laugh at my efforts. I watched his face while he read my childish scrawl:

There is a pretty garden
with flowers of every hue,
A rosebush in the corner
does credit to the view

A man stands in that garden
My Dadda is his name
He's loved by every person
And he loves them all the same

He's old, he's gray, he's wise,
And that's the reason why
He is the Dadda that I love
And shall love 'til I die.

Dadda put the paper down on his knee and cleared his throat. He didn't speak for a minute, and then he frowned. I knew I had utterly failed.

"Say something," I begged. "Is it all right?" I wanted him to like my poem and tell me I had done a good job of putting the poem together. Finally, he smiled and said the magic words I wanted to hear.

"Yes, well, so now I'm old, am I? Yes, beauty, I do like it and I'll keep it here beside me on the shelf." He did, too. He folded it in half and used it for ages as a bookmark in whatever book he happened to be reading.

From Miss Danford's class, we graduated to Miss Piper's room. She was a young unmarried woman, who would normally have been called a spinster. Rumour had it she was courting a young man from Halesworth. None of us knew for sure, but she was very attractive. She was quite tall with, as Lenny remarked, a "very good build," and carried herself well. Her best features were her beautiful blue eyes and naturally fair hair which she kept in a tidy bun at the back of her head. Most of us were fascinated by her fastidious grooming habits, for even on the playground she never had a hair out of place or a wrinkle in her skirt.

It was the teachers' habit to take a tea break during the morning and afternoon recess, and watching Miss Piper sip tea was a lesson in true British social grace and elegance. Imagine our consternation one day when we discovered she wasn't drinking tea at all, but plain hot water with a slice of lemon floating in it. On several occasions some of us, thinking this might be a magic potion for flawless skin, tried to emulate her. After several attempts, we went back to drinking our standard brew of strong, sweet, milky tea.

Lessons were harder in her class. All of our writing had to be done in ink instead of pencil, with no blots or cross-outs. We had to clean the glass inkwells in each of our desks thoroughly before refilling them from the large bottle at the front of the room.

Twice a week in Miss Piper's class, the girls and boys were separated. The boys went off into Mr. Sangster's room to learn heaven knows what, but the girls who stayed with Miss Piper learned the niceties of "deportment," the art of walking with a book on one's head, reciting sophisticated poetry, working with raffia, caning chair seats, sewing, knitting, and even the rudiments of cooking.

On rare occasions we marched, boys and girls together, down to the village Hut, where Mrs. Bailey came to bang away on the out-of-tune piano while Miss Piper called the sequences for a folk dance lesson. One of our favourite numbers called *Rufty-Tufty* was a particularly lively and noisy dance. Though we wore our plimsolls, the wooden floor of the Hut seemed to buckle under us as we hoofed up and down like a herd of young elephants.

There was always some good-natured shoving and buffeting as girls and boys lined up in rows facing each other. We could make ourselves even by lining up two extra boys or two girls, but when there was one too many it meant that the odd man out had to sit on a chair by the window and wait his turn at the next dance. Next we formed into sets of four, spacing ourselves an arm's length from each other. When Mrs. Bailey struck up the first note on the piano, it was our cue to place hands at our waists, elbows akimbo, and begin the first phase of the intricate dance pattern.

We leapt and swung first one foot and then the other in time to the music. When the tempo changed, we charged across to the other side of the line, danced in place to the beat, pivoted and returned to our starting places. From there we began a series of complicated maneuvers of crossing over, first to one partner and then another, swinging our partners down the line on the left, then to the right, breaking away, and eventually reforming into the original line, to begin again.

The pattern was one thing; it was quite another to keep up the lively skipping pace and clap our hands over our heads at the proper time. To us, it was a delightful romp with much noisy laughter and eventually even some systematic rhythm, but I can't say the same for our teacher. Her usually soft voice became positively raucous, trying to make herself heard over the thumping on the piano, our stomping, clapping, and fits of giggling. But she did her level best to instill a sense of grace and to keep us all in some semblance of order. It was the only time we ever saw Miss Piper the least bit ruffled.

In later classes she coached us in the basics of ballroom dancing the waltz, the two-step and the foxtrot. We learned to hold our hands in the proper position with our bodies at a respectable distance from each other. The boys put their handkerchiefs over the spot where their hands touched the girl's shoulder, so as not to dirty her dress. Whenever possible the girls were teamed with boys, but it never fazed us for two girls to dance together. We were all intent on getting it right, counting off the steps and trying not to trip over each other's feet. We always ended the sessions by standing at attention and singing the National Anthem. Then we'd scramble to find our shoes and coats and march back to school in proper formation.

It was at about the time of the dancing lessons that Lenny taught me to whistle. My front teeth had finally grown all the way in, and I thought this was a wonderful skill. At first all I could produce were little squeaky noises, but with dedicated practice, and I did practice diligently, some recognizable tunes began to emerge. It was at one of the afternoon dance lessons when Mrs. Bailey struck up *God Save the King* that I dishonoured myself and the whole school by whistling the tune instead of singing with the others. When the music stopped, we noticed Miss Piper quivering. Nobody moved. We all waited, knowing there had been a huge breach of etiquette.

None of us were prepared for the words that cut through the still air and landed like icy shards on us. Looking straight at me, she proclaimed in no uncertain terms that no one *ever* whistled the National Anthem. Apparently whistling not only desecrated the royal honour, but also brought shame on the school. Furthermore, she added with a slight toss of her beautifully combed head, only boys and tomboys whistled. She ended by quoting an old saying that rang in the hall and bounced off each one of us: "A whistling woman and a crowing hen are neither fit for God nor men." Then she ordered us to line up to march back to school.

I was struck dumb. Here I had imagined she would applaud my genius and congratulate me. Instead, she had castigated my efforts, and for once some of my boldness left me. But as we collected our lunch pails and prepared to leave, a sense of the ridiculous swept over us.

Once we were properly dismissed and outside of the school grounds, someone snickered, then someone else. I glanced over at Walter, who had his mouth clamped shut, but his eyes were watering the way they did when he had a laughing fit. I punched him in the ribs and he exploded. He held his stomach and headed for the grassy bank where he sank down and rolled over and over, laughing his head off. The others joined in, and soon we were all rolling about holding our stomachs and laughing at the huge joke. The idea that I had insulted the school and even Royalty was too much for us to bear. We laughed until we were exhausted. Our lunch pails scattered and shoelaces untied, we straggled home content that the day had taught us a lesson in deportment that we should not soon forget.

Lenny also taught me to play the mouth organ and a few tunes on the accordion. My practice sessions caused consternation to everybody; even the dog covered his ears and occasionally howled. Dadda was patient with my renditions of *Now the Day is Over*, and *My Bonnie Lies Over the Ocean*, but Mrs. Saunders found it hard to bear. She issued an order that I was to practice only in Lenny's room while he was absent, and only after the shop was closed on Wednesday afternoons, and Sunday after church.

From Miss Piper's class, we reluctantly graduated into Mr. Sangster's class. The headmaster was an imposing gentleman, with ramrod straight back, always very serious with piercing eyes and sharp tongue. All of us respected and somewhat feared him, and none of us wanted to cross him or feel the lash of the thin cane he carried. At age eleven, in his class, if we passed our "O" and "A" level tests, we could go on to normal school in Beccles. If we didn't pass, we would stay in Mr. Sangster's class for three more years, until we completed the school's curriculum and were ready to leave school at age fourteen.

Life outside the classroom was always busy. School hours were from 8:00 a.m. until 4:00 p.m., with an hour for lunch and short recesses mid-morning and mid-afternoon. There never seemed to be enough hours in the day to complete all the projects we made for ourselves. Most of the children had chores of some sort. In the winter when the daylight hours were short, there was no time to gather again after tea for a game of rounders or hopscotch. That was for summertime only, and we looked forward eagerly to the lengthening days.

The long winter evenings were wonderful in a different way. At the kitchen table under a paraffin lamp Dadda helped me with my schoolwork, and afterwards would play a board game: "*Ludo,*" "*Snakes and Ladders,*" or draughts (checkers). He was a keen competitor and didn't allow me to sulk my way to winning a game.

No fear! In draughts he was particularly astute. But once he'd swept the board of all my men and cornered all my crowns, he graciously showed me his winning strategy and we'd start all over again.

"Best out of three," I'd say and then, "best out of five," or "seven," until it was well past my bedtime.

Dadda's habit after the evening meal was well defined. He consumed two bottles of Guiness in small sips as he paced back and forth from one end of the house to the other. It was a familiar ritual that went on without fail every evening. He would stop to tap out his pipe at the kitchen fire, then go over to the table to make his move on the board. Then he went on through the front sitting room to the barometer on the far wall, stopping to sip his Guinness on the way, then back to me in the kitchen, where the whole routine began anew. Up and down he paced, always pleasant, chatting with Mum and our house girl Letty, who sat by the fire knitting or hooking a new fireplace rug.

Sometimes he examined the barometer that hung on the far wall between the family portraits. I could hear him tap the knob in the middle of the huge dial and would know he was peering intently to see what change had occurred since the last time he'd checked it. When Dadda tapped the barometer, we got a reliable weather report on his return to the kitchen, and I would know whether or not I should wear my mac and rubber wellies to school in the morning.

When the winter wind howled, the bedrooms were icy. Though there were fireplaces in most of the bedrooms, we seldom lighted them. My room was the warmest, because in addition to being the smallest, it was located just above the kitchen. The kitchen chimney went right up the wall near the foot of my bed. I sometimes had two hot water bottles, one for my feet and another to cuddle to keep me from freezing to death. My favourite bottle was a triangular one of polished stone. It had a cozy, fleecy cover that was cut out to fit around the stopper. Once it was filled with near boiling water, it would stay warm for hours. The other was a squishy rubber one that also had a fuzzy cover. That was for cuddling.

Just before bedtime, I would take a torch, race up the cold stairway, tuck the stone hot water bottle in the middle of my bed, find my flannel nightdress and race back down the stairs to the warmth of the kitchen to wash and change. It was a nightly ritual, lingering by the fire, kissing everybody good night a dozen times, including Goofie. Finally I made a second wild dash up the cold staircase to pop under the covers and nestle snugly among the lovely warm feathers.

I never knew what time the grown-ups went to bed, but many nights I saw the beam of Dadda's big torch and felt his good hand stroke my forehead in that way he had of letting me know that all was well with our world.

Chapter 4

This England

This blessed plot, this earth, this realm, this England.

Shakespeare

Casual visitors hardly ever came to Wenhaston. Though throngs of summer visitors frequented the nearby seaside resorts of Southwold, Felixstowe, and Dunwich, Wenhaston had nothing much to offer sightseers. Many tourists came within a mile of us on their visits to the Blythburgh Cathedral, but few ventured farther to our snug little village. For Wenhaston, as attractive as it was to its inhabitants, had few historical landmarks of note.

It was with some surprise that half-way through the first year in Miss Piper's class, the Girl Guides in our Form were chosen to represent Wenhaston County Council School as part of a welcoming committee for some distinguished visitors. Miss Piper told us that a delegation of church dignitaries were coming to the village to get a first hand look at the rustic old Church painting, the "Doom," which took up one wall of our village church. Though none of us could imagine what interest anyone might have in the painting, it didn't matter. It was springtime and we would be out of the classroom for most of the day, and in the centre of all the action.

We looked forward to the event almost as eagerly as we looked forward to the annual Armistice Day service. On Armistice day we paraded from the school to the church, each wearing a poppy, to participate in the rememberance service for the dead heroes of our village from the Great War. We felt the reverence and sadness of those days, and we knew the service almost word for word. On the eleventh hour of the eleventh day of the eleventh month each year, as the church bell sounded the death knell, we children, along with the whole village, stopped to solemnly remember them.

On this splendid, festive, and rather auspicious occasion, the atmosphere was totally different. We were unashamedly showing off. It was lovely to be the chosen ones. Like me, most of the girls had only just joined the Guides. We had learned to say the Girl Guide Pledge, and had been drilled in the proper way to salute, how to form a line and march in step. Apart from that we were rank novices at being Guides. Oh, but we were thrilled to show ourselves worthy of our brand new navy-blue uniforms, to wear our wide brimmed felt hats and our thick leather belts. There were many useful gadgets that clipped to the rings on each side of our belts. So far, most of us only had two.

One of these was a huge penknife that included a can opener, a corkscrew, a screwdriver, several small spanners, a pair of scissors, and three different sized knives. It was weighty and brand new as was the gigantic whistle that hung from the ring on the other side. What with the weight of these items added to the enormous belt buckle with the Guide emblem, I, like the others, had difficulty keeping the belt positioned at my waistline. Unless we strapped them tightly, the belts had a tendency to sit at precarious angles on our hips. On this day, we sacrificed comfort in the interest of vanity. We were strapped so tightly we could barely breathe, but we thought we looked very smart in our uniforms. We relished the opportunity to be useful, and to be diverted from our daily routine.

That was how we learned more than we ever wanted to know about the Doom. Up until then, none of us had ever really looked at the dusty old painting, covered as it was by a thin drapery that was drawn back on special occasions. In later years we would come to appreciate this piece of mediaeval history, preserved for centuries in our ancient parish church, but for this moment we were both unaware and ignorant of its inherent value. Neither had we given a thought to the fact that the old stone church that was so familiar to us all, was also of interest to historians.

St. Peter's Church that stood in the centre of the village, we now learned, had been entered in the Domesday Book in 1086, and was in itself a monument of some note. Evidences of Saxon stones in the walls and windows from Norman times gave proof to its antiquity. It was pointed out to us that changes in its structure, to the chancel, sanctuary, nave, bell tower and porch were well documented. These changes attested to the fact that men in every age since before the Norman conquest had attempted to restore and preserve this special place of worship. One could almost imagine the myriad feet that had trodden the uneven cold stone floor down through the ages and bowed the knee in worship in this ancient building.

The rood-screen painting on wood of the Last Judgement presented its own difficulty in interpretation for us. But we accepted its importance, and struggled to make sense of it. It showed the figure of the Divine Judge sitting on a faded rainbow, with St. Michael weighing souls and what appeared to be the Devil making notes on a scroll. St. Peter held the key to the gate of Heaven, and an oversized fish head that we were told represented the jaws of Hell, yawned widely.

Three wooden figures were attached on the front of the painting. The central figure was obviously Christ the Saviour, with St. John on one side of him and the Virgin Mary on the other. The outline of the rood, a wooden cross removed ages before, could still be detected. Other painted figures, all naked except for their headgear, we were told represented a king, a queen, a bishop and a cardinal. In the top right hand was the fully clothed figure of John the Baptist, thankfully with his head firmly attached.

We stood quietly while the dignitaries coughed and pointed out their various bits of knowledge, and shuffled our feet ever such a little on the hard stone floor during the lengthy lecture. After the viewing, there was a bit of a scramble for seats. All of the visitors sat together in the first four rows to the right of the pulpit. This grouping displaced some of the regular members whose seats were held in trust for them alone. The congregation was so well-trained that even when the seat owner was not in church, the others reverently left those seats unoccupied. Today, a faint clucking and a collective sigh of resignation was heard as the congregation settled themselves for the remaining ceremonies. This, after all, was a special occasion that called for some sacrifices.

We Guides regrouped ourselves to march up the aisle singing a hymn, just as we did on Sunday mornings, except we were all wearing our Girl Guide uniforms instead of our choir robes. Margaret Hazel, the tallest and most sensible of the lot of us, led the procession. She was flanked by Gladys and Clara. All three carried flags, with the largest being the Union Jack, the smaller ones being the Church flag and the St. George's Cross. The rest of us followed in pairs, splitting a bit untidily into two groups at the choir benches. Miss Piper, who walked alone behind us, did a beautiful genuflexion and flowed into the front left hand seat, presumably so she could watch all of us and keep us mindful of her presence. The Vicar, Mr. Hardingham, and one of the visiting Bishops walked firmly behind us all, but far enough behind not to run over Miss Piper who spent the fleetest of seconds bowing the knee and moving gracefully into position.

They too divided at the front and each squeezed into the back choir bench behind us on either side. First one and then the other would pop forward from their seats to speak in those special voices men of importance use on weighty occasions. We sang several hymns lustily, but we hoped with grace, all the while watching Miss Piper's face for the least sign of displeasure. Mr. Hardingham made a long prayer, and he and the Bishop led the processional back down the aisle singing *Guide us, O Thou Great Jehovah.* Then he closed the curtain over the great painting.

After we sang *God Save the King,* we were free to go home, but none of us would go home just yet. The best part of the whole event was ahead of us. The Church Guild ladies had prepared tea for the visiting dignitaries in the Sunday School building just down the lane to the left of the church, and we were invited. What a feast it was. There were tiny cucumber sandwiches and bread spread with many different jams and marmalades. There were sponge cakes and treacle tarts, sugar biscuits and strawberry scones with mounds of double cream, gingerbread with white icing, and chocolate cake slices arranged on lovely platters. The room smelled of fresh tea, and the women, dressed in their best pinafores, dispensed trays of steaming teapots to each of the tables around the room. Mrs. Ellis directed our Girl Guide delegation to a table in the corner. Our help would be needed to serve second and third cups to the noisy crowd, and to refill the serving plates as they became empty. We plopped our hats and coats on the chairs, and followed her to the kitchen.

Mrs. Ellis was a kindly lady. Her husband, Mr. Wallace Ellis, was the Clerk for the Parish Council, an important position in the village. The Ellises were a prominent Wenhaston family and there were a lot of them. Three Ellis families lived within sight of my house, and there were others scattered about the village. Mr. and Mrs. Percy Ellis lived next door to us on the Bramfield Road. Mrs. Percy Ellis was my favourite of all of them, but they were all genuinely nice people. Though our side yard and their front yard were separated only by a low wall, I hardly ever went to their front door when I went to see them, which was often.

It was much easier to go to their kitchen door, and a lot less formal. If I were going to stay for a while, I could leave my shoes in the tiny mudspace just inside the back door. If I went to the front door, I had to remove my shoes outside. I think most of England in the 1930s had the same system for mud removal: take the shoes off completely. It was an unwritten law called "not tracking in" and there were penalties for any infractions. I had to pass the Ellis's back gate every time I went to fetch water from Miss Danford's pump. They had a little terrier, "Mitzi," that was friendly and playful. When I walked past their gate, she would always greet me with a happy little bark.

Next to the Percy Ellis house, farther down the Bramfield road, lived Mr. and Mrs. Wallace Ellis. Across Back Road in front of the shop there was a duplex house where "old" Mrs. Ellis lived on one side and Mrs. Louie Long, who was related in some way, on the other. It was only after I was grown up that I fully realized that nearly all the villagers were related in some way or other. The Saunders were an exception. Their nearest relatives that I knew of lived in Colchester and Ipswich.

Most of the village women, including all of the Ellis clan, belonged to the Church Guild. Because of the shop, Mummy was severely limited in the number of functions she could attend. But she contributed in many ways, providing boxes of tea, and sometimes baking sponge cakes for various events. She was always eager to hear the details and especially to hear "who did what" at any gathering I was allowed to attend. I viewed it as quite a responsibility to take note of everything, so that later I could give an accurate accounting.

We children knew for sure that there was always an abundance of food, and nearly always much left over. We knew that at this special function, there would be plenty of good things for us to eat after the adults had been served. There always were. We knew too that we'd be in the kitchen helping with the washing up once the hall was empty of guests. But that was part of the fun, being with the women in the kitchen, listening to their gossip and light banter as we cleared the tables and swept the floor. Best of all, we liked to hear them singing.

Florrie Wilson, Walter's mother, loved to sing as she worked, so someone would always start her off with *Annie Laurie* or *Isle of Capri,* and the rest would join in. Florrie was from Yorkshire, and had a broad north country accent. There was a clipped sharpness in her voice, which contrasted distinctly with the soft Suffolk inflections we were used to hearing. When she sang, however, her voice was clear and lilting and a delight to hear. This day, the women were happy; they sang as they worked, and we helped them. We knew we had been a part of something special in our village. At the end, we each wrapped leftover jam tarts and bits of sponge cake in serviettes to take home with us. It was reward enough.

Singing was a great part of growing up in our small village of Wenhaston. The children sang because the adults led. We mainly sang old folk tunes that lent themselves well to the mouth organ or accordion. Songs like *Clementine*, *My Blue Heaven* and *I'll take you home again, Kathleen* were favourites as we walked over the gorse-covered heaths, or as we picked blackberries and bluebells on one of the many "commons:" open areas of grass, bordered by hedges and trees. The young women walked with the children, picking wild flowers for their tables or gathering berries to make steamed pudding or jam.

I especially remember Walter's Mum, and Mrs. Spenser, Gladys' Mum being among the women who foraged with us for wild gooseberries on the common near Bicker's heath. We had to walk down a footpath along the edge of a sugar beet field to get to the best places for picking berries. I loved to take home some bounty for our own table. Mummy made a wonderful steamed pudding using blackberries and apples, which was one of Dadda's favourite "sweets." She topped it with warm custard, the same kind she used for Christmas pudding. It was delicious.

The *Compasses Inn*, which the villagers called simply "The Compass," was the undisputed heart of our village, the entertainment

Compasses Inn

centre for most villagers. Music and song were very much a part of pub life. Lucky was the village pub that had an old piano as ours did, and someone who could play a tune. No matter that the keys were yellow and cracked, and the once polished top was stained with hundreds of rings from mugs of ale. It was an instrument that could and did accompany singing. Besides the piano, the mouth organ was particularly popular, and the concertina and the accordion were also good "travelling" instruments.

With the increased popularity of the wireless our world was expanding, and that was especially true with music. Romantic tunes from America such as Bing Crosby's, *Did you ever see a dream walking?*, Kate Smith's, *I don't know why I love you like I do,* and Guy Lombardo's, *It looks like rain in Cherry Blossom Lane,* were beginning to be mixed in with *It's a long way to Tipperary, Bless 'em All, Roll out the Barrel,* and Vera Lynn's *Be like the kettle and sing.* Sing we did. Whether old or new, the songs became familiar because we joined our voices together, learning the words and melodies from each other in joyful repetition.

We sang in church, in school, on school outings, riding our bikes, or walking across the meadows and heaths. The most memorable singing we did was on chilly spring mornings on a farm on the Blyford Road. We went to pick strawberries and we were instructed to sing as we picked. The adults in charge realized that some of us would eat all the profits. They gave us big baskets to carry and as we went down the field singing *Three blind mice,* we were told to concentrate on three things: staying in our appointed row, putting only ripe berries in the basket, (no overripe or yellow ones) and keeping in tune.

Time was money; the faster we picked, the more money we made. When our baskets got full, we ran with them to the lorry at the field entrance. We ran back to the stick we'd poked in the ground to mark the place where we'd left off. It didn't seem like hard work, and the season was short. On rainy days we couldn't pick at all, and the next day the berries would be mud-splatted and hard to find. For our efforts we earned tuppence a basket. It was a great incentive, and even though we sang, there was always a way to taste a lovely ripe strawberry or two.

On week nights the *Compass* clientele consisted mainly of regulars of every age, single or married, who stopped in for "a pint" on their way home. Saturday night was family night when young parents with school age children would gather along with the regulars for the early part of the evening. There was always a dart game going. Some who sat on the sidelines kept up lively conversations and banterings. Dart competitions were an essential part of the British social scene, and some of the young, single adults traveled to pubs far and wide to compete.

Lenny was a keen dart player and was on several teams. He taught me the correct way to hold a dart between the thumb and forefinger, and how to control the weight of the throw to hit the mark more accurately. Once or twice a year, when the wooden dart boards at the Compass began to dry out, Lenny would bring them home and soak them for several days in one the huge galvanized tubs we used for laundry. He seemed to know exactly when the boards were ready to be remounted. They'd hang dripping in the back yard until they were at the right consistency to be returned to the pub. The temporary boards that had been used in the absence of the resoaked boards would now need renewing. Someone else would volunteer to take them home and go through the soaking process. There were always good dart boards at the *Compass.*

Lenny was also quite a musician, having taught himself to play the mouth organ and the accordion. We sang a great variety of songs and sea chanties in the pubs. Many times I've heard Lenny play *Down among the dead men* or a rousing rendition of *Blow the man down* on his accordion at the *Compass*. He took me with him sometimes on Saturday nights. He'd buy me a lemon squash and let me stay for a game of darts with some of my friends.

At eight o'clock I had to leave, as most of the young children did. I would run home to Dadda, sometimes taking him his Guinness, and I'd tell him about everything: who was there, what we sang, and whether we'd won or lost our game of darts. Mummy seldom went to the pub. I think she preferred staying home with Dadda. I never thought of it then, but I've wondered many times in the intervening years if they both longed to go with us and be part of the jolly crowd at the village pub. I still don't know. No one ever mentioned any frustration or expressed a desire to change a difficult situation. I accepted things the way they were, and never questioned or expected that anything was unusual about our family.

The Village Hall, usually referred to as "the Hut," was another important part of village life. It was a wooden building built shortly after the Great War ended in 1918, which made it the newest building in the village. It was larger and better appointed than the brick and stone Church Hall where the Sunday School classes, Girl Guide and Parrish Council meetings were held, having a more complete kitchen and inside toilets. The two places were within a stone's throw of each other, but served to accommodate the needs of the villagers in completely different ways. The brick Church Hall, located in the lane that ran between the Cemetery and the side or "Porch" door of the church, was built in the 1600s as Wenhaston's first school. It was still used only for church connected functions in the 1930s.

The Hut, on the other hand, was used for many social functions. It was on the main road often called "The Street" leading to the school, just beyond the blacksmith's shop, and catty-cornered from the church yard. There was nearly always something going on there. On certain afternoons, it was used for holding "whist-drives," a competitive card game competition similar to today's bridge tournaments. Alternately it was used by the school for teaching dance lessons or for practicing the annual school play, and by the

Women's Guild for activities that required more space than the smaller Church Hall would allow.

The Hut's most popular function was for the "Wenhaston Village Club." This Club was a group made up mainly of young people, roughly between the ages of early teens through about thirty-five, who met together for dancing and socializing on Friday and Saturday nights. Members took charge of things such as getting the dance floor ready, hiring the bands, collecting money at the door, and sweeping up afterwards. Anyone who wanted to attend the dances could do so by paying sixpence at the door. The money paid for hiring musicians, who came from neighbouring towns when our own local talent fell short. Sometimes the out-of-towners brought along their own pianist, but more often than not, the bands were accompanied on the piano by our own talented Mrs. Bailey, who could rock the walls with her rhythmic thumping.

Lenny and his friend Jimmy Broom were staunch members of the Village Club. The dance floor had to be waxed to make it slide easily. This was done by strewing a white powdery substance over the floor. When the powder was ground in a bit, the floor became shiny. The more it was rubbed in, the glossier it got. We children helped by sliding over it before the music started. Sometimes it was a challenge to stand upright, let alone dance, when there was a good job of waxing. During half-time, when the band took a break, it would be waxed again. It was even more of a challenge to stand upright for those who had run down to the *Compass* for a quick pint between dances.

The quality of the music depended mainly on the experience of that evening's band. Most of them played a combination of tempos, alternating between the fast and slow numbers. At some point in the evening there would be the "rompers," a time when rollicking group dances like *The Lambeth Walk, The Hokey-Pokey,* and *Knees up Mother Brown* got the ball rolling for sing-a-longs. I remember one well that was entitled *Who's taking you home tonight?.* Sometimes somebody in the band sang the melody. But no matter how many waltzes, foxtrots, tangos, and rompers were played, the dances always ended with a waltz tune and the lights were dimmed. When the lights went up again and the music stopped, every one stood to attention to sing *God Save the King.*

Another important building stood beside the Hut. It was a small building down at one end of the Hut enclosure. This was Mr. Woolnough's fish and chips shop, one of the busiest places around. The memory of the wonderful aroma that wafted through the whole village makes me hungry even today. If you were going to buy fish and chips for the evening meal on Friday or Saturday nights, you had to be sure and get there before the dance started, otherwise you might have to stand on line a long time. Cod from the North Sea was delicious and plentiful, and was a staple in our diet. Dipped in batter and deep fried, the succulent white meat was the best in the world. Mr. Woolnough had a marvelous device to cut chips. He would take whole potatoes, scrubbed, but with the skins still on, and put them in the top of the large square cutting machine. He would then pull the handle down with a bang and force the potato through a kind of grill work of sharp knives. The chips fell out the bottom, to be scooped up and thrown into a vat of sizzling grease.

Fish and chips were wrapped first in a square of greaseproof paper, and then in newspaper. If you were buying chips alone, they would come wrapped in a cone of waxed paper so you could eat them walking or riding along. The cone not only kept them warm, but allowed the vinegar to stay in the bottom without soaking through.

Apples from local orchards were plentiful in season. Our parents provided us with lots of ripe, palatable fruit. But "scrumping" (stealing) apples was a pastime we children couldn't resist. That we got caught out was beside the point. It was the challenge that tempted us. Usually we scrumped when the trees were loaded with apples in a small orchard on the Bramfield road. It was one of the few times we didn't sing as we worked. In fact we did our best to be as quiet as possible. We whispered in falsetto voices as we helped each other form a strategy. On a dare and with a little help, I could be counted on to climb over the fence and into dangerous territory. If the farmer's dogs were out that day, I had to beat a hasty retreat. But the dogs usually stayed near the house at the other end of the orchard, so we could often get in and out before our intrusion was discovered. Our efforts to be quiet and stealthy were limited. Mostly we were noisier than when we sang, crashing around under the trees.

Those of us on the dangerous side of the fence inside the orchard clambered up the trees or jumped up to reach the apples on the lower branches. The cohorts on the safe side of the fence waited for us to throw the apples to them, often missing the best ones. They, of course, could see danger coming from a long distance away. So with a warning shout, they turned and ran, leaving the brave few up the trees to scramble down and over the fence any way we could. The apples we got were nearly always green and sharp tasting. Besides stomach aches and bruises from climbing the fences, we got chased by the owner and chastised at home when we got found out. I often wonder why we continued to find it such enormous fun.

Near the beginning of each school year in late August, our families traditionally purchased new clothes for us. The basic elements were woolen underwear, some of it knitted, white blouses, wool socks, big navy blue bloomers used for athletics, stout shoes, and a good, warm coat. There was a new wool skirt or dress that was considered "Sunday best" to be worn only on high days and holidays. This once a year event was meant to clothe us decently not only for school, but for Sundays and all the special occasions that we participated in connected with the church. In our day, and possibly to the present time, the Church of England had Holy Days and festivals for every prominent Saint, and we children were very much a part of these frequent festivities. We, therefore, were schooled religiously in the art of making ourselves presentable: no stains on our gym-slips , our shoes polished, with black knee socks, darned, pulled up and well gartered.

On the Sunday in September closest to Michaelmas, the festival to honour the Archangel Michael, we wore our new winter clothes for the first time. Besides new skirts, blouses and blazers, we also had new gloves, hats, scarves, socks and shoes. Usually the shoes squeaked for the first few Sundays until we got them broken in. We did look smart in our new outfits. Toward springtime our school uniforms and our best winter clothes began to show signs of wear. Also, as the weather warmed, we had a special need for something lighter than our winter woolies.

Between Easter and Whitsun, the seventh Sunday after Easter, there was another flurry of new clothes, though not on quite the scale as our winter wardrobes. The girls got new cotton frocks, and the boys got new short trousers and shirts. These new spring clothes also served us for our annual school photographs. So it was that none of us were ever photographed in our school gym-slips and white blouses, only in our Sunday frocks and best shoes.

Most of the girls' mothers bought material and sewed their spring dresses for them. But since Mrs. Saunders was busy with the shop, she had little time for sewing. Instead she would send me with a length of cloth to Mrs. Barber, the village seamstress, to be fitted for my new clothes. Mrs. Barber lived in the second house in the row at the top of Cole's Hill, almost next door to Ivy Cottage, Kathy and Walter Wilson's home. I could stop in to see them on my way to or from Mrs. Barber's. Sometimes I stopped only for a few minutes, depending on how much time there was before tea.

There was always something interesting going on at the Wilson house. The most exciting thing in my memory that happened at their home was the installation of a modern "flushing" toilet. It was installed upstairs off the master bedroom, and all the neighbours where invited in to inspect it—to ooh and aah and make clucking noises over the new white porcelain, pull-chain toilet.

When the newness had worn off a bit and the neighbours stopped coming round to have a look, we children were allowed to see it anytime. However, we were never allowed to use it, only to LOOK. One day when I was there playing, I thought I'd test the water, so to speak. Walter egged me on to ask Kathy, who being our elder by five years, was in charge of us. I started by cajoling to be allowed to "see" the new toilet. Walter chimed in and we all trooped upstairs through their parents' bedroom to have a look. We did our usual inspection, noting the tall tank up near the ceiling and the nice wooden handle on the end of the chain.

Then Walter and I began to pressure Kathy, to no avail. I pleaded with her to let me use the new toilet. I persuaded her that I really did "have to go" but only "number one." I thought that would do the trick. But Kathy had strict orders not to let anyone use the lavatory, especially while her parents were out of the house. Her mind was made up. She knew there would be dire consequences for disobedience, and she wasn't going to risk it. She knew as well as we did that if she relented, one of us would brag about it to our mutual friends, either accidentally or on purpose, and she would be in trouble.

Kathleen, at fourteen, had already left school and would soon be going to work. In fact, Kathy worked as a "shop-girl" for the Saunders for a year during the war. That was an enjoyable time for both of us. But on this day she was "in charge" of us.

Walter and I were both a few years younger than Kathy, and we were supposed to mind her. With pressure from both of us, Kathy would often give in to us and join in our games. But not this day. We tried several of our childish wiles on her, but she was adamant. I danced and hopped on one foot, held my stomach and made unseemly grunts and groans, but nothing worked. By this time, Walter was giggling and Kathy was threatening us with mayhem. We realized her patience was wearing thin. Finally, Kathy wrung her hands and in exasperation pulled out a huge ornate chamber pot from under her mother's bed and told me in no uncertain terms to use it and be done. I knew she was serious.

It was a disastrous move. No sooner had I positioned myself on the ornate chamber pot, than we heard a loud "crack." The pot shattered into several pieces with one sharp piece attached to my bum. It took us an hour to clean up the mess. Kathy swabbed my backside with iodine and found a plaster to put over the wound. All the while she swabbed, she scolded me, and Walter rolled on the floor, laughing his head off. His laughter was always infectious, and soon all three us were holding our stomachs and wiping our eyes. I got another scolding from Mummy when I arrived home late for tea, with a fairy tale version of how I got my bum cut.

We girls began to learn many skills in Miss Piper's class. We learned hand-sewing first, making endless practice rounds of "blanket stitch" with embroidery thread on kitchen towels and hankies. We learned to iron "transfer" flower patterns on pillow-slips, and embroider the leaves and petals. We also learned how to hand-sew lace on ladies handkerchiefs, and embroider an initial in one corner. For several years, the finished products were our special Christmas presents to our mothers, aunts and friends.

Our regular lessons: Scripture, math, reading and writing, were held in the morning hours. The afternoons were used for developing us in many different ways. The girls, and occasionally the boys, learned to crochet, hook rugs, weave with raffia and cane chair seats in the afternoon hours. There were always multiple projects that challenged us.

One of the most challenging projects we ever did was to make our own dresses for Easter and the spring class photograph. It was our first attempt at dressmaking, and we had some doubts about the outcome. We were encouraged to get our measurements at home, and cut the fabric to the pattern of our choice. We were to work on sewing the pieces together during class time. I was able to sew the side seams together with little difficulty. Then came the fiddly bits—setting in the sleeves and attaching the little "eton" collar with the rounded edges. At first it was a challenge, but then it became a battle of wills, and the dress was winning. I was beside myself.

Barbara's mother helped her to make lovely petal-type sleeves to go with her collarless dress, and Gladys made delightful little cap sleeves to match the V-neck front of hers perfectly. I struggled on with mine, tearing the sleeves out many times over, as well as my hair. Finally, Dadda, tired of my nightly tirades, persuaded Mum to help me. She sent me and my disaster to see Mrs. Barber on Coles Hill.

Mrs. Barber was a nice lady who always smelled faintly of lavender. She had a huge pin cushion permanently attached to her left arm. She greeted me with her usual warm smile, then looked aghast at the bedraggled mess I carried. She made me stand on her little stool, pulled the dress here and there around me, and proceeded to stick hundreds of pins the whole way around my neck and armholes. Trying to get the dress off again without damaging myself seriously was an exercise in dexterity, but a few scratches were a small price to pay for my sanity. Mrs. Barber coached me through the remainder of the project.

Each afternoon before tea, I would run to her home to sew seams and get a new fitting. At last I had only to make the belt and smooth it with the iron for it to be completely finished. Ironically, since Easter Sunday turned out to be cold and rainy that year, I had to wear my green macintosh over my lovely new frock. The day the school photographs were taken, however, was fine and warm. We giggled and shuffled and looked resplendent in our "almost" hand-sewn dresses.

Miss Piper's Class 1938

Chapter 5

The Bells of St. Peter's

Come all to church, good people
Oh, noisy bells, be dumb;
I hear you, I will come.

Housman

St. Michael's Church Lane

St. Peter's Parish Church was the undisputed centre of spiritual activity in the village of Wenhaston. It was the heart and soul of village life. No matter what phase of life one was in or what social standing, whether rich, poor, or somewhere in between, the villagers turned to the church as their catalyst for many of life's solutions and endorsements. In short, the village moved in time with the sound of the church bells.

It was the place where everyone gathered for joyful occasions such as weddings, christenings and confirmation rites, when the bells rang joyfully and the sound of them reverberated gladly throughout the village. We didn't need a newspaper to tell us what events were taking place. The church bells told the story and set the mood for the occasion.

The church was the first place a newborn was taken, to be baptized. It was also the last place the young soldiers going off to war visited before journeying to the battlefields. It was the place they came home to, to give thanks for their safe return. It was the place of constant remembrance for those who were killed in service to their country. It was a place where grief and loss were not strangers, and the place of consolation for those who needed it.

It was, without a doubt, a big part of daily village life. Certain of the villagers, and especially the older ladies, attended both morning and evening services at the church. We often saw them coming out of the church gate in the mornings as we were going to school, their prayer books clutched in their hands.

We children were hardly ever expected to attend church for the daily morning prayer or the evensong service on weekdays. For special services, our classes formed up and marched from the school to the church, but that was on infrequent occasions. We were expected, however, to pay full attention during our class devotions at the beginning of each school day. This involved spending much time learning parts of the Bible. We memorized scripture—the Sermon on the Mount and long portions from the Psalms, repeating verses for the day as designated by our teacher. Before we broke at midday for the noon meal, we sang grace to the tune of *All People Who on Earth do Dwell.* It went like this:

Be present at our table Lord
Be here and everywhere adored
His Kingdom come, His mercy praise
Come ye before Him and rejoice. Amen

Upon our return, we stood at attention for a moment and sang our thanks to the tune of another hymn:

Thank you for the food we eat
Thank you for the world so sweet
Thank you for the birds that sing
Thank you God for everything. Amen

Though I never understood the need for this endless recitation at the time, I have been thankful many times over for this early training. Many times in my life have the old familiar words come back to my memory, giving me renewed joy, hope and spiritual uplifting.

On Sundays, almost everyone went to church. The Church bells pealed to notify the village that the service was ready to begin. When they tolled, we knew we only had a few minutes left to get in the door before the processional began, or we'd be late and embarrassed. Until I became a choir member, I walked with and sat beside Mummy. She carried her own *Book of Common Prayer* and had a special kneeling cushion on the left hand side near the pulpit, so she could hear every word of the Reverend Mr. Hardingham's sermon. The choir members went earlier and were pressed into services for lots of other duties. We took turns tolling the bells, pumping air into the wheezy old organ, and gathering prayer books that were scattered about, putting them in tidy piles on the table beside the door.

I sat through the service being especially careful not to wriggle. The stone floor was uneven, and with each movement, the chair wobbled and made a squeaky, scraping sound. I always thought Mummy seemed edgy on Sunday mornings. She wore her best hat to church, the tan felt that had a long brown feather that swept from the crown past her left eye to just below her ear. Whenever I was being a fidget, she would look through the feather. I would catch the gleam in her eye and know I needed to sit still. It was with a sense of relief for both of us that she allowed me to join the choir.

It was at choir practice that I first learned the meaning of enunciation. The Reverend Hardingham was a hard taskmaster. In his rectitude he was much like our headmaster, Mr. Sangster. But in his attitude toward us there was a big difference. Mr. Sangster carried a long thin cane that he was quick to use on any of us who crossed him. The Reverend Hardingham was insistent, but never cruel. He would make us repeat the things he wanted us to know over and over, and clap his hands in delight when he was satisfied we had "got it." He had his work cut out for him. In our daily speech we were used to slurring our words and using Suffolk colloquialisms, but he would have none of that. He taught us to pronounce words clearly, and clip the ends off them precisely.

During our weekly practice he would fasten on a word or phrase we were singing, wave his arms and stop us mid sentence. "It's not 'nutty'," he would say in exasperation, "but 'nity', e-ter-NITY." And we would practice first saying the word, and then singing it again until he was satisfied we had it right. He used the same patient coaching for "ever and ever." He made sure we clipped the "d" and would not allow "and" to run together with the final "ever." "It's not 'ANEVER'," he'd say, wrinkling his brow. "Separate the words and enunciate clearly." He'd make sure we had it right before we left. But he was kindly, and we tolerated his instruction more or less graciously.

He made us practice the responses to the morning prayers that we sung without the aid of the organ. He would begin: "O Lord, open thou our lips," and we would reply: "And our mouth shall show forth thy praise." "Remember," he would say, "the choir leads the congregation, so you must get it right for all of them."

I loved being in the choir for other reasons. One was that the benches we sat on were attached firmly to the floor, so they didn't budge when any of us moved. We also wore choir robes over our clothes; that added an extra layer of warmth on chilly mornings. We were part of the processional too, actually leading the adult choir down the aisle each Sunday morning. At the close of the service we marched down the aisle first, waited while the Vicar gave the benediction, and then joined in singing the three part amen before racing into the stone cubby where we kept our choir robes.

Our part in the service was very small, but our attention to detail was essential. At the beginning of the Apostles' Creed, it was important that all of us turn toward the altar in unison, and bow our heads together at the proper moment, as we said the name of Jesus Christ our Lord.

The best part was having the freedom to read during the sermon. Since the only books I had at my disposal were the hymnbook and the prayer book, I read through the entire "Solemnization of Matrimony" service on numerous occasions. The imperfect memorization of it came in handy for our theatre play days. Though occasionally I would liked to have played other parts, I was always the one chosen to be the Reverend who solemnly intoned, "Dearly beloved, we are gathered together here in the sight of God..."

We loved to act out plays. Every year at Christmastime we would be part of some play that was a combined effort of the school and the church. We practised saying our lines for weeks before the great event. The Hut was cleared, a stage erected and chairs were placed for the expected audience. Our dramas were always well attended, and we were proud of our accomplishments. But the plays we enjoyed most were the ones we put on for our private audiences, mainly our families. In fact, as long as we were together, we children liked doing almost anything.

When we weren't at home, we were either in school, in church or Sunday school, on our bikes, or playing. Whatever we did, we did together, nearly always in small groups, but sometimes en masse. We went through childhood fads and phases as thousands of children had done before us, and thousands more would do in the years to come. Our games were simple, but intense: hopscotch, marbles, rounders, and hide and seek. Our toys were mostly homemade: spinning tops with string, yo-yos, and conkers made from horse chestnuts.

The playground just behind Miss Danford's room had a wonderful big seesaw and some swings. We skipped rope on the playground, sometimes with double ropes going in opposite directions. Two of us twirled the ropes while others hopped in and out, not missing a beat. We also used the brick wall expanses between the windows and doors to play countless games with a simple rubber ball. Since a ball would bounce easily off the walls and pavement, we were able to work out a whole series of procedures that we played against the school's brick walls.

Miss Danford's room wall was the best because there was some good open space between the window and the corner. We took turns doing each portion of these complex routines that sometimes had as many as ten parts. Each part involved an increasingly difficult strategy. One I remember was throwing the ball from behind one's back, twisting around and then catching it as it bounced off the wall. If you missed it or dropped the ball, you were out and it became the next person's turn.

Sometimes a ball went astray and hit the window. Miss Danford would push open one of the small windows, thrust her head out gingerly, and reprimand us. When we left Miss Danford's class, we graduated to the front playground, which was much more spacious. It had an iron railing and two gates that separated it from the street. Some small trees were planted along the grassy strip between the railing and the pavement, so the playground was somewhat hidden from pedestrians. Occasionally a passerby would glance at us through the fence, or a dog on a leash or an old person who had wandered away from Bulcamp Union would stop and press close to the iron railing, wistfully watching us playing.

The whole asphalt playground was painted with white stripes and half circles for playing netball, with a tall metal hoop on either end of the playground. Netball was only for girls, and we played it on Friday afternoons, during the winter. The boys had their own games of football (soccer) for Friday afternoons, which they practiced on the playing field directly behind the school. We formed four athletic teams each spring in Miss Piper's class, two for the boys and two for the girls. All of us vied to become team leaders, but our teachers decided. I was once appointed captain for the Cavell team. It was a defining moment for me. Each team member wore a coloured band across her chest in the colour representing her team. The team captains wore two bands, proudly crossed over their blouses.

The boys' teams were named for Great War generals Allenby and Haig. Allenby's wore blue bands and Haig's wore red. The girls' teams were named for famous nurses of the same era, Cavell and Florence Nightingale. Cavell's wore yellow bands and Nightingale's wore green. On regular Fridays, the girls' teams challenged each other to netball and the boys did likewise for soccer.

In the spring the girls joined forces with the boys for cricket practice on the playing field, choosing up sides by grouping our normal teams in different sequences each week. Sometimes Cavell and Haig were teamed, at others Cavell and Allenby would play against Haig and Nightingale. We merged as one team when other school teams such as Halesworth or Bungay came to challenge us. When that occurred, our games took on new meaning. Though contests between our home teams were always energetic and often there was heated rivalry, we stood together staunchly against any "outsiders." We were often out-classed and out-sized, but never out-daunted. What we lacked in expertise, we made up for in spunk and plain hard-headedness. We played our hearts out, and win or lose, we thoroughly enjoyed being tested.

At one of these test matches, I was to discover my head was not as hard as I had originally thought. Georgie Sturgeon, a likeable and good-natured classmate who also happened to be from Dr. Barnardo's, was up at bat and it was to be my turn next. I took my position behind him to wait. Unfortunately, I stood too close. Georgie was a strong hitter who frequently twisted his whole body completely around to gain momentum. His aim was good. As he slung the bat over his shoulder in preparation to whomp the ball, I caught it full in the face. I heard the "crack" as it hit my nose, and then didn't know anything else until I woke up on the schoolroom floor sometime later.

Someone fetched the District Nurse, who lived just down the road from the school. I discovered her kneeling over me when I regained consciousness. I was covered in blood, and my face and head hurt horribly. I could smell the "smelling salts" under my nose. It was an amnonia smell that was too strong for comfort when you were awake. The nurse rinsed off my face with cold water and eventually helped me sit up. When the blood gushed anew, she made me lie down flat again. When the bleeding slowed, I was able to get up. I was a bit unsteady, but she helped me get my legs going. I must have looked a sight, as I had to walk with my head thrown back on my shoulders and a great wet towel over my face.

I knew I was hurt physically, but more than anything else, my pride was shattered. This had been an important game, one in which every team member was expected to give his very best. To lose one player and disrupt the play in this way was almost as bad as giving the game away. I had brought shame on myself and on my team by my stupidity. I was devastated at having let the team down in such an ignominious way. So the pain was more than skin deep, and I fretted inwardly while I bled outwardly.

I was partially mollified by being given a ride home in the nurse's car. Mummy looked aghast as the nurse led me through the shop door. They talked briefly, and then together they led me through the front hall and through the other door into the lounge, where they put me flat on the floor. The nurse gave Mummy some tablets for me to take, gave instructions about keeping cold compresses on my face, and said she'd ask the doctor to pop in to see me in the morning. I knew from experience that the doctor held office hours each morning at his surgery. Depending on how many patients he had, would stop in to see me after his surgery was over. For the remainder of the afternoon, I stayed on the floor, flat on my back, while the blood continued to run down the back of my throat. My head throbbed.

Dadda was in the bird shed when the nurse brought me in, so Lettie went to tell him the news. He came straightaway to survey the extent of my wound, and Goofie came in with him. Because of his "wobbly" head, Dadda couldn't get down on the floor beside me. But he did sit in a chair beside me, talking to me for what seemed like hours. With his good hand he steadied the dog, who thought I was playing some sort of new game for his benefit. Goofie finally stopped trying to play, and resigned himself to spreading out on the floor beside me. The afternoon slipped away to evening, tea time came and went and I remained on the floor with Dadda talking to me and then reading to me from *Oliver Twist*, the Dickens novel we were currently reading.

Mummy and Lettie took turns putting cold wet towels on my face, "to keep it from swelling" they said. But swell it did, and for several days I could hardly see at all. Mummy gave me tablets to take away the pain, which was really fierce at times. She also tried to tempt me to eat "something nourishing." She had a theory that food had curative powers. Whenever I was ill I had to eat certain things that I didn't like, but which she said were good for me. A beef broth known as Bovril was one of my least favourite cure-alls. It was said to have lots of protein and vitamins in it, and I did manage to please her by getting some of it down.

Some of the things she offered I considered "treats." I loved a bowl of "milk sop," buttered and sugared white bread in warm milk. I also liked warm custard over cold strawberry jelly (gelatin), and there was always chocolate! I was never a finicky eater, but there were times when I had bronchitis when my appetite waned briefly. This was not one of those times. My only problem was being able to sit up to eat. It was just too painful. In a few days, I was able to eat again without difficulty despite the swelling. I even began to enjoy the extra attention I was getting, with all my chums coming in to visit me and exclaim over my misshapen, black, blue, purple and green face. I was a sight to behold.

Wenhaston is a hilltop village that was first settled during the Bronze Age. It has been torn apart many times by war, ravaged and restructured time and time again by the Romans, Saxons, Normans and lesser known hordes and scalawags who had strewn bits and pieces for countless generations of school children to muddle over and discover anew. Through the ages, much memorabilia had been unearthed in the surrounding countryside, and eager historians and curiosity seekers had thoroughly scrutinized each new find. Headmasters and school teachers, especially those in my era, continued to speculate about treasures that might remain buried in the wind-blown mile that stretched between Wenhaston's North and South hills.

Through all the years and all the changes, the church had stood stoutly, its stone walls renovated to suit each new conqueror. Its windows were altered and steeple changed to reflect the architecture of its current tenants and landlords. But through it all, the old church has stood, in one form or another, as a reminder of man's dependence for spiritual consistency on an outward form, a symbol of worship beyond his humanity and beyond his comprehension.

Speaking boldly for most of my contemporaries, I know the pupils at Wenhaston County Council School were vastly more interested in the more practical aspects of everyday life than they were in the Norman invasion, or in the tools and weapons they left behind them. We accepted our village as our own. The feet that had trodden over the heaths and forded the streams were long gone. In our time it belonged only to us. Its foibles and eccentricities were part of our identity and minutiae of life, and Wenhaston's church, fields, hills and valleys served as a daily reminder of our tangible links to it in the very present tense.

No matter which way you left the village by bicycle, toward Halesworth at one end or toward Southwold on the other, it was a freewheel ride down a hillside. Halesworth, the nearest town, was a mere three miles away. The journey began with a glorious swoosh of power downward past the stile on the left and round several curves, past cottages with white picket fences, across the lane and past a meadow at the bottom and a final splash through a small run as the road flattened out near the humpback bridge over the River Blyth. Of course adults never splashed through the run's stream as there was a perfectly good, narrow bridge running across it. Indeed, when the stream was swollen, the challenge was too much even for our hardy souls. It was an easy pedal beyond the humpback bridge and onward down the tree-lined lane. Then turning left past Blyford Church on one side and *The Queen's Head* pub on the other, it was a fairly comfortable spin past spaced out farms, fields and cottages, through Holton's tiny burgh and on into the town of Halesworth.

Once there, the adventure began. Halesworth, unlike Wenhaston, boasted many shops and interesting places. There was the busy train station and the bus depot, which were next to each other at the top of the hill on Station Road. Directly across from the railway station was Halesworth's largest hotel, named appropriately the *Railway Inn.* Down the hill on the left, there was a row of "alms houses," whose widowed occupants were sustained by the church. At the very bottom, across the road on High Street, was the house where my friend Owen lived. It was a very steep hill to the station and a real challenge to pedal all the way up. But as hard as it was, I struggled and strained my way to the top every time I went to Halesworth, just in case any one was watching. It was a matter of maintaining one's honour.

Owen's father, Mr. Summerfield, was the Station Master. He wore a shiny navy suit and a cap with the British Rail insignia on it. He was a pleasant man who never seemed to mind when we children came down to the station to pick up parcels or just to be there when the trains came in, provided we stayed out of the passengers' way. In his private office at the station, he had a fascinating piece of machinery that he operated to send messages about the arrival and departure of each train. Whenever a train was due, he closed the street gates and set the alarm bell ringing. Within a few minutes a train would come lumbering in, growl and hiss to a noisy stop, and there would be a few minutes of noisy confusion while the incoming passengers alighted with their luggage, and those who were leaving got aboard.

Once the platform was cleared, the Station Master would go down the line, checking doors to make sure they were all properly closed. Then he would raise his flag and blow the whistle to signal to the engineer that all was clear. After the train's departure, and if it was my lucky day, Mr. Summerfield would allow me to help him push the gates open to let those that waited to continue on up the road. Then I would be off down the hill to the main part of town.

There were many shops that we did not have in Wenhaston, and there was even a cinema. In the centre of town was a large space that on certain days became the Market Place where farmers and small business entrepreneurs set up their stalls and sold their wares. Down from Market Place on High Street, there was a Boots chemist's shop, a ladies' and gents' clothing shop, a Clark's shoe shop, a greengrocer's and a Lloyds of London bank.

I seldom had occasion to enter the bank, but when it fell my lot to leave a signed document for the Saunders, what an awesome experience it was. The entrance itself was impressive enough, with its wide stone steps and highly polished brass handrails, but the

Market Place, Halesworth

interior, with its tall counters topped with glass panels, was intimidating indeed. I entered the bank with the same reverence I mustered for Sunday church, whispered my mission to a man in a black coat, handed over a manila envelope, and waited breathlessly while he inspected the contents, cleared his throat and gave me a nod of dismissal. Back out on the Halesworth High Street, I could breathe normally again and continue my rounds to the fishmonger, the butcher or wherever else my errands took me that day.

Right in the centre of town by the war memorial were the public toilets. There was plenty of room to park a bicycle by the iron fence round the stone stairway, but I worried about leaving my parcels unattended too long. So I hurried down the steps, tried every door to each stall in case some kind person had left one slightly ajar, inserted my penny on my unlucky days, and hurried back up the steps two at a time to claim my parcels. I didn't need to worry. Though there were plenty of people milling about, I never, ever found anything missing. But there was a sense of real importance about being protective.

On the way back through town, I sometimes saw Owen playing in the street with his brothers, and we'd call to each other as I rode by. His school cricket team came to Wenhaston sometimes to play against ours, and there was always a lot of good-natured teasing about the games no matter who won. Going home was always a little less exciting, especially when there was a head wind coming in from the sea, which was often the case. Invariably loaded down with shopping bags and boxes collected from the shops and sometimes the train station, the bike was more difficult to maneuver and the Halesworth road seemed a bit longer on the return.

Even when the wind was favourable, the hills at the end of each journey were formidable. By some unwritten law, we instinctively knew there was a definite order to traversing the inclines. The children and men pedaled up, albeit with varying degrees of difficulty, sometimes wobbling this way and that across the road, barely moving forward, with much huffing and wheezing. Meanwhile the more sensible women dismounted halfway up the hill and walked sedately, pushing their bikes laden with parcels to the level space at the top.

By 1935, the year I arrived in Wenhaston, train service from Halesworth to Southwold had stopped, and most of the railway tracks had been removed. There were vestiges of railway travel still in evidence: a converted train station at Blyford, and a beautifully kept steam engine on a single looped track that was used for holiday makers.

Regular bus service to our village and to Southwold ran from the Halesworth train station three times a day. There were numerous stops along the way, but the main ones were at the pubs that dotted the route. Coming up from the northwest, the bus from Halesworth stopped at the *King's Arms* in Holton, came through Blyford, stopping at the *Queen's Head*, then turned right to travel the short stretch to the river where it slowed, squeaking the brick sides of the narrow humpback bridge, before climbing the steep hill leading to the village centre. At the centre of the village, the bus made its most important stop at the *Compasses Inn*.

At the other end of the village, past the church, the village hall, and the school, the bus made its last stop in Wenhaston at the *Star*, halfway down Star Hill on the way to Southwold. There was very little traffic through Wenhaston in the early days, but motorized vehicles were gradually beginning to replace the standard horse and cart, and for the young lads, the motorbike was slowly replacing the bicycle. Large vans from Halesworth began delivering goods to the shop on a weekly basis and more and more motorcars were appearing in the village. Mr. LeCroix who lived in the large house beside the village green had a shiny black Daimler. My friend Gwinny's father, who must have been very rich, not only had two motorcars, but a chauffeur to drive them and keep them spotless.

Gwinny didn't go to school with the rest of us, nor did she join in our outdoor games. There was a pond in the field within sight of her home, where in the winter we worked diligently to make a slide clear across it. I imagine from her window she had a wonderful view of us, but she never joined us. I'm not sure whether she was not allowed, or whether it was her own choice not to play with us. In our day there was a disease known as "consumption." It was a totally debilitating disease of the lungs that I later learned was tuberculosis. One never spoke of diseases in polite society, so I never knew whether Gwinny was "consumptive" or not. I only knew that she declined our many invitations to join us.

Beside her nanny and tutor, Gwinny had other servants that "took care of things" for the household. There were servants that cooked and kept house and an old man who did the gardening. I don't know what her parents did for a living. I only met her mother once or twice and never saw her father at all. I was nearly always welcome to play with Gwinny on rainy afternoons. Sometimes I delivered groceries to the kitchen door and was invited in. On other days, I was given tuppence immediately and sent away.

Gwinny was a nice, if rather fragile, little girl who had lots of toys and masses of pretty clothes. Adjoining her bedroom was another room called the nursery that was filled with nice toys and a collection of dolls stacked on the bookcases that surrounded the walls. I had a sense that she must have been very lonely, but we never discussed her situation, or mine for that matter. I often wondered why her family didn't seem to be part of village life, why they weren't part of the normal activities of the church even on Sundays. Perhaps because they were rich, they were somehow set apart from the rest of us.

I never discovered the answers, but I did enjoy the time I spent with Gwinny. She might have been lonely, but she was certainly well-provided for. She had stacks of jigsaw puzzles, the thick wooden kind that had pictures on both sides and took hours to put together. Besides the dolls which we dressed and undressed regularly, she had many board games and books that she would sometimes let me take home for a few days. Her private tutor came from Bungay in the mornings, but her nanny lived with her all the time. When it was time for me to leave, the nanny would bustle into the room in her no nonsense way, give me my tuppence for delivering the groceries, and see me to the door.

Though the village was getting more modern and motorized, some of the merchants held out, reluctant to change. Mr. Parry, the butcher, rode round the village on his trade bike, which had a big boxy front and sturdy frame. He continued to ride his bike for several years after Mr. Sterry the milkman traded in his horse and cart for a white van It had open sides for the driver, and wide doors on the rear to hold the milk canisters. But as lorries and cars became more prevalent in the village, the number of accidents on our dangerous corner increased.

None of us will ever forget the day of Jimmy Broom's fatal accident. It was the sixth of August 1936, a nice warm day toward the end of our school holidays. We were congregated on the Village Green in front of the Bakery. Mr. Youngs, Joy's father, was baking the afternoon "tea bread" and it smelled absolutely delicious. I would have to carry a loaf of "Hovis" home shortly; that's the brown bread that Mummy said had the most vitamins. Though she maintained it was easier to cut straight pieces once it was cool, it always tasted the very best while it was still warm.

We were just hanging about on the village green, drinking in the marvelous aroma of the freshly baked bread, when Jimmy went by us on his noisy motorbike. Though the bike sounded as if it were going a hundred miles an hour, it really wasn't. Jimmy was a careful driver and for all the noise he created with the bike, he was not reckless. Without question it was a noisy monster, but it sounded loader to us because the village had not quite got used to having any motorized vehicles. We children thought the noise made it all the more exciting, and we thought it might be thrilling to ride on it sometime.

He had no sooner gone past us when we heard the screech of brakes and the sound of grinding metal. Mr. Crisp, our village constable, was just coming out of the post office when he heard the crash. Mr. Kett the postmaster ran with us quickly to the scene,

The Village Green, Wenhasten

along with several other men. It was easy to sum up what had happened, but it was hard to take it in.

A lorry coming up Back Road from the direction of the Newby's Clock shop had struck Jimmy's back wheel a glancing blow as Jimmy attempted to cross over to the Bramfield road. Just before impact, the lorry must have swerved trying to miss the bike. It had come to a stop at an angle in Mrs. Long's hedge. When we arrived on the scene, the driver was just alighting, and stood dazed and trembling by the lorry's open door. Jimmy had been thrown off his bike, and was lying up against the Saunders wall in a pool of blood. Bits of metal littered the road, and the twisted motorbike, its front wheel still spinning crazily, lay a few feet away. It was a gruesome scene.

Mr. Crisp, a tall young man with an air of authority, took charge immediately. He went over to the crumpled heap and kneeled down beside him. He then turned round to anyone in earshot and began issuing orders. He was wearing his full uniform, and the silver badge on his navy blue cap glistened in the sun as he bent his head. He waved everyone out of the way so that Jimmy could "get air." He then sent someone with a bike to fetch the doctor, if he was still in the village, or the District Nurse if not. Then he sent someone else for water and something to put under Jimmy's head. Someone rolled up his jacket and helped Mr. Crisp carefully move the inert body to a better position. Mummy and some of the shop customers came pouring out of the shop door into the street. When she recognized who was lying beside the wall, Mummy gasped and almost fell over. Mrs. Stockdale steadied her for a moment until she regained her composure.

Just then the nurse drove up and Mr. Crisp again ordered everybody to stay back while she bent over Jimmy's inert body. A large crowd had gathered by this time. "He's breathing" the nurse said, and there was a collective sigh of relief. The lorry driver kept shaking his head and wiping his forehead with his big hanky. "I swear I never soar 'im cummin," he repeated over and over, to no one in particular.

The men carried Jimmy into the shop, and laid him gently on the stone floor. Mummy ran and got towels from the scullery, and some of the women helped her to make him comfortable. Mr. Crisp ordered all of us gawking children to move away so the lorry driver could move his vehicle out of the middle of the road. The driver was still shaking and acting confused. One of the men got in the lorry and backed it out of Louie Long's hedge and across the road. He parked it in the space leading to Miss Danford's pump, just beside the shop wall.

Mr. Crisp got his notepad and pencil out of his pocket and began taking notes from the lorry driver. "I never soar 'im cummin," he said in a plaintive voice. "I swear, I never soar 'im cummin," he reiterated, shaking his head and wiping his face. Mr. Crisp inspected the front of the Lorry, made some notes and returned to the driver once more. Finally, Mr. Sperry drove up in his van. We couldn't hear what the men were saying, but we could see them clearing out the churns from the back of the van and setting them in the shop yard.

They carried Jimmy out of the shop and laid him in the back of the van. Mr. Crisp and one of the men climbed in with Mr. Sperry and they drove off for the hospital in Halesworth. The District Nurse followed behind in her black Austin, and the men that were left began disconsolately to pick up the pieces of the motorbike that were strewn in the road.

It was a very long night. Mummy and Letty stayed in the shop long after closing time, scrubbing the floor and putting things right.

Lenny was working in Bungay. He must have heard the news on the way home. He came in hurriedly, changed from his work clothes into his good trousers and wool jacket, said a few words to his mother and left again for Halesworth. I don't know what time he arrived home that night, and he was gone before I got up the next morning. Dadda said that Jimmy was still clinging to life, that he had a concussion and was still unconscious. Dadda said that as long as he was unconscious he could feel no pain, and that we would have to wait until he "came to" to know the extent of his injuries.

The horrible news came later that day to say Jimmy had died without regaining consciousness. Lenny was distraught and seemed unable to comprehend how the world could have turned upside down so quickly. Jimmy had touched so many lives and was so well liked that the church could barely hold all the mourners. There was such an outpouring of love and sympathy, the likes of which had hardly been seen before. Most of the shops including ours were closed all day. People pulled down their blinds along the funeral route. Some, like Mummy, covered up their mirrors the way they did for a thunderstorm. Dadda didn't laugh at her though, because he said this time it wasn't funny. He said it was just her way of showing respect for the dead.

The solemn tolling of the church bell poignantly called the village together to pour out their grief in their most familiar gathering place. The children couldn't crowd into the church, as there was hardly room for the adults. So we gathered together over against the churchyard paling and watched and listened in hushed silence as first the bier and then the coffin were carried into the church. There must have been a representative from almost every family in Wenhaston, and every one, including the children, wore a small black armband to show we were mourning.

Jimmy's parents, his sister Louise and his brother Peter all looked gaunt and haggard, their eyes red-rimmed from weeping. The number of floral arrangements was staggering by any standard. We watched as they were carried into the church, and later out again and placed around the newly dug grave. Our weekly newspaper had quite a long and detailed column about Jimmy's death, a list of the people who attended the funeral and the names of all those sending floral arrangement. It was an impressive number. I have copied one small part of the report verbatim. The reporter has long since been forgiven for misspelling not only the family name, but many others as well:

"MANIFESTATIONS OF SYMPATHY AT FUNERAL"

"There were many manifestations of sorrow at the funeral of Mr. Walter Robert James ("Jimmy") Broome, at Wenhaston Churchyard on Tuesday afternoon of last week. Mr. Broome, who was only 20 years of age, passed away in the Patrick Stead Hospital, Halesworth, on Friday, August 7th, 1936, following a motor cycling accident at Wenhaston on the previous day. Of a quiet yet amiable nature, Jimmy was well liked by all with whom he came in contact, and was well known among a large circle of young people. Evidence of this was seen at a dance held in Wenhaston Village Club, on the evening following the inquest, when a large company of dancers stood for one moment in memory of one who had been a familiar and popular figure. Much sympathy is felt for his parents, Mr. and Mrs. J. Broom, Low Farm, Wenhaston, sister Louie and brother Peter in the sad loss they have sustained.

"The Vicar, Rev. J. Hardingham, M.A. conducted the funeral service. May he rest in peace."

Chapter 6

Along a Briny Beach

O oyster, come and walk with us!
The walrus did beseech.
A pleasant walk, a pleasant talk,
Along a briny beach.

Lewis Carroll

Some of the most exciting days in the summer were our Sunday School seaside outings. Normally Sunday School lessons were held on Sunday afternoons, but for the month of July the schedule changed. Mrs. Sangster, our Sunday School teacher, supervised the outing. Mrs. Hardingham, the Vicar's wife, and several other adults went with us on the Southwold bus to the seaside. I relished these wonderful outings and tried hard not to do anything that would interfere with being allowed to go. I ran errands and fetched the water without being told twice. I tried to remember to be quiet and fairly respectful without being told to do so. Our only deterrent was rain. If it was raining, it was no use going to the bus stop. Instead we stayed at home and put a jig-saw puzzle together, or read our books. We looked forward to sunny Sundays in July, and we were not often disappointed.

On the big day, Dadda always gave me sixpence to spend. It was a reward for "being a good girl" he said as I kissed him good-bye. That sixpence, added to the shilling and fourpence ha'penny I'd saved, was an absolute fortune. Mummy complained that he spoiled me, and she was right. After last minute instructions from her, I took my bag with dry clothes and towel, my shiny new pail and shovel, and ran to the *Compass* where a crowd was gathering in the sunshine to catch the bus to Southwold.

Bathing costumes were low priority items in Wenhaston. Many adults didn't own any beachwear at all. It was quite normal to see ladies dressed in their summer frocks and straw hats, sitting in deck-chairs, removing their shoes and heavy lisle stockings so they could paddle gingerly at the water's edge. Occasionally there were men dressed in one-piece costumes who dove in the surf and swam out beyond the breakers. More often the men from the village wore their white summer cricket trousers, rolled up to the knees, and walked along the wet beach. They also wore summer straw hats and open-necked shirts with rolled up sleeves.

The boys were luckier than the girls, because until they reached a certain age, they wore short trousers every day. Parents did try to provide the girls with something that passed as seaside wear. If we acquired our bathing costumes during the winter months, we prayed they would still fit when summer rolled around. Some of the girls tucked their dresses or blouses into bloomers the way we did for our "keep fit" classes at school. Others, like Gladys, had pretty one-piece sundresses that their mothers had made for them.

The year I turned eight, my costume was knitted red wool with a white band around the mid-section. The following year, we cut it across the mid-section and put elastic through each piece. That bathing costume served me for three years. The first year I had it was the most memorable. The night before our first big outing of the summer, I got it out of the drawer. It smelled powerfully of camphor from the mothballs in the drawer, but it fitted fine. I was so anxious to be ready in the morning that I slept with it on. I hoped some of the smell would diminish, but it didn't. It not only smelled of camphor, but it itched like anything. By the time I arrived at the seaside, my skin was fiery red and quite painful.

No matter that the adults complained that the water in the North Sea was frigid, it never deterred us children. The sea had its own special sound and scent. The moment we got off the bus we could smell the salt air and hear the pounding surf. Down the steps from the promenade, along the sea wall, there were several beach huts that provided a modicum of privacy for changing our clothes. These were small gaily painted cabins with pointed roofs and doorways that had striped canvas across the openings. Four or five girls shared a beach hut, and as soon as we had plonked our bags and towels in bundles, we raced for the water's edge.

First we put our toes in tentatively to test the temperature. Then as the cold water penetrated our bodies, we dared each other to jump in and get wet all over. It took courage, but one plucky one would start us off, and the rest, shrieking with excitement and fright, would follow suit. Usually the bolder we got the louder the screams. We let the sand and surf roll around us as we darted in and out. We sat in the wet sand and waited for the seventh wave, which we believed was the biggest one, to tumble us over and over. Then the surf bore us back to the beach and spit us out unceremoniously on the sand. We squealed with fright and excitement at every big wave. Our noses became raw from the salt water. Our hair was matted, and our skin tingled from the tiny pebbles mixed with sand that thrashed against it.

Finally we would give up "swimming," and shivering happily, we shared our pails and shovels to build marvelous castles with lots of turrets and deep moats around them. Someone would find a shell on the beach and we would take turns holding it to our ears to listen to the roar of the ocean. At home for days afterwards we didn't need the shell to remind us. We could feel the motion of the waves and hear the roar of the sea, and there was always the residue of sand that stubbornly stayed between our toes.

Later in the day, bunches of us would carry our empty pails and climb the steps to the promenade, stopping at the little beach hut to change into dry clothes. It was a long walk to the amusement pavilion. We had to walk past all the hotels, tea rooms, and houses with steep steps going up to their glass fronted doorways, that were lined up in tall rows on the opposite side of the wide street. You had to pass the lighthouse in the open space and a large steepled church, and another row of large houses that the locals called "summer cottages." Though there was a pavement on the other side, we seldom crossed over, preferring instead to walk with the crowd on the ocean side, on the promenade.

On our side, we could look down at the sand and the people lolling about in deck chairs. We could inspect the fishing boats pulled up high on the beach. Sometimes we could see the fishermen mending their nets or spreading them out in the sun to dry. It was well worth the walk, as there was much to see along the way. The sea always looked alive from up on the promenade and you could see its different colours. It changed from green to blue to almost purple, from the higher vantage point of the promenade. Sometimes

Southwold Lighthouse

we hung over the heavy rails to wonder how the sea met the sky, and occasionally we would see a huge ship moving slowly far in the distance.

We would finally reach the outer edge of the amusement pavilion, a bricked over entranceway that was lined with bicycle racks. The pavilion itself was a cavernous building with wide doors that were flung wide open. As we approached, we could see the long wooden pier that seemed to stretch for miles behind the building. Lots of people walked up and down it or sat on benches down the middle and along the sides. Fishermen cast their lines over the sides, wearing hats tied under their chins, their basket-like creels beside them. The building housed an enchanting array of games of chance as well as food stalls that sold sandwiches, ice cream, cakes, and orange squash. It was darker inside, and we had to wait a few minutes to let our eyes adjust.

Gladys and I nearly always decided first to try our luck on some of the many "grab" machines. These were glass enclosed cases with a claw-like grappler. Some of them were filled with coins among little pebbles and some had toy trucks half buried in sand and shells. We liked the one that had the stuffed animals buried among wrapped sweets, tiny combs, and doll toys. We each had a try to get a dear little fuzzy white rabbit that we thought would be easier to get because it didn't look as heavy as some of the other stuffed animals. We took turns at putting our pennies in and moving the arm of the claw over the toys strewn on the bottom.

Time was of the essence for our penny's worth ran out in what seemed a few seconds. We manipulated the arm and managed to get the claw to hold the prize for a breathtaking second, but before we could get the arm over the opening in the bottom of the case, we lost it. A few times we were lucky, but not very often. Most of the time all we got for our money was a ha'penny's worth of toffees and some silly little trinkets. Undaunted, we trooped around to look at all the other amusements before finally spending our last pennies at the ice cream stall.

We'd get back to our place on the beach just as a crew was putting the finishing touches on the housing for the Punch and Judy show. This was a show with puppets on sticks, and the characters were familiar to all of us. Punch was a lazy husband who was always getting into scrapes. Judy was his demanding wife who took great delight in chasing her husband with a broomstick whenever he did something wrong. The script varied as the story unfolded, and the activities created depended a great deal on the volume of laughter that came from the children watching. Sometimes Punch got in trouble with a policeman, a portly man with a big black moustache, who chased Punch with his club up and down the perimeters of the makeshift theatre. It was a delightful show, and as the ice cream melted and ran down our arms, we basked in the wonder of a summer day at the seaside. We sang songs on the bus on the way home. To this day I never hear *Row, row, row, your boat* or *Ten green bottles* without remembering the joy of those special outings.

That August was blissful. The weather was hotter than usual, and there was not much rain. In addition to everything else, I had the freedom of having a good bike and time to spare for many outings. The longest journey I had made on my bicycle to this point was the three mile trip to Halesworth. I only went there when I was sent on specific errands. There was always so much to do in my own village, there had seemed no reason to wander far.

That summer I wanted to branch out and explore other places that were within the range of possibility. Southwold was only eight miles from Wenhaston. The idea of spending time at the sea-side apart from our Sunday outings was very appealing. So one bright morning a few of us set off on our bikes for Southwold. We didn't follow the bus route past the *Star Inn*, but went the other way toward Halesworth, turning right at the *Queen's Head* in Blyford instead of going left to Halesworth. It was a shorter way for us, and the bus route would intersect at about the half-way point.

We started out with much enthusiasm, over hill and valley toward Southwold. It was a warm August day, though clouds were scudding through the sky, sometimes darkening our pathway as they hurried by. Dadda had predicted rain when he tapped the barometer earlier in the morning, but as warm as the day was, a hint of rain couldn't deter us. What was more troublesome, as we pedaled into unfamiliar territory, was the strong head wind that was growing stronger with each mile. The sky had turned a rather dull gray and the sun had gone behind the clouds.

We reached Southwold tired and out of breath, but elated that we had reached our goal. We parked our bicycles near the promenade and walked down the stone steps to the beach. The wind was stronger now, and the clouds looked darker and more ominous. Looking over the sea, we saw a storm would soon break over us. We were resourceful and determined to have at least one paddle in the water's edge before it began. We had barely sat down to take our shoes and socks off before we heard a rumble of thunder. A gust of wind blew sand in our faces as we frantically picked up our scattered shoes.

People everywhere up and down the beach were gathering their belongings into bundles and calling their children. The men in charge of rented umbrellas and deck chairs came hurrying along the beach. A brightly coloured umbrella suddenly became airborne and a man in white flannel trousers gave chase. Another man snatched up deckchairs whose canvas seats billowed like sails in the wind, and ran with them to the nearest beach hut.

The beach was clearing fast, and the moment we heard the second rumble of thunder, we too scampered up the steps to our bikes, heading we knew not where. The sea heaved darkly and the waves crashed and roared. We could barely stand upright, let alone walk. Our hair stood straight out and the girls' dresses ballooned around them. We saw a flash of lightning and felt the first splashes of rain, and our hearts were filled with fear. The only instructions any of us knew about thunderstorms was to never stay close to water or take shelter under a tree.

In our part of the world, thunderstorms were very rare, not more than one or two in a summer At home we had learned to cover the mirrors and stay away from the windows. Other than that, we had heard a rumor that our bicycle tyres, being rubber, would help to "ground" us, if we got caught in a storm. None of us wanted to chance it at this time, so we ran alongside our bikes down the promenade hoping to find a place to duck into.

The lightning flashed and the thunder roared as we raced along the promenade. It had begun to rain great fat drops that plopped on our heads and bounced on our backs as we ran helter-skelter, pushing our bikes. We had no idea what we should do, only that we wanted to escape the storm. Fortunately, we were headed in the right direction. We saw the outline of a familiar building up ahead. We recognized the pavilion as a place of refuge, so we raced toward it, past the hotels and the lighthouse on the opposite side, and up to the open expanse leading to the entrance way. It was raining hard now, and the lightning and thunder rolled around threateningly. We threw our bikes in the metal stands willy-nilly and raced for the building. The large doors that were normally wide open were closed, and one small door was the only way in.

It was crowded inside, and the air smelled a strange mixture of musty dampness, hot tea and cigarette smoke. The refreshment counters were crowded with adults and children in various attire getting trays of tea, lemonade and sandwiches. Few of us had thought to bring money. Each of us had a sandwich in our saddlebags, but with the storm so fierce, no one volunteered to run get them. Between all of us we had about seven pence ha'penny. It was enough to buy some lemonade, or by pooling our money we could indulge in a little luxury.

We decided to share what we had, so there was a time of much calculation. Frozen ices were the cheapest thing available. They cost tuppence each and came on sticks, two to a packet. We were able to get three of those and break them in half, so each of us got one. We were also able to buy three sticks of peppermint "rock" which was only available at the seaside. We broke this in halves so there were six pieces, one for each of us.

The storm raged around us as we sucked our flavored ices and pushed our way through the maze of bodies swarming over the claw machines and the "shove-ha'penny" tables. We were damp from the rain and our shoes were full of sand. We worked our way to the claw machines and watched others play them. Some were lucky winners and we watched enviously. Some others lost their money in the shove-ha'penny games. We made the rounds checking the empty machine "return" pockets and someone found thrupence. We were able to play some games, a rare treat indeed. We had our usual silent contest to see which of us could make our peppermint rock last the longest, and watched enviously as Gladys licked daintily her last half inch after ours was totally gone.

The storm moved on, but it continued to drizzle. We were still damp, but we each pulled out our ponchos and macs from our saddlebags, found our crumpled sandwiches and headed back to Wenhaston, riding and eating and feeling exhilarated for having had a wonderful adventure.

Our next adventure came two weeks later. I suddenly got the idea of bicycling to Peasenhall. Since I had come from there by train and bus, I thought it must be a hundred miles away from Wenhaston. Imagine my surprise to find it was only about six miles by road. Lenny had been working in Peasenhall, and he was going there by bicycle daily. He knew all the back lanes and was glad to give me directions. Dadda said it would be all right to go as long as I didn't go alone. He must have understood my curiosity about seeing the place where I had once lived.

At the time of planning, I had no intention of going to see the woman in whose foster care I had been for a year and a half before going to the Saunders. In fact, I was not sure I would recognize her, and I still did not know her name. But my ego got the best of me, and I wanted to show off in several ways. First I wanted to show this nebulous foster parent how I had grown up, and how independent and clever I had become, because I remembered only being very young and "naughty" during my stay with her. Second, I wanted to show her that I could ride my very own bicycle. Third, I wanted to show the three friends that went with me that I really had lived in Peasenhall before going to Wenhaston. To my friends it was rather a heroic feat that I had lived somewhere else and was returning in this rather victorious way. They were thrilled to be included in such a grand escapade.

Gladys had a lovely new bike, a girl-sized "Hercules" that had shiny rims and the original pump. Walter's was one he shared with Kathleen, but was his for the day. Bernie's was a third-hand, serviceable bike that was a shared blessing among the farm boys he lived with. Mine was Lenny's old bike that he had especially restored for me. It was a boy's bike, and it was sturdy. Lenny had put on a new seat, lowering it to where I could reach the pedals. He had fitted new tyres and inner tubes, put on a new bell and a good pump. It was in fine shape and reliable.

Father Christmas, who was either Uncle Aubrey or Dadda, had given me a brand new black leather saddlebag for Christmas. I found it on Christmas morning in the pillowcase at the foot of my bed. I'd never seen a nicer one. It was large enough for carrying my hooded rain poncho, and still had room left over for all the essential things one must put in a proper saddlebag. It had two small pockets, one on each side of the large pouch, that strapped down with buckles. These were for carrying bicycle tools, a patching kit, and a torch, and a soft cloth for wiping off a wet seat and handle bars. It smelled of new leather and was a great addition to the bike.

I was now adept enough that I could mount the bike wearing a skirt and still maintain my dignity, which was quite an accomplishment. It pleased Mummy that the old trousers she had provided for me in the beginning to preserve my modesty were now put away, and used only for harvesting and other dirty jobs. In the 1930s it was not thought "proper" for girls of any age to wear trousers, not in Wenhaston anyway.

So the four of us: Bernie Mansfield, Walter, Gladys and I, began our Peasenhall adventure. It was a Wednesday and early closing for the shop. Lettie, our shop girl who lived in Bramfield, was finished for the day, so she rode along with us part of the way. We started out on the Bramfield Road about noon time, with a promise to be back before dark. The first two miles to Bramfield were easy, then we veered off to the left as Lenny had told us, down a narrow lane. We rode for what seemed like many miles, between steep hedges on both sides of the lane, chattering as we rode.

At one point we met a horse and cart and had to scramble up the side of the bank to give the farmer room to get by. We asked if he could tell us the way to Peasenhall, and while the horse lumbered slowly past us, the farmer shouted directions. He told us we had about a mile and a half to go "til ye cum to the Harper's farm gate, whar thar's a fork. Go left right at the fork," he said pleasantly, "and you'll see the sign post what says Pissanall." "Mind how ye go then" he said cheerily, as he went on past us.

We climbed down the bank yelling "thank-you" to the farmer's back, who lifted his hand to wave at us. We continued our journey, finding the sign post just as he had told us. The sign post read Peasenhall 3/4 mile. We stopped beside it to get our bearings, when someone remembered the farmer's pronunciation of the village name, and we began to giggle. We then took turns trying to say it just the way the farmer had, with a huge emphasis on the "piss" part.

We rode into the village about half-past two. I located the school, and we climbed off our bicycles and ran over the vacant playground. Until that moment, I had not realized how similar in structure this school was to the one in Wenhaston. But it was. There was something about it that seemed familiar even though its doors and windows had different placements. It was smaller than our school in Wenhaston, but it had the same colour brick construction and the same multiple pointed roof treatment. The playground was smaller, and there were no white-lined diagrams for netball. We kicked some loose stones around to each other on the playground and then went around back to the brick toilets that were exact replicas of ours in Wenhaston.

I showed the others the stream that ran down beside the roadway. Walter was wearing his wellies, so of course he had to have a splash in it while the rest of us stood on the bank. Wild horses would not have dragged me into that particular stream, even had I been wearing my wellies. The stream was just the way I had remembered it, and I realized that by following it, I would come to my first foster house. I was a bit nervous about actually going to knock on the door, but when I hesitated, Gladys urged me on.

"It will be all right to just call in" she assured me. I was reluctant to do that, and we stood out by the gate contemplating my next move. Bernie said I was too scared to meet my old "Mum." It was a challenge I couldn't resist. Before I got to the front door, a rosy-cheeked woman with her head wrapped in a colorful scarf flung open the door. A flood of memories rushed into my mind. It was not so much her face as it was the scarf that I remembered. She always used to wear it when she had her hair put up in curlers. Before I had a chance to speak, she came forward to meet me. Holding out her arms, she welcomed me as though I were her long-lost child, pulling me in to the house and beckoning to my friends to come in also. I could not fathom her exuberance. It was the last thing I had expected.

She was so excited at seeing me that it was hard to get a word in, even if I could have found my voice. That she had recognized me at all was surprising; that she had invited us all into the house, into the sitting room no less, was a miracle. She made us all sit down in chairs draped with sheets. It was summertime and I realized that in Peasenhall, as in Wenhaston, when the sun might fade the upholstery, the settee and chairs were covered for protection.

We all sat obediently, albeit carefully, on the sheeted chairs. Walter nudged a ginger cat out of its spot in order to have a small space to perch on one of the high backed chairs. He looked across at me with his eyes wide, hoping I'd change places with him. The cat stood up and arched its back, annoyed at being displaced. My "ex-foster mum" regaled us with a constant stream of information, much of which we didn't understand. She must have thought I had perfect recall for all the names of people she threw out at me. I sat silently, trying to look intelligent, while she continued to tell us about so and so who had got married to a man of means who held an important position on the Council.

That nice Mrs. so and so "what used to cut your hair" had run off to Wrentham with a "traveling man" and no one had heard from her since. Someone else was in the "family way" and Mrs. Strickland, "poor old dear" had fallen and broken her arm in two places. She babbled on a bit more and then flew to the kitchen to put the kettle on, still talking from the next room. She told us that she didn't have a wireless, that they were bothersome, newfangled things. But she did own a gramophone and had lots of recordings of beautiful music. I started to tell her about Uncle Aubrey and the gramophone he had brought us, but she hurried on, hardly pausing for breath.

"Maudie said you was a-cummin' when she read the tea-leaves this morning," she told us. "I must go and get her. She'll be ever so pleased her forecast has cum true." Off she went out the back door. The cat hastened after her. I expect he too was a bit overwhelmed by the proceedings. I sat thoughtfully, remembering snatches of things, and realized with a start that her friend Mrs. Harper who lived next door read tea-leaves. It seemed incredible that this woman had such powers of discernment, and I was heartened by the thought that perhaps she would tell our fortunes. It would be something to tell our friends about at school. Not knowing what to say, and not getting much opportunity to talk anyway, we sat in expectant silence.

My ex-foster mum came back quickly from her errand. We could see her moving about in the kitchen, opening tins of biscuits and slicing cake. The kettle boiled and she made tea in a large brown pot. Still chattering complacently, she put a green cozy with a fluffy tassel over the pot and brought her second-best cups to the table. Mrs. Harper, "Maudie," came in excitedly through the kitchen door, carrying a tray of jam tarts. She set them down on the kitchen table and moved breezily into the sitting room, clapping her hands gleefully. To our surprise we all stood in unison to greet her as she entered the room. Our school training served us well at that moment.

It was always expected of us to rise from our seats whenever an adult entered our school room. In the classroom, we tried to stand with as much clatter as our folding seats would allow. In this room, we surprised each other by remembering to stand, and we did it instinctively, without being ordered to. It was an unbidden and slightly embarrassing inspiration. It impressed our two ladies no end. "Maudie" clapped her hands with excitement and came to pinch our cheeks and peer into each of our faces.

"I knew you was a-cummin'" she said, and clapped her hands again. "I saw it in the leaves we was a-havin' company." She could hardly contain herself. She was a small woman with bony arms and tiny hands. She had bright eyes like a little bird's, and she fluttered about the way a canary hen would do building her nest. We weren't sure whether her delight was in seeing us or in the fact that she had had success with one of her predictions, but her exuberance was infectious.

My ex-foster mum called us into the kitchen for tea. We each took turns dipping our hands in the white enameled bowl in the sink, and wiping them off on the towel she offered us. Then we crowded round the table to have the cake and biscuits she and Maudie had laid out for us. We were ravenous as usual, and we soon emptied the plates of every crumb, drinking down our tea with relish. While we ate, she continued to tell stories of my exploits during the time I stayed there. She talked about the parade I was in, which I could not remember at all, and recounted stories that seemed totally unrelated to me.

I couldn't help wondering if she had me mixed up with someone else. I tried unsuccessfully to get the conversation going in a different direction. I began talking about school, our netball team, and the sports day fete that would soon be held in our village. I looked to the others to help me, but except for murmured assents now and then, they stayed mute. At one point, Bernie, who was usually quite talkative and self-assured, attempted to enter the conversation by bringing up the topic of war.

"If we have a war," he said stoutly, "I'm going to join the army." All the young boys that year were itching to wear uniforms and go off to war. The fact that they were far too young and therefore ineligible never seemed to faze them. Maudie clapped her hands and clucked her teeth together.

"My word," she said, "what nice children you are" and proceeded to tell us about how she'd known this would be a red letter day, and how she was glad we had come. At the end of tea, Maudie gave each of us a reading of our tea leaves. As I recall, Walter was going to be very rich and marry young. Gladys was going to be a teacher and would have her heart broken. Bernie was going to be a fine soldier and have lots of children. I was going to get married and would live a long life.

We were nearing the end of our visit. We felt satisfied that we had acquitted ourselves well until Maudie clapped her hands and invited us to come to "Pissenhall" to see them again. We had been serious and tense for more than an hour. Something was bound to set us off, and that was it. We said our goodbyes quickly, thanking them for tea and hardly managing to get out the door until we began giggling in earnest. Our laughter was muffled and intermittent until we pedaled a good distance, until we reached the signpost. At that point we threw our bikes in a heap and lay on the patch of grass beside it and howled like idiots, until we could laugh no more. We mounted our bikes and headed for home, singing and talking noisily all the way.

At home Dadda and Mummy were having a late tea. They had been listening to the six o'clock news, and their faces mirrored their growing anxiety. War with Germany seemed inevitable. It was uppermost in everybody's minds. There had been nothing but talk of it for months on the wireless. The growing unrest among the leaders of our own country about their roles seemed even worse.

In February, the Foreign Secretary, Mr. Anthony Eden, had resigned over policy differences with the Prime Minister, Mr. Neville Chamberlain. Dadda sided with Mr. Chamberlain, but did not agree with the way he went about appeasing Adolf Hitler. Dadda felt strongly that there should be no appeasement whatsoever. He felt that Hitler was a tyrant who should be dealt with swiftly. War was not something Dadda wanted, quite the opposite. But if it came to that, then war was a necessary evil to rid the world of a despot like Hitler, who was becoming an ever more dominant force in Europe. His rise to power in Germany, and the ruthless way his army had marched into Austria and taken over the city of Vienna seemed preposterous.

I did not fully understand much of what was going on around me. I only knew that the preoccupation of most adults, especially men like Dadda who had been in the Great War, was intense. Words and phrases like "Alliance," "League of Nations," "German Reich," and names such as "Munich," "Poland," "Czechoslovakia," "Russia," and "France" kept cropping up in every conversation. Hitler was vilified by every means possible; his haughty stance and silly moustache were the butt of many cruel, but justifiable jokes.

It had struck me while we were visiting Peasenhall that the two women we encountered seemed detached from all talk of war. When Bernie had broached the subject it had fallen flat, as though it was an unmentionable topic. I mentioned this to Dadda when he asked me about the journey.

"Some people don't want to talk about war, Dadda said. "They are afraid if they talk about it, it will somehow make it happen." He asked about the ride, had we got lost, and especially did we mind our manners. He smiled when I told him we had stood at attention and how much the ladies had liked that. I told him about the tea leaves and that Maudie had predicted our visit, and he chuckled. I knew by his attitude he thought it was all nonsense.

The following weekend I went camping with the Girl Guides. It was the first time I had slept outdoors and the first night I had stayed overnight anywhere, so it was an exciting event. Our Girl Guide leaders lived about two miles outside Wenhaston in a town called Thorington. We had been learning to mark a "nature trail" and then to follow our markings back to where we started. Additionally, we had practiced gathering wood, lighting a fire with no more than two matches, and cooking a simple meal. We had done these things for several weeks when our Guide leaders informed us that we were ready for a "camp-out." We were going to hike to their farm, pitch the tents they had waiting for us, cook our meal, and sleep on the ground.

We met on the Black Heath on the appointed day in full uniform, wearing our wide brimmed felt hats and carrying a knapsack full of articles we would need for an overnight stay in the outdoors. It was an exciting time, our chance to show our mettle. Of course, we each carried more "stuff" than we would ever use, but our creed was:

"Be prepared and don't be scared by difficult things to do.
"To fry an egg or mend a leg is all in the work for you."

We carried a box of matches, a magnifying glass, and some pieces of flint that were to be used to start fires. Our Bryant and Mays matches were in a small, flimsy wooden box with a. tin cover that fit exactly over it. The cover was made with holes in the sides to expose the striking area. In addition, we carried some large wooden matches that would strike on a stone, in tin cough lozenge boxes. It was a bit difficult to make flame with the flint, but not impossible. We enjoyed using the magnifying glass most, but this was only possible with bright sunshine. On a cloudy day we had to resort to one of the other methods for starting fires. We were not lacking in provisions. In a word we had enough flame-producing equipment to set the Guy Fawkes bonfire alight. Later we would only be allowed to carry the magnifying glass and two matches without the box to strike them on. As beginners we had an excess of everything.

We carried a tin fold-up container that doubled as a frying pan and serving plate, and little cups that folded down like a telescope into their own covers. We carried a huge utensil on our belts that contained several different sized knives, a fork, spoon, screwdriver, bottle opener and various other useful pieces of equipment. Each of us packed tins of "Bully-Beef," Heinz beans, sardines, sausages and our favourite staple, bread and cheese, that would have fed the lot of us for a week. In addition we each carried an old army blanket, rolled up, a rain poncho, and a warm jacket. We could barely move with that lot strapped to our backs. Fortunately, our leaders had the tents at the other end, so we didn't have to carry them.

Our leaders left us with a "trail map." We were to follow the marked trail and rendezvous with them at their farmhouse. Since none of us knew where they lived or had ever been there on our bikes, we had to pay close attention to the broken sticks and makeshift arrows that marked the path. We started over the Black Heath with confidence, but became a bit anxious as we traversed through some woods, across the corner of a field and over a stile. We discovered with delight that our way had lead us to a familiar stream, the "run" across the road at Thorington where we often played. We could have got there in half the time on our bicycles by the road. But this had been a training exercise, a test of sorts, and we had met the challenge. There were many farms close by, and we were glad to follow more signs that led us to the right one. We knew it was the right place when we saw the Leader's estate wagon with wooden sides parked in the barnyard.

By the time we arrived we were glad to put down our bundles. It had been several hours since we had eaten, and we were famished. We were ready to start opening tins and lighting fires, but our leaders got us busy erecting two large canvas tents instead. It was not an easy assignment, and we struggled with it. Our leaders watched and gave us detailed instructions, sometimes raising their voices to be heard over our yammerings. It was a team effort, with some of us holding the heavy canvas upright while the rest got the guy ropes steadied and hammered the wooden pegs in with a mallet. We got it halfway up, only to have it collapse on top of us. After several attempts we got the hang of it, but by the time we got the second tent pitched, our stomachs were rumbling uncontrollably. That first meal, prepared without the aid of fire or frying pan, was the best I'd ever eaten.

We talked and played guessing games far into the night, until the damp night air made us crawl into our blanket rolls. We were supposed to take turns keeping the fire going, but no one woke up to take care of it. In the morning there was a mad scramble to get it going again and get some water boiling. After a strange breakfast of half-cooked eggs, eggs our leaders provided from the farm, and some stale, burnt bread, we set about disassembling the tents and packing our gear. Camping was enjoyable enough, but after one night on the hard ground, I was ready to go home to my comfortable bed.

We loaded each other up, got our trail map from our leaders, and hiked back through Thorington run, over the stile, through the woods and across the Black Heath for home. Our loads seemed much heavier than the ones we'd gone with. I felt wretchedly dirty and unkempt by the time I arrived home, and was glad it was Saturday, my bath night. Camping was fun, but I sank into my clean feather bed that night, grateful to be home again.

Chapter 7

What's in a Name?

Who hath not own'd, with rapture smitten frame,
The power of grace, the magic of a name?

Campbell

On spring days the house shone and winked; its faded brick seemed not so dull when the pale sun began to warm it. Easter had barely passed before there was a great stirring both inside and out of the old house. On the first sunny day, we took the feather mattresses and pillows out to be "aired" and shaken. We boiled bed covers and curtains, and hung them across the back yard lines to dry, the poles in the centre straining under their weight. Sometimes I was pressed into service to help put the linens through the mangle. It was a huge wrought iron contraption with smooth round wooden rollers that could be set to squeeze water out of the heaviest or daintiest piece of cloth. Occasionally the handle needed oiling to ease the going. Often it took Lettie and I both, pushing with all our might, to get the heavy mattress covers through, while the machine groaned and squealed, and the water squished down to the galvanized tub below.

The shop was next. Usually the storage room behind the shop proper where the bulk items, sacks of flour, sugar, and dried beans were stored was the starting place. It was a cold room with a brick floor as in the shop itself, except that in the winter months the shop was warmed by a paraffin heater. We kept the door to the storage room closed to keep the warm air out in winter. In the spring, the door was open to allow the air to circulate in the hope that the room would stay cooler.

In the springtime everything changed. The fires were not kept lighted and we gave the fireplaces an overhaul, blackened the kitchen cooking stove, and polished the low brass hearth fender. A chimney sweep came to clean the cold chimneys, and the window washers came with their tall ladders to clean off grime that had collected through the winter.

After the ritual spring cleaning, the windows were then officially opened to let the "fresh air" in. Mrs. Saunders, like most of her peers, was obsessed by fresh air. "Fresh" to her could mean "freezing" to me, particularly first thing in the morning. Spring also meant we began the weather watch for rain showers, which in our part of England occurred almost daily.

For the entire spring and summer months we were on constant alert for rain. Dadda took care of the bird shed windows that were able to be cracked open in a way to deflect the rain. But with the house windows open and increased washing on the lines in the back yard, it was a mad dash in several directions when a rain cloud appeared. When it thundered there was double panic. In addition to the window closings and laundry rescuing, we went into a flurry of activity to cover ALL the mirrors in the house. I never understood why, but at Majuba House on those rare occasions when there was a thunderstorm, the rule was to cover the mirrors. We never deviated from the practice. Mummy once said that her mother had begun the tradition. She said something about the "reflection" of the lightning being harmful. Only after the storm had passed could we uncover them, fold up the sheets and open the windows again.

There were a few other eccentricities peculiar to our household. One of my most favourite eccentricities was a person, Uncle Aubrey, Dadda's brother from Ipswich. He had a motor car, so naturally he was considered by all my friends as being a real "toff." He'd arrive unannounced some Sunday afternoon, and immediately the fun began. He was a bit younger than Dadda and slightly taller, but with the same brown eyes and hair and a definite family resemblance around the mouth and chin. But in personality they were as different as chalk and cheese. Though Dadda loved a joke and could see the funny side of things, he was also quiet and subdued most of the time.

Uncle Aubrey could not be serious if his life depended on it, and it was only in Uncle Aubrey's presence that I heard Dadda laugh out loud. It was a wonderful sound and the old house echoed the merriment. In addition to his home in Ipswich, Uncle Aubrey also maintained a flat in London. His business connections were there. He liked to spend the weekends in his country home to get away from the mad rush of London. I had never seen either of his homes, but I heard a lot about them and I knew that some day I would have the opportunity to visit.

Uncle Aubrey's visits were far too brief. Occasionally during Christmas Holidays he would spend the night. Lenny would willingly move into the back bedroom for the night and give Uncle Aubrey and his wife his room. I never knew Uncle Aubrey's wife's real name. He always called her "Carly-luv" and sometimes "curleytop" because her head, what could be seen of it under the marvelous big hats she wore, was a thick mass of beautiful golden curls. Carly-luv didn't say much, but she smiled a lot and bent her head toward you in a gracious way letting you know she was listening to every word you uttered. She called her husband "darling" in the softest voice I've ever heard. When she spoke about him, she called him "Orb" in the most delightful way.

I thought she was the most beautiful woman in the world. Mummy, whose hands in winter were always red and sore, called Carly-luv, whose hands were delicate and white, a "gentlewoman" which was a somewhat envious complement. She was a tiny wisp of a woman with an air of elegance, and gave the impression that she was used to being entertained for tea in ornate drawing rooms. Her hands and feet were tiny and her features reminded me of a lovely china doll. Her eyes were blue with thick, dark lashes and her skin, without cosmetics, had a vibrant, polished look that poets of old might truly have called alabaster.

Uncle Aubrey spoke in riddles and he had funny names for all of us. Dadda was "Gorgie-Porgie" and Mummy was "Liddy-Lou." I was "Ditsy-Doo" and Lenny was "Henny-Penny." As soon as he entered a room, he was the centre of attention. He was "pickled tink" to visit us and said the current news about Prince Edward abdicating his throne to marry an American divorcee (Wallis Simpson) was an awful "fettle of kish." He nearly always brought unusual gifts, magic tricks, or Chinese paper puzzles. He knew the latest tricks to do with wooden match sticks, how to lay them out to create a puzzle that kept us guessing for ages until he showed us how to work it out.

With Uncle Aubrey we were always surprised and delighted by new and adventuresome things. I was also on alert for some of his old and shaggy sayings that he pulled out frequently. He would say for instance: "An apple a day keeps the Doctor away." My response had to be: "An onion a day keeps everybody away." He would invariably ask me if I "was all right?" "No," I would respond without hesitation, "I'm half left." On and on we went in this bantering vein.

On one of his visits, he brought six pomegranates, a fruit none of us had ever seen before, let alone tasted. "Good lore," Mummy said, as he spread the funny looking fruit on the kitchen table. "What use have we for the likes of those?" She wasn't quite sure whether they were edible, whether they needed to be cooked, dried or just put out in a bowl for show. So Uncle Aubrey proceeded to cut the red, rather tough, rind off in strips to reveal the meaty and very seedy innards. He told us it was "passion fruit." That it was exotic we had little doubt. Uncle cut through the core so we could see the "cross" outlined, and then he gave each of us a juicy morsel of the strange, seedy, but rather nice tasting fruit.

Uncle Aubrey also occasionally brought us whole coconuts, another rarity in our part of the world. These had to have a hole drilled through one of the "eyes" in the hard outer crust to get the "milk" out first. Then we would take a hammer out in the back yard and smash the brown hairy hull so that we could get at the white meat that was stuck like glue to the inner shell. I could eat the pieces I got immediately, if I could worry them from the shell. Mummy had the best luck removing the meat from the shell. She was able to get great chunks out with a thin, flexible knife. She would only eat little fragments of it. Rather she would lay the meat all out on a wooden tray, cover it with a clean cloth and put it on a top shelf in the pantry to "dry." Later she would get it down and grate it, saving it for Christmas cooking.

It seemed to me, growing up, that nearly everything from Harvest Festival onward for the rest of the year was "saved" for Christmas. In the autumn, we painted paper doilies with red, green and gold edges, and stored them away. We dried fruit, particularly black currants, certain grapes and apples in trays, and stored them high on the pantry shelves. We made ginger marmalade and gooseberry preserves in the summer, and saved them as gifts for special people. We also stored nuts of all kinds, especially chestnuts and walnuts. We particularly prized and saved almonds, with their light, porous shells. We used almonds throughout the year for many cakes, as decoration as well as for flavouring.

At Christmas, almonds were the essential ingredient for the paste we used to coat the top and sides of the Christmas cake. This thick cream-coloured layer, a mixture of sugar, eggs and finely ground almonds, was the extra special "under" icing for the dark, rich fruit Christmas cake. White, hard, shiny icing went over the top of this, and a band of corrugated silver paper, the official Christmas Cake "ruffle" saved from other Christmases was wrapped round the sides and tied with a thin strand of red ribbon. The top of the cake was always beautifully decorated. Some of the decorations could be eaten: tiny chocolate snow-covered yule logs and chocolate letters that spelled out "Happy Christmas." Other decorations could not be eaten: tiny fat metal robins, silver "thrupny" bits, called "Joeys", and shiny sixpences, little horseshoes and other trinkets adorned the luscious, rich cake. These non-edibles, along with the silver accordion-pleated ruffle were carefully cleaned and stored away again for another Christmas.

The saving for and significance of the once a year Christmas cake was rivaled only by supplies and preparations for the Christmas "plum puddings." Before Guy Fawkes Day on the 5th of November, the ingredients for the Christmas puddings were not only collected, but sometimes already assembled in crockery pudding bowls. While we children were occupied with assembling the yearly "Guy" and pulling him about the streets of Wenhaston, and fetching loads of faggots and hauling them to the heath for the bonfire, our mothers were preparing the Christmas puddings.

Mummy ordered pieces of special suet from her favourite butcher, "the fat from the kidneys only, if you please," and hung them on strings in the coolest part of the shop storage room to dry properly. Sultanas, raisins, dried apricots, plums and pears and a wide variety of spices came by the case-load in lorries from Halesworth, to be sold for Christmas fare. We had to protect then from damp that came up through the stone floor, and from mice that nibbled their way through the wooden crates.

We set the traps nightly and listened for the tell-tale snap so we could re-set them. If we discovered mouse holes in the walls, we bunged them up with odd scraps and covered them over with tin. The storage room, in fact, was so "mouse-proof" that the poor creatures spent much of their time running up and down the walls, between the joists and along the ceiling laths. We could often hear them rustling around in the night, squeaking and gnawing in great agitation.

At Christmas Uncle Aubrey was extremely generous. His presents were sometimes nonsensical and funny and occasionally mildly risqué. His conversations were like that, too. If I was in the room when he started one of his famous stories, Dadda would shoot him a warning look and motion toward me. I always listened a little more attentively when I saw the exchange. I think he did save some of his raunchier tales for a time when I was out of earshot. But the ones I heard were simply "gigglers." This is one I still remember:

"Old Jimmy Roper thought it was a sin
To rub his poor old leg with gin
So he let the gin run down his throttle
And rubbed his leg with the empty bottle."

He also taught me several verses of a ditty entitled, *"In Father's Little Short Shirt."* The verses I learned then were quite harmless, but later when I was old enough to hear the pub version I realized why Dadda gave him warning looks.

Uncle Aubrey's generosity was not only bountiful, but also predictable. We all knew, and waited in certainty, for the special "chock of boxlettes" in beautiful wrappings he would bring us for Christmas. Dadda's chocolates were shaped like tiny bottles and were filled with different kinds of liqueur that he liked. I thought they tasted awful. Mummy's were cordials, with mushy, runny orange, peach, and mint centres. Lenny got "Quality Street" toffees, in a tin with a picture of people wearing long scarves, skating on a pond with snow piled around it, and children and dogs running with sledges.

Mine were the best. Uncle Aubrey brought me *"Cadbury's Finest Milk Tray Assortment"* in a luxurious dark blue box with gold lettering and a lovely gold ribbon round it. The box contained every kind of chocolate imaginable. There was a diagram of each chocolate by shape with a description of its "middle" inside the lid. I liked all of them, but some better than others. The cremes were my least favourites, but there were only a few of those in the double tiered box. There were solid chocolate squares, coconut mounds, bite sized marzipans and turkish delight. There were oblong nougats and chewy caramels. But the ones with nuts in them were best of all. There were little round ones with hazelnuts, and those with bits of almonds. Then there were the large, strangely shaped ones that had a whole brazil nut encased in chocolate.

To be polite, I had to hand the box round the room before I could take one myself. Uncle Aubrey always took the ones with mushy middles. I've never been sure whether it was because he really liked them, or whether he understood my preferences and was being kind to me. In any case, I was grateful for his choices.

Uncle Aubrey was generous in other ways. At Christmas time he brought his car full of gaily wrapped packets, presents for everyone. He brought us all the things we liked best: books, puzzles, games, and wonderful things to eat. Among other things he sometimes brought a great round tray of Christmas delicacies that included dates, figs, glazed pineapple, and cherries. The tray was attractively arranged and there were always some small ivory forks with which to spear the fruit. These unique forks were "saved" every year for, as mummy said, "the time when we might need them again." As I recall, we hoarded quite a stack of them.

One Christmas Uncle Aubrey had brought us a gramophone, probably the first one in Wenhaston. It was a huge contraption that took up the entire end of the dining table. It had a wooden case with places fitted in the lid for the handle, and several records. The sound came through a large horn that came in a separate soft bag in another container. To make it work, Uncle Aubrey took the lid off completely, attached the horn to the top, put the handle in the side of the box and a record on the turntable. He then wound the handle, being careful not to overdo the winding, put the silver "head" with the needle onto the record and pushed a lever. There was a bit of crackling, then suddenly there was music and sometimes singing.

I remember the Strauss waltzes, especially the *Blue Danube* and *Tales from Vienna Woods,* and Uncle Aubrey clearing a space between the fireplace chairs to do an impromptu little dance with Carly-luv. What a sight they were, and how merry the day. Uncle Aubrey, dashingly handsome, would hold Carly-luv ever so gently, while her silky dress swished gracefully around her. When the record ran down he'd spin Carly-luv to a stop, bending her almost to the floor while we all clapped our hands and Dadda said, "Bravo!"

Many of the records were "modern" love songs: Gershwin tunes such as *Embraceable You, 'S Wonderful,* and *Lady Be Good.* What delicious fun it was to learn the words as we sang along with the gramophone. With each subsequent visit, Uncle Aubrey brought new records for our wonderful machine. The one that got the most laughs and was played frequently was *Miss Otis Regrets.* It was a song about how Miss Otis shot her unfaithful lover and therefore "regretted" she was "unable to lunch today."

Our gramophone was a novelty, an expensive luxury that we probably would not have had, had it not been for Uncle Aubrey's generosity. It was a beautiful instrument manufactured by RCA. It had a picture of the little spotted dog with his ear cocked to the huge horn attached to the top. Underneath the picture the caption said "His Master's Voice."

To my knowledge no one else in Wenhaston had a gramophone at the time. But Gonie Spindler's father had a "player piano" that played dozens of songs. It had a round tin drum with holes in it that turned round and round inside the open-fronted piano. We watched in fascination as the drum turned and the keys went up and down as though someone were playing the notes. There was always something pleasant about visiting Gonie's house at the bottom of Coles Hill. There was a welcome and warmth and much laughter in that cozy home.

Gonie's name was really "Begonia" but I didn't learn that until I was about ten years old when the subject of nicknames came up. Gonie let me plait her hair. It was always a special pleasure to do that. Gonie had the most remarkable head of hair: thick, brown, luscious locks that were long enough for her to sit on. She wore her hair in two long braids that had to be disassembled daily, brushed three hundred strokes, and replaited. As I wielded the brush, we talked. She was trying to console me about the nickname "Sidney" I had recently picked up from a bully at school. She quoted the old adage about sticks and stones not breaking any bones, but my tormentor had hit a raw nerve.

Gonie knew that I wanted desperately for the Saunders to adopt me and give me their family name of Saunders. My last name was Sidey, an unusual name that no one in the village had ever heard. The nicknames and taunting would not have hurt nearly so much, except that I was at a most vulnerable position at home. The Saunders had made application to Dr. Barnado's Home who were, I now believe, negotiating with their higher powers. I wanted to be adopted so badly and have their name as my own that I sometimes inadvertently gave my name as Saunders. So did some of my friends.

I remember one incident in particular. It was a few nights before Guy Fawkes and we were up to our usual pranks. One of these was the "parcel" game. This involved wrapping a cardboard box in brown paper and putting string around it to make it look like a parcel from the post office. We'd tie a long string to it and knock on the door. When the door was opened and the householder went to pick it up, we'd jerk the string and run like the dickens, dragging our box behind us. Sometimes we didn't bother with the parcel on a string. We simply knocked on the door and ran a few yards away, so we could see and hear the reaction of the one who opened the door.

There was an elderly couple who lived in a cottage half-way down Coles Hill, not far from Gonie's house. The old man was a bit of a grouch and though he knew our game, he invariably opened the door and tried to catch us. On this particular evening we had already made two or three passes, knocking loudly and racing away to safety. But he was wiser than we knew. On our last pass I was on the tail end of the group. I had banged the knocker and turned to race up the hill. The rest of the group were already most of the way up the hill. I turned to look back, expecting to see him opening his door and making strides behind me. In the next second I ran into a howling monster.

He had waited behind a bush by his garden gate. When I banged the knocker, he strode forward with arms outstretched and I ran into him full tilt. I have never before or since known such pure horror. He was my worst nightmare come true. He was snorting and raving and I was screaming my head off. My friends up the hill thought he must be killing me. Someone, I don't remember who, came back down the hill to try to rescue me, but the old man had me in a vice-like grip.

"What's yer name?" he bellowed. For once in my life I had no words to say. I was shaking like a leaf in a windstorm, thoroughly and completely terrified. When I opened my mouth to speak, nothing would come out but gibberish. I squirmed and twisted, but the old man would not let go until I had given him an intelligent answer. Fortunately, my friend grasped the situation. From somewhere above me he yelled,

"It's Joicy Saunders, you old sod. Let her go." For just a split second the old man turned to see who the impudent lout was behind him, and in doing so loosened his grip on my arms. I squirmed away and ran up the hill as though the Devil himself was on my heels, collapsing in a heap at the top, outside of Walter's house. Mr. Wilson came out to see what all the shouting was about, gave us all a scolding and sent us home. Whenever I remembered this nightmarish incident, and I frequently did, I also remembered the sweet sound of being known as "Joicy Saunders."

I wasn't in the habit of keeping anything from Dadda. As soon as I flounced in the kitchen door he knew something was wrong. I was still trembling uncontrollably. I was getting too big to sit on his knee as I had once done. But now I sank down beside his chair and buried my face in his knee and sobbed. He stroked my hair and made me tell him the whole story. While he knew, as I did, that I was in the wrong, he still tried to comfort me. Mummy was not so charitable. When she learned the truth, I got a good tongue lashing and was sent to the scullery to get myself washed and ready for bed. I knew I'd get no supper, which I'd missed anyway.

But Mummy believed in keeping me "nourished" so she gave me a mug of Bovril, a thin beef broth that was rather distasteful to me. It was some consolation that she allowed me to drink it at the table with Dadda before packing me off to bed. I made it last as long as I could, dawdling between sips of the warm, brown liquid. She was very angry with me, roundly scolding and giving me "what for" in no uncertain terms. She was also upset with Dadda for coddling me, and promised both of us we hadn't heard the last of the affair.

She was right, too. The next day at school Mr. Sangster took some of us out in the boys' hallway one by one. He questioned me about whether I had been the "ringleader" in the pranks on Coles Hill the night before, and though I hadn't really thought of myself as that, I did confess my guilt as being part of the marauding group. He asked me to hold out my hands and before I knew what happened he gave me a whack across the palms with his thin cane. I yelped and drew my hands back. I had never been caned before, and I vowed at that moment never to be again.

Mr. Sangster steely eyes looked through me. His lanky frame was rigid as in icy tones he informed me that for every time I drew my hands back, he would add strikes. Something told me that he meant what he said. I gritted my teeth and closed my eyes. It was the most difficult thing to do, but I put my hands forward for a second and then a third time. I was then allowed to go back to my desk in the classroom and sit in the "rest" position, which meant sitting up straight with my arms behind my back. This was our normal position when we were simply "at rest," that is to say, not actively writing or doing something that required hands on our desks.

When I entered the classroom from the boy's hall, all my classmates were sitting at rest. None of them dared speak to me, but their eyes spoke volumes of understanding. With the back of my hands I quickly brushed away the tears that would have disgraced me and peeked furtively at my palms to make sure they weren't bleeding. They weren't, but ugly red welts were already rising and they burned like fire.

None of the other girls who were with us got caned, possibly because no one in authority knew who they were. But for the next hour, several of the boys were called into the hallway, one after another. We could hear the muted "crack" of the cane as each was made to bend over, drop his trousers and take three lashes across his seat. Occasionally we could hear a sharp cry of pain, but not one of them came back in the room crying. George Sturgeon, a fellow Dr. Barnardo's friend who wore a perpetual smile of good humour, came back in the room looking strained and pale. But Harold King came back to the classroom with thunder in his eyes. We knew from experience that he hated the headmaster and would one day try to take revenge. That day came, just before we left school in the year we reached the magic age of fourteen.

Harold, a tall, rugged farm boy who wore hobnail boots, was being punished for some infraction when he fought back. Though none of us actually witnessed the event, we all knew it was plausible. It was said, and we believe it's true, that when the headmaster told Harold to bend over for some infraction of the rules, that Harold defied him, kicked him in the shins with his hob-nailed boots and ran from the school, never to return.

A caning was hard to bear, but the wounds were temporary. The headmaster was a common enemy that we could identify with en masse. We could escape his wrath by not getting caught disobeying the rules. When we did get caught, we could lean on each other for support and sympathy. Like the time I moved the clock hands forward and was kept in to write a hundred "lines" during playtime. No one "tattled" that I had done it and I don't think old Sangster had any proof. But he was right, and I was punished for it and my classmates had much empathy for me. Beyond the sympathy was also a faint tinge of respect for the martyred one that helped tremendously heal any pain.

Much harder to bear than caning was being taunted and bullied by one of my own fellow classmates. Out of the whole school I had only one enemy. He was a particularly loathsome lout whose name was Eddie Ferguson. Not only was he teasing me verbally, but he was physically obnoxious as well, chasing me down the hill from school, pulling my hair and punching me. His unflattering rhyme about me went like this: "Sidney-Si, piddled in a black man's eye." He had a perpetually runny nose and his face, covered with pimples, was constantly contorted into an ugly sneer.

The bully was a newcomer to the village and I was not his only victim. Gonie and I decided to join forces against the intruder. We referred to him mainly as the "snot-nosed twirp" but later branched out to include many rude names including "Fergi the turdi." It was the cruelest thing we could think of at the time. I don't know why this boy took a dislike to me. Dadda warned me not to goad him. Gonie and I were no match for him, so in the end I did my best to avoid any contact with him. My silence and avoidance seemed to antagonize him even further. I couldn't seem to get away from him, no matter how hard I tried. In desperation, I took one of Dadda's walking sticks to school with me.

I knew I couldn't actually take it into school with me, so I hid it by the church yard steps at the bottom of the hill. It gave me much satisfaction to see the surprised expression on my adversary's face as I turned toward him brandishing my stick. Unfortunately, my advantage was limited. It was only a matter of time before the "twirp" outran me and used my own weapon against me. That day, to my surprise and pleasure, some of the bigger boys came to my defense and chased him away. It was a small, but most enjoyable victory. Thankfully there was only one bully throughout my entire school experience, but that to me was one too many. The rest of the children in school I counted as friends, though I saw some less frequently than others.

Mary Gillingham lived next door to Mr. Hammond's cobbler shop on Front Street. Whenever I had to leave shoes to be mended or pick up some that had been repaired, I would call in on her. We loved to watch Mr. Hammond cut the leather and shape it over the sole of a shoe. His shop smelled wonderfully of new leather, and lasts of every size and shape were on his wooden bench. The main last was attached to the bench. It had a metal base and wooden pieces shaped like a foot cut in half on the top. Many times we watched him put a shoe to be repaired on the wooden pieces then crank the metal handle until the last fit the shoe exactly. Then he would begin his work, placing the leather sole and hammering tiny nails all around the edges. He would then hold the edges up to a sanding wheel that he operated with a foot pedal, and smooth off all the rough edges. When he had it just right, he painted round the outside with black paint to finish it off.

Sometimes he had to sew up a shoe that had come apart. He had a special machine for doing that. It looked like an unwieldly and rather spindly sewing machine. He operated it by a foot pedal that was half hidden under the well-scarred bench. Mr. Hammond was a kindly man. His son Willie, who was in our class at school, would sometimes be in the shop with his dad, waiting on customers. One day when I was sent to leave some shoes to be repaired, Willie was outside the shop talking with Mary. As I came up they turned toward me, and began telling me about the Gypsies that had come overnight to the caravan down the lane by the Hut.

It was a strange phenomenon in our village, this caravan. Painted in gaudy yellow with orange, green and blue markings, it looked suspiciously like a left-over circus caravan, which in truth it probably was. It was located up the lane that ran between the blacksmith's shop and the village Hut. It was nestled in a clump of high bushes, partially hidden from the main thoroughfare. Margaret Hazel who lived much farther down the lane had to pass it every day on her way to school. Most of the year it sat empty, but then suddenly from nowhere the Romanies, as they were called, would appear. They normally only stayed a few weeks and then they were off again. No one knew where they came from or where they went. They just simply appeared, and just as quickly they were gone again.

Gypsies dressed in strange circus-like garb. The men wore scarves around their heads. The women wore colourful dresses and big earrings, and often were seen smoking pipes. They had a cart they pulled round the village, and they sold glass beads and wooden clothes pegs. Everyone said the Romanies made the best clothes pegs, and were ready to buy them when they came to the village.

The Gypsies would read your fortune for sixpence, but you had to go up to the caravan to get it done. We were supposed to stay away from them, but our curiosity always got the best of us. We'd hide in the bushes close to the caravan and watch for them to go in and out. Sometimes we were lucky and could watch them as they cooked on a little camp stove outside the caravan steps. We always imagined it was witches brew they were stewing.

We knew we weren't supposed to go near the caravan, but curiosity got the best of us as usual. Nothing would do but that we go see what was happening, so without wasting another minute, off we ran. When we arrived at the caravan on this day, we were surprised to see not Gypsies as we'd expected, but two nice ladies dressed in ordinary clothes. One of them was a bit heavy set with rosy cheeks and a wide smile. The other was of slight build, younger than the other. She had black hair that was caught in a heavy netted snood around her shoulders.

The two spotted us immediately and invited us to come in the caravan. We hesitated, not really knowing whether to run away or accept their invitation. In the end the smaller of the two walked over to us and extended her hand toward us.

"Come along" she said, "I've got something to show you that I think you'll like." We couldn't resist her offer. Without a word, we followed her into the tiny caravan. None of us had ever been inside before, so it was quite exciting to see the interior. The area we came into was a small room with a door leading to what we assumed was the sleeping quarters. The cramped space we entered had built-in cabinets above a tiny counter, which must have been the kitchen. There was an oil lamp hanging from a ceiling hook and a Primus stove on the end of the counter. Further around, there was a window that looked out onto the lane. Under it there were cushioned seats that looked large enough to hold two or three people. A small table attached to the floor was placed in front of the seats.

When the ladies indicated, we three squeezed around to sit behind the table, and the ladies, whose names we learned were Miss Constance and Miss Faye, brought over some books from the counter and spread them in front of us. They told us they were missionaries who traveled around the country to tell people about the good news of Jesus Christ. They told us Jesus loved little children and wanted them to come to Him. They talked about how Jesus had come to "seek and to save those who were lost." They showed us the books they had, that had religious pictures on them of Jesus with children crowded around Him. They quoted John 3:16 to us: "God so loved the world that He gave His only begotten Son, that whosoever believieth on Him should not perish, but have everlasting life." On and on they talked, pointing out to us that we were in grave danger of being eternally lost if we didn't know Jesus as our Saviour.

We listened with rapt attention until there was a pause. Willie and Mary said nothing, only exchanged glances now and then. It was obvious to me that Miss Constance and Miss Faye didn't know much about Wenhaston or the church-oriented villagers who lived here. I then piped up with words of wisdom for these two sweet ladies. As usual my mouth ran away with my brains. "We know about Jesus," I said. "Everyone in Wenhaston believes in Him," I said with great confidence. I was trying to let them know that they were wasting their time in Wenhaston. We already knew the "good news," as they called it.

It made me feel smug and very knowledgeable. I went on to tell them about how we went to church and to Sunday school and how we recited the psalms and other scripture at school. The ladies waited until I ran down a bit and had to catch my breath. Then Miss Faye looked at me kindly, took my hand and told me that going to church and reciting the scriptures wasn't enough. She said that everyone had to make a personal decision to follow Jesus. She said that each person needed to confess his sin and accept the forgiveness Jesus had sacrificed His life to give him.

She wanted to know if we were ready to receive Him. We must have nodded our heads in assent. At that point we were a bit confused, and didn't really understand what was expected of us. No one had ever talked to us like this before. In fact, we never heard people talk about God or Jesus at all, outside of church. The people we knew, even Mr. Hardingham the Vicar, didn't talk about Jesus in this way. There seemed to me to be something very wrong and irreverent about it all.

By this time Mary, Willie and I were squirming uncomfortably in our seats and wishing we could make our escape. Miss Faye asked us to bow our heads, which we did obediently. She prayed over us a prayer such as I had never heard before. She talked to God as though He were right there in the room with us, telling Him how we were special children, and asking Him to forgive our sin, to wash us in His blood and to watch over us and bless us. When she had finished she said words that stunned me and struck a vulnerable place in my heart: "You are now adopted into the family of God and He will watch over you all your lives." On the way out the door Miss Constance pressed a little pamphlet into each of our hands, smiled and said "cheerio" as we scampered down the wooden steps.

I ran all the way home to Dadda. The word "adopted" ringing inside my head. I suddenly believed that God had given me a sign, that now the adoption into the Saunders family I had been looking for would be a reality. The rest of the session had been a jumble. But that one thought remained. Dadda was just coming out of the bird shed when I reached the gate, so we walked to the house together. I was talking so fast and the sentences tumbled together in such a way that Dadda could not make head nor tail of anything I was saying.

"Hold on, Beauty," he said, guiding me into the kitchen door. He wanted me to sit down at the kitchen table, but I was too excited. I finally sat on the floor, and while Dadda cleaned out the bowl of his pipe with his penknife, I began at the beginning relating as best I could what had transpired. At first he made me talk about why I went to the caravan to begin with. I admitted I had been wrong to go there, and I suffered through his scolding, impatiently promising not to go anywhere near the caravan again. He questioned me closely about the missionary ladies and looked over the little pamphlet they had given me. I was anxious to hear what he had to say about the adoption they spoke about.

"Is this a sign from God?" I wanted to know. In the Bible I knew that God sent signs to many people. I was always willing to believe God could work "in mysterious ways His wonders to perform." Dadda laid his pipe down for a minute and looked at me steadily. He explained to me that what the missionaries were talking about had nothing to do with my physical adoption. He reassured me that if it were possible to do so, I would be adopted into the family. If not, and he looked at me steadily, "you will always be my special little girl," and he smiled to let me know that everything would be just fine. I understood what he was saying, but pressed him to let me change my name so that it would be legally Saunders.

"I can't do that, Beauty," he said. "Not now, anyway. Be patient just a little while longer." He picked up his tobacco pouch and began to press the aromatic tobacco into the bowl of his pipe. I knew I needed to stop pestering him, but I didn't want to drop the subject. Mummy came in from the shop, calling me to take an order out. Dadda urged me to be a good girl and help Mummy. So I got up from the floor, kissed Dadda on the cheek and prepared to go. As I was turning away, Dadda spoke softly. I caught his words as they trailed after me.

"What's in a name, Beauty?" he said softly. And again, "What's in a name?"

Chapter 8

Summer's End

To Thee, in whom we live and move, we come
To praise Thee for the sheaves brought safely home
With Harvest-tide Thanksgiving.

Old Hymn

I had my ninth Birthday in July 1937. It had been a lovely summer and now at the beginning of August the days stretched wonderfully long. We lingered in the evenings playing "rounders" outside Joy Youngs' house on Front Street. Grandmother Youngs knitted in her chair by the window, watching us play. The men worked in their garden plots over the wall behind us, gathering the late vegetables and clearing away the dead runner beans and other vines.

When we heard the mothers calling us, we pretended not to hear. We wanted to make the evening last forever. One and then another soon called "cheerio" or "see ya" and ran off home. Harold left with Tom, and Norman followed them toward Back Road. Primrose and her sister Marjorie went the other way. They lived in the house right next to the school, so they had the longest distance to go. Soon we all had gone our separate ways. Tomorrow was another day, and we'd got the word the men were harvesting wheat up at the field on Bramfield Road. It was something to look forward to.

Though harvesting may have been a stressful time for the farmers, who worried about getting their crops in and stored before the bad weather set in, it was a joyous time for the children who counted it a privilege to be allowed to help. Wheat, corn and hay harvesting were especially delightful. Sugar beets and potatoes were much harder. Thankfully we children seldom helped with those. When the men were cutting hay or grain, we would gather early in the morning in the field that was being cut, with flasks of lemonade, fresh bread, chunks of cheese, and jam sandwiches. We also brought along our heavy sticks with which to kill the rabbits that hid in the field.

The wheat and corn harvesting progressed differently from the hay harvesting. The reaper would make swathes round the edge of the wheat or corn field, throwing out bundles as it went. We would then help the men gather three or four bundles together and stand them upright in sheaves all around the field. The sheaves might stand in that same way for several days until the farmer was ready to gather them in for stacking and later threshing.

As the reaper progressed in its rounds, the rabbits that were hiding amid the tall stems ran for cover, some darting in front of us while others fled to the centre of the field. At a certain spot, while there was still wheat standing, the reaper would stop cutting, leave his tractor and help us encircle the remaining wheat. We then "ran" the rabbits, whacking them as hard as we could across the head so as not to ruin the body. Since rabbits were plentiful in those days, and were a desirable source of food, our "catch" was an added bonus to the enjoyment of the day.

The men partly dressed the rabbits on the field and helped the children with theirs. We'd tie the rabbits up to tree branches by their hind legs, and watch the deft process as the men slit them down their mid sections and emptied their innards on the ground. Later I would proudly take my portion of the catch home and would watch fascinated as Mummy chopped off the heads and skinned them. She skillfully separated the limbs in all the appropriate places, and thoroughly washed each piece.

By all accounts, Mummy made the best rabbit stew in the county. First, she stripped off the meat and cooked it with seasonings to make a broth. She then filled a deep crockery pie dish with cut-up vegetables, meat, and broth, and encased it all in thick pastry, putting an egg-cup in the middle to keep it from sinking in the centre. It was truly a delectable and savory dish that we all enjoyed.

Harvesting hay was different. We did flush and chase the odd rabbit, but we concentrated on getting the harvesting done. The grass was usually cut, gathered and stacked all in the same day. The huge steel comb-like rake on the back of the tractor left rather untidy heaps in places round the field. If the men were using a lorry for gathering, one of them would drive it onto the field and begin work at the farthest point of the field. More often than not, they would be using the horses and carts, which we children liked better. Two or three of us would jump in the empty cart, catch the hay as it was thrown, and "bed" the hay evenly, filling the cart almost to overflowing.

New-mown hay has the most marvelous, fresh aroma in the world. Its unique fragrance lingers down through the years in a most pleasant way. When our cart was filled and could hold no more, we would ride on top of the hay back to the farmyard, sometimes wobbling mightily as the horse lumbered down the road and up the lane. Back at the farm, we would help unload the hay with our pitchforks while the men on the ground fashioned a "ragged stack," a squarish pile. Time after time up and down the road we would go, stopping only briefly to eat our meal at midday. That it was work, we didn't know then. We knew that it was delightful being together in the fields, tossing the hay, chasing rabbits and laughing together in the sunshine.

It was because of my good experiences with the harvesting that I decided one summer to try my hand at farming. I went to work at Vale Farm, which was located directly across the road and down the lane from Walter's house. The owner, Mr. Freeman, also owned the coal business that supplied most of the village. We children often went to the coal yard to watch the men load up the wagons. Some of the coal was put in big sacks that the men toted on their shoulders, but most of it was put in half-ton loads and delivered in loose piles. At the Saunders house, the coal pile was put through a chute in the corner of our bicycle shed. A big load of coal in one corner lasted through the winter.

Walter's father, his grandfather, and his uncle Mr. Page, Doreen's father, all worked on the farm. They were kind to me, if sometimes a bit gruff. They let me know there'd be "no loafin' or muckin' about" while I was working. Whenever they needed anything I was to "hop to it." They were hard working men, and expected no less from everyone else. From the start I knew I would have to "turn to" to earn my pay. I can see the men's weathered faces in my minds eye now: the dark, leathery complexion of their cheeks contrasted by the whiteness of their foreheads when they removed their sweat-stained caps.

I was glad to dress up, if a tad baggily, in a well-used pair of Lenny's outgrown overalls with the too-long legs stuffed inside my "wellies." These rubber boots were the most practical for the farm, and were comfortable without socks because they had a thin insulating lining. Mummy didn't want to cut the legs off the overalls; she said, "Next year you'll be grown taller," meaning I could use the overalls again.

It was years later that I thought back and remembered how frugally we lived, and yet how bountiful our lives seemed to be. I recall now that nothing was ever wasted. Certainly no piece of clothing was ever thrown away. There was always another use for everything. Either we gave it to a less fortunate person, or if it was too far gone for wearing, we cut it into strips to be used in making fireplace mats.

I started my farming chores at Vale Farm as a "fetchit," doing a little of everything, like carrying pails of milk to the separator house or helping to clean out the tall churns. My main responsibility was to see to the cows, and get them where they were supposed to be at the right time. It was a small herd of about fifteen cows. They all had names and individual personalities. I drove them out to the grazing fields after they'd been milked in the morning and then returned them to their stalls in the evening. They were such creatures of habit that when I went to bring them in, they immediately began lumbering down the lane toward home.

I worried only about one certain gate in a narrow lane that was kept closed. The herd would stop and bellow, waiting for me to get through them to the front and open the gate for them. I was a bit intimidated by their size and their ability to cast a level stare at me whenever they felt cornered. To avoid being crushed, I climbed all the way up a steep embankment, traversed the hedgerow, and climbed back down on the other side of the gate. The cows looked at me with their big, soulful eyes as though I were totally daft. When I'd opened the gate, they would put their heads down, flick their tails defiantly and lumber on up the lane to the barnyard. They knew the way. They didn't need me to show them. I was only needed to open and close the gates for them.

I'd only been a cow herder for a few weeks when I was pressed into learning how to milk. I began my apprenticeship on one of the more tractable cows, named Ruby. What an experience that was! First I had to scrub my hands with red carbolic soap in icy cold water from the well. Sometimes if Ruby's udder was mud splashed, or worse, caked with bits of poop, I had to take a flannel in a pail of water and wash her clean also. She didn't much care for that procedure. I think it was because the water was so cold. She'd swish her tail around and turn her head to gaze at me with the most sorrowful look, bellowing softly. Sometimes she'd move her feet slightly in protest, but she was never cranky, nor did she flail about and bellow wildly as some of the other cows did.

Walter Wilson's father, "Ollie," as the grown men called him, showed me how to squat down on the stool, tuck the milk pail at the right angle between my knees and put my forehead right into the cow's side. I then learned how to curl my fingers, begin at the top of the teat and squeeze gently while pulling down firmly. After much practice and many false starts, I knew I was doing it correctly when the squirts rattled against the side of the shiny pail in just the right rhythm and with that certain "zing."

My farming tasks took only a small part of the summer days, in the early mornings and late afternoons. I had many activities that kept me busy for the remaining time. My main job for the shop was going to various homes to pick up their weekly orders, then packing the groceries at the shop and making the deliveries. The shop closed at noon on Wednesdays, as did all the other shops in Wenhaston, Halesworth, and in cities such as Colchester and Ipswich. Though the custom has mainly gone out of style now in the cities, "Wednesday half closing" is still practiced in small towns and villages all over England.

In the spring and summertime the bird shed was busier than at any other time. With more free hours, I was able to help Dadda in many ways, particularly shipping the various birds. The birds were able to survive a two day journey in their special traveling cages, with air holes all around and a handle on top. Sometimes Dadda had them traveling in pairs. I went by bus to the train station in Halesworth, paid the freight charges, and waited for the right train to come in. I loved watching the trains lumbering in to the station, blowing and hissing steam and clattering noisily to a stop. It was delightful to be part of the excitement of people arriving and departing, and watching the porters bustling about with their laden trolleys. I would take the birds to the luggage car and hand them over to the porter in charge. It was not unusual to see other animals that were traveling by train, in crates or cages.

After delivering the birds, I usually had an hour or two to wait for my bus to return home. Nearly always I would skip down the hill to look in the shop windows, and as I passed by Owen's house would call a cheery "Hello" to him. Sometimes I would get involved in a game with Owen or his brothers and sisters. I had to stay close to the station so as not to miss my bus home. Occasionally the bus would begin its descent toward us and someone would shout the alarm. I would have to race to the corner bus stop and climb aboard.

Since my first bus ride, I seldom sat down below on the double-decker. I wound my way up the stairway to sit at the top, out of breath, and huffing and puffing. From that vantage point, I waved to my chums and sat down to enjoy the ride home, past Holton and Blyford Inn and especially the "whoosh" over the humpback bridge. I loved being able to see the green and lush countryside, and watching the wide-open expanse of sky. Sometimes I imagined the clouds formed shapes of people or animals and as the bus moved along, the patterns disintegrated and reformed into other things. Always the bus ride was too short, and I would be at the Compass Inn before I knew what was happening.

I had regular commitments on certain afternoons: choir practice, tennis lessons, Girl Guides, and other activities. Dadda said I was "always on the go" and wondered where I got the energy. To me, there were never enough hours in the day. One of my favourite summer activities was playing in the "runs" at Blyford or Thorington. Some of us would gather spontaneously of an afternoon as though we had planned for weeks to meet at that particular spot. We had a curious fascination about the streams of water that ran across the road in these areas. It was especially nice in summer, because the water was usually quite low. In the rainy season, wagons had a difficult time getting through the Thorington run. At Blyford run, there was an alternative route: a roadway with a very low bridge along one side of it.

Humpback Bridge

My friends and I could amuse ourselves for hours wading in the water or building makeshift dams. The Blyford run was located right next to the humpback bridge, on the Wenhaston side. When we got tired of playing in the water, we would dare each other to run across the wide cement top of the arch that curved across the humpback bridge, which was about twenty feet above the river. It was a dangerous game. Though none of us who attempted to run across it ever fell, it was truly a miracle. As I look back on it, I shudder to realize that had any of us fallen, we would surely have been killed. The river bottom was full of stones and huge rocks that jutted up out of the water when the river ran low.

I didn't work on the farm on Sundays, but they also were full days in the summertime. There were church services in the morning, and there were wonderful visits to Southwold with the Sunday School Class in the afternoons when the weather allowed. God must have been smiling on us, because it seldom seemed to rain on Sunday afternoons in July. When it did, it was disappointing not to be able to go to the seaside, but we had plenty to keep us busy. It was a great opportunity to visit each other's, homes, to play board games or put together a jigsaw puzzle. We were never bored!

That year at Girl Guides we began to learn First Aid. We spent much time bandaging each other's arms and legs, and improvising stretchers to carry wounded bodies. We were becoming most adept at "setting" an arm with two pieces of wood and bandaging the splint with torn-up sheeting. All of us began to think nursing might be a good career. Certainly, we found the nurses uniforms to be very attractive.

We worked hard at memorizing the names of items placed on a surgical tray, and in practicing the art of making and applying a tourniquet to stop the flow of blood. I was lucky to get additional instruction at home from Lenny's friend Joyce Borrott who was a nurse. Lenny was seriously courting Joyce, and brought her home now and then for tea.

Lenny was rather shy in many ways, and had seemed lost and lonely since his friend Jimmy's death. But Lenny always seemed strong and confident in Joyce's presence. She was, without a doubt, the right girl for him. To my knowledge, she was the only girl Lenny was ever serious about; at least she was the only one he ever brought home to the family. Joyce was a tall, big-boned girl with a wide smile. Like her cousin Gonie, Joyce had an outgoing personality and a generous heart. Unlike Gonie, she had fair hair, blue eyes and freckles across the bridge of her nose.

Joyce Borrott

As I was now beginning to consider a nursing career, I plagued her with questions about her duties and responsibilities. She was a nurse at Bulcamp Union Hospital in Blythburgh, which was located just beyond the limits of Wenhaston. I knew from experience that it was not the most popular place to work, as there was a certain stigma attached to the place. Joyce let me know there was a great deal of satisfaction in working with patients, particularly those who were not only infirm, but who were also the peculiar "misfits" in society.

According to her philosophy, Bulcamp Union's poor patients deserved every bit as good nursing care as did London's Harley Street wealthy patients. She made sure the patients on her ward got the best she could give. I loved her philosophy and wanted to grow up to be just like her. I was going through a stage of being a dramatic idealist in those days. I could visualize myself as the world's next Florence Nightingale, and longed for the day when I could grandly show kindness and bring comfort to the sick and needy people of the world.

The Workhouse, as Bulcamp was generally known, was an institute for the poor. The men and women who came there could work on the surrounding farms during the daytime for meager wages, if they were able. Thus they were able to contribute something toward their bed and board and have some pocket money too. Some of the occupants were feeble-minded, or in our local vernacular, "daft as dish-water" and unable to cope with reality, let alone be gainfully employed. Though a good many of them were unable to care for themselves properly on the outside, they were able to contribute quite well to the workforce of the institute itself. Under supervision, all had mandatory jobs and most of them went about their assigned tasks in the kitchen, scullery, dining hall or gardens with a sense of childlike enthusiasm.

Bulcamp Union was a sprawling group of brick buildings that were built in 1765 as a community poorhouse. It had the capacity to house close to four hundred residents, including more than a hundred beds in the infirmary. The women and men were strictly segregated in the living quarters as well as in the hospital wards. The residents were allowed freedom to mingle as they went about their daily tasks on the grounds, and in the huge dining hall where they met for meals. Married couples presented all sorts of problems, especially in the hospital, as men were not allowed to visit in the women's ward and vice versa.

The workhouse was supported financially by perhaps as many as forty surrounding Church Parishes, including Wenhaston. Some of the residents came by choice, seeking sanctuary. But many who came to live there were either vagrants, or had been committed through proper channels by relatives who could no longer care for them.

Though Bulcamp residents did a good percentage of the menial tasks in running the institute, there was employment available for young apprentice housekeepers and for assistants in the hospital wards. One matron supervised the entire staff of nurses, housekeepers and groundskeepers, who in turn, appointed supervisors over the underling apprentices and residents. The whole place was run very efficiently, and though the building was old, it was in excellent condition and kept in good order.

Joyce had taken her nurse's training at Halesworth, and at graduation had opted to go on staff at the workhouse, rather than taking a more prestigious placement. That Bulcamp was close to her home may have had some influence on her decision. Knowing her, I believe that she truly had compassion for the people whom she thought needed the most care. I admired her so much. I was glad she was engaged to be married to Lenny. I was especially glad her name was Joyce like mine. It gave us a bond.

As summer slid into autumn, the women began to collect the last of the fruits and flowers to decorate the Church for the Harvest Thanksgiving service. For the better part of a week, they enlisted the children's help to carry pails of water, immense flower jugs, and baskets of fruit to St. Peter's for the ceremony. Every nook in the stony walls, around the chancel and high window ledges was covered with straw and twigs to cradle colourful wild flowers, small boughs of elderberries and loaves of bread. Great urns of wild flowers: Harebells, Persicaria, Heather, Knapweed and Goldenrod interspersed with heath Gorse, Seabious and wild rose hips were arrayed in every available space. The covered entry porch, whose stone seats lent themselves to many purposes, were cleaned of all the accumulated papers, children's hats and broken brollies, and decorated with small sheaves, vegetables, and urns of flowers.

Everyone agreed the church looked its best when it was decorated to the hilt for a festival. But for the harvest there was a unique sense of God's bountiful mercy and grace. We always acknowledged the physical harvest with thanksgiving to God for His earthly provisions. Always the harvest was connected with God's word and the spiritual needs and nurturing that only God could provide for our souls.

Reverend Hardingham's prayer for the blessing of the Harvest, the "collect" of the day, though beautiful in its familiarity, was somewhat troublesome for those of us who had not yet grasped the significance of "the fruits of the spirit." From my front row seat in the choir stall I followed along silently in my prayer book as our Vicar intoned the words:

> *"O most merciful Father, who of thy gracious goodness has heard the devout prayers of thy Church, and turned our dearth and scarcity into cheapness and plenty; we give Thee humble thanks for this special bounty; beseeching Thee to continue Thy loving-kindness unto us, that our land may yield us her fruits of increase, to Thy Glory and our comfort; through Jesus Christ our Lord."*

And in unison the choir, the people and the Vicar said a solemn "AMEN." Thus the busy, carefree summer ended. It was a bit difficult to get back into the routine and discipline of school. But as September approached and the annual rituals of Michaelmas and of new winter clothes arrived, I began my own adjustment to the changing season. It was not easy this particular year. My new shoes squeaked dreadfully, and they felt clumsy to me after I had been barefoot or wearing wellies and plimsolls without socks all summer. I had a tendency to blame the shoes and not my own clumsiness for a series of events that took place in quick succession.

It had been obvious for several weeks that our beloved Alsatian Goofie was not well. The once lively and attentive dog was not himself; his pattern of seeing me off at the garden gate and welcoming me home had changed noticeably. He slept most of the time, and when he was awake, he was alternately listless or very snarly. His habits were becoming erratic and unpredictable. Now instead of curling up to sleep in his own space between Dadda's chair and the bookcase, he uncharacteristically sprawled full-out wherever he plopped, sometimes in the heavily traveled area beside the kitchen door. Dadda was concerned about him, especially when he observed him having an epileptic seizure one afternoon.

I understood something about epilepsy because there was a boy named Harold who had occasional seizures at school. When he began to jerk around and eventually fall to the floor, we who sat close to him knew to move our desks so he wouldn't hurt himself. Miss Piper would come and stand near him and wave all of us away, to give him room to struggle. We would wait quietly until he stopped flailing and was able to sit up on his own again. Often the "fit" only lasted a few minutes. When it was over, Miss Piper helped him back into his seat, gave him a drink of water, and went back to the lesson at hand. Harold, who was normally a placid youngster, hardly seemed the worse for wear after his fits, and seemed to take them in stride.

What was happening at home with Goofie was much different. His whole personality seemed to be changing radically. I was bewildered by his new behavior toward me, which was becoming increasingly intolerant and snappish. At the same time, Goofie was acting more and more protective of Dadda, not letting him move out of his sight and sometimes growling at the rest of us when one of us came too close. On many occasions Dadda had to speak sharply to him. I felt that I was to blame for Goofie's venting his frustration on me. For years I'd tripped over him in haste, not looking where I was stepping, and he'd yelp and limp away. I was always sorry I'd hurt him, and up until now he'd always been very forgiving.

But something was drastically wrong with him now, and none of us quite knew how to handle the situation. We knew that he was suffering. Dan Norman, the local veterinarian who treated all the farm animals, came to see him several times. He gave us hope that given the proper treatment, Goofie would probably recover. He left some powdered stuff that was to be mixed with some special dog food. The only thing was, Goofie would hardly touch it, so Mummy and Lettie mixed the powder with warm milk and tried to ease it down his throat. It did not help matters that Goofie would only let Dadda touch him. Dadda wasn't able to bend over and wrestle with him, but had to sit on the sidelines and give commands, holding onto one side of his collar.

The powder did calm Goofie's epilepsy somewhat, but did nothing to improve his newly acquired bad temper. Twice, when I accidentally stumbled over him, he snapped at me and bit right through my new shoe to my big toe. The first time it happened, I was shocked and confused by his behavior. It was quite a nasty wound, and hurt a lot. Mummy sent for Mrs. Parsley, the District Nurse, to bathe and bandage my foot. The second time was not as bad, more of a big scratch than a wound, really. I didn't want the nurse to come, so Mummy bathed my toe, smothered it in iodine and bandaged it herself, scolding me the whole time for being so clumsy.

In November, just after Guy Fawkes Day, Goofie snapped at me and caught my hand in a savage bite. He was not himself, and I was beginning, too late, to be very cautious where I stepped. This time the doctor was called in to see to me and the District Nurse came to change the dressing every day until it was better. She was insistent that Dadda "put the dog down." Even Mummy stopped scolding me and sided with the nurse. I begged Dadda not to put him away just yet, feeling sure that when he got well, Goofie would revert to his normal self. I promised fervently I would be extra careful not to step on him again.

I knew Dadda was struggling with a hard decision. It was a difficult time, and to make matters worse, I had my hand bandaged when the "Home" lady came to pay her semi-annual visit. She'd just finished measuring my increased height on the door jam when she noticed my bandage. Mummy explained the details of my accident and assured her the doctor had been tending to it and that the wound was healing.

Later, after the Home lady had left, Mummy and Dadda spoke to each other in muted tones. I couldn't hear what they were saying, but both of them seemed subdued during the evening meal. I dreaded what was coming. When I returned home from school the following day Goofie was gone. Dadda said I needed to be brave and realize it was "for the best" and then we sat by the kitchen fire and wept together, our hearts totally broken.

This was my first experience with feeling the pain that comes with losing a loved one. Though I had been touched by Jimmy's Broom's death the year before, this was different. I had felt terribly sad about Jimmy mainly because I had watched Lenny hunched over the kitchen table, head in hands, sobbing uncontrollably. I cried then not only for Jimmy, but for Lenny, whose stricken face revealed the depth of his agony.

Goofie's death was more personal. It was as though a part of me had suddenly been torn away. I was hurting on the inside far worse than I'd ever been hurt physically. Much more, indeed, than when I'd had my nose broken or from any of the bites to my foot and my hand. I could not explain or escape my sorrow. It went down deeper and touched a place within me I hadn't known existed. My physical wounds healed quickly, and over the years, I have rarely noticed the small scars I still carry on the back of my right hand. But the memory of the pain in my heart from that fateful day and the closeness of sharing my grief with Dadda continues to live on.

In the next few weeks I began to think about death and search for information about it. I became almost obsessed by my need to know about what happened to people, and especially to dogs after they died. I put aside my usual reading of the "Solemnization of Matrimony" in the Prayer Book during the Sunday sermon, and instead began to peruse the order for the "Burial of the Dead." I felt sure I would get some answers to my questions. Actually, the Prayer book ultimately raised more questions for me than it answered. The very first passage caught my attention:

> "*I am the resurrection and the life, saith the Lord;*
> *he that believeth in me, though he were dead, Yet shall he live;*
> *And whosoever liveth and believeth in me, Shall never die.*"

I thought about this a lot. I was familiar with the resurrection, and knew that Jesus had risen from the dead. But now the words seemed to suggest that resurrection was not limited to just Jesus. I wondered if this meant that if we believed hard enough while we were alive, we could live forever. I liked that thought and wanted to know how to make that happen. But what about Goofie, who couldn't reason? What had happened to him? Perhaps there was a way that we wouldn't have to die; that we could just go right on living. I questioned Dadda about this.

"We all have to die," Dadda told me quietly. "Some of us live longer than others, but all ultimately die, animals as well as people." He went on to tell me that though animals can't think and plan for themselves, God has given them special instincts to live by, so their lives are sinless and when they died, they went straight to heaven.

"The difference between animals and people," he said, "is that people have the power to choose how they will live, whether to love God or to turn away from Him." He told me God loved animals and that he was sure God had reserved a special place for them. He said he thought that place for Goofie would be a lovely big field without any fences, where he had lots of other dogs to run and play with. He also reminded me what Jesus had said about the sparrows. He said that God had His eye upon them and that not one fell to the ground without His notice.

Dadda went on to explain that our Heavenly Father loved people more than birds, so we could depend on it that He would get us safely to heaven. He quoted part of a poem to me that I had heard many times before:

"Only be faithful, never waver
Nor seek earth's favour, but rest.
God knoweth what His will to be
For all his creatures, so for thee, the best."

Why then, I wanted to know, does the Vicar have to ask for special favours when someone dies? Why were prayers said that indicated a person needed special deliverance and help to enter heaven? One phrase in the prayer, "deliver us not into the bitter pains of eternal death," made me question my assumption that everybody automatically went to heaven. I worried about whether I would be "good enough" to get to heaven, and would the Reverend Hardingham know how to plead for me.

Would God count all the bad things I did, and there were many, and perhaps not let me in? Dadda said I was a Christian and that all Christians went to heaven. He said that bad people, those who were thieves or murderers, didn't go to heaven, that they went to hell. The Prayer Book, he said, was meant to cover all possibilities. In case the Vicar didn't know what kind of life the person had lived, he prayed for him at his funeral just to make sure.

It was a tangle and I couldn't quite understand it all. Dadda assured me that I was a Christian. When I asked him how he knew I was a Christian, he said because he knew I believed in God, therefore I was a Christian. I was, in the words of the lady missionaries, adopted into the family of God. He indicated that the way we behaved toward others was the best measure of whether or not we were Christians. He said that Christians don't lie or steal, because that would be displeasing to our Heavenly Father. The Prayer Book said that God knew the secrets of our hearts.

This troubled me as I knew my heart was treacherous, that I was willful, "cantankerous" Mummy called me, and an accomplished liar, never hesitating to bend the truth when it suited my purpose. I tried never to lie to Dadda, but the thought that God knew my secret self was unsettling. So why, I wanted to know, did the Vicar pray for a person who was already dead? If a person had to choose his destiny in life and a person chose to be bad, would the Vicar's prayers at his funeral make everything all right? Dadda looked at me a long time and relit his pipe.

"Well," he said, at long last. "I'll have to think on that." It puzzled me that Dadda didn't give me a conclusive answer. To my way of thinking there was nothing beyond Dadda's comprehension and nothing he couldn't readily resolve for me. The next Sunday I found another difficult passage:

"We meekly beseech Thee, O Father, to raise us from the death of sin unto the life of righteousness."

Now I posed some new questions about resurrection and "rising." I needed to know if after people died, did they come back to earth and live again. I had a friend whose aunt had told her that after people died they could come back as anything they wanted: dogs or cats or butterflies. I wanted to come back as a person, but I wanted to know the details of how to do that.

There were so many things I didn't understand about all this and so for the next few weeks, I badgered Dadda for answers. It was not a subject he really wanted to tackle, but he tried. He repeatedly told me that no one totally understood all the answers. He pooh-poohed with disdain the idea that anyone came back to earth at all, either as an animal or as a human being. Once a person died they were dead forever, he said. Jesus had risen from the dead and this was why we celebrated Easter Sunday.

He said that resurrection for the rest of us would take place in a different way. We would not come back to earth, but would enter a new earth that Jesus was preparing for us. Those of us who were Christians would live in heaven with God forever. No one, he said, had ever returned to earth to tell us what it was like in heaven. How we lived on earth would determine whether or not God thought us fit enough to enter heaven. He believed we would have to wait until we got there to find out what happened next.

From our conversation then, and from other bits of information I gleaned along the way, I got the idea that God had a pair of giant and exacting scales. My sins and my good deeds would be weighed out one against the other. If I had enough good deeds to my credit, I would be let into heaven. I recalled the poem about Abou Ben Adhem and the way he found the angel writing in the book. I remembered how at first his name was not written, and how Abou had put things right and found at the end that his name was written in the book.

I remembered Scrooge, the hard-bitten Dickens character who hated Christmas and was cruel to people. In a series of nightmarish dreams, he had been converted and his life changed dramatically. I began to have a germ of an idea that only "good" people would go to heaven. As long as one was alive, even when one grew old, he still had a chance, a choice to change his sinful attitude, and then he would be acceptable for heaven.

I wanted to know where heaven was located. Dadda told me that the Bible said it was "above" the earth, so he was sure it was in the sky above the clouds. He could not tell me what heaven was like, only that it was reputed to be a wonderful place, and that God and the angels lived there. It was the place everyone wanted to go to when they died. I know Dadda believed the Bible was true. He loved to read from it, and had a particular fondness for the Psalms. But he, like most of his generation, believed that the earthly church, the church hierarchy, and the rituals and repetition of creeds, plus an upright life, were all that God required. He believed that if man would obey the church laws and adhere to the golden rule, he would go to heaven.

Dadda pointed to a passage in Luke's Gospel where a certain man had come to Jesus to ask how to obtain eternal life. Jesus, instead of giving him a direct answer, had asked him what was written in the law. The man had answered Jesus, "Thou shalt love the Lord thy God with all they heart, and with all thy soul, and with all thy strength, and with all thy mind; and thy neighbour as thyself." Jesus then answered the man, "Thou hast answered right; this do, and thou shalt live." Christians, Dadda said, loved God first and then their fellow man. This, he believed, was what God required of man, faithfulness to God and service to his neighbours.

Dadda believed that God was a just God and that He was all-knowing. Therefore, if a man was honest in his dealings with others, God would know and forgive any past sins. His was not a personal relationship with the Lord Jesus Christ, but his faith in God was real. Dadda lived by a moral code that was impeccable and sometimes frustrating for those around him who would attempt to bend the rules occasionally. As a child I accepted his wisdom and his perception of God as my own. I trusted him implicitly, even though I had endless questions. I sensed that I was simply not able to understand the hard concepts with which I was grappling. I hoped that somehow I would naturally come to a better understanding as I matured.

Dadda tried hard to satisfy my curiosity and to answer my questions in a straightforward manner. I realize now, after having children of my own, how difficult it must have been for him. Many of my questions were ones that he himself was still pondering. It is obvious to me now that he had not been able to resolve them adequately. I've come to realize that he was unsure about life after death and couldn't or wouldn't venture into unknown territory for fear of leading me astray. In answer to my question about how it felt to die Dadda answered confidently,

"It's just like going to sleep. No one, not even dogs, suffers after he is dead." Dadda said we should let the dead rest in peace and that we should not continually fret ourselves about those who were dead, particularly those who had had Christian burials. He quoted a poem that day that I committed to memory and still recall frequently:

"Come not when I am dead to drop thy foolish tears upon my grave.
To trample the unhappy dust thou couldst not save
There let the wind sweep and the plover cry, but thou go by."

Though I hadn't learned much about death, heaven or life after death for humans, Dadda's words satisfied my curiosity about Goofie. For the time being, I could picture Goofie asleep better than I could think of him suffering. I could imagine when he was awake that he would be running free across a beautiful meadow. It was nice to know he was no longer ill or in pain or having fits. It was comforting to know he was living in a special place in heaven that God had provided for him.

Chapter 9

Bleak Midwinter

In the bleak midwinter
Frosty wind made moan,
Earth stood hard as iron,
Water like a stone;
Snow had fallen, snow on snow,
In the bleak midwinter, long ago

Rossetti

In the first weeks of 1938, there was an air of something indefinably odd about the old house. There was a restlessness, a new undercurrent stirring in the wainscoting and a trembling around the house's foundation. The feeling of agitation was not confined to our old house alone, but was echoed everywhere in the streets throughout the village.

At home, I thought it might have had something to do with our new dog Lu Lu, a huge St. Bernard puppy that had come to us the week before Christmas. She was placid to the point of being lackluster. Dadda said her movements were too slow for such a young dog. For the first few days, he thought she might just be weary from her long railway journey. But when she didn't improve, he suspected Lu Lu might be suffering from some malady. Dr. Norman, the local veterinarian, called in to see her, and quickly declared that Lu Lu had distemper. He gave her a hypodermic needle full of medicine, left some smelly liquid to cleanse her runny eyes, and said he would be back in a few days to see her again.

Lu Lu was a rather nice dog, very hairy, with eyes that drooped downwards and always looked sad and watery. She slobbered constantly from her jowly mouth, sometimes dropping great gobs on the kitchen carpet or on us when we petted her. Her body was massive and rather cumbersome, and as she was covered with an incredibly thick coat, she looked even bigger than she was. Wherever she walked, touched or flopped, she left long trails of yellowish-white hair. Our woolen winter clothes, skirts, coats and trousers all bore telltale signs of Lu Lu. No amount of brushing could remove it all.

From the beginning Mummy wasn't sure she wanted Lu Lu, especially not anywhere near the "good" furniture and rugs in the Front room. But in spite of her shedding and slobbering, the dog was housebroken and well-behaved. Since she was ill, Mummy didn't have the heart to turn her out. So Mummy resigned herself to taking care of Lu Lu, and decided to give the dog a kind of probation period until after the Christmas holidays.

The restlessness that pervaded that winter was not altogether to do with Lu Lu. There were other factors. War talk was creeping into every conversation. Memories of the Great War with Germany were still fresh in the minds of those who had fought in it twenty years earlier. Hitler's name was being bandied about in the shop, on the bus and on the six o'clock news as a fanatical and ruthless person to be dealt with. There was a fearful kind of uncertainty about the whole village concerning armed conflict. The young men, including Lenny, were being "called up" according to their age and marital status. They were eager to put on uniforms, leave their homes and go off to war, while their parents trembled. People in the shop sometimes spoke in hushed tones about rationing, and wore worried expressions. Mummy fretted more than usual, not only about the dog, but over minor details in the house and shop.

Dadda became absorbed in the news broadcasts, pulling thoughtfully on his pipe as he did his evening pacing. The news from Europe was disturbing. It was obvious that Dadda was anxious by the new agitation in his voice as he discussed current affairs each evening at the dinner table. Some of his anxiety I sensed was for Lenny, whom he knew would be among the first to "join up" for the armed service if war broke out. Perhaps he remembered his own enthusiasm in 1914 and shuddered at the reality that had followed. I wished I was old enough to be called up. It all seemed terribly exciting.

After supper one evening Dadda took down a large leather bound volume from the top shelf in the Front room cupboard. It was entitled "The Great War, 1914-1918." It was full of brownish pictures from the war. There were pictures of the battlefields where young soldiers lay huddled in damp trenches, their canvas knapsacks strapped across their backs. Dadda let me thumb through the photographs of contorted bodies strewn helter-skelter, their mud splattered faces grimacing terribly. I saw scenes of men with canvas stretchers racing with wounded soldiers, while above them the sky was murky with smoke and shell bursts. I saw it and was fascinated, but it looked to be so long ago and far away. The soldier's uniforms were ancient; their leggings were tight below the knee and wrapped in bands of cloth. It was a different time, a different era, and I could not conceive of any of it being able to touch us here in Wenhaston.

"War is hell in any time for any country and all people," Dadda said, as he put the book back on the top shelf. Some of the restlessness that winter might have been due to the weather, which after a strangely mild and snowy December had turned miserably cold and wet. The north wind howled savagely round the old house, screeching in the night and rattling the window casements. The days seemed to march by in almost endless dullness, the skies overcast and grey.

It might have been due to the normal post-holiday letdown. After a wonderful Christmas with Uncle Aubrey showering us with presents, we were bound to feel gloomy as we took down the shriveled holly boughs and paper chains over the Front room mirror. How quickly the holiday had passed, and how long it seemed before the next one would come. Lenny hoisted the gramophone up to the "box room" at the head of the stairs for safekeeping. We would bring it down again the next time Uncle Aubrey visited.

It might have been due to the especially severe sickness that touched so many villagers that year. The church bell solemnly tolled the death knell for three parishioners in quick succession. Our blinds were drawn and the mirrors covered more frequently in one month than they had been in the whole prior year. The year had started on a strange note.

My own annual bout of bronchitis arrived almost before the Christmas decorations were put away, and it progressed to pneumonia in short order. The doctor came on several visits, and declared I had caught the influenza epidemic that was going round. He prescribed his horrible elixir, an expectorant that made me gag and sometimes vomit. Mummy covered my back and chest with mustard plasters that nearly overpowered me. She then wrapped me in flannel from head to toe, and replenished my hot water bottles frequently. What with my feather mattress and down coverlet and the warmth from the kitchen chimney that ran right up beside my bed, I perspired profusely and alternately shivered. The heat was presumably a big part of my cure.

The more I perspired, the sooner I would be rid of the infection, went the theory. The heat treatment from the mustard plasters was also meant to get the phlegm moving from my lungs to my stomach and throat, which it did. A ghastly "slop-pail" beside the bed served as my spittoon. My usually hearty appetite left me, and I had difficulty eating anything. Nothing tasted the way it should, while I was ill. Though I couldn't eat, I had to drink gallons of everything liquid: broth, juice, herbal tea and especially water.

Dadda couldn't come to visit me until the Doctor pronounced me "past the worst," which translated meant "no longer contagious." Each morning during the "worst" of it, Dadda would give me a brief rundown of the day's weather, Lu Lu's condition, and the latest bird shed activities, from the top of the landing. It was a happy day when the doctor pronounced me no longer quarantined. My appetite soon returned, and my convalescence began. Dadda could now come and sit with me a little while before he went downstairs to begin his daily chores. His visits were the bright spots of my confinement, and I looked forward to them with much eagerness. It was on one of these brief visits that I learned one morning about the large painting that covered the wall opposite my bed.

Lettie had come in early to "see to me." She brought me a kettle of hot water to bathe with, while she changed my sheets and tidied the room. Mummy brought up a softly boiled egg and buttered bread cut in fingers to dip out the yoke. She brought it all on a tray, and plumped up my pillows, so I could sit up like royalty and have breakfast in bed. Dadda came in just as I was finishing my tea, and sat on the side of the newly made bed. I got a brief whiff of his eau de cologne as he brushed the top of my head with a kiss.

I'd been meaning to ask him about the painting for a long time. It showed the deck and rigging of a large sailing ship. Along the sides of the deck, sailors were firing cannons, and there were puffs of smoke from an unseen vessel. Dadda said that it was a scene from the battle of Trafalgar. Admiral Nelson was half sitting, propped by the cabin wall on the poop deck, a black patch over one eye. He had one arm tucked inside his ornate uniform jacket, and was looking up at another man in uniform who was obviously ministering to him.

"Did he die?" I asked, indicating Lord Nelson.

"Yes he did, Beauty," Dadda said. "He died at the battle of Trafalgar."

"Who was he?" I wanted to know. "Was he famous?"

Dadda shifted his position slightly so that he was facing me. I could see by his expression that he was serious, that this was important to him.

"Nelson," he said solemnly, "was a great leader and one of the greatest Admirals the world has ever known." Looking at the rather diminutive form lying crumpled on the deck, it was hard to imagine him as a great hero.

"What did he do that was so great?" I asked. "Well," said Dadda, "for one thing he had great courage in facing the enemy and wasn't wishy-washy about making decisions." I knew from experience that "wishy-washy" was a terrible defect in a man's character. One strove to be remembered for attributes such as being "stalwart," "valiant" and "courageous."

"By his decisive actions during the heat of battle, he was able to defeat Napoleon's fleet." Dadda paused momentarily and then continued. "Except for Nelson, we might all be speaking French now." I wrinkled my nose in disgust. Dadda always said that the French were turncoats. He said they looked to England to help them when they were in trouble, but that they could not be trusted.

"One year they'll be fighting with us and the next year they'll be fighting against us," he would say. It was obvious to me he didn't care for them. I, on the other hand, had little reason to like or dislike the French as a nation, but if Dadda disliked them, I trusted his judgement. I certainly had reason not to like their language. We joked about French words that made us sound as though we were clearing our throats, or trying to cough up mucus from our lungs.

"Was Nelson in YOUR war?" I asked innocently. Dadda smiled.

"Good heavens, no," he chuckled. "Nelson died during HIS battle of Trafalgar in 1805," he said. "MY war, as you call it, was from 1914 to 1918." "Someday when you go to London you can see the monument that's been built to him. It's in Trafalgar Square" His mention of London triggered a dark thought that had been swirling unspoken between us for several weeks. I knew little about Dr. Barnardo's Home, but the one thing I did know was that it was located in London.

"Will I ever get to London, Dadda?" I asked him.

"Yes, Beauty," he said, "I expect you will, but not just yet." This last was said with confidence and reassurance, to let me know that all was well at the moment.

We kept having these conversations, skirting around the subject of my adoption. Apparently adoptions were complicated and hard to attain. I later learned that there were very few, if any, formal adoptions that were done from Dr. Barnardo's in my era. Foster families and their charges made agreements with each other when the child was of an age, and the foster parents agreeable, to make more permanent living arrangements possible.

I also learned that Dr. Barnardo's or "the Home" as we usually referred to it, dropped responsibility when the child's biological family requested to have the child returned to them. Apparently the family had to show financial stability and a desire to have the child returned to the family in order for this to happen. Another alternative seemed to be that the foster family could make a claim on the child when he or she reached the age of fourteen. That was the normal age for children to leave school and begin making their own way in the world, either by being apprenticed or by going into service.

Service, for girls in peacetime, meant becoming a maid servant in a private home, or for the more fortunate ones, in a large well-established hotels or another institution. There was very little pay for these beginning positions, but the on-the-job training, food and lodging were ample rewards. Parents were glad to have their daughters go "in service" in reputable establishments. It was one less mouth to feed at home, and at the same time, the girls received excellent training for the time when they would be mistresses of their own homes. There was also the possibility of advancement to the upper levels of servanthood, should the girl remain a spinster.

Dadda's plans for me were on a somewhat loftier scale. We both knew I would sit for my "elevenses" exams the following year

(1939). The tests would be administered through the school in Wenhaston on an appointed day. Dadda had great faith in my ability to score high enough that I would be eligible to attend teacher's training at Beccles Normal school. Though tuition was nominal, there were certain other fees involved that Dadda had already taken into account. If nothing went wrong, that is if I weren't recalled to Dr. Barnarndo's Home, I would be launched in a suitable career early on in life. It was my dream too. I longed for it to become a reality. I was determined to work hard and make Dadda proud of me.

There were other compensations in going to Beccles that appealed to my childish mind, that had nothing to do with getting a better education. Topmost on my list was being able to escape from Mr. Sangster, the headmaster at Wenhaston County Council School. Though I only received one caning from him during my time as a student, I lived in dread of his swift punishment for any infraction of the rules. There was, too, the status of living away at school during the week and coming home on the weekends, laden with books to study and papers to write.

Additionally, and almost as important to me, Beccles Normal had its own emblems enblazoned on everything. The school uniforms, including hats, socks and ties, tennis racquets and bicycles all carried the school emblem. Its prestige was well established, and I would be fortunate indeed to be able to attend.

Each year, sometimes twice in the same year, a person from Dr. Barnardo's Home came round to inspect my living conditions, take note of my physical welfare, which meant measuring my height against the kitchen doorway, asking Mummy how much weight I'd gained and whether I'd been under a doctor's care in the interim between visits. They always asked about my behavior and whether there was any reason to return me to "The Home." There was always the reminder during these visits that I didn't yet "belong" to the Saunders' household, which gave me a peculiar awareness of my vulnerable position. After these visits, life quickly reverted to normal and I was once again confident in my standing. Though he didn't tell me so, I knew in my heart that Dadda was doing everything possible, writing letters to those in authority, to try to change my status from "Home girl" to "daughter."

When I recovered from my bout of bronchitis, and the weather broke in March, the spring ushered in warmer winds and lighter showers. But the talk of war grew stronger and more insistent. Lenny was engaged to Joyce Borrott, a nurse at Bulcamp Union. She was a tall and attractive, fair-haired girl from a large Wenhaston family. That they were in love was obvious to everyone, and their wedding at St. Peter's in May was well attended. Despite the knowledge that Lenny would soon be leaving to join the army, it was a joyful wedding.

Joyce & Lenny's Wedding

The sun shone on the silver horseshoe the bride carried, and the village doused the pair of them in the churchyard with an absolute deluge of confetti. There was an early evening party at the *Compass,* and a crowd of ribald friends saw them off on the last bus to Southwold later in the evening. After the bus left, Mummy let me stay with her for a short while in the crowded pub. The smoke got so thick you could hardly see across the room, and the singing got a few decibels too loud for comfort.

Mummy was the only person I knew over the age of twelve who didn't smoke. In those days, everybody smoked. It was the thing to do. I watched those who inhaled deeply and then let the smoke come out in short puffs with each word they spoke. Uncle Aubrey could blow perfect smoke rings through constricting his throat in a certain way and pursing his lips. It was jolly nice amusement and I set my heart on learning how to do that.

When we arrived home from the wedding celebration, Dadda was pacing about with a more than usual intensity. Lu Lu had crawled under the kitchen table and had vomitted. The stench was terrible. Worse than that, the dog had choked on her own vomit and died. I helped Mummy get the dog outside and together we got the mess cleaned up. Both of us were in our "dress-up" clothes, so after we got the kitchen cleaned up, we had to clean ourselves.

We hadn't known Lu Lu long enough to get totally attached to her, but there was still a sadness that hung over the house for the next few weeks. Dadda immediately began the process of finding a suitable replacement for Lu Lu. He felt the kennel was at fault for sending her in her distempered condition. The papers that came with her had guaranteed she would be distemper free.

So began another letter writing campaign and the search for another house dog. Mummy requested it not be another St. Bernard as she was still working to get hair out of the Front room carpets. Dadda agreed with her. I think the memory of Lu Lu's sad, droopy eyes, her smelly medicine, and constant slobbering were still fresh in all our minds. In May we received a huge crate on the midday bus with our new dog in it. He was a pointer, white with brown spots, short-haired with a long tail and an amazing amount of pent-up energy. His pedigree was long and impressive. His full name was a tongue twister that was unpronouncable. Dadda suggested we call him "Fleet" because he could run fast and we could all pronounce it.

The spring was full of new beginnings. Fleet settled in well with our household routine, but needed to be exercised in a way that neither of the other dogs had. Thus he came with me on long runs whenever I was going to collect a grocery list or to deliver an order. I had to have him on a long leash, which in the beginning was very awkward, especially when my bike was loaded. A few times he darted in front of me and nearly sent me flying. In spite of his nervous energy, he was a quick learner and very tractable. We got along very well.

I was now beginning to study to take my "elevenses" exam that would make me eligible for secondary school if I passed. It was a

goal I was willing to work for. I studied hard and Dadda helped me each evening with the long practice papers. He encouraged me when my spirits flagged, and cheered me on when I made measurable progress. The tests would be given in several parts, on the Saturday following Whitsunday. They were to be given in Mr. Sangster's classroom, and there would be eight of us taking the tests.

It was a heady experience. Each of us had two brand new pencils, a copy book in which to write answers, and butterflies in our stomachs. Mr. Sangster looked especially officious and sanctimonious as he distributed test papers and gave us instructions on how to word our answers. We were spread about in the classroom so there would be no chance to copy from one another or communicate in any way. Not that we would have deigned to talk to each other in any event. In Mr. Sangster's classroom, we didn't dare to even look at each other, let alone talk.

The clock on the wall ticked loudly, and there was occasionally a muffled throat clearing or an exasperated sigh. Each test was timed, and on the hour, Mr. Sangster rang a bell to signal us to lay down our pencils and sit up in the rest position while he came to collect our test papers. We had ten minutes recess between tests, to stretch our legs or go to the toilets. Then we returned to our desks and went through the whole procedure again.

At three o'clock it was over. Drained and empty and not a little anxious, we wended our way home. Margaret Hazel and I commiserated on the road down the hill toward home. Both of us felt we had failed miserably, especially in the "earth science" questions. One question that had given us both trouble had to do with stratum layers of sand and rock in the earth. Neither of us could remember the details of the earth's crust and how the layers were stratified. We had missed our Saturday Girl Guide meeting as well, so we parted at the lane, waved goodbye to each other and ran the rest of the way to our respective homes.

Lenny left for the army soon after I had taken the elevenses test. I had been allowed to move into his old room since his marriage. The bed seemed enormous after my small one, and it had the added advantage of having a bolster and several extra pillows which made it wonderfully comfortable for reading in bed. However, Lenny's room was not near as warm as my room over the kitchen had been. I missed the kitchen chimney that kept my small room toasty, but I would not exchange the pure pleasure of having Lenny's big, cold room for a bit more warmth.

The electricity had been laid on in the village for nearly a year by this time. The lights in each room were ceiling fixtures. In the kitchen and Front rooms, the ornate hanging paraffin lamps were converted to electricity. we were blessed to have light switches both at the top and the bottom of the stairway. The only problem with having more light on the stairway was that Mummy could see that the brass rods that kept the stair carpet flat needed more polishing. So, along with the benefits of better lighting, there was also the disadvantage of having extra work created for us.

Like most of the villagers, we were just getting used to having the electric lights in place of our paraffin lamps and candles. It was an expensive commodity and could be a bit unreliable at times. We had to adjust ourselves to this new luxury that had come to our village, and we couldn't dream of wasting it. It was something of a scandal to leave a light on after one was in bed. So reading by electric light was not a possibility, and I was not allowed an oil lamp or candle in the bedroom. Fortunately, I was able to improvise. Before he left for the army training camp, Lenny had given me several of his most valued possessions. One of these was a three battery torch that was ideal for reading under the covers. I could pull the warm down coverlet around me, even over my head so my nose wouldn't freeze, and spend many happy hours with my beloved books.

Lenny also had given me the use of his small green Brownie camera, with a lens that folded away like a telescope. I was able to take lots of photographs with this treasure, some of which I still have. One shows Gonie standing in the street astraddle her bicycle. One shows Lenny and Joyce's wedding outside the church, and shows Kathleen by the bridge at Blyford. One of my most precious is that of the shop with Mummy standing in her morning "pinny," just inside the shop door. Until she was dressed in her afternoon best, Mummy wouldn't show herself outside the door for the camera.

Gonie Spindler

Dadda, who would never under any circumstances come outside to have his photograph taken, stood at the upstairs window in his shirt sleeves, looking down at me. Though I could barely see his face, I know he was smiling. That night at bedtime I told Dadda that I was going to write a book about him and Majuba house someday. As I reached up to his cheek to kiss him goodnight, he looked at me and said softly, "Yes, you do that, Beauty." He paused to kiss me and said again, "Yes Beauty, promise me you'll do that."

The Shop

It was several weeks before we heard the results of the elevenses tests. In fact I had almost forgotten about it when the letter came giving us the good news that I had passed the exam with a comfortable margin. It turned out that Margaret Hazel and I had each scored about the same and we had the highest marks in that particular grouping. It was indeed a happy thought.

Lenny had been away in the army for about six weeks, and had just come home for a week's leave when the test results came in. It was double excitement that called for a celebration. I was allowed to join him and Joyce, Gonie and her family, and many other families as they gathered at the *Compass* for an exuberant evening of laughter and song.

But the restlessness that had begun the year was determined to linger. Within days of having good news from one quarter, the ghastly news came from another that I was to be recalled to Dr.

Barnardo's Home. Both Mummy and Dadda were noncommittal with their responses to my questions. I sensed they were obeying orders and did not want to unduly influence or upset me. They gave me to understand that neither they nor I had any choice in the matter.

I was to leave as soon as the school summer holidays began. I would be going to the home at Stepney Causeway in London. Uncle Aubrey had once told me the streets of London were paved with gold, so I could look forward to seeing that spectacle with my own eyes. Mummy helped me find a suitcase from the box room at the head of the stairs and together we packed all my nicest things, nothing with holes or even socks with darned places. I must take only the best with me. My Easter dress that year was emerald green taffeta with a small white collar. Mrs. Barber had made it a little too big for me on purpose, because Mummy said I was growing so fast I would outgrow it before summer was over. My shoes were brown leather sandals, with enclosed heel and toe and a pretty cut-out pattern across the front. My blazer from winter also had been purchased a size larger, so fitted me nicely and was still smart and wearable.

I couldn't take many of my treasures, but then I knew they would be safe until I returned. The thought never entered my head that I would be gone a long time. Looking back, I have wondered whether the Saunders knew but never told me. I had very little information, but lots of confidence, about my inner assumptions. I fully believed that Majuba was my home, and I would soon be coming back to it. Therefore the fact that I had to leave behind my bicycle, the board games and jigsaw puzzles, my tennis racquet, Lenny's camera and all my books except one did not faze me. The one book I carried was *"The Three Desmonds."* It had been a Christmas present and was a wonderful story about the adventures of three children who lived on a cliff overlooking the sea and who discovered a pirate cove. I had already read it through twice, but wanted to be able to read it again.

Dadda gave me a small folding writing case made of white cardboard with pretty flowers painted on it. When it was opened, it revealed sheets of paper in one side and envelopes in the other. Down the middle, on the fold, held in with a cardboard loop, was a brand new dark green fountain pen. The envelopes already had postage stamps attached. I was to write as soon as I arrived so that he and Mummy would know I was safe.

"I shall want to know everything about the journey, the Home, and London," he said. I promised I would write often. Dadda had given me an important assignment; one he knew I would execute faithfully.

I began to get excited about going. I was to leave on the first bus for Halesworth, and at the last minute had to hurry to get my things together. I crammed the last things into my suitcase: my toothbrush and tin of toothpaste, with my hair brush and comb, in a little oilcloth bag. Mummy had put labels with my name in big letters on my suitcase and on my jacket lapel. I ran up the stairs two at a time and found Dadda's door ajar. He was just finished shaving and was applying cologne as I ran in. I climbed on the side of the bed so I could reach him, gave him a quick kiss on his freshly smooth cheek and was down the stairs again in two minutes flat.

"Don't forget to write," he called after me as I raced down the stairs. "I won't," I promised, as I joined Mummy at the front door.

We walked to the *Compass* together. When we got to the Newby's house, I turned back to look at our house. Dadda was at the window of my old bedroom watching us go. He raised his good hand to wave, and I waved back and blew him a kiss with my fingers. Mummy rode with me to the train station in Halesworth, and waited with me until the London train came in. She told me that a lady from the Home would get on the train at Ipswich, and would look for me in the third class carriage. Her name was Mrs. Farnsworth. As I boarded the train, Mummy pressed a half-crown into my hand, and pulled a paper bag from her carrier bag and handed it to me.

"In case you get hungry on the way," she said. "There's a sandwich and some chocolate biscuits. You can buy a lemon squash from the dining car, but mind you don't spill any on your good clothes," she said. The train doors were slamming shut up and down the platform. Mummy leaned forward and kissed me on the cheek. "Mind 'ow you go then, my dear," she said, and turned away quickly, but not before I saw the glint of tears in her eyes.

Owen's father blew his whistle and the train began to move. I pushed my suitcase into the luggage rack above the seat and ran to the window. I tugged at the window strap to let the window down and leaned out to wave to Mummy, but she had already disappeared from the platform.

Chapter 10

Thursday's Child

The London North Eastern Railway that came through Halesworth, known by its initials to most Britishers as the L.N.E.R, ran all the way from beyond King's Lynn in Norfolk down to Liverpool Street Station in London, with Halesworth in Suffolk being about a fourth of the way. The journey from Halesworth to London covered a distance of about a hundred miles. The enormous engines were coal fired, and the engineers sweated profusely as they stoked the fires, their faces blackened with soot.

In that era, the British train service was enormously proud of its ability to run on schedule. Except for catastrophes, a train that was due at 10:21 A.M. could be counted on to come steaming into the station right on time. By the same token, a three-minute stopover at the station would be just that: three minutes. The British public was well disciplined in trusting rigid timetables, and expected promptness not only in travel, but in other areas of life as well. It was part of the regimen of self-control that was built into the country's very fiber, that lent structure and reliability to our well-ordered lives.

The train stopped at every small station for only a few minutes, but stopped at the larger stations for longer periods, long enough to dash out to buy a paper, a magazine, or a sandwich, and return to the same seat. Halesworth was a small station, and the next two stations, Saxmundham and Wickham Market, were about the same size as Halesworth. The first large station was at Ipswich. It was at Ipswich that I was to meet Mrs. Farnsworth.

When I got on at Halesworth, I had my choice of seats, as there were so few passengers. I seated myself in an empty third class carriage by the window, where on one side I could watch the passing scenery and on the other I could watch the passageway for Mrs. Farnsworth. At each stop, more passengers got on, and the compartment I was in began to fill up. At one of the stops, a large pleasant man sat down opposite me in the window seat. He smiled as he breezed in, said "good morning, Miss," and settled down with his newspaper. At Ipswich there was a great exchange of passengers, with hordes moving noisily up and down the passageway. I had remained in my corner, hardly daring to move, until we stopped at Ipswich. Now the carriage was full, and there were some people going up and down the passageway looking for empty compartments.

Three ladies who were traveling together spread themselves out on the seat beside me. I shifted over as far as I could into the corner to give them room. They were talking noisily when they got in, and continued talking non-stop as the train began to move. The one next to me brought out her knitting and scrunched her overflowing knitting bag down between us. On the opposite seat across the aisle, two young women and a young pale-faced boy had got on at Wickham Market, filling the remaining seats next to the man with the newspaper.

The farther I traveled, the more I realized I didn't want to go to London after all. The excitement of the adventure was wearing off, and I was beginning to feel anxious and a little afraid. I fretted that Mrs. Farnsworth would not find me, squashed in the corner as I was, and I actually began to hope that she wouldn't. I knew the way home would be easy, and I was just beginning to form a plan to get off at Colchester and catch the next train back to Halesworth, when I heard a "take charge" voice directed at me. She didn't come inside the compartment, but Mrs. Farnsworth had slid the glass divider open just enough to put her head through.

"There you are, Sidey," she boomed, not unpleasantly. "Come along now, and bring your case."

I could see she was tall with a thin, sharp face. I knew it must be Mrs. Farnsworth, and my heart sank. There was to be no turning back after all. She was dressed all in navy blue, wearing a navy blue dress, hat, and jacket with the Dr. Barnarndo's emblem on her hat and jacket pocket. There was no mistaking who she was. I had a little difficulty extricating myself from my corner and from the passenger's knitting paraphernalia squeezed in beside me. Finally, I stood up and attempted to get my case from the overhead rack. I hadn't realized what a struggle it would be to stand up with the train moving, let alone reach the luggage rack.

When the train had been standing in the station and the seats had been empty, it had been easy to reach the overhead rack by climbing up on the seat. Now it was impossible to reach. I clung for a moment to the handhold near the window with one hand and attempted to reach the case above me with the other. "Come along, child," Mrs. Farnsworth said again, a little impatiently. The large man sitting opposite me in the window seat kindly offered to help me.

"Here yer are," he said, smiling as he handed my case to me. He had to lean over me in order to get to it, with one hand on the rack to steady himself. The train was moving fast and swaying badly. As he handed me the suitcase, I let go of my handhold and rocked forward on my feet. I put out my hand to grab something to keep from falling, and wound up knocking the nice gentleman, my suitcase and myself into the laps of the three ladies. The knitting lady gave a piercing shriek, which added to the confusion. I was mortified. But the nice man easily righted himself and pulled me to my feet.

"Yer alright, luv," he said with a laugh. I nodded miserably, ashamed of myself and very disoriented.

"Sorry, Mum," he said brightly to the ladies who were huffing at the indignity of it all. I gathered myself together as best I could, and slipped out the door into the passageway. Mrs. Farnsworth led me down the passageway, past the door marked "Toilets" and through the connecting doors to the next carriage. There were quite a few empty seats in the compartment that we entered. After she had put my case in the overhead rack, Mrs. Farnsworth indicated I was to sit next to a girl in a navy blue wool gym-slip and white blouse. She was wearing a green wool tam similar to one I wore to school, and she looked to be about my age. Beside her, leaning against her half asleep, sat a young boy whom I thought must be about six years old. Mrs. Farnsworth picked up a valise, sat down, opened it and sorted through some papers that were inside.

"We've a long way to go," she said, "so you three can get acquainted while I fill in some of my notes." The girl's name tag said "Dulcie Smith" and the boy's said "Robin Smith." They, too, were obviously going to Dr. Barnardo's Home. The girl seemed friendly enough, and her brother, after looking me over a bit suspiciously, went back to sucking his thumb with his head on his sister's shoulder.

I was glad to have Dulcie to talk to. I told her about my friends in Wenhaston, Margie and Primrose, whose older sister's name was Dulcie. I thought it was a pretty name. She told me she was going back to the Home for three weeks and then afterwards was going to live in Watford with her Mum and new Dad. Dulcie was twelve, two years older than I. She said she had been living with her brother in a place called Claydon, not far from Ipswich, for the past three years.

Before that she had lived with her Mum until Robin was three years old, and then the two of them had been put in the Home in London. I was eager to know about the Home, and she was glad to tell me except that as she talked, she was watching Mrs. Farnsworth guardedly. I suspected she had secrets she wasn't allowed to tell, so I didn't press her. I hoped we could stay together while we were in the Home. It would be nice to have a friend.

The train moved on at a rapid rate. We stopped at several stations along the way. At Colchester station, Mrs. Farnsworth leaned over and told us she was going to get us some refreshments and we were not to move from our seats. She was back in no time with a tray of wrapped sandwiches, cake, and small cartons of milk. Until that minute I had forgotten about the lunchbag Mummy had made for me. I had squirreled it away in my suitcase before the train started. Now I decided to leave it for later. As we pulled out of the station at Colchester, I had a fleeting thought that my last chance to go back to Wenhaston had passed. But with Dulcie to talk to, the journey was beginning to be more interesting. Her brother Robin perked up a bit when Mrs. Farnsworth brought the food in. As we ate our sandwiches, our talk was light and cheerful.

As we neared London, the scenery changed drastically. For miles and miles we had seen open fields and farmhouses, and occasional rows of houses near the larger city stations. Finally, we had left the countryside. Here the scenery changed to row upon row of houses whose sides and chimneypots nearest the railway line were covered with sooty grime.

"Are we in London yet?" I asked Mrs. Farnsworth.

"Yes," she replied, "London spreads out a long way, and we're going through the outskirts now." I peered closely at the streets between the rows of houses.

"Whatcha lookin' for?" Dulcie said, thinking I was playing a game.

"For the streets that are paved with gold," I said blithely. Mrs. Farnsworth looked up and smiled broadly, but Dulcie giggled out loud.

"Whoever told you that," Dulcie said, "was pulling your leg. It's just an old saying." I looked across at Mrs. Farnsworth, a question forming in my mind.

"It doesn't mean the streets are literally paved with gold," she said, "only that many rich people live in parts of London."

I was a bit disappointed about the streets, but I hadn't long to wonder about it. We were coming in to the largest station I had ever seen. Trains were everywhere, some racing past us going in the direction from which we had just come, and some shunting off to sidings. Across the wide expanse of rails, passenger and freight trains were lined up, some moving and some standing still with steam hissing around their engines.

As the train came to a stop, we could hear the stationmaster shouting, "All out for Liverpool Street Station." There was a great banging open of doors, and people thronged in the passageway. Mrs. Farnsworth helped us with our cases. Dulcie carried one case for herself and her brother in one hand, while holding Robin's hand with the other. I was thankful for Mrs. Farnsworth, as the station was so big and noisy, with people hurrying every which way. I would have been overwhelmed without her.

She charged ahead and we hurried to keep up with her up steps, over to another platform, through gates and ticket windows and eventually down many stairways to another platform where we stood to catch another train. This was the Underground, "the Tube" as it's known in Britain. This was to be my first ride on it. As the train came to a stop, the doors opened with a "swoosh" and the four of us stepped in. We had hardly got in our seats when the doors closed and the train whispered as it moved forward. Dulcie had ridden the tube many times before and showed me how she would ride the train to Watford to her Mum's house, on the map above our seats. I was in awe of someone so talented and knowledgeable.

When we neared our stop, Mrs. Farnsworth warned us to get ready to get off. Dulcie stood up like a professional and held on to the upright post by the door. She had Robin beside her and the suitcase firmly in her hand. I wasn't sure I'd be able to stand without falling, so I waited until the train came to a full stop to make a move. I made it safely to the platform, and followed the rest of them up lots of steps until we finally reached the street.

It had been dark below in the underground, and I was surprised that it was still bright daylight as we emerged onto the street. The streets were busy with motorcars and lorries near the station, but we soon branched off down a long street lined with the same rows of houses we had seen from the train window. Finally we came to a large complex of houses, and Mrs. Farnsworth consulted her papers. Robin was to go in with the boy's housing, she said, and Dulcie and I were to go across the walkway to "Heather House."

Dr. Barnardos Home
Girl's Village (1930's)

When Robin realized he was going to be separated from his sister, he kicked up a fuss. Mrs. Farnsworth took him by the hand and led him into a building marked "Hope Cottage." He began to cry and beg to stay with Dulcie. His sister implored Mrs. Farnsworth to let him stay with her, but she said there were rules at the Home that the boys couldn't stay in the girls' dorms and vice versa.

"He'll be taken good care of," she told Dulcie, as she held his hand more tightly. "You two report in to the office over there," she said, pointing to Heather House. "I'll be along shortly to see to you."

It was a sad scene. As Robin was led away crying, Mrs. Farnsworth and Dulcie both called out reassuring words to him.

"It will only be for a little while," Dulcie said. "I won't be far away." Dulcie was upset and was near to tears herself. She felt responsible for her brother and was anxious about him, but she was putting on a brave front for his sake. She bit her trembling lip as we walked together across the grass to Heather House.

We were greeted by a young woman dressed in a dark blue uniform with a white starched collar and belt that looked very similar to the nurses' uniform that Lenny's Joyce wore. Her name tag said "Miss Parker" and we were to call her "Miss." The reception area was a large paneled room with chairs and small tables meant to be small group seating. Miss Parker led us through the reception room to the door at the far end, then down a hallway and into a smaller room that looked like an office. An older woman greeted us by our surnames.

"Ah, yes," she said brightly as we entered, "Smith and Sidey. We've been expecting you." She shuffled through some papers on the desk in front of her, asked us questions to verify who we were and where we'd come from. Then she proceeded to give us multiple instructions about the house rules and regulations.

Each dorm was assigned household tasks on a rotating basis, one week laundry duty, and the next kitchen or floor duty, and the next lavatory cleaning, and so on. Each of us was expected to make up our bed and to tidy around it on a daily basis. In addition to our other chores, we would take turns cleaning the dorm floors. Two different girls each day would be in charge of sweeping the dorm, and once a week another two would be assigned to scrub it down.

While I stood there trying to assimilate the plethora of regulations that included cleaning duties, meal and bedtime schedules and general house rules, Dulcie, who was fairly familiar with all of it, stood by calmly. The dormitories all had numbers, and we were given beds in different ones. I was totally disappointed, but was afraid to speak up. Dulcie ventured a request that we be allowed to be in the same dormitory, and I could have kissed her. But it was not to be. I was assigned to Dorm Two and Dulcie to Dorm Three. At least, we comforted each other with a look, we would be near by.

Miss Parker showed us the dining hall, a large room with four long tables and benches, and the "recreation room" that had a large table tennis table on one side, and a piano, several round tables and chairs along one wall. The floor was shiny brown linoleum. Behind the piano were bookshelves with lots of well-thumbed books and boxes of puzzles.

We would not even be at the same table in the dining hall, since the tables were numbered to coincide with the dorm assignments. There were several girls working in the dining room, spreading cloths and setting out cutlery on the tables. After showing us round the bustling kitchen and scullery, from which came the wonderful odor of the evening meal, Miss Parker preceded us up the wide, polished wood staircase. We could hear scuffling feet and many voices coming from above as we climbed the stairs.

The upstairs landing was wide with corridors going off at angles. There were four large dormitories, each with about twenty beds, ten down each side, and a window at the end of the room. All four dormitories shared one central bathroom, which turned out to be an enormous tiled cavern with two gigantic tubs. There was one tub on either side of back-to-back basins down the middle of the room, and a dozen or more doorless toilet stalls down the outer walls.

Next to the bathroom there was a huge linen closet, with floor to ceiling shelves that were all labeled. It smelled nicely of clean fresh-laundered clothes. Miss Parker gave us instructions and took us to our beds to leave our suitcases. We were to wash ourselves and comb our hair, and be ready to meet in the dining hall at five o'clock. Dulcie remembered that she had her brother's things mixed in with hers and asked if she could take them over to Hope house before the dinner bell rang. Miss Parker said she could, but to leave the things at the front desk, as she was afraid Robin might get upset again at seeing his sister.

There was a little cabinet by each bed with space to store clothes in the bottom, and a little drawer at the top. I unpacked my suitcase and put away the clothes in the bottom part. I put my book, my writing case and my packet of sandwiches in the drawer, and put my suitcase under the bed as I had been told to do. There were girls milling about everywhere, and I had hardly time to think before the dinner bell sounded. I followed the others down to the dining room, realizing I was ravenously hungry.

We formed a line outside the dining room door and marched in together to our assigned tables. We stood at attention until all the others had trooped in. We were given a signal to bow our heads to say Grace before we climbed over the benches to sit at the table. The food was set before us in several bowls and was passed around for each of us to take our own servings. The food was quite good; pieces of meat in gravy, mashed potatoes and cabbage, and pudding for "afters." I was glad to have a proper meal, and I know I gobbled up more than my fair share.

Just as we were finishing our meal, the Matron came in to give us instructions. My seat mate Peggy and I were fully engaged in a conversation about exchanging books. She was telling me about some George Formby comic books she had that I could read in exchange for my book *The Three Desmonds*. We hadn't noticed that the room had grown quiet, or even that the Matron was trying to get our attention.

"Will the two gulls at table two who are talking, please stand." We stood, a bit fearfully, trying not to knock over any dishes in the process. The Matron assigned us "clearing tables" for the evening, and we were to report to the office as soon as we had completed the task. As it turned out, the assignment had hidden benefits; we were able to talk quite freely once the dining hall was cleared.

The other girls who were on duty were a big help in showing us where everything was kept and what was expected of us. We had the job done in no time, and I had made some additional friends in the bargain. I felt better about things knowing that Peggy and I were in the same dorm and would be together frequently.

We reported to the office and listened respectfully to the lecture about not talking out of turn. We were made to understand that when the Matron came in and the "charge person" rang her little bell, we were to stop talking and pay attention. We had been so engrossed, neither of us had heard the bell. I made up my mind I would be more alert in future. Penalties for infractions of the rules were cumulative, and punishment would be meted out accordingly. It was not a very favourable beginning.

I was to report to the bathroom immediately for something called "delousing." I recalled hearing something about a family that had lice in our school at Wenhaston. The District Nurse had come round to the school and had inspected all our heads, but nothing was found. Except for the shocked aftermath of the mothers gossiping and keeping closer watch on our heads for several weeks, that was the end of it. I felt confident as I entered the bathroom that the same situation would apply now. How naive I was to the ways of the world of the orphanage.

It was a strange feeling to have so many naked bodies milling about and it was a bit intimidating to have to use the toilets so publicly. But since the other girls seemed not to mind, I supposed I would get used to it also. What I couldn't quite reconcile was the method used for delousing.

There were several attendants running what appeared to be a production line. First, we girls lined up beside one of the sinks for a treatment that consisted of rubbing some awful smelling, thick pasty stuff all over our heads. We then marched to the next station where we cleaned our teeth at one of the other basins. We had each been given a flannel and a towel and I struggled to continue to cover myself with the towel in one hand while brushing my teeth with the other. We were to wait ten minutes while the delousing stuff "worked" on our heads. After that we were dunked in the tub by one of the attendants, laid backwards while she rinsed us off first in the bath water and then with the faucet running clear water.

I had not realized until the minute the attendant put me backwards in the water, that I had a phobia about going backwards. It was not something I had ever thought about, and I was surprised by my own reaction. Today it might be called a panic attack. I don't know. All I could do was scream in terror as I felt myself being lowered into the water. The attendant tried talking to me, telling me it would be over quickly, but I couldn't control my hysteria. I struggled and screamed, my soapy body making it more difficult for the attendant to do what she needed to do. I thrashed about and the attendant called for help. Two of them together managed to force my head under the water once, thereby removing some of the gunk, but some remained.

It was a nightmare for all of us. They finally hauled me out of the tub and let me go, telling me that I must rinse off the residue quickly before it did permanent damage. I raced to the dormitory, grabbing a towel on the way out. I could not listen to reason, and I could not understand what had happened. Suddenly I was somebody else, someone I had no control over. It was horrible. My scalp was beginning to feel very warm and tingly, but I remained stubborn and intractable. The attendants tried many tactics to make me come back into the bathroom, but I would not.

I crawled under the bed and would not come out. They cajoled and threatened, and finally left me to return to the rest of their charges. I had upset their entire routine, and I was mortified by my own behaviour. I knew my punishment would be dire, but I couldn't help myself. I eventually crawled in bed, with my unrinsed head wrapped in a towel. I lay there shivering and crying, wanting for all the world to be back in the safety and sanity of my Dadda's house in Wenhaston.

I must have slept, because the next thing I knew the sun was coming through the window at the end of the room, and the Matron came to wake me. She was quite stern, but practical. She told me I was to come with her immediately and she would see to it that my head was properly rinsed. My scalp felt as though it were on fire. I wanted to get the smelly, hurtful stuff off. I also wanted to salvage my dignity. She supervised while I ran water in one of the basins and plunged my hair in. She took a cup and while she talked soothingly, filled it with clean water and rinsed my head numerous times.

When we were done and I was dressed, the Matron questioned me closely about what had happened the night before. I did not know. I could not tell her anything except that I was frightened. For some reason the whole business about my falling on the radiator at Peasenhall came up and she wanted to know the details. I couldn't tell her much, but she examined the back of my head and located the scar. She told me she had to punish me for my disobedient behavior of the night before, and assigned me some extra duties.

I did not get off to a very good start at Dr. Barnardo's. After the bathroom incident, the other girls were noticeably cool toward me for a few days. I must have seemed completely crackers to them. I wanted desperately to have some friends, and over the next few days sought out Dulcie, who in her own placid way took everything in stride. She had a letter from her Mum, and she would be leaving soon. Her brother Robin had settled down, and she was allowed to visit him daily during recreation time in the early afternoon. I had not much spare time, but Sunday afternoons were set aside for walking in the park or writing letters. I had already been writing letters each night before I went to sleep, adding to the pages with an account of everything I had done throughout the day.

I quickly used up all the paper and envelopes I had. We were not allowed to seal the envelopes, but the letters had to be put unsealed into a special basket in the recreation room. They were gathered on a regular basis, and I assumed they were being posted regularly. My first letters were full of complaints about the home and full of questions about what was going to happen to me. I had no idea what to expect, but I felt sure Dadda or Mummy would be able to tell me. Two weeks passed and I had no reply to any of my letters. I was beginning to worry during the third week, when one of the attendants came with a letter for me. It was Dadda's handwriting and I could hardly wait to read it. I was surprised to find it had already been opened.

"My dear Beauty," it began. "Mummy and I are worried about you as we have received no word from you. We hope you are well and are adjusting to Home life." The letter went on to tell me about all the latest goings on in Wenhaston, to ask about my situation, and to tell me that Lenny had been home on leave. It also gave a brief account of Fleet's naughty escapades in jumping over the gate and taking himself for a run, and of the three new families of canaries. It ended by telling me how much they all missed me, and wanted me to write to them.

I was stunned that Dadda had not yet received any of my letters, and fretted about it a lot. One of the attendants brought me notepaper and said I was to write an answer immediately, which I did. I wrote in it that I didn't like Dr. Barnardo's very much and asked him if he could get permission for me to come home. The attendant then told me that my mother was coming for me in a few days, and I would not be going back to Wenhaston for a while, and probably not at all.

She told me I was not to write asking for Mr. Saunders to get permission for me, but to write to him that I was very well, that I had received his letter and tell him not to worry about me. I did as I was told, reluctantly, and she took the letter and sealed it in my presence.

Later that day, Dulcie told me that all our letters were read, and they would not be sent unless I said nice things about the Home. We devised a scheme in which I could write a letter and put it in my last envelope with a stamp on it. Dulcie would take it with her and post it for me in a pillar-box in London. I wrote on both sides of the remaining notepaper in small print to tell everything. I loved the clandestine adventure, and knew Dadda would enter into this with me. I wanted to set his mind at ease and at the same time wanted to beat the system that would try to interfere with our relationship.

In a few days a big box of food arrived: homemade cakes, biscuits, and chocolate bars. Mummy had sent a veritable feast, and it arrived on the eve of Dulcie's departure. We made our own little farewell party during the recreation hour, inviting Peggy and some of the other girls to join us. The next morning as Dulcie was leaving, I wrote on the outside of the envelope of my cached letter: "Thank you for the parcel." Dulcie hid it and promised to post it for me.

One morning about a week after Dulcie had left, the Matron called me into her office and told me she had news for me. She said my mother was coming to get me, and I was going to go home with her. She told me to gather my things together, wash myself and comb my hair. Miss Parker was to help me pack my suitcase, and she would bring it down to the office. I was scheduled to do bathroom duties that day, but Matron said that after I was dressed, I was to stay in the recreation area until I was called.

I did as I was told, packing the empty writing case and the now very mouldy sandwich that was still carefully wrapped in one of my "nice" hankies. Miss Parker told me I was to throw the sandwich away because it was very nasty. I don't know why I had kept it so long, or why I hadn't eaten it. I just felt I needed to keep it intact, as security perhaps. Anyway, I reluctantly put it in the rubbish bin, then folded the hanky and tucked it in a corner of my suitcase.

I hadn't many of my own clothes left, as the ones I'd brought with me were now mixed in with others in the linen cupboard. Miss Parker found one set of underwear that I identified as mine, but the rest of the things she took down for me must have belonged to someone else. My green dress and my good skirt were still folded in the cabinet beside the bed. I had given my favourite book, *The Three Desmonds,* to Dulcie, so my suitcase was a bit lighter than when I arrived.

I went down to the recreation area to wait for my mother to come, wondering as I tried to settle down to read and wait what she would be like, and what I would say to her. It seemed like an eternity, but in fact I didn't have long to wait before Miss Parker came to fetch me to take me to the office.

My first impression of my mother was one of sheer delight. I don't know what I expected, but if I had conjured up a thousand idealistic images, the real person would have exceeded all of them. I saw her eyes first, bright blue and smiling. There was love and acceptance in her eyes, and it was enough for me. Whenever in the future I was to think of her, even today, I see those smiling eyes.

My memory of the journey home to Wembley is etched indelibly in my mind. My mother was not much taller than I was, but her short legs were quick and agile. We walked long streets, rode the bus and then the underground, and then walked again. As we went, I noticed nothing of the surroundings because we talked incessantly. I must have asked a million questions, and she tried to answer them all in her soft Welsh brogue. I had never felt so free in adult company to question and to receive responses.

I found out my father's full name and that my eldest brother was named after him: Reginald Maurice Sidey. I learned he was a shrewd businessman and had owned a motorcar, a sure sign of success. My mother told me that he was a good man and very likeable.

"Did you love each other?" I wanted to know. Mother looked at me seriously for a minute.

"Of course we did," she said. "Why did you ask that?"

"Well," I ventured, "I just wondered why you didn't stay married to each other. I thought you had to stay married 'till death did you part." Mother looked at me strangely. She couldn't know I had done at least sixty-two readings of the Solemnization of Matrimony ceremony, and I didn't think this was the time to tell her I hadn't listened to any of the Vicar's sermons. She told me that she and my father had loved each other very much and had been very happy together for several years. But he was very charming, a "ladies man," as she called him.

"He left us for another woman soon after you were born," she said with a sad little smile. Mother told me that she had grown up on a farm in Abergavenny in Wales. She said that after she was married she went back there to live, and that some of my older brothers and sisters were born there.

"Where was I born?" I wanted to know.

"You were born in London, within the sound of Bow Bells," she told me. "That makes you a true Londoner, a Cockney." I felt very pleased to hear that I was a true Londoner. It seemed somehow to be a special honour, a good, solid connection for me—something of interest to tell my friends about. I discovered that I was the youngest of five children, and our birth order was two girls, Betty and Phyllis, two boys, Reginald and Eric, and then me, each of us eighteen months apart. I learned why my mother had named me the way she did.

"Why did you give me so many names?" I wanted to know, and her answer delighted me.

"First of all, I named you Joyce because your birth was a joy to me," she said. "Your other two names, Muriel and Florence, were for the two people who came to help me during my confinement." Though I didn't understand much about the birth process, I knew that babies were usually born at home with a midwife in attendance. Family and friends stayed to help with the household chores and with the other children until the mother was able to "get on her feet" again. Florence was mother's sister who lived in Wales, and Muriel was either a friend or someone from my father's family; I've never really known. We continued to walk and talk, pausing once or twice to clarify some point I didn't quite understand.

I learned so much about my birth family that first day, and in the years that followed I was able to build upon the relationship that we established on that journey. My mother had a quick wit and was steeped in Welsh country lore. She knew dozens of old adages that she loved to quote.

"A stitch in time saves nine." "You can lead a horse to water, but you can't make him drink." "You can always stoop down and pick up nothing" " Smile and the world smiles with you, cry and you cry alone." These were a few of her favourites. She was practical, but not prudish. She could be serious and often was, but she could see the funny side of things too, and could laugh at her own mistakes.

As we walked that day, I learned my life's history, how Mother took my brother Reginald and my sister Phyllis and me to the Home, and how it was only supposed to be for a little while until she was able to take care of us. She told me Eric couldn't go to the Home because he had a weak chest and was ill a lot, and how my eldest sister Betty remained at home to be a comfort and a help to Mother. We talked about my birthplace and the lovely home we lived in. Mother said she thought that I was born on a Thursday, and repeated an old saying I hadn't heard before:

Monday's child is fair of face
Tuesday's child is full of grace
Wednesday's child is full of woe
Thursday's child has far to go
Friday's child is loving and giving
Saturday's child works hard for a living
But a child that is born on the Sabbath day
Is fair and wise and good and gay.

We trundled on. Mother questioned me and asked about the Saunders, and I told her everything about Dadda and Mummy, the bird shed and the sunflowers that Lenny planted, and about Goofie and his fits. She told me that I had a new stepfather, that his name was George like Dadda's, and four younger half brothers and sisters, two girls and two boys. The youngest was still a baby not quite a year old. It was a lot to absorb, but my insatiable curiosity could not be quenched. Mother had her share of questions for me, too. She could not understand why I hadn't received letters from her or certain gifts she had sent. I didn't know the answers to that, but since they were filtered through Dr. Barnardo's and not sent directly, it is not surprising that I didn't receive them.

Meeting my stepfather and brothers and sisters was a new and enjoyable, though somewhat hectic, experience. Of my older four siblings only two were home all the time, Reg and Eric. I looked somewhat like each of them, except that they had blue eyes like

Mother. It was not until I met my sister Betty a few days later that we recognized in each other many similar traits, including the brown eyes that obviously came from my father's side of the family.

The house in Wembley, though nice in its own way, was vastly different from the one in Wenhaston. It was much smaller and much more modern. A hallway with a stairway going up one side ran from the front door to the kitchen in the back of the house. The upscale kitchen had no room for a table and chairs; these were in the comfortable dining room next to the kitchen. The other downstairs room was a large front room with bay windows overlooking the street. It was only used, as Mother said, "on high days and holidays," and was called the Lounge. It had a pretty carpet, lovely comfortable chairs and an overstuffed sofa with lacy doilies along the back and across the arms.

The kitchen was compact, but very serviceable. It was well equipped with a large sink with hot and cold running water, floor to ceiling cupboards, and counter space. It had a white enameled gas-fired cooker with four burners on top and a large oven beneath. There was a gun-like device attached by a springy black wire that lighted the stove somehow with a bang. The gas meter in the hall cupboard under the stairs required feeding with pennies or shillings whenever the gas got low. It was a daily sprint to make sure there were enough "coppers" in the house to keep the gas going. In one corner there was a small coal-burning stove that was cheerful on winter mornings.

The piéce de resistance, though, was the fully equipped white tiled bathroom at the head of the stairway. The door had a lock for privacy, and a wide window ledge that held soap and toothpaste and nice smelling talcum powder.

I began to settle in with my newfound family, and though it was all very nice, I missed Wenhaston and especially I missed Dadda. His letters were always full of cheerful news, but I sensed he missed me too. The thought of starting school in Alperton near Wembley, at the enormous city school where I was scheduled to go at the end of August, was daunting. Though I felt sure my place at Beccles was filled by this time and my chances of getting in would be slim, it was worth a try. I pondered whether I could deal with being in Mr. Sangster's class again if the Beccles School couldn't have me. I decided that being with all my friends again in familiar surroundings would be far better than facing hundreds of strangers.

Mother's house at 3 Vincent Road in Wembley was over-flowing with all of us. For a while it had been fun to sleep in a bed with my younger sister, June. We had talked and giggled endlessly. But now I longed for my own room again, and reading under the covers and waking up to the sound of Miss Danford's cockerel crowing his head off. I began to think of harvesting, the Harvest Festival at the church, the Girl Guides, tennis lessons, and practicing for the Christmas play. I missed having my bicycle and knowing the names of everyone in the village. When I asked her, Mother said if I really wanted to go back to Wenhaston and the Saunders were willing to have me, she would consider letting me go.

So began a letter-writing blitz of mammoth proportions. The letters flew back and forth over the hundred-mile distance that separated us. First I wrote to Dadda explaining the situation and asking him if he would consent to let me come, at least during the school year. His first reply was directed to my mother, assuring her that it was indeed a good arrangement, and that they would be delighted to have me come back and live with them. He also wrote to me, and we shuttled letters back and forth, ironing out details of my travel, which train I was to get so Mummy could meet me at Ipswich.

I wrote back and assured him that Mummy needn't come all that way to meet me, as I would catch the right train that came all the way to Halesworth, and then catch the bus for Wenhaston at the station as I had done so many times before. It took several letters to convince him, but at last he was satisfied that I would be careful and could manage. He enclosed a pound note for my train and bus fare and "some left over for something to eat along the way."

Mother came with me to Liverpool Street Station to see that I got on the correct train. I found myself once again feeling awed by the massive number of trains, the noise and confusion of this huge station. But mother led me to the ticket window and stood by while I bought my own ticket. "Never be afraid to ask for directions," she said, and proceeded to demonstrate by asking the ticket seller where I needed to go.

"Platform nine, Miss," he said, pointing in the direction we were to go. They were well marked and easy to spot. When we got to it, the train was already standing with all the doors open, ready for boarding.

"Goodbye, Pet," Mother said, as she kissed me on both cheeks. "Be a good girl, won't you, and write often." I promised I would as the train began to move, and she smiled her beautiful smile and stood on the platform waving until she was out of sight. I settled back in the carriage for the long ride. The train stopped long enough at Colchester for me to hop out and buy a sandwich and an orange squash. It was heady business traveling alone and being responsible for watching the stations and feeling the exhilaration of going home. It was with joyful anticipation that I stepped off the train at Halesworth, called "Hello" to Mr. Summerfield, ran across to the waiting bus, and hopped aboard, bounding up the metal stairway to the upper deck.

The farms and friendly fields seemed to smile in acknowledgment as I rode by, and I giggled as the bus bumped over the humpback bridge. I was down on the bottom step, ready to jump off before the bus stopped at the *Compass*. I was through the *Compass* yard and onto Back Road in a second. As I approached Mr. Newby's Clock Shop, I looked up the road toward the house. It had not changed one whit in my absence. It looked warm and inviting, and there was a wonderful familiar face watching for me at the kitchen window.

Chapter 11

Gas Masks, Evacuees, and Air Raid Sirens

Wish me luck as you wave me goodbye
Cheerio, here I go, on my way.
Wish me luck as you wave me goodbye
With a cheer, not a tear, make it gay.

Popular WWII song

The sounds and sights of war that had been hovering over us for nearly a year reached our small village with a flurry of activity in 1939. The BBC news broadcasts that Dadda always followed with great care now became galvanizing for more than just him. The whole village buzzed with a new vocabulary of war talk and names hardly mentioned before. People formed opinions about Neville Chamberlain, the Prime Minister, and the results of his attempted peace negotiations with Germany in 1938. They spoke almost daily of Anthony Eden, the Foreign Secretary, and the vocal Winston Churchill, then a Member of Parliament. Churchill, whose fame as First Lord of the Admiralty in the Great War lingered for the older generation, was a popular figure. People spoke of having him as Prime Minister instead of Mr. Chamberlain.

Every conversation was sprinkled with these names and others that we did not know as well. We began to hear of events in Austria, Poland, the Soviet Union, and Turkey. We heard on the news that Germany had invaded and suddenly conquered Czechoslovakia. People discussed the League of Nations, Marxism, Fascism, and National Socialism. We heard the talk, the names and the opinions, and while we didn't understand the details, we knew which side we were on. We confidently expected our leaders in the government and in the armed forces to "take care of things" for us.

Germany attacked Poland on the first day of September, 1939. On the third of September, England declared war on Germany. Our wireless, which we now called a radio since the electricity was laid on, was tuned in for an unprecedented number of hours during those critical days. Dadda paced the floor, almost neglecting his duties in the bird shed. Our village became mobilized, like the rest of England. A "Home Guard" was formed in which the older men with families were drilled to protect their home territory. Spare guns were rounded up from private collections. Dadda took his double-barreled shotgun and two other prized guns from their glass encased rack and offered them voluntarily to the cause.

The strong spirit of patriotism that was evident in peacetime gained momentum, and suddenly became a torrent that swept the country like a tidal wave. The young men and women eighteen to thirty years old who had been leaving the village by ones and twos were now departing in droves. Some, like Lenny, had been "called up" early on, and others had gone voluntarily before they were called. Some eager sixteen and seventeen year old boys lied about their ages so they would be accepted in the Forces. The boys and girls who were younger, the eleven year olds like me, were envious of their older siblings who were able to go off to war. It didn't seem fair somehow that we were left at home.

We children tossed around the name of our major enemy, the fanatical Nazi party leader in Germany, Adolph Hitler. It seemed like great sport to blacken our upper lips, pull down a lock of hair across our foreheads and make rude gestures while proclaiming loudly: "zieg heil." Hitler's two most disliked generals were Goebbels and Goering. We saw them many times on the *Pathé News* at the Saturday afternoon picture show, between the Disney cartoons and the feature film. They were both ugly, fat men with squinty eyes, so it was easy to poke fun at them. We imitated the "goose step" that Hitler's army used in marching, and learned to dislike everything German. Years later we learned of the thousands of "good" German people who were swept along with Hitler's philosophies against their own better judgment. But for this moment in England, we children vied with each other to see which of us could give the best expression of our hatred for the enemy.

In the competition for most hated, even Goebbels and Goering paled beside one of our own countrymen who called himself "Lord Haw Haw." This man, who set himself up as leader and very vocal spokesman for the Fifth Column operating in Britain, was slandered and ridiculed at every opportunity by adults and children alike. His radio messages always began with, "London calling, London calling" and then he would launch into a diatribe of lies and vile anti-British speeches attacking the government, our royalty, and the armed forces. I never heard what happened to him, but his messages ceased early on in the war.

For several months, plans for fortifying our village and protecting our homes had been subjects of long conversations in committee meetings, pubs and private conversations. Now preparations got underway in earnest. Air Raid Wardens, who took turns watching the skies and listening for incoming reports about enemy planes, were appointed to drill us in safety procedures both at home and at school. If there was an air raid while we were at school, we were to get under our desks or be led out into the hallways, depending on the amount of response time we were allotted. At home we were to get under tables, or for those homes that had them, run to the shelters in the back yards.

Preparations were underway for every possible emergency. We brought out the oil lamps that we had so recently stored away, and put them in prominent places, filled them with oil, and trimmed their wicks. My Girl Guide troop stepped up its First Aid program to include more practical training and rescue techniques. Each home and public building was issued rolls of sticky paper, similar to the kind used to seal parcels. It had to be wet thoroughly and then attached in criss-cross patterns to all window panes. It was meant to prevent glass from shattering and throwing shards across a room. Though it looked unsightly, we accepted it as a sensible defense against injury from flying glass.

While we children adapted readily to the necessary changes, our parents didn't adapt quite as easily. The blackout seemed to be the biggest trial for the adults. Most of the homes had heavy lace curtains covering the windows, with drapes down the sides made of thick materials, held back with shiny tassels on ornamental hooks. Our Front room drapes were green velvet and were only pulled across the window on winter evenings to help keep the cold out. They were never intended to block out every sliver of light. Now, in addition to pulling the drapes across, we also had to put a blanket over the centre slit where the draperies didn't quite meet. It was a job getting it right each night and disassembling it each morning.

If there were the smallest sliver of light, the warden would come round and yell at us to turn off our lights. Opening a door after dark also became a challenge for everyone, particularly for pubs and other places of business that operated at night. The owners built box-like contraptions around doorways with a curtain at one end, so that customers could come and go without violating the blackout.

We learned that the merest chink of light could tip off an enemy aircraft. Even a match flaring or a lighted cigarette were potential hazards. We put black fabric over our bicycle head lights and aimed the light to shine on a small patch of the road just ahead of the front wheel. When we traveled at night we could barely see each other in passing, let alone see the road. When the siren wailed, we immediately put our lights out. Fortunately, the roads were familiar to us, and we learned to sing as we rode, so that we could hear each other even though we couldn't see or be seen.

The air-raid wardens also taught us the sounds and meaning of the three sirens. The first, a mournful wailing sound, was cautionary: "get ready, we've spotted aircraft that are headed our way." The second, a more insistent, broken wailing meant: "get to shelter NOW, the planes are over us and attack is imminent." The third siren was a long, thin sound. Though tonally unattractive, it was the most pleasant sound of the three. It was the "All Clear" it meant the enemy had gone, and we could come out of our shelters.

There was one familiar sound that was soon taken from us. The church bells that were a huge part of village life were stopped for the duration. We missed the bells' pealings keenly, for they were part of our daily lives. But newer, more modern sounds: songs about love, courage and seeing things in a positive light were very popular. Whacky songs such as *Be Like the Kettle and Sing* filled the airwaves and gave us something to smile about. A new midday program called "Worker's Playtime" was broadcast from one or another of the munitions factories throughout the country. The workers from various plants played host to singing celebrities, who in turn entertained them and the radio audience during the noon lunch hour. In this way we learned the words to all the newest hit songs, and we children especially loved them.

Vera Lynn's songs about the war were very popular. Songs

such as: *When the Lights go on Again* and *The White Cliffs of Dover* made reference to ending the blackout and hearing the church bells again. *We'll Meet Again* and *Yours* reiterated the themes of love and faithfulness until the war came to an end, and the men were back home again. My parents and some of their contemporaries who had cut their teeth on chamber music were slower to respond to the new songs, but eventually they too were humming along with the catchy tunes.

There were other sounds that were new to us that we became accustomed to hearing and distinguishing—those of aircraft engines. The British Spitfires had bright, fast engines that quickly became familiar to our ears. The RAF bomber engines made a somewhat somber, but steady sound. We didn't know it then, but within a year we would also learn the sounds of the German aircraft engines. The Luftwaffe bombers sounded heavy with an uneven throbbing that distinguished them from ours. The enemy fighter plane, the Messerschmitt, had a heavy, uneven, almost staccato throbbing.

We were all issued gas masks. They were made of black rubber and had a peculiar smell. We children queued up outside the village Hut, talking and laughing as though we were in line for the Saturday picture show in Halesworth. We were instructed in how to put them on. They had adjustable straps that went over the back of the head, a bulbous piece to breathe through under the chin, and a plexiglass eyepiece that got steamed up the instant we put them on. They made us look like weird creatures, so we giggled at each other until the Wardens in blue overalls reprimanded us. When we pulled them off, our faces were sweaty and the rubber bands caught and pulled strands of our hair.

We were told we were to carry our gas masks everywhere we went, to school, on errands and even to our bedrooms at night. They were always to be available on an instant's notice. With so much carrying about, we knew the brown cardboard gas mask boxes we were issued would soon be worn out. The village set to work devising covers for them. Some made theirs with fabric in pretty colours, and some made theirs of string or leather. Gladys and I made ours of wool taken from jumpers that had become too small for us. We knitted a piece on big needles in the shape of a strange cross, then continued knitting a piece that tapered to a point that would be the front flap. We then sewed up the sides and put a wide crocheted band, sewn on three sides of the box to form a shoulder length handle. Lastly we attached a large button and loop to form a proper closing.

We were in our knitting mode at school that autumn. Someone had devised a scheme for making what we called "poke bonnets." They became all the rage, and even the men wore them underneath their caps to keep their ears warm. A poke bonnet consisted of an elongated knitted scarf made of used wool. We plagued every one to give us their old jumpers and cardigans, and in return we gave them a new poke bonnet. With the remaining wool, we made our own bonnets and made others for Christmas presents.

After knitting the long straight piece, which was fraught with many knots, we sewed the scarf part way down to form the head piece, the poked hat. Then we decorated around the face part with different styles to suit the person. For some it was just a finishing touch in the same yarn. For others we either knitted a contrasting bright border, or sewed fabric edges. The final touch was to make a pom-pom for the poke at the back of the head. Poke bonnets were easy to make and lent themselves well to our creative talents for trying out fancy stitches and blending colours to make every one of them a little different.

Our village was quickly and willingly pressed into service to accommodate children under the age of twelve who were being evacuated from London and its surrounding counties. I hoped that perhaps some of my own brothers or sisters would be among them, but they were not. Most of the evacuees that came to Wenhaston were from Dagenham or Romford, which like Wembley are located on the outskirts of London. Each village home was inspected for unused bedrooms, and wherever children could be doubled up, boy with boy or girl with girl, we fitted them in.

I moved back into my small bedroom happily, hoping we would have some children placed with us. Instead of children we were given two Irish soldiers who were billeted in Lenny's old room. These remained for a few weeks and then two more came to replace them. We didn't get to know them very well because they came and went so rapidly, and hardly were in the house except to sleep and eat the morning and evening meals.

Almost every home had either children or soldiers billeted with them. Though our own young men were gone to serve in other places, the village population did not significantly decrease. In fact, we were suddenly teeming with new life and every home was packed to the limit. Next door, at the Ellis' home, there were two girls named Adele and Phoebe. Both were from Dagenham, but they had not known each other before they were evacuated. We walked to school together sometimes, and spent a good deal of time in each other's homes, learning new games from each other. Walter's family had a brother and sister, Eddie and Maurie, billeted with them and Joy Youngs shared her home with an evacuee named Ivy Lee.

Our school, which had always seemed so large to us, suddenly was bursting at the seams. In fact some auxiliary classes had to be taught at the village Hut. New teachers came with the evacuees and the school classrooms were divided with curtains down the centre of the rooms. The evacuees were more used to large groups of children than we were. They also had the advantage of having had a much easier rapport with their teachers than we had ever experienced. The nearest we had come to rapport was a healthy respect for our women teachers, Miss Danford and Miss Piper. None of us would have dared to question Mr. Sangster, our strict and rigid headmaster.

Mr. Clark was one of the two teachers who came to the village with the evacuees. He was an extremely affable young man with a shock of ginger hair. He did not carry a cane, and his scoldings were delivered in a firm but good-humoured manner. It was a new experience for Wenhaston scholars to actually relate to their teacher in a relaxed way. Mr. Clark and Miss Marshall taught children in the middle forms, those who were aged eight to eleven, and thus they divided responsibility with Miss Piper. Unfortunately, Miss Piper's room could not hold all the students, so the largest classroom, Mr. Sangster's, was eventually divided. It was all fairly muddled for a time, but none of the students minded the confusion as much as the teachers did.

The over-elevens, including a few evacuees, had no choice about their teacher. We were all in Mr. Sangster's class. If we'd had the option, we all would have gone down a grade to be in Mr. Clark's class. I believe Mr. Sangster may have learned some valuable lessons in his method of administering discipline from our evacuees' teacher. I know that my contemporaries and I did.

We children were too young to fight, but we loved to pretend. One of our favourite war games was locating enemy spies, which we assumed were everywhere. Any stranger, particularly one with a foreign accent, was suspect. We had what we thought was a very efficient network. A dozen or so of us took turns following any stranger to keep watch on all his activities. A family, who must have escaped from Poland or perhaps Czechoslovakia, moved into the LeCroix's large house by the village green. We had not seen them move in, but we knew they were there. I now realize that they were quite innocent, but our "job" then was to monitor their movements.

The house was almost hidden by large trees, and the grounds were completely hemmed in by a brick wall that was slightly higher than the tallest of us. The LeCroix family was not very well known in the village. We occasionally saw them driving their black Daimler out of the garage before the war, but now that petrol was rationed, we had not seen it in a long time.

Our network moved in around the house to spy out any strange activities. One elderly man in a trilby hat and long overcoat made several trips to the post office and to the bakery across the green. He held his head down and steadied his hat against the wind with his black gloved hand as he crossed the common. As he walked, he looked furtively to the right and left as if he knew he was being followed. Surely, we thought, there was some skullduggery going on in the house that we could discover and report to the authorities.

We scouted the front gardens for secreted weapons and equipment, finding nothing but some old garden tools. We got as close to the house as possible, listening for the sounds of espionage: a radio transmitter or encoded messages that might be going out. We had been learning the Morse Code at Girl Guides, and how to send messages using signal flags, so we thought we might send an encrypted message to higher authorities if we were able to pick up anything.

Our lookouts were supposed to be alert and warn us of approaching danger. But they sometimes gave us false signals, to make our foraging a bit more interesting. When one of the lookouts rang the bicycle bell twice in quick succession, it was the signal that someone was coming. After about the third time we were made to leap over the wall for nothing, we had some heated discussion. Walter said it was practice, to see if we could improve our escape time. The rest of us were not amused. After several attempts with nothing gained, we decided the front garden was too obvious a search area.

So we decided to investigate the back garden. It was very overgrown, and seemed to be a good place to hide things. I was the first over the wall to reconnoitre the area, and I was to give the signal. Throwing a small stick back over the wall meant that the area was safe for the rest of the group to follow and help with the search. As I came climbing over the back wall, I startled someone or something. I thought it might have been a cat or rabbit, but as I crept over toward a big bramble bush there was the unmistakable sound of heavy breathing. A young girl about six years old was crouched down behind an old rusty wheelbarrow that was upended against the wall. She was bent over with her back to the wall, peering with fearful eyes in my direction. I took a step toward her.

"I came over to find my ball..." I began, hoping to start a conversation and find out all about the new family. But as I approached, the girl let out a scream that could have been heard in Southwold. She bolted away from me as though the Devil himself were after her. Without waiting to find out anything more, I scrambled back over the wall, landing helter-skelter in a patch of nettles, recovered my bicycle and took off after my fleeing teammates.

Though the experience put a damper on our spying efforts, it by no means scotched them completely. We began to make several hideouts in each other's sheds and on the heath, rough places of refuge were we could bring our intelligence together, plan our strategies, and if necessary, escape from the enemy. Sometimes one of us made a stop at the bakery and for tuppence-ha'penny got a fresh, hot loaf of bread to sustain us while we did our deep planning.

Being so close to the coast made our village in some ways vulnerable, but the defenses around us were good. We were surrounded by small pockets of "ack ack" guns, which were most numerous toward the seaports. The Forces used our heaths as training fields, and billeted soldiers in our homes.

Southwold beach was mined, and we were no longer able to

touch our feet on the sand. The fishermen who had for centuries launched their boats at will through the surf, now had to limit their launchings to prescribed places, and ran the risk of being killed by a mine that had strayed from its moorings. Many years after the war ended and the mines had been removed, a stray mine now and then continued to wash up along the shore.

Early in December 1939, only a few months after the start of war, a new diversion captured our attention. The news broadcasters had been talking for weeks about elusive German battleships that had slipped into the open ocean before war was officially declared and before the British blockade was in place. One of these, the pocket battleship *Graf Spee*, was wreaking havoc with British and French merchant ships in the South Atlantic shipping lanes. As October ended and Guy Fawkes Day approached, the toll of merchant ships became staggering. Three, four, five, then a tanker and then a sixth merchant ship was lost to the *Admiral Graf Spee.* She was a new ship and her captain was able to use her skillfully to slip in, attack and move on.

Dadda silently paced the floor, utterly preoccupied with every fresh sinking. For a few weeks, as new information filtered into our living rooms, a pall seemed to hang over the entire village. At church the Reverend Hardingham took the situation in hand and from the Prayer Book led the congregation in an earnest plea for God's divine intervention:

> "Thou, o Lord, art just and powerful; O defend our cause against the force of the enemy.
> "O God, thou art a strong tower of defense to all that flee unto Thee: O save us from the violence of the enemy.
> "O Lord of Hosts, fight for us, that we may glorify thee.
> "O suffer us not to sink under the weight of our sins, or the violence of the enemy.
> "O Lord, arise, help us, and deliver us, for Thy Name's sake."

And the congregation, choir, organist and visitors said a heartfelt and collective AMEN! I fully believed God would hear and answer our prayers, and deliver our ships from the hands of our enemies.

Dadda said it was good to believe, but that I shouldn't think that God always answered prayers in the way we hoped for. He said that very often God worked in ways we couldn't understand, and we should be willing to accept whatever came to us as His answer.

In the weeks that followed, news came steadily of more sinkings of our merchant ships. Nine ships in all had been lost by the first week in December. But on the thirteenth of December the evening news reported the stunning news of victory, that after being chased and damaged by our cruisers *Achilles, Exeter,* and *Ajax*, the Germans had scuttled their own ship. Through the rejoicing, the details were forthcoming. The *Graf Spee* had finally come up against three of our own cruisers that had been searching for her. Our ships had damaged the *Graf Spee,* and though *Exeter* herself was badly damaged, they had continued to give chase as the *Graf Spee* fled to Montevideo. The damaged *Graf Spee* had to leave the neutral port. Our cruiser *Cumberland* sped to the area. Perhaps the Germans thought that they were overmatched and that there was no escape for them. In any event the German crew scuttled their own ship in the River Plata on the 17th day of December 1939. The Captain—Langsdorff—then committed suicide. It was a glorious victory at sea which I saw as a direct answer to prayer.

Christmas Bazaar

Christmas, later that month, was a joyous celebration, though restricted in some ways. We had rehearsed our school play well, and the costumes were fitted and ready. Because of the larger crowd of children, some of the scenes were revised to include more than the original cast, and extra group songs were added. There was a chorus as a grand finale, in which all the children could take part. It was arranged so that the girls and boys sang some parts in unison and some antiphonally. We rehearsed this many times, and it sounded splendid. At one point the girls and boys sang in harmony, then the girls were quiet and the boys came in strong with their richer voices, and then finally all sang together. As we rehearsed, there was a slight tendency for the boys to miss their cue at the point where they were supposed to come in, but it was worked out nicely in rehearsals and by an evacuee from Dagenham named Clifford. His strong, confident voice adequately glossed the slight pause, and his outgoing manner made up for anything the rest of the group lacked. Our director encouraged Clifford to lead the others boldly, and we felt sure he would.

Instead of the Sunday School building, we had to use the larger Village Hall, the Hut. Many extra hands helped erect an elevated stage and get the props together. The men of the Home Guard had made shutters for the windows at the first hint of blackout, and now they built the enclosure surrounding the door. The sewing ladies, who made our costumes and the stage curtains, also made a heavy black covering for the doorway enclosure. Gladys and I, along with several others, climbed on rickety ladders, and strung colourful twisty crepe paper and paper pompoms in every direction across the ceiling and around the walls. Some ornaments from Christmases past were hung with care on the small tree at the very edge of the stage.

Lenny was now gone, and I would miss his being at the school play. He had been the family representative for most of my school performances. I was surprised and pleased when Mummy promised to attend in his stead to watch the play. I was glad she was coming, and worked especially hard to learn my lines to make her proud. The Women's Guild organized themselves to prepare wonderful refreshments for the audience, to be served after the performance was over. It was very exciting, and despite the war we were enjoying the bustling activities immensely.

On the night of the big event everything was ready. All day the men had been carrying chairs from the Sunday School building across the road to the Hut. The ladies had been preparing sausage rolls, mince pies, and other goodies and bringing them to the tables at the far end of the hall. The players arrived early, and there was much scrambling backstage finding the right costumes and getting ourselves sorted out. The curtain, which didn't quite reach the floor, was pulled across the front of the stage, and the audience began arriving.

All went very well. The Vicar made his customary welcome and introduction; the stage curtain was pulled back, and after an initial wave of nervous anticipation, we collected ourselves and remembered to speak our lines on cue. As the play progressed, we could smell the brewing tea and see the movements at the back of the hall. When we got to the group singing, we were flushed with success. It was not hard to tell that the audience which up to now had been enthusiastic, was beginning to get a bit restless. We heard their chatter between scenes becoming a bit louder, and it was obvious their attention was waning. But they were a loyal lot and weren't ready to give up just yet.

It was getting late and we children had poured forth great energy. We were headed for the finale and we knew it would soon be over, so we dredged up our last reserves. It was strange that we should be edgy now, but we were. There was some nervous twitching as we assembled ourselves in our proper places, tallest in the back row and the shorter ones in front. Mrs. Bailey thumped out the introduction to our piece and we started out in unison, then changed to the antiphonal where the girls sang their part. The boys, who were to come in strongly with their responsive part, missed their cue. They hesitated in confusion a mere second or two, and then attempted to forge ahead with Clifford in the lead.

Everything would have been fine except at that moment, Clifford, whose voice rang out over the others, had his voice change. The rasping notes that came out were startling. They jangled against the walls and echoed through the hall. The audience came awake abruptly, some holding their ears. Clifford stopped, red faced and shocked, in mid-sentence. The other boys, not knowing whether to laugh or cry, bumped labouriously through the remainder of the piece. The girls picked up the refrain on cue, frantically hoping to save the day.

A ripple of laughter came from the audience, and after a horrified few minutes of maintaining some sort of dignity, the cast too began to waver. Walter's eyes were watering and his stomach was shaking. Everyone knew he would be rolling on the floor in another minute. Mrs. Bailey, thumping as hard as she could on the piano, attempted to drown our voices altogether.

We managed somehow to get through the rest of the song, grateful for the curtain being pulled across in front of us before we had finished taking a bow. The audience applauded appropriately, between outbursts of laughter and loud jovial comments. For us the magic moment of success had been tempered by the incident. Clifford disappeared backstage immediately. The rest of us stumbled through the curtain and down the steps to join the audience in singing the national anthem. Afterwards, someone turned on all the lights, and the cast along with the audience, gratefully turned to the heaping plates of refreshments laid out on the tables in the rear of the hall.

Uncle Aubrey and Carly-luv arrived on Christmas Eve, and the holiday spirit arrived with them. I had just returned from taking the last order out to the Malcolms' farm. There had been lots of orders to deliver on this day, and I had earned more than a shilling in generous tips. The shop closed early on Christmas Eve and would remain closed through Boxing Day, so my chores for the day were all done. As I swung my bicycle into the shop yard, I heard the sound of the car's hooter. I knew the sound of it, and turned to wave a welcome. Uncle Aubrey pulled the car into the slot beside the shop wall, and in a second he was bounding out of the car door

"Hullo Ditsy-Doo!" he called out as I ran into his outspread arms. "Your cheeks are like tricycles," he said, rubbing them between his gloved hands. I understood his rhyming game. My cheeks were cold, like icicles, and probably a bit red too. "Are you all right?" Uncle Aubrey said mischievously, hoping to catch me off guard.

"No" I replied with great haste, "I'm half left." He grinned as he turned back to scoop up bright parcels from the boot of the car. Carly-luv smiled, and came over to enfold me in her soft coat.

"Darling, you are frozen solid," she said, bending her head

toward me in that gracious way she had. "And you've grown so tall, nearly up to my shoulder," she said, her eyes shining. I ran ahead of them through the shop and into the front hallway to unlock the front door for them. They were our special guests, and it was an honour to be the first to greet them heartily and welcome them through the front door.

Lettie had gone home to Bramfield at midday to be with her family for Christmas. A few days before, she and I had made lots of paper chains and brought in branches of red holly berries to decorate the Front room , knowing it would be the central gathering place throughout the holidays. We had draped the whole room, the mantelpiece, the mirror, the clock and the pictures round the walls, with colourful chains and branches of cedar, pine and holly. The room looked festive and smelled officially like Christmas.

Before Lettie left, she had laid a fire in the Front room fireplace and left the scuttle filled with coal on the hearth. It was a bitterly cold day. The ponds were frozen solid, and even the cisterns beside the house were iced over. One of our billeted soldiers had gone home on leave, and the other one had not yet come in for the day.

Lenny had been home on leave a few weeks before, and we had been glad to see him looking fit and well and very handsome in his army uniform. Since he was now married, he no longer stayed with us when he was home, but he and his wife Joyce visited us frequently. He had been moved several times to various bases during his training, and now had told us another transfer was imminent. He didn't know where his next assignment would be; he knew only that his battalion was being shipped overseas. We accepted the fact that he would not be coming again for at least six months.

Without Lenny there, no one had made provision for obtaining the Christmas tree. We had stashed presents that we'd been working on laboriously for weeks in cupboards, under beds and in various little "hidey-holes." They would miraculously appear in the morning, to be opened with delight. Mummy had made the Christmas cake and decorated it with the usual "saved" silver ornaments, and the plum puddings were ready. Sausage rolls, mince pies and custard tarts had all been baked a few days before. These and a fat goose, stuffed and ready for the oven, were in the pantry waiting to be savoured on Christmas Day.

Uncle Aubrey had brought his usual load of presents for each of us. He brought them in by armloads and stacked them on the floor in front of the settee, their colourful wrappings and mysterious shapes bringing warmth to the cold room.

"Where's the tree?" he asked, rubbing his leather gloved hands together.

"Lenny's not here and I couldn't get one on my own, but I know where to go to get one," I said eagerly.

Dadda came in from the bird-shed. "Hullo, old man," they greeted each other affectionately. Dadda was always pleased to see his brother Aubrey. Carly-luv was pleased too, and stepping gracefully around the gifts on the floor, swept her arms around Dadda's neck, planting kisses on both his cheeks.

"It's luvly to see you," she said, smiling her sweet smile. Dadda smiled back, a bit shyly. He never quite knew how to respond to Carly-luv's overtly kind affection. Mummy came in from the shop.

"My goodness," she said after greeting the guests, "Isn't anyone going to light the fire?" Dadda handed the large box of Bryant and Mays matches to her from their place on the mantel, and soon the paper and kindling came to life. Even before the coal caught, the warmth spread from the hearty blaze and began to fill the room. Both Uncle Aubrey and Carly-luv were wearing long fur coats that reached almost to their ankles, and hats to match.

"Where can we find a tree?" Uncle Aubrey said, looking at me. I told him about the patch of woods beside Gwinny's house where Lenny had taken me the year before. I hesitated a moment, remembering that Lenny had put last year's tree over his shoulder and ridden home with it perched there.

"We'll take the car," Uncle Aubrey said. Mummy was aghast at the thought of them going out into the woods with their gorgeous coats on. And the car, she fretted, would not be fit to sit in. She gave us all the necessary tools, and armloads of old blankets to wrap the tree in. I was thrilled to ride in the car, even though it was less than half a mile. I wanted so much for all my friends to see me riding in Uncle Aubrey's car, but no one was anywhere to be seen.

We left the car in the lane and tramped into the woods, miraculously and quickly finding a tree that looked to be perfect. It was beginning to get dark when we arrived home. The blackout curtains were already in place, and the aroma of something delicious greeted us as we brought the blanket-covered tree into the house. Mummy searched the shed and found the official Christmas tree pail, still with sand in it from the year before. After much laughing, measuring and advice from each other, we finally got the tree to stand up, albeit slightly wonky.

We brought the gramophone down from the box room and the tree ornaments from their storage place. While Uncle Aubrey played his newest recordings, we decorated the tree. In a little while, our resident soldier Ian came in, cold and very hungry. He gratefully joined us at the supper table. After we'd eaten our meal and done the washing up, we sat by the fire and opened the chocolates Uncle Aubrey had brought for us. There'd be presents for each of us under the tree in the morning, but for this night we were content to sit back and enjoy the moment.

Carly-luv and I had just got the border done on our new jigsaw puzzle, when a band of carolers gathered around the front door. It was lovely to hear them on such a cold night. They were nearly frozen solid when Mummy invited them in to have a warm drink by the fire. It was obvious that they'd made a few stops prior to coming to our house. They joked about not being able to find their way in the blackout and told us they'd had to get the Wardens to guide them to each house. Mummy, understanding immediately that the mates of the group were Wardens, laughingly opened the door and called them to come in too. The room was crowded, and soon was ringing with laughter. Uncle Aubrey was in his element, and entertained everyone with his lively and witty humour.

The gramophone played and our guests touched glasses in many toasts to the King, to those away in the Forces, and for the welfare of relatives, real and imagined, spread around the world. Before the group left to wind up their evening at the Compass, they led us in singing *Good King Wenceslas* and *The First Noel.* It was a special time and a special season for all of us. Our hearts as well as the fire burned brightly and wonderfully warm that night.

Little did we know what horrendous changes we would endure before Christmas Eve came again.

Chapter 12

War Efforts, Shelters, and Growing Up

They also serve who only stand and wait.

Milton, quoted by Churchill 1940

Christmas had been an especially joyful time at Majuba House. The New Year 1940 began with freezing temperatures and rather bad weather, though we had a brightened outlook. Uncle Aubrey and Carly-luv had left on Boxing Day. The house felt empty and a bit dismal to me after they left. They had told us they would be putting their motorcar in storage at their home in Ipswich, so they wouldn't be traveling to see us by car any more. With tightened petrol rationing due to the submarine warfare, they were not going to use their motorcar for the duration. Dadda expressed his approval of that decision. He thought his brother was doing the right thing in not trying to get special favours from some of his well-placed acquaintances. Uncle Aubrey said he couldn't justify enjoying extravagant luxuries while "our chaps are dying over there."

It was unusual for me to see Uncle Aubrey in deep conversation, but several times during the holiday he had soberly discussed his plans for doing his part for the Country. "I'm too old to go to the Front," he said ruefully, "but I can jolly well muck in here at home." He had obviously thought long and hard about his war effort, and he was chafing to be part of the fray. He said that his London business office connection gave him the best opportunity to be part of the action. He had lost no time in making arrangements for the Hospital Corps to take over their home in Ipswich for billeting wounded army personnel. He said he had been approached and given several choices about uses for their home for the duration of the war.

They had opted for the house and grounds to become a kind of hospital halfway house: convalescent quarters for returning soldiers who needed rehabilitation. Uncle Aubrey was pleased with the arrangement, which he felt would give their home a prominent place in the war effort. He and Carly-luv were moving to live in their small London flat, so he could be close to his central office. Unspoken but clearly understood was the idea that he would also be part of the London air-raid warden brigade. It was well known that with the young men gone, the middle-aged men for these jobs were in short supply.

Dadda and Uncle Aubrey debated train and bus schedules between London and Halesworth. It was good to hear Uncle Aubrey speak about continuing his visits. The talk of train schedules sparked the memory of my own recent adventures on the London North Eastern Railway. They smiled as I recounted the story for the umpteenth time, and I couldn't help but wonder if they had contrived the talk about schedules to bait me. They both agreed that I was a brave and accomplished traveler. Uncle Aubrey made a point of saying that as soon as the war was over, I perhaps could find my way to their London flat. He and Carly-luv would take me round London, to see the places I'd only heard about.

"Nelson's column?" I said, thinking that Dadda would like me to see that so that I could tell him all about it. "Yes," he said, "of course, and Trafalgar Square, Marble Arch, Tower Bridge, and Buckingham Palace." "And Madame Tussaud's," Carly-luv chimed in.

It was a happy thought, and something I could look forward to. For the present time, though, I would not be able to travel to London. "Not while all those perry jots are flying around making a mess of things," Uncle Aubrey said with a toss of his head. He waited to see if I'd caught his inverted joke. I was pleased that I had. He had many names and many witty jokes about chamber pots. Sometimes he referred to the chamber as a "thunder jug," and sometimes as a "respectable receptacle," or as "the big teacup" under the bed. More recently he had dubbed it the "Jerry pot," and his joke was meant to associate Germans with the pot's contents. The talk turned to air-raid shelters, and Uncle Aubrey asked Dadda what he was doing about getting one for our protection. Dadda said he hadn't quite made up his mind about it.

"Well," said his brother, "don't wait too long, will you old chap." He went on at great length to describe how the Civil Defense was working to make different types of shelters available to every household. Dadda listened thoughtfully and pulled on his pipe.

They discussed London's shelter system and talked about how the Underground stations provided natural shelters all over London. He went on to talk about the miniscule Quonset hut-type shelters that were popping up in people's back gardens, and the sturdy steel indoor shelters that doubled as tables. He went on to tell us about the concrete, above-the- ground bunkers being constructed along the streets in places located away from the Underground stations.

"Really?" Dadda asked, interested. "They look a little bit like the booths along the streets of Paris," Uncle Aubrey said, with a merry twinkle, "except they're not as colourful; they cover the feet and you're not allowed to do in ours what they do in theirs." Dadda chuckled and looked at me. I was curious to know what Frenchman did in their street booths and when I discovered the Paris booths were men's toilets, I was appalled. My consternation made the others laugh, and the conversation was not so serious after that.

I understood that I could not travel to London to see Uncle Aubrey for the time being. But it was not lost on me that he assumed I would someday want to visit my Wembley family. He said that when I did travel to London, I had a standing invitation to visit him. Meanwhile, for the duration, they would be coming to see us, traveling by train and bus. We agreed I was to meet them at the Halesworth train station when they returned to Wenhaston in the spring.

The powers that be had taken off the big red double-decker buses on the Wenhaston route, and had replaced them with smaller, sleek looking coaches. We believed it was a move to save petrol during this tightened rationing period. Where the double-deckers had the open door in the rear where the conductor stood, the new coaches had a door in the front, opposite the driver, that could be closed tightly against the weather. Though the new coaches were not nearly as exciting to ride in from my point of view, the older people found the padded seats more comfortable and the ride less drafty. I was sorry Uncle Aubrey and Carly-luv would not have the thrill of riding over the humpback bridge on the double-decker. They would have liked that. However, I relished the thought that they would visit us, and did indeed keep that appointment with them when they came during the summer holiday.

Early in the new year, our shop girl Lettie was called up to military service. She opted to serve in the newly formed Land Army that had been created to fill the void of young men who had gone to fight in the armed services. Since she had grown up on a farm, the Land Army was a natural choice for her. Though she didn't want to leave us, she was anxious to do her "bit" to help fight the enemy. We were sorry to see her go, as we were all quite fond of her. She worked out her two weeks notice at the shop, and promised to come round to see us whenever she could.

For a few weeks, I was pressed into doing several additional duties. I enjoyed being a help, as it made me feel very grown up. But Mummy was, to quote her: "run off her feet." I came home from school one day to find our new shop girl Lily Brown had arrived and was beginning to learn the household and shop routines.

Lily was probably sixteen years old and mature beyond her years when she came to work for the Saunders. She came from a large hard-working family, and had learned to shift for herself. She had what country people call a sturdy character. She stayed with us through the next two years. Though she was a likeable and reliable helper, I didn't have the same comfortable understanding with her that I had enjoyed with Lettie.

Lily saw it as her duty to keep me in line, and I did not respond very well to this new imposition. Lettie had hardly ever corrected me, so the new regime was something of a trial for me. I found myself sparring with her verbally on more than one occasion. I learned some swear words from her. Dadda was not any help; engrossed as he was with the war, he seemed to have less time and stomach for sorting out my bibs and bobs. I was left to get on with it on my own.

I don't really know when it started, but there was an increasing undercurrent of antagonism in our household. I know that it began some time after I returned from Wembley. Mummy seemed a bit fed up with me much of the time. Even Dadda had times of impatience with me, but his scoldings seemed not that serious. I felt secure in my standing with him.

All of us seemed to be changing in rather indefinable ways. I realize, looking back, that I was becoming ever more demanding of

Dadda's time and attention, and that I was seeing Mummy in an altogether new light. I was beginning to make comparisons between my biological mother and Mummy, who had been her stand-in for the past six years. I was also beginning to exhibit some horrid behaviour. It aggravated me that Mummy allowed Lily to discipline me. When I was told to do something that I didn't want to do, I found myself answering back in a defiant way and actually goading Mummy to punish me. Mummy would never box my ears, even though she threatened to. I tested the limits of her endurance constantly. Down deep I knew I was causing problems, but I didn't seem able to control myself.

One Saturday when I "pitched a right fit," as Mummy said, her patience snapped. I had been helping Lily to clean out the bicycle shed when Gladys came to call for me. The shed had become almost unusable for parking our bikes because of the vast accumulation of junk that filled it. I had forgotten that Gladys and I were supposed to meet for Girl Guides that morning instead of the usual Saturday afternoon. I was angry with myself that I hadn't left enough time to get myself ready.

Lily and I were knee deep in old bicycle tyres, rims, and rusty mudguards when Gladys came round. I told Lily I had to leave, but that I would come back later to finish sorting and carting away the rubbish. Lily would have none of it. On Saturdays she left early to go home for the weekend, and she didn't trust me to finish the job for which she would be held responsible. At first I pleaded with her, telling her "on my honour" I would complete the job, but she wouldn't budge.

"You're not going today 'til the job's done and that's an end to it," she said with finality. "You can catch up with 'em later and no harm to anyone." With that she sent Gladys away and let me know she was in charge of the situation. I was furious. I called her an ugly name and told her what she could do with the shed and its contents.

"You're not my boss," I shouted; "I don't have to listen to you," and on and on, working up a head of steam and righteous indignation as I went.

"You keep that up, young lady," she said threateningly, "and you'll get a good dose of what for from me." I stuck my tongue out and made a rude noise at her. In two strides from the workbench where she had been standing, Lily was beside me. She pulled back her arm and boxed my ears, WHAM! I literally saw stars. No one had ever hit me like that before and I was stunned, but only for a second or two.

"Don't you come the lady with me," she said, "I won't be talked to like that from the likes of you," she huffed at me. I turned to go into the house, to find Mummy and report this monstrosity, but as I turned Mummy was right behind me. She had witnessed the whole scene. When I began to protest, she told me I deserved punishment for having such a fit, that I was to get on with the job and finish it before I got a good hiding in the bargain.

So I seethed as I worked. Lily directed my every move. I threw clutter willy-nilly into a wheelbarrow and carted it off to the rubbish bin. I worked harder and faster than I ever had before, gritting my teeth and vowing revenge on Lily at some time when she least suspected it. But I was cautious about what I said to her, knowing that she had a wicked right hand, and that she was authorized to use it on me.

When she was satisfied with the shed's appearance, she let me go. I ran up to my room, defiantly threw clothes everywhere, hurriedly washed, and changed into my Girl Guide uniform. As I passed through the Front room , Dadda was tuning the radio. He looked around as I flashed by, waiting for me to stop as I usually did for a brief hug or pat on the head. But today I passed him wordlessly, looking straight ahead. I hoped he would see how offended I was and perhaps ask me what was the matter.

It would give me just the opportunity I needed to pour out my frustration and indignation for the way I had been wronged. I had no time for tears just then, but when I did, I guessed I would be able to get lots of sympathy from him. When I turned at the doorway to catch his expression, he had already gone back to twiddling the knobs on the radio. He seemed to have forgotten my existence already. I was thoroughly incensed.

What happened next haunts me to this day. Dadda was particularly sensitive to loud, sharp noises. They hurt his head in ways I could not understand. I had always known this and tried to be respectful by always remembering to close the doors gently so as not to hurt his "wobbly head." This day in a fit of frustration and uncontrolled anger, I slammed the door as hard as I could. "There," I thought to myself, "he'll notice me now." It was a cruel thing to do, and immediately I began to feel remorse. I ran off without stopping to apologise. I would tell him I was sorry when I got back. I knew he would forgive me.

My return to Wenhaston from London the previous fall had been at first a glorious reunion with everything seemingly the same as before I left. However, it soon became obvious that changes had occurred both to me and to the Saunders during my absence. The physical changes were obvious. I was much thinner than when I had left, and I had grown several inches taller. My arms and legs seemed to be too long for my body, and none of my clothes seemed to fit right anymore. But the more subtle changes were psychological. I was becoming more aware of the world around me and of how I fitted into it. I was also beginning to form ideas and opinions of my own, rather than accepting what others said I ought to believe. It manifested itself in small ways, but nonetheless generated prickly issues that I stewed about silently. One of these small annoyances was about my name.

In Wembley I had decided that I no longer wanted to be called "Joicy," as some of my Wenhaston friends were used to calling me. I was beginning to get finicky about things like that. On my return to Wenhaston when Mummy started calling me Joicy, I was a bit put out. But because it seemed to be a way for her to express her affection for me, I didn't protest at first.

When I first got back from London, Mummy had seemed genuinely glad to have me back in the family circle. In the beginning she had asked many questions and had seemed interested, but as the months went by, I noticed a definite change in her attitude. Eventually as I chattered on and on about my family and made many allusions to the differences between city and country life, a kind of coldness crept in. Both Dadda and Mummy listened, mostly without comment. Dadda had accepted what I said with cheerful thoughtfulness, but Mummy snapped her lips closed and sniffed disdainfully. I did not quite understand her reaction.

After the first few weeks of my homecoming, Mummy seldom asked any questions or spoke about the Home or the Wembley family. Finally she said she didn't want to hear any more about any of it, and brushed off my attempts to understand why. I sensed an underlying resentment toward my other family. In fact, I was uneasy about which was my true home, Wenhaston or London. Both claimed me more or less, but to which family did I owe my greatest allegiance? I couldn't answer that. I only knew that I did not ever want to be separated from my beloved Dadda.

Letters and parcels from my mother had begun to arrive at regular intervals. Mummy had received them and handed them over to me without comment. I shared the letters with Dadda, who gave me advice about how I should answer them. He had insisted that my replies be done promptly and with good grammar. He monitored and coached the whole process. Mummy wanted no part of it, being too busy with the shop to worry about such unimportant pursuits.

The adults had agreed that now that there was a war going on, and London had evacuated as many children under twelve years of age as they could, it was logical for me to stay with the Saunders family. I had become, in a sense, an evacuee like the boys and girls from Dagenham. But I was not. I had yearned for so long to be a "real" part of the Saunders family and to bear Dadda's name that I could not separate myself completely from that ideal. Yet there was a part of me that wanted to enjoy the benefits and bonding of my newfound blood relations.

How strange it seems to me now that I did not understand the ambiguous feelings that had been going on inside of me, and were increasing in intensity in the early months of 1940. On the one hand, it was nice not to be a "Home girl" any longer. On the other hand I felt more of an orphan than I had ever felt, before I met my biological family. I struggled to find a happy medium. I had a recurring fantasy that perhaps a miracle would happen and my biological mother and Dadda would somehow be married, and we could all live together in a new harmony.

It was an absurd and hurtful daydream that I may have expressed in some form in Mummy's hearing. It's hard to recall all the details, but I'm sure she must have sensed my devious machinations. Though she was not overtly hostile, there was a definite coolness in her attitude that had not been there before.

For the moment the war provided me the best of my two worlds. I had friendly and frequent contact with my biological mother, yet I could live physically in the sheltered warmth the Saunders provided and enjoy uninterrupted friendships and activities in the village. Why suddenly did I begin to rebel against both worlds? I don't know the answer to that, but I do remember the turmoil and the aggravation my attitude caused, and the dire consequences that eventually followed.

The British Expeditionary Force had joined French forces in 1939 to block the German army from overruning France. It had been a prudent decision for our armies to engage the Germans and beat them on French soil. The news broadcasts from the fighting fronts in France and Norway now became alarming, but were tempered by the victorious reports of the Royal Navy sinking enemy ships. There was an air of hope that we had the enemy at bay. Many people thought that there would be a quick end to the war, and the world would get back to normal in short order.

Dadda didn't share this view. He listened with interest to the speeches by our Government leaders: Neville Chamberlain, the Prime Minister, Lord Beaverbrook, Minister of Aircraft Production, and Lord Halifax, the Foreign Secretary. There were a number of others. The news talk seemed to go on interminably. Dadda would call me in to listen to the King's speeches and some of the others that he thought were important for me to hear. King George's speeches were a little more palatable than some of the others, but the lengthy speeches and news reporting began to get a bit tiresome to me. Sometimes, when "the wind laid wrong," as Mummy said, the radio messages were filled with static, and barely understandable. Dadda thought they were of great interest, and struggled to hear even the most garbled messages.

Then Norway fell, and our ships and soldiers had to withdraw. Dadda said that it was a major loss to us.

A few days later, our lives were shaken to the core by the turn of events of the war in France. Belgium and Holland, France's nearest neighbours though allies, had declared their neutrality early on. We knew that only a slim body of water, the English channel, stood between France and England. If the French were defeated, it could mean that we would soon be fighting on British soil. The tension was growing intense, and war talk that had been jovial at the sinking of the *Graf Spee* was now subdued. Suddenly there was a threatening change in the tenor of the evening news. Dadda began his pacing in the middle of the day, not the usual exercising stroll he had in the evenings, but a nervous march across the carpet, head bent forward, lost to all that was going on around him in distracted thought.

On the 10th of May, 1940 the Germans marched through Belgium and Holland, violating those nations' neutrality and gaining the upper hand against our troops. Our forces were pushed to within 30 miles of Dunkirk with their backs to the sea.

We could easily hear the guns across the English Channel, booming night and day relentlessly. At the time, we couldn't make out whose artillery it was, nor could we fathom what devastation it was causing. We felt the impact of the bombardment from a considerable distance, and yet it seemed close. King Leopold capitulated, leading Belgium to surrender. It was a grave situation, but total rout of our forces was not to be. Our fighter planes from the aerodromes around us continually roared overhead to the French Front. Though we didn't know it at the time, we later learned that the Royal Air Force was responsible for holding back the enemy planes that would have wreaked havoc on our ground troops trapped at Dunkirk.

That much we knew from the BBC evening newscasts. We heard the news that Neville Chamberlain had resigned and Mr. Winston Churchill was to replace him as Prime Minister. There was great rejoicing at that one bright part of the otherwise alarming news. Dadda was well pleased, and called us all in to hear the acceptance speech on the radio. Mummy left the doors open between the shop and front hallway. Doreen Page's mum and Mrs. Goddard who had come in for groceries, followed Mummy across the hallway and into the Front room where Dadda, Lily and I were already crowded around the radio.

Mr. Churchill's speech that day was powerful and very stirring. His deep and sonorous voice quickly became the most recognizable in all of England. Though I'd sat through many speeches, sometimes squirming and bored, Churchill's were different. I sat transfixed to hear him make pronouncements about the war that day that even I, a child of eleven, could comprehend and appreciate. It was anything but boring to hear him address us with these memorable words:

> "I would say to the House, as I said to those who have joined this Government," he began in the inimitable style that was soon to become familiar to the whole world, "I have nothing to offer but blood, toil, tears and sweat. We have before us an ordeal of the most grievous kind. We have before us many, many long months of struggle and suffering. You ask: What is our policy?
>
> "I will say: It is to wage war by sea, land, and air with all our might, and with all the strength that God can give us; to wage war against a monstrous tyranny, never surpassed in the dark lamentable catalogue of human crime. That is our policy. You ask: What is our aim? I can answer in one word: Victory! Victory at all costs, victory in spite of all terror, victory however long and hard the road may be; for without victory there is no survival."

We listened eagerly. There was something captivating not only about his words, but in the halting, yet rousing way he presented them. At the end Mummy broke our awed silence. "Run and put the kettle on, Joicy," she said to me, and we'll have a cup of tea." It was Mummy's way of celebrating. She needed to bustle about a bit, especially when something unusual or exciting like this happened.

Many families, like ours, had little knowledge of where their loved ones were. We thought perhaps Lenny might be in France, which added to our anxiety. From his recent correspondence, letters that were censored and cut in ribbons, it was impossible for us to guess where he was. Our worst fear was that he was lying wounded or even dead. Though no one dared speak the words, the thoughts and fears hovered over us constantly.

The only way to endure the uncertainty was to push aside the negative thoughts and get on with daily living. I recall part of a poem Dadda and I were reading during that time. Though I cannot remember the source, I remember these lines:

> *Only be faithful, never waver, nor seek earth's favour, But rest. God knoweth what His will to be, for all his creatures, so for thee, the best.*

It comforted me to have the hope that God was watching over our lives, and that He would keep Lenny safe. When we read poems like this one, it was the closest we ever came to praying out loud at home. There were occasional whispered and silent prayers, and the dutiful prayers at meals and bedtimes, but nothing more. We understood that "real" prayers were done only in church services, led properly by a man of the cloth. In that regard, our churches were not slack in their responsibility. They lead the people faithfully to depend on God for deliverance.

The spirit and intention of the church were true, but the worship was formal and ritualistic. I can now see that through the formality there was a deep reverence for a Holy God. To put it in the vernacular, there was always a reaching UP to God through proper channels. God was "up there" somewhere, and it was our job to plead in a correct and orderly way, hoping beyond hope that He would hear us and answer favourably. There was, to my knowledge, no other way of communicating with Diety.

Our war-torn household, as our counterparts in the village and throughout the country, continued to wend its way to the church. The Vicar led us through prayers of confession and prayers of supplication to seek a merciful God who would hear from heaven and answer our cries for help. We well knew about a God who was out there, above us, watching over all of us. We did not perceive Him as a personal God who was interested in each of us as individuals, or in any way connected with our day to day existence. The message that was clearly conveyed as coming to us from heaven was to stand firm, be patient and never doubt God's mercy. Our country, in the end, would be victorious.

On the 26th day of May, 1940 the most remarkable rescue by sea the world has ever known began. It continued for the next several days and nights. "Operation Dynamo" had started only about a week before the situation became critical. The orders were given to begin gathering boats of every description. They began to assemble at Dover and Southampton as a "mosquito armada," as Churchill called it. He recalls in his memoir: "Lifeboats from liners in the London Docks, tugs from the Thames, yachts, fishing-craft, lighters, barges and pleasure boats were all called into service."

This fleet, along with many larger Royal Navy vessels, evacuated approximately 200,000 men in the most strategic and well-executed rescue operation ever attempted. We felt that we had out-witted the enemy. But our Army had been forced to leave most of their weapons behind at Dunkirk in order to escape. Churchill warned us that we should not mistake this grand manoeuvre for victory. He said, "Wars are not won by evacuations," and that it was not time to let down our guard. He spoke from Parliament with resolute determination for our nation, encouraging us not to give up the fight for our freedom. We listened with renewed hope as he intoned these now famous words:

> "Even though large tracts of Europe and many old and famous States have fallen or may fall into the grip of the Gestapo and all the odious apparatus of the Nazi rule, we shall not flag or fail. We shall go on to the end, we shall fight in France, we shall fight in the seas and oceans, we shall fight with growing confidence and growing strength in the air, we shall defend our island whatever the cost may be, we shall fight on the beaches, we shall fight on the landing-grounds, we shall fight in the fields and in the streets, we shall fight in the hills; we shall never surrender, and even if, which I do not for a moment believe, this island or a large part of it were subjugated and starving, then our Empire beyond the seas, armed and guarded by the British Fleet, would carry on the struggle, until, in God's good time, the New World, with all its power and might, steps forth to the rescue and the liberation of the Old."

In our village, life followed its familiar schedule, even in the midst of the war. On the first warm Saturday in June the village held its annual Field Day Festival on the school playing fields. There was much excitement leading up to this event every year, but this year seemed even more frenetic. It was as though the rest of us had to make a special effort to make a go of things, with our young men gone from the village. For weeks our school teams had been competing against each other in a five hundred yard relay race.

Opposing team members scrutinized the starting line. If even a toenail was over it, the race was held up until the offending foot was moved to its proper place. At the cry "Ready, steady, go," we would leap from the starting position and run like the wind to the end of the course, and touch hands with the team mate, who then ran the length back to the starting line. The two boys' and the two girls' teams competed together in the relay races, but some of the other events were divided by sex. While the boys competed against each other in the "long jump" competition, the girls competed against each other for the "high jump." Winners were given buttons to show how they placed, which we wore proudly on our collars for the remainder of the year.

The weather for the Field Day Festival was balmy, with only a small breeze to push the feathery clouds along. The sunshine warmed us, and it seemed good not to have to wear our jackets. The women had set up tables for handcrafts, knitted jumpers, hooked rugs, crocheted doilies and pots of homemade jam and honey to be judged and sold. The Wall's ice-cream man brought his square bicycle cart and parked it at the side of the field, next to the lemonade stand. The field was packed with people, the ladies wearing their best hats and the men dressed in their good clothes.

Annual Field Festival

We older girls wore our running clothes early in the morning so that we could participate in the school sports that would establish our team standings for the following year. When the foot races and the older children's meets were over, we changed into our Sunday cotton dresses for the rest of the day. Some of us then helped with the younger children's sports program as their parents looked on.

The day was filled with activities for all ages throughout the day, but none quite as strenuous as the official competitions.

Gladys and I were partners for the three-legged race, in which we tied our ankles together and in unison raced for a prize. We then competed against each other in the sack race, in which we hopped in a burlap bag as hard as we could go. The grown-ups grouped themselves around us for each new event, and some of them held the ribbons to mark the finish lines.

The "egg and spoon race" that required us to race holding an egg on a spoon was delightful. Our eggs were made of some hard ceramic material that didn't break when they fell on the grass. Even though we lost time picking them up, we still had a chance to place first, second or third in the race. The grown-ups loved to tell us that when they were our age, they had to use real eggs, which meant that when they dropped them, they were out of the race.

Wenhaston "Dig for Victory" 1940

Only a few weeks after the Festival, the boys at school were encouraged to be part of a "Dig for Victory" campaign. Some of the evacuees joined the village boys in this worthwhile effort. There were several community vegetable plots scattered around the village, but most of them were located down the slope on Front

Street, opposite Joy Youngs' house. Most of the dads and young men who had once tended these plots were now away, either in the Forces or working at munitions factories.

The boys worked hard to clean away the stubble and vines left over from the prior year's crop. Then they turned the soil with their spades. They planted potatoes, runner beans, peas, cabbage and cauliflower, and watched carefully over the next weeks to see the fruit of their labour. Some of the city children learned much about farm life during that experiment. All of them were rightly proud of their accomplishment, as the crop was shared round the village.

The skies high above our village had been festooned with barrage balloons, a constant, silent reminder of the war. We were on the playing field one afternoon when the siren sounded the alert. A barrage balloon had torn loose from its mooring and was almost over us. We were quickly herded into the classroom and made to get on the floor under our desks in case it crashed into the school building or the electric wires along the street. The All Clear came eventually, and hours later we learned the fate of the errant balloon. It had drifted several miles until finally its mooring wire had become entangled in a tree near Wrentham. Airmen from a nearby airfield were able to get it back to its proper position, undamaged.

With so many balloons in the sky around us, it was hard to see how any aircraft, enemy or friendly, could manage to manoeuvre its way through such a barrier. But some planes did get through. Most of the German planes had no reason to bomb the coastal villages, devoid as we were of munitions factories and airdromes. Wenhaston was occasionally on the way for enemy planes headed for more important places such as an RAF aerodrome or Birmingham, and again as they were leaving after their deadly work was finished.

The enemy planes that were deflected away from their targets without using their bombs were the ones that were the most frightening. Before they left our coast, they would sometimes drop their bombs indiscriminately, presumably so they didn't feel their mission had been a total loss. Some said it was because it was dangerous for them to land their planes in their home airport with a load of bombs. Others contended that the enemy had lost his way and thought he was somewhere other than over an inconsequential village when he let his load loose. In any event, we awoke one morning to huge blasts that shattered windows and rocked the very foundations of our home.

It was barely daylight that morning when we were startled from our beds by the sound of the second siren blasting. Almost before the siren stopped, the bombs rained down on our village. By the time we'd roused from our beds, men from the Home Guard were running and shouting in the streets outside the shop. The men were shouting "Stay inside" and "Take cover" into each doorway as they made their way down the road toward the *Compass*. Dadda had pulled on his old maroon robe, and Mummy hurried into my room with her hair in disarray. A fresh breeze with a hint of acrid smoke caught my nose as I sat up and pulled the covers tightly around myself. Dadda's torch light first fell on me, and then as he panned the far end of the room, it showed shards of glass littered about the floor. Some pieces still hung at crazy angles, attached to the sticky paper on the window panes.

We could see the outline of the crater through the window and the torn curtain, in the pale light of dawn. From this distance it looked to be an enormous gaping hole in the middle of the road just past the Newbys', close to the *Compass*. The large oak tree that had been on the bank opposite the back entrance to the pub was completely gone. We speculated about how the *Compass* had fared, as there was no way to be able to see it clearly from my bedroom. Mummy glanced at the broken window and came over beside the bed to look things over. There were no fragments of glass on the counterpane or even around the washstand. The sticky paper crosses we'd put on the panes had stopped the glass from flying across the room.

When Mummy was satisfied that I wasn't hurt, she hurried off to get decently dressed. If she were needed, she didn't want to be caught in her nightdress. Mummy thought it was important to be properly dressed to face a crisis. From that day until the end of the war, to my knowledge, she never took off all her underclothes when she went to bed. She removed her long pink corset with its wire stays nightly, but kept her petticoat and stockings on until her regular mid-morning bath.

After she left the room, Dadda sat down on the side of my bed. In the pale morning light his face looked stricken and very gray. His good hand was visibly trembling, and his breath came in short quick gasps. He was not wearing his prosthesis, and the loose sleeve over the nub of his arm quivered ever so slightly. I sensed a strange air of unguarded apprehension, of cringing fear that suddenly seemed to blanket the small room.

I had never before thought of Dadda as being afraid or upset about anything, but the sight of him at this moment sent a qualmish shiver through the whole length of me. He must have become aware of my thoughts, because he quickly gathered himself together and smiled at me.

"Well," he said a bit hesitantly, "the old wobbly head doesn't like to get up so abruptly." Then as he got up to leave, he pointed toward the window. "The Jerries have gone now. We'll be safe from them for today. Mind the glass when you get up, won't you, Beauty?" He kissed my forehead on his way out the door.

We had heard the engines of our own planes roaring over the rooftops, and marveled at how quickly they had sprung to action. We were in an agony of suspense for several hours, wondering where the other bombs had landed, who if anyone had been killed, and what damage they had done. Finally, the all clear sounded, and we were allowed out of our homes to survey the bomb damage. My window and the kitchen window below it were the only two that faced the crater. Mine was the only one damaged. It made me feel rather important to have had my window shattered by a bomb. As the day wore on and I told the story over again to my friends, I basked in the attention it afforded me. But it was short-lived. The real excitement was inspecting the craters that were scattered over the Wenhaston countryside.

Mummy put the kettle on for tea and pulled up the window shade on the shop door. She was preparing to greet those who needed a cup of tea after their early morning rout. Mr. Woolnough was one of the first to come in. He was grateful for the tea Mummy offered him. He was disheveled and tired, but full of pride and wonderment at the way things had worked out.

"Only one plane it was, with a stick of four bombs dropped," he said, gulping his tea. "But no one hurt," he said cheerily, "and never hit one building neither." He pushed back his Warden's cap in a self-assured way, revealing his matted grey hair beneath, and wiped his handkerchief across his forehead.

"The *Compass* has a bit o' damage, but everyone safe inside. There's another crater behind the Napthines' house that's broken all the windows and thrown muck all over their house, but nobody hurt," he said with a broad smile.

The other men began coming in the shop now, and there was much good-natured banter between them. Mummy supplied plenty of hot, steaming tea. They were glad for the Jerry's miscalculations, if that indeed is what it was. They felt somehow that they had gained a victory over the enemy, simply because there was no real harm done except for the mess. "Besides," someone remarked airily, "Our boys shot his arse off before he reached the channel. There's one less Jerry going home to Germany today."

Walter's dad "Ollie" Wilson came in dressed as usual in his overalls and wellingtons. He was hastening to the farm to get the cows in for milking. He had already been around to survey the bomb craters, and had stopped in to buy a packet of Woodbines before he went off to work. We found out from the men's talk that the bombs had struck in a straight line starting from the one at the *Compass*, then the next behind the Council Houses, and the remainder strung across the Black Heath and the fields beyond the pub on Star Hill. Each bomb had left a tremendous hole and scattered shrapnel in the surrounding area. The children were warned not to jump down in the craters for fear of sharp pieces of metal that would be dangerous.

In the following week, crews of men with shovels filled in the gaping hole beside the *Compass* and lorries full of stone and tar lumbered past the shop and down Back Road past the Newbys' house. The Newbys' windows were repaired quickly, as was mine. Soon we could once again ride our bikes down the road past the spot where the first bomb had hit, and except for getting fresh tar on our shoes and socks, there were few reminders of our first attack.

There were several dogfights over Wenhaston, but never another bombing in our village throughout the remainder of the war. Our Spitfires and Hurricanes defending the coastline would come in swarms against the enemy planes as they lumbered in. An enemy plane shot down in a field somewhere was an absolute delight for the children. The news of the downed plane's location would spread round the village like wildfire. We would dash off on our bicycles to see the wreckage, getting as near as we were allowed.

The most perplexing part of the war for Dadda was providing us with an air-raid shelter. Uncle Aubrey had tried to pin him down to a solution during the Christmas holidays, but he had been reluctant to discuss details at that point. We understood why he didn't want to get one of those tiny little rounded shelters that were sprouting up in everyone's back garden. One of those might be useful for some of us, but for him it would present untold problems. The "oversize dog kennels" as he called them could only be entered by getting down on all fours and crawling in, something that was impossible for him.

Remodeled Bomb Shelter

Finding the right solution was difficult. Though the house had a solid foundation, it did not have a cellar or even room enough under the house for us to crawl into. Reason told him we were in a relatively safe part of the country, but the bomb that had landed at the *Compass* had made him conscious of how vulnerable we were. I know he must have given the subject much thought before he decided on a plan of action. He would put the large sturdy section of the bird shed underground, fortify its sides and roof, bank it with soil, and stock it with emergency provisions.

It was the perfect plan. It would have an upright doorway with a few steps leading down. There would be room for several cots and a large chair for Dadda. He laid out the plans on the kitchen table, consulted with Mummy and then with workmen. In a matter of weeks the project was underway.

It seemed very sad to me to sell and ship all the birds except for one prize canary which came into the house. But Dadda said it was "for the best" and the birds were going to good homes. None of them would be going to the Welsh coal mines, but were going to reputable places where they would have the best of care. It was a heartening thought that none of them would be used to detect the gas in the mines. But Dadda had said earlier on that it was a "noble calling" for canaries to be used to save the lives of coal miners. I think that now, perhaps he couldn't bear the thought of any of them being sent out to die.

He also sold all the equipment, cages and carrying cases. The bird shed rooms were strangely bare. Workmen came to tear down the open carriage shed, that fine place next to the bird shed where I had given many tea parties and put on several impromptu dramatic plays with my friends. I was sorry to see it go. Next the workmen divided the bird shed, removing the L-shaped portion from the main and larger section. After they'd carried away this smaller part, they moved the other portion over to the place where the old carriage shed had been. It sat at a crazy angle while they dug a tremendous hole at its original site. It seemed odd to watch it happening.

After school each day, some of my friends would come and inspect the progress. Dadda would stand at the kitchen window and watch. He was having a difficult time controlling Fleet. The dog was young and very energetic, and thought the workmen had come just to play with him. Whenever he could, Fleet would run round the garden barking and wagging his tail, getting in their way. If someone didn't stop him, he was soon out the garden gate taking himself for a good old run. I'd be sent to find him and bring him home again.

The wire-netting fence was torn down and our lively dog saw this as his opportunity to run free. If he couldn't get past the men and out the gate, he found a way to jump over the brick wall. Once in the street, Fleet would then stand outside the gate wagging to be let in, obviously so he could play with the men digging the enormous hole for the bird shed. The men carried on working despite the dog's antics.

Once the hole was big enough and the bird shed was put underground, the men fortified its roof and outer shell, and mounded soil over it. Inside, they fitted shelves, and we carted in cots, the Primus stove from the bicycle shed, and lots of tinned food. It was dark inside the shelter, and there was a mystical air about the bird shed now that it was underground. There was a faint and lingering smell of the birds that was almost overpowered by the musty smell of damp earth. But it was the cloying silence within its dank walls that was most off-putting for me.

On the outside the strangeness was sharply defined. From the garden door, which was an extension of the kitchen wall, the bird shed had blocked the view of the side gate, the Bramfield road and the field across the road. Now there was a tremendous empty place that was grayish brown and starkly bare, with unsightly bits of roots and small rocks littering the landscape. The tall sunflowers and the happy windows they covered were gone. The earth looked bleak and rather untidy, a mound of dirt stretching nakedly from the garden door to the gate. The ugly expanse was broken only by the hump over the entrance door. The same three steps that once led up to the bird shed doorway and opened to the light, now led downward to the darkened space beneath the surface.

Mummy kept us busy stocking the shelter with necessary items, lamps, jars of water and tins of sardines and meat paste, that had to be rotated at regular intervals to keep the items fresh. Everything that went down there eventually acquired the same dank odor of the shelter itself.

For the next few weeks, Dadda's nervous pacing was somewhat abated. But the wear and tear of apprehension was beginning to show in many small ways. His regular routine had been disrupted now that he no longer had his beloved birds to attend. His time and energy were consumed by the war reports. His anxiety about Lenny's welfare was an unspoken agony for him. His face seemed perpetually worried and haggard, and his normally cheerful disposition seemed forced. Mummy, who now more than ever needed his support and expertise, struggled to get his attention almost as much as I did. It was the worst time of all to have another disaster happen.

This time the calamity came in the guise of helping with the war effort and the results were totally unexpected. The country had a great need for scrap iron and was collecting it from any available source. Across the lane from our house on the shop side there was an old forge that had lots of this scrap. Men came early one morning and began loading huge lorries with rusty looking stuff, shouting and banging about with gusto. We thought they must surely be finished after the second day, and all would be quiet again. Dadda was having some difficulty with the noise, but seemed to be coping rather well under the circumstances. We were unprepared for the next and noisiest phase of their scrap gathering.

The Saunders had not realized that some years in the past, a huge iron tank of some sort had been buried underground. It was located right next to our house, along the wall between the pump house door and the shop wall. The job foreman came into the shop to tell us they would be digging it up, then cutting it in pieces and taking it away. He apologized in advance for any nuisance this would cause us, and promised to have the job done as quickly as possible. Mummy warned him that Dadda had shrapnel lodged in his head that made him vulnerable to loud, sharp noises, and asked if they could possibly by-pass this one piece of scrap. But the foreman said they had their orders and had to go ahead with the job.

In the house the noise of digging and the lumping of their machines now became horrific. Nowhere in the house was there any escape from it. Mummy and Lily persevered in the shop, but had a difficult time making themselves heard above the din. They bore up fairly well. Dadda, on the other hand, was not faring well at all. His head hurt him terribly, and he had no place to go to get away from the noise. The bird shed under normal circumstances would have been his place of refuge, and even now, underground, it provided some sanctuary for him. When I came home from school one day at lunchtime, I found him down in the shelter with the door open, sitting in the chair, trying to read by the light of an oil lamp.

When the workmen took a break, he came back into the house for a respite. I noticed his face looked even more drawn than usual, but he said he'd grit his teeth and he'd be able to endure it if they would just get a move on and finish the job. Unfortunately, none of us had counted on things getting worse. But they did. When the workman began using pneumatic drills to cut the tank in pieces, it was too much for Dadda to tolerate. Even in the bird shed bomb shelter, he suffered the effects of not just the noise but the vibrations of the hammering and thudding of heavy equipment. Mummy and Lily had to help him into the house and upstairs to the bedroom when the work finished that day. I was sent to get the District Nurse, who came immediately.

After only a few minutes in the bedroom, the nurse came out and spoke to Mummy. She said she was going to fetch the doctor for him. Meanwhile Dadda was to be kept perfectly still and quiet. We crept around the house making the dinner, and we found ourselves whispering to each other as though it would make a difference. Our resident soldiers came in just as Mummy was closing the shop and helped us put the blackout curtains in place before sitting down to the evening meal. We were doing the washing up when the doctor arrived. He and Mummy went up the stairs while we waited below in anxious silence.

The doctor told Mummy that Dadda had an internal hemorrhage around the old war wound in his scalp, and that they would have to relieve the pressure somehow. I don't know what the treatment was or how it was administered, but when the doctor and the nurse finally came downstairs, they looked disheveled and very tired. We were to give Dadda complete rest and quiet for the next few days. Mummy said she thought the scrap iron workers had finished the job, but the doctor left a paper that would order them to stop work immediately, should they begin again.

Thankfully, they did not return. Their work must have been finished. The doctor came twice a day for the next week, and each day we were encouraged by the progress he reported. At week's end, I was allowed in to see Dadda. The nurse, with her helper, had been in earlier to see to him. When Mummy and I went in, he was awake, with a fresh bandage round his head. Mummy's bed was on the other side of his, with the foot board adjacent to the windowsill. All of her pillows as well as her bolster were gone. They were propping Dadda who looked almost lost in the white wilderness in his half-sitting position. We couldn't sit on the side of his bed for fear we would upset his balance, so we went round to sit on Mummy's bed, where he could see us without having to move his head.

We didn't stay long, but before I left he asked me to come and read to him the next day. I was happy to be able to do that. Every chance I got for the next several days, I was beside him on Mummy's bed, sprawled out with whatever book, magazine or newspaper he wanted me to read to him. By the following week he was coming downstairs and taking up his favourite position in the kitchen chair, happy to have his pipe again and his meals sitting at the table with his family around him.

Uncle Aubrey and Carly-luv came for a short visit during that summer holiday from school. I went to meet them from the train in Halesworth and helped them with their cases and parcels. Dadda's birthday fell on the fourteenth of July, and mine fell on the thirtieth. It was natural that we should celebrate the birthdays together in the middle of the month, and it was doubly delightful to have Uncle Aubrey and Carly-luv to celebrate with us.

As usual he had brought us wonderful gifts, books, jigsaw puzzles and some trick chains that kept us guessing and working for hours. First we worked to get them undone and then to put them back together again. They defied all attempts at being separated until he showed us how to do it. Even after that, the puzzle remained a challenge. One of his many gifts to me that year was a matchbox snake. When the top of the box was pushed back, a long, green paper snake jumped out. I wore it out making it jump out at Fleet, who of course wanted to capture it and eat it.

Only a few days after their visit, we received word about Lenny. An official looking telegram came that stopped our hearts. After stating his name and serial number, it said only: "Missing in action." We were devastated by the news, and Mummy closed the shop early. That evening Lenny's wife Joyce, her mother and her brother Derek all came to the house to sit quietly in the Front room to try to make sense of things. Our soldiers came in that evening to a subdued and grieving household. Derek, who was getting ready to leave for the service, suggested that "missing" very often meant there'd been a "cock-up," that some official had made a mistake in the count. Our soldiers concurred with him, citing cases they'd heard of others declared missing who were suddenly "found" again.

It helped to ease the tension somewhat to have this possibility before us. None of us ate very much, and Dadda did his nightly pacing in utter silence, not stopping to tap the barometer or check the clock on the mantel. He had not been recovered from the scrap iron injury very long, and was slowly regaining his full strength. He did stop once to cover Lucy the canary's cage with its wrap-around curtains. He retired to bed early, which had become his practice since the hemorrhage ordeal. Mummy let me go in to say good-night, and when I leaned over to kiss his cheek, I realized from the wetness on his cheek that he was crying.

That night I prayed for Lenny. I asked God to please take care of him and send him home to us. I didn't think God would respond to me. I hadn't any right really to pray in such a bold fashion. But I thought I'd ask anyway.

Not many days afterwards, we received several letters from Lenny. It was obvious from their dates that they had been written at different times and that they had been a long time in transit, but it was impossible to tell where they had originated. We knew he was somewhere overseas, but we had no idea where, and there were no intelligible clues in the letters themselves. Each letter had been censored thoroughly, and great chunks were cut from the paper. Whole sentences and sometimes whole paragraphs were missing. The letters gave us renewed hope that there had been some "cock-up" as Derek had suggested. Of course, I hoped my prayers had been heard and answered. All we could do now was to wait and see.

Chapter 13

There Let the Plover Cry

Summer was over more quickly than usual in 1940. The Germans were bombing England with increasing fury. The RAF was fighting back tenaciously. The beaches at Lowestoft, Yarmouth, Felistowe, Dunwich and all along the East Coast were mined. Our beloved beach at Southwold was a dangerous place to be. Several concrete bunkers had been built at intervals along the retaining wall. Large wooden barriers that looked like overturned sawhorses had been erected and entwined with barbed wire all along the shore line. Sinister notices were posted up and down the beach and especially at all the steps warning trespassers of danger.

The colourful huts used for changing our clothes, the deck chairs, the sun shades, the fishing boats, and even the rubbish bins were all gone. The sand, bristling with barriers and concrete bunkers, looked forlorn. The Sunday School outings to the seaside were suspended for the duration, but groups of two or three of us children could not resist forays there by bicycle during the heat of the summer.

By intuition and familiarity we gathered together on several occasions that summer, and made our way to the seaside, with sandwiches and flasks in our bicycle saddlebags. My friend Owen came from Halesworth and met our Wenhaston group at the *Queen's Head* in Blyford, and we rode the rest of the seven mile journey to Southwold. Though we couldn't walk down the steps onto the sand, we could walk along the almost deserted Promenade, hang over the railing and gaze out at the ocean.

The sea was never still. The restless waves showed different colours as they curled over and crashed on the shoreline, just as they had always done. Though the beach was barricaded and drastically changed, the sea was still there, its colours and churning ever changing, but yet in essence unchanged, holding the same fascination for us as it always had. In the distance we could often glimpse Navy ships moving slowly along the horizon, and we had a sense of uneasy excitement in their presence.

Autumn came swiftly and with bluster. The north wind swirled the dry leaves across Back Road on our way to school. Their untidy eddies seemed to express the strange restlessness that had settled on all of us. It was a new and disturbing sensation that seemed to permeate the very air around us. We could not identify the cause as any one thing in particular. It was a feeling of general discontent that came from many sources.

For one thing, the school was crowded with evacuees, and classes that had once been extremely well ordered were now in disarray. A temporary structure had been built to divide Mr. Sangster's classroom into two areas. The "upper form" classroom for the eleven and over age group was a very large room with windows on two sides. Sturdy steam radiators that sometimes to our delight, hissed and clanged during class, were under the high windows. Two thirds of the room was normally filled with our desks, Mr. Sangster's lectern where he stood most of the day, his table-sized desk, bookcases, and two large easel blackboards. The other third of the room was a little-used section that had functioned as an indoor game area and as a practice place for school plays and after-school meetings.

The evacuees far out-numbered our original class, so it was practical for them to occupy the larger of the two areas. The new room division was made so that the smaller space with one window, now cleared of the piano and an accumulation of clutter, could function as the upper form classroom. Our entire class, consisting of about twenty-two children plus a few of the older evacuees, was packed into this newly created space. Most of the evacuees, along with their effusive teacher Mr. Clark, were crowded into the larger area.

In the interest of space, we did not use our desks. Wooden chairs were brought in from the Sunday School building. The back portion of each chair had a built-in book rack that served as limited storage space for our inkwells and excess books. To relieve the tedium, we could surreptitiously jiggle our seats and with some luck cause the inkwell of the student behind us to tip over, or at least slosh about a bit. Mr. Sangster would pause in his lecture and rap on his desk with his thin cane when there was any disturbance. Talking, chewing or even sudden movement were strictly forbidden.

We dreaded to see him begin to walk toward us, cane in hand, for some infraction of discipline. We knew his punishment was swift, and none of us would risk anything too outlandish. A slight, almost undetectable skirmish was all any of us dared. Air raid drills were fairly frequent, and these also provided a break in the routine. In one way the new order and the crowding seemed something of an adventure. We did not realize that in other ways it was adding tension and anxiety to our daily lives.

At home, my life was also taking a disturbing new turn. I was becoming estranged from Dadda in ways I could not grasp. My normal bedtime routine had been to wash and change into my nightdress in the pantry just off the kitchen, kiss every one good-night ten times and scoot up the stairs with my hot water bottles. When the soldiers came to share our house, I had to be more circumspect, being careful to keep my bedroom door closed. I understood the reasons for that, and complied readily.

I didn't understand Dadda's growing reluctance to let me have physical contact with him. Increasingly he rebuffed my excessive hugs and waved away my kisses. I knew I was now too big to sit on his lap, but I still loved to sit at his feet with my head resting against his knee when we read together. These times of intimacy were becoming less frequent. More often than not, Dadda would ask me to sit on a chair beside his, telling me I was getting too big to sit on the floor. This was another in a series of seemingly insignificant details that gave me a sense that he disapproved of me.

He also rebuffed my overt attempts to fondle his arm while we strapped on his prosthesis. In earlier days when I was a small child, Dadda had rolled up his shirtsleeve on one or two occasions and allowed me to see his injured arm. The sight of it fascinated me. The bone had been cut just below the elbow and the skin folded over envelope fashion on the stub end. As young and unlearned as I was, my intuition told me that he thought of his injury as a deformity: unnatural and rather ugly. Partly because I was curious to touch it and partly to show him affection, I held the white stub lovingly against my face. It felt soft and smelled faintly of his special soap. I called it my little teddy and tried to cuddle and kiss it, but he would always laugh and pull away, telling me to run and fetch this or that for him.

He sometimes let me help him tuck his sleeve neatly around the bottom of the stub, so that the prosthesis would sit more comfortably. Though he could, and most often did fit the heavy artificial arm in place himself by a series of manoeuvres, it must have been a boon to him to be assisted. I loved to help him and often begged for the chance. He was always slightly wary of my profuse affection and exuberance, but now, without any explanation, he suddenly was becoming almost hostile to my overtures.

In retrospect, I see clearly how my little-girl maudlin clinging to him was no longer appropriate. But it was all I had ever known. A secret fear was beginning to haunt me that growing up was something undesirable. If I grew beyond childhood, I might lose Dadda's affection. I wanted to stay a child forever, and never let go of the safe haven of his loving embrace. More than ever, at this stage in my life, I needed his attention and his counsel. But there was a wall developing between us that was indefinable and almost impenetrable. I longed for the early days when I was his whole world. Then I could freely fly into his arms and be held and kissed affectionately, with no tension or discernible anxieties, only joy and laughter.

If only he had been able to explain to me in a reasonable way that he could see me developing and changing physically, it might have been easier for both of us. But in the straight-laced world in which we lived, it would have been an impossibility for him to have held a discussion of sexual matters with me. He maintained a friendly but more distant bearing, and I was left to sort out the whys and wherefores on my own. I truly believe, looking back, that he hadn't a clue to the emotional storm that I was experiencing, nor the havoc his circumspect behaviour was creating for me. I'm inclined to believe that he left the difficult subject of explaining my physiological maturation to Mummy, who was of all people the ultimate example of prim and proper. There were certain subjects that were taboo for her.

Sex was definitely at the top of the taboo list, but certain diseases such as tuberculosis and cancer ran a close second. In Wenhaston, at least in shop conversations, cancer was a disease only touched on lightly, never openly discussed. It was a foregone conclusion that anyone who had it was ashamed to speak about it. Pregnancy was well hidden, and during the final months, expectant mothers weren't seen either at church or in the shops if it could be avoided. Women who were pregnant and married were respectfully said to be in the "family way" and the women nodded knowingly to each other in a kind of comradely fashion. Nearly everybody shunned girls who were pregnant and not married, and talked about them in shocked whispers. It was no wonder I was totally ignorant and somewhat appalled by my changing situation.

There were times when I appealed to Mummy to help me to understand my constant frustration and discontent. But my attempts were clumsy and may have been construed by her as being crass and unladylike. Mummy was stoically distant and unreachable. I well knew that she was busier than ever trying to cope with new government regulations, ration books, and the beginning food shortages. But her attitude toward me had changed noticeably since my return from London. There was a sharpness to her tone that had not been there earlier. I had the vague feeling that I was doing something to displease her, but I wasn't sure what it was. My own inconsistent behaviour challenged her patience. I had fits of temper and argued over simple instructions in a way I had never done before.

Physically and mentally I was becoming a study in contrasts. Some days would find me listless, quiet and disconcertingly sleepy. Other days I was energetic, boisterous and unabashedly rude and defiant. There were times when I didn't recognize myself. Sometimes I felt totally exhausted all day long. When I arrived home from school, I wanted to find a comfortable place to curl up and sleep. Getting up in the mornings began to be a chore, and often before the evening meal was over, I was ready for bed. It appeared to be an acute attack of laziness, at least that's what Mummy called it.

Mummy was put out with me. I was not pulling my weight in the shop, and I knew it, but I had no reasonable excuse for being so sluggish. In an impatient gesture and against my wishes, Mummy took me to see the doctor one morning. We sat in the Surgery waiting room while I fidgeted and fretted. I didn't feel sick, just tired. Therefore, I reasoned, I didn't need a doctor.

The doctor's diagnosis was that I was anemic and was suffering from a common malady known as sleeping sickness. He gave me an evil tasting tonic, a mixture of cod liver oil and honey, I think, and told Mummy not to worry that it would soon run its course. He was right, too. Whether it was the medicine he gave me or not, I don't know. The physical lethargy soon left me, but the moody disposition lingered on.

It was in late October when a strange combination of events brought all of us to the brink of disaster. I had been indignantly vying with Lily about whose responsibility it was to do some task. Lily never minced words. A hard worker herself, she expected nothing less than prompt obedience from me, whom she considered her underling. But I decided to be stubborn and answered back with a cheeky rejoinder. It was the wrong thing to do. Before I knew what was happening we had a major war of words flying between us.

We were in the back part of the shop where the cheese was kept, and there were customers waiting to be served at the front counter. As she had been doing more and more frequently of late, Mummy stepped in to sort things out between us. Reason told me that all I had to do was close my mouth and get on with the job at hand and this incident would pass. But my foolhardy head wasn't listening to reason. When I began to protest loudly about the injustice being done to me, Mummy tried to warn me. When I continued to shout abusively, she ordered me out of the shop.

Walter Wilson's mother was in the shop with Julia Ethridge's mother and two other ladies. They stopped talking to each other and made a path for me to run out the door. The bell jangled horribly as in my haste I tore the door open and as swiftly closed it with a bang. It hurt my pride to be scolded in front of witnesses, especially since I thought I heard a muffled giggle as I raced by them. I was in "a right good huff" as the Suffolk natives would put it. I stood against the shop wall in a terrible black mood, muttering unkind epithets to no one in particular. I was feeling miserable, and was not sure what my next step should be.

Mrs. Wilson came out of the shop and put her string bag with its contents in her bicycle basket. I didn't want to face her, so I looked down at the ground and kicked sullenly at the loose dirt.

"You should be ashamed of yourself," she said. "A big girl like you making such a fuss."

"Lily started it," I said defensively, hoping she'd be a bit sympathetic. But Florrie Wilson was not the type to be taken in by familiar excuses. She tossed her head and gripped the handlebars of her bike to turn it toward the gate. She looked straight at me and clucked her tongue.

"You should be ashamed of yourself," she repeated. Her eyes snapped and her head bobbed to emphasize how strongly she felt about my misbehaviour. "If you were mine, you'd get a good clout and no mistake," she continued. She went on in this vein, castigating me for being ungrateful for all the kindness the Saunders had shown me, and letting me know I was letting them down at a time when they needed my help.

Ordinarily I would have felt justifiably chastised and accepted her strong words as my due. She was, after all, someone I liked and respected, and I was used to being reprimanded mildly by her. But in my current unhinged temperamental state, I reacted without thinking. Her words had cut and wounded me deeply. I shouted a popular swear word at her retreating back. Without so much as a glance to see her shocked expression, I ran full speed round the corner of the house, through the pump door and into the kitchen.

Dadda was sitting in his chair reading when I burst into the kitchen. He looked up in surprise as I stormed in and slammed the door behind me. He winced from the noise of the slamming door, but said nothing. Fleet moved out from under the table and wagged his long, thin tail. It thumped against the table leg as he looked expectantly at me.

"He'd like to go for a run," Dadda said gently. Then, looking at the dog, he reached out his good hand and stroked the sleek head. Fleet snuffled Dadda's hand with his wet nose then bounced over to where I stood and excitedly began to dance around me. His leash hung on a peg by the door and I reached up to take it down.

In the next split second something like a thundercloud settled over me. Suddenly I was jealous of the dog and I was angry with Dadda. I wanted to lash out at the whole world. I don't know what possessed me, but I was furious at both of them. In one swift spiteful movement I took the leash and whacked the dog with it.

"Damn dog," I said belligerently. "I hate you, I hate you," It was as though a dam had burst inside me. I began to thrash the dog unmercifully. I couldn't control myself. I was screaming now, yelling hateful, abusive words. It made no sense whatsoever. The dog yelped and at first crouched down at my feet, then bounded to safety under the kitchen table. Dadda was appalled at my outburst and started up from his chair with his hand outstretched to snatch the leash away from me.

"Stop it," he shouted at me. "Stop it this instant. How dare you be so cruel?" His face was vivid red and his eyes looked wild. As he lurched toward me, he lost his balance and stumbled against the table. Until this moment, I had never seen Dadda angry, but now I saw him enraged and ready to strike me. I was shocked at my own behaviour, but once started down this path of venting my fury, I couldn't switch it off. I was beside myself. I started screaming at Dadda who put his good hand up to his head, trying to shield himself from the onslaught. I called him ugly names and accused him of untold injustices. I told him over and over that I wished he were dead. On and on I ranted.

Dadda sank down into his chair and I had a horrible glimpse of him as a weak and helpless old man. The vision terrified me. I wrenched open the door and began to run as hard as I could, through the gate and up the Bramfield road as fast as my legs could carry me. I kept running, past Gwinny's house, down the lane and into the woods where the Christmas trees grew. I threw myself against a fallen tree and screamed my heart out.

I don't know how long I stayed there, alternately crying and beating my fists into the rotting bark, but finally I ran out of steam. It had begun to get dark and I realized it was cold and damp in the woods. I had run out of the house without my coat and I had been wallowing about on the ground for hours. I was wet and disheveled. When I sat still I could hear creatures rustling among the wet leaves. Their scratching made me feel uncomfortable and a bit frightened.

I didn't have the slightest idea what to do next. It must be long after supper time, and I was getting desperately hungry. I toyed briefly with the possibility of spending the night in the woods so that our household would have the added benefit of worrying about my safety. Then at last my better judgment took over. I reasoned that it was better to go home and face the music and get it over with. I would tell Dadda I was sorry, and he would forgive me. Mummy would punish me and life would be restored to normal. As I walked home, I planned my apology strategy. I didn't want to be too humble, but on the other hand I needed to make a good excuse for acting so irrationally. I would make up to Fleet by taking him for an extra long run tomorrow, and everything would be as it was again. Yet I could not shake the gnawing fear inside me that nothing would ever be normal again.

Lily was sitting beside the cleared dinner table when I arrived home. She reprimanded me sharply for my appearance. She said I looked like I'd been dragged through a hedge backwards. She saw my questioning look toward Dadda's empty chair.

"He's gone up early," she said brusquely, "and so's Ma'am." Though she chided and fussed, telling me to get off my wet things and get washed, her natural acceptance of me as a normally naughty girl somehow helped restore my balance. There was a lovely fire burning in the kitchen, and a saucepan off to the side gave me hope there was still some food available. Though Lily continued to berate me, telling me I needed a good hiding, she nonetheless helped me get washed and into a clean nightdress. Something told me she had saved the mashed potatoes just for me. It made me look at her in a new light. I gulped down the food she gave me, and slunk upstairs to my bed. With a twinge of regret I realized Dadda would not come in to see me, to touch my forehead or murmur "goodnight Beauty."

For once I was glad Dadda was not up when I left for school the next morning. I did not really want to face him just yet. I could smell porridge cooking as I came down the stairs. It was a cold morning and the porridge smelled wonderfully warm and inviting. Lily had taken the dog out early and was now gone to Miss Danford's for water. Mummy was bent over the stove when I entered the kitchen.

"Well," she said, straightening herself and facing me. "What do you have to say for yourself, Moor Charlotte?" she said. The name was meant as a derogatory term and her voice dripped with nasty sarcasm. I stood, not daring to speak lest I said the wrong thing. I wished with all my heart I could just blurt out that I was sorry for my awful behaviour and ask for forgiveness. I was trying hard to think of the right words.

While I hesitated, she caught her breath then began the longest diatribe I had ever heard from her. She let me know in no uncertain terms I had crossed the line of her good will. I was untrustworthy, impertinent, ungrateful and rude. She let me know I was a great disappointment to her and Dadda; that I was selfish, spoiled, and rotten to the core. Part of her anger was directed at my mother, who at one point she called a slut. She told me I would never amount to anything and that I was destined to grow up to be just like my boorish family.

Just as she was winding down, Lily came in with the water. It broke the spell somewhat and I managed, with Mummy's prompting, to say that I was sorry. I promised never to kick up such a fuss again. I truly was filled with remorse, but I didn't know how to express it. I wished with all my heart she had asked Lily to "clout" me. Her words cut deeper and stayed with me longer than the worst whipping ever could have.

In the weeks following the temper storm, I was careful to behave myself with the utmost decorum. I walked the dog, fetched the water, ran errands and generally made myself useful. I was working hard to make up for all the trouble I'd caused, and trying my best to get back into everybody's good graces. It was an uphill task.

Dadda stayed in his room for several days after my tirade. Mummy told me he didn't want to see me. I learned from Lily that he was having intermittent bleeding and needed to lie flat, so he didn't trust himself to come downstairs. Mummy took his food up to him and stayed with him in the evenings. When he finally came down, he was very pale, but otherwise seemed to be just fine. Though our relationship was rather strained, I was able to tell him how sorry I was that I had been so awful. He waved his hand as though to brush away the memory, and quickly changed the subject.

"The clock in the Front room needs winding," he said. "Be a good girl and find the key for me, would you? I think it's fallen on the floor again." Though I wanted to linger and talk to him, it was obvious he didn't want to talk. I ran off to search for the clock key, wondering if things would ever be back to the way they used to be.

Somehow, I didn't think they would.

Practice for our school play began as the Church Harvest Festival ended in late September. The autumn was always a busy time for children and adults alike, and after the rush and hurry of the fall season, we could look forward to Christmas, our most favourite time. Before we knew it Guy Fawkes Day was upon us. It was one of the coldest Guy Fawkes days on record. It would have been perfect weather for a great bonfire on the heath. But we were not allowed to have a bonfire that year. The air raid wardens said it would take too long to extinguish it if there was an air raid. But they would allow us our private fireworks displays, provided we understood to quickly put them away at the first warning siren.

I'd saved up some fireworks over the weeks and on the fifth of November a few of us pooled our resources and gathered to set them off outside Walter's house at the top of Coles Hill. I had taken mine over to his house because I thought the noise would upset Dadda. Mummy had thought we were all going to gather in the field across the Bramfield road and had kept the kitchen window shades open with the light out so she and Dadda could watch the show. She was upset with me when I finally arrived home empty handed. It seemed no matter what I did, I couldn't get things right anymore. I was getting too headstrong for my own good. I would have to try to do better.

Mummy's birthday on the 28th of November provided me with a good opportunity to partially make up for past discrepancies. It was a school day so I was up early in the morning to greet her and give her a packet of three handkerchiefs I'd embroidered with her initials. I hadn't anything to wrap them in, but I had found a length of blue ribbon to tie round the flimsy paper box. She was stoking the kitchen fire when I went in to give her the gift. I hadn't been in her good graces for several weeks, so it was something of a relief to be able to exchange pleasantries with her once again. She seemed pleased that I had remembered her birthday.

She accepted my gift graciously and thanked me for the nice work I'd done. She was always pleased but yet a little embarrassed to accept gifts, but my tiny little gift made her smile and she put the present on the kitchen mantelpiece above her head. It was a Thursday morning, and as Lily had gone home for the Wednesday half-closing, she hadn't come in yet. I wanted to please Mummy today, so without being asked, I took the empty water pail and hurried off to Miss Danford's pump to fill it. It was bitterly cold and the wind seemed to cut right through my coat and my woolen gymslip under it.

I hurried, and just as I got back to the pump door, Lily came in from Back Road on her bike. We had the porridge Mummy had made and I hurried off to school. For one brief moment I wondered if Mummy would let me take Dadda's tea to him this morning, but then thought better of it. I missed so much having that friendly five minutes with him in the mornings. I remember thinking that I would see him at lunchtime and I would try to be extra nice to him then.

My bicycle was being repaired, so I had to walk to school. But since I had begun coming home for lunch the year before, I continued to do so even when I didn't have my bicycle. The two evacuees from next door, Adele and Phoebe, met me outside the garden gate and we joined others in the road. The wind was icy cold, so to stay warm we ran all the way up Back Road, past the church, the cemetery and the council houses to school. On the way home we'd look in at the blacksmith's forge. He'd have a big fire going in there.

The classroom air was chilly. Our breath made miniature clouds of steam when we talked. We could see the edge of Mr. Sangster's brown woolen pullover under his suit coat. He only wore it during the coldest part of the winter. The steam radiators clanked noisily, so there would soon be warmth in our crowded classroom. We had recited the Psalm for the day and were deeply involved in maths when something seemed to hit me in the back of my head. It was a stunning blow and I looked round the room to see what it could have been. My head hurt, but there were no giggles and no one close to me seemed to be paying any attention.

I began to feel ill physically, and suddenly I was overwhelmed by a strange blackness. I struggled to maintain an upright position, but could not. I slumped over my desk and my books clattered to the floor. I must have fainted briefly, but in seconds I had regained my composure and rescued my books from the floor. Gladys gave me a strange look, but did not dare to speak to me. It must have been a happy accident that Mr. Sangster's face was turned to the blackboard. Just as I recovered my books and straightened myself, he turned to glare at me. I was quite a troublemaker and from his glance toward me, I knew I had better get control of myself quickly.

I did get through the class without another incident, but my emotions were in turmoil. Something was wrong, and I didn't know what it was. I wasn't able to concentrate on anything going on in the classroom. Only my body stayed in the chair; my mind was completely scattered. There was something unreal and very eerie going on inside of me, and only a small part of it was physical. My head thumped miserably and there was a horrible sense of fear and trepidation that permeated my very soul. I was powerless to shake it off. It clung to me with frightening tenacity. I still don't know how I got through that morning.

The hands of the big round clock on the classroom wall moved with sepulchral slowness. Finally the hands pointed to half-past eleven. In another half-hour I would be able to go home. With my whole being I longed for the time to pass quickly. Whatever was wrong could be put right again, if only I could go home. I endured each minute with mounting frustration. Just at that moment there was a knock on the classroom door. Mr. Sangster stopped abruptly mid-sentence and faced the door.

"Come in," he said loudly, and as the door opened the class stood to attention to welcome the visitor. It was always a wonderful diversion to have a guest come to class, so we could scrape our feet noisily as we sprang to attention from our seats. Whoever it was did not come completely inside, but must have motioned to Mr. Sangster through the half-open door. He laid his cane over his desk and turned to us.

"Be seated," he said curtly and "rest," which meant we were to fold our hands behind our backs and not speak to each other. He was gone for several minutes and when he returned he called my name and instructed me to go out into the girl's hallway. I was surprised to find Lily there waiting for me. Her normally controlled demeanor seemed to have vanished. She held out a brown paper bag with a sandwich in it.

"Yer Mum wants that you have yer lunch at school today," she began. She looked quite disheveled as though she'd come in haste. I couldn't believe my ears.

"Why?" I protested. "Please, not today, Lily. I've got an awful headache and I'm not feeling well. Please," I begged, "I want to come home today." I went on and on beseeching her, not wanting to make her angry, but trying to persuade her that I truly did want to come home. She looked at me steadily, her eyes imploring me to be reasonable.

"Why can't I come home. What's wrong?" I asked again.

"Yer Dadda's taken ill and the doctor's with him," she said unsteadily. "It's best you stay at school." Her voice wavered a bit, and I could tell she was struggling to stay calm. Her whole body seemed to plead with me to accept her news graciously. Alarm bells were going off in my brain. I knew something was beyond the ordinary, but I couldn't guess what it could be that I wouldn't be needed or wanted at home. I tried to convince Lily that Dadda would want me to be there if he was ill, but knowing how things had been between us lately made me hesitant. I realized that she was probably right. She wouldn't budge, anyway.

I felt a terrible fear down inside my stomach; it had something to do with the way she was looking at me, and the solicitous way she spoke to me that raised a warning flag. Usually, she was rather bossy, but now her tone as well as her bearing was subdued. It frightened me. She asked me kindly and softly to be a good girl and not make a fuss. That, she said, would be the greatest help to Dadda just now.

Something in her tone, the quiet pleading so uncharacteristic of her, made me give in without a struggle. But I could not return to class. After she'd gone, I sat on the floor in the corner of the hallway while the class recited the meal prayer. It seemed so strange to hear their voices from outside the door. I'd never had that experience before. When they were dismissed, there was the usual orderly filing out into the hallways and the usual stampede and clatter once they were safely out of Mr. Sangster's classroom. For those who were going home, there was a noisy din of changing into boots and the frantic calling to "wait for me" as coats and hats were pulled hastily off the pegs. The rest chattered as they collected their lunch bags and flasks.

Barbara English and Gladys came over to where I was sitting on the floor. I got up and moved over to the washbasin with them so we could wash our hands and dry them on the roller towel. They saw the lunch bag I was holding.

"My Dad's ill and I'm staying at school. Lily's brought me a sandwich," I said by way of explanation. Mr. Sangster had a motor car and always left for home at lunchtime. It was a relief to be free of him for the noon meal. Gladys led the way back into the classroom. We stopped at the milk crate in the corner to pick up our bottles of milk and a straw, and went on to desks in the far corner of the room.

Since the war started and the evacuee children had come to the village, the school had begun to provide milk in small bottles to all the children. We could have the milk during the mid-morning recess or at lunchtime. Having milk in bottles was a new thing for us in the country, and particularly these small individual bottles. I had seen larger bottles in Wembley when I had been there. Mother washed out the empty ones and put them outside the front door for the next morning's delivery, sometimes with a little note, ordering eggs or cheese. In the city, the milk crate's rattle was one of the first, rather pleasant, sounds of the morning.

Here in Wenhaston, our milk didn't come in bottles, but was delivered to each of our houses from Nolloth's farm in a tank with a tap on the bottom. The tank sat upright in his open horse drawn cart. We had special jugs for keeping the milk, and we kept them in the coolest corner of the pantry. Once the milk had a chance to settle, we skimmed the cream off and used it for other things. So it was a novel thing to have our own lunchtime milk bottles with two inches of cream on the top. The small shapely bottles had stoppers made of little rounds of cardboard with an indented tab for lifting them off, or to poke the straw through. We had to shake the bottle to mix the cream up so we could get it through the straw. Sometimes we took the top off completely and scooped the cream up with our fingers.

The school also provided Horlick's malted milk tablets. They tasted delicious and normally I looked forward to this treat. But today was different. My head continued to pound and I was anxious and miserable. My sandwich seemed tasteless and neither the milk nor the Horlick's tablets gave me any of the usual enjoyment.

Though I sat in class for the remainder of the day, I cannot recall anything except my anxiety and restlessness. The day dragged on unmercifully. At half-past four I was ready to race home. I stood in line impatiently to march into the hallway. As soon as I was clear of the classroom, I dashed over to collect my coat and hat from the peg. Miss Danford was standing by her classroom door. She beckoned to me as I pulled on my coat. I walked over to were she was standing.

"I want you to walk home with me," she said, pulling her wool scarf round her shoulders. I know my jaw must have dropped a foot. I was dumbfounded and speechless. Though we lived next to each other, I had never walked home with her. Miss Danford put her hands on my shoulder and looked into my face.

"There's been an accident at your house and your Dad's been hurt. I want you to come home with me while it's being sorted out." I knew it was no use to protest, but I couldn't make myself understand why everyone seemed to want to keep me away from the house. I was being left out and I didn't know why. Why couldn't I go home? My heart told me I could make everything all right if they would just let me see Dadda and talk to him. I tried to convey this idea to Miss Danford, but to no avail.

My old bicycle was in the shop being mended, so the excuse of having my bike wouldn't wash. If Miss Danford hadn't stopped me, I would have darted out the door and run like the wind. Walking with her sedately, while my counterparts chased each other and trotted in noisy groups around us, was a trial. It was a miserable and tedious walk home. Several times Miss Danford tried to draw me into conversation, but the idea of being seen by my classmates as actually talking in a friendly fashion to our old teacher was unthinkable. I kept a respectable distance and fretted inwardly.

My head was thumping painfully and my spirit was so troubled and confused I had no words in which to express myself or even answer her in a logical fashion. I wished I could find a valid excuse to pull away and run home. There was something so strange about this circumstance that I didn't dare be belligerent, or even protest. We passed the Newby's shop in silence. By force of habit, my eyes focused on the kitchen window of our house. There was no one there. I felt a twinge of nausea at seeing the ugly blank ground where the bird shed had once stood. It was a terrible eyesore.

The wind was bitterly cold and the sky was overcast. From the Back Road angle, with the grey sky above, the house looked strangely dark and uncomfortably sinister. As we approached the front of the house I could see that the blackout curtains were drawn across the Front room window. For this time of day it was very odd indeed. I felt my throat constrict. The front door looked forbidding and unlovely. As my glance took in the shop, I saw that it was closed, and the green blind was pulled all the way down. My heart skipped several beats. Something was terribly wrong, and much was happening over which I had no control.

The lane up to Miss Danford's house had a slight incline. By the side of the shop where the scrap metal had recently been retrieved there was parked an unidentifiable big black van beside the familiar black Morris that was the doctor's car. The thought went through my mind that Dadda had hit his head somehow, that he was bleeding and the doctor was treating him. Everything would be all right in a little while. I could have raced away from Miss Danford and darted into the house. But if I did that, I would be letting myself in for more trouble. I dared not upset Dadda further. Lily had said that I could help him most by being obedient and not making a fuss. I hoped her analysis was correct.

Miss Danford opened her gate for us and the silly notion that I ought to run to the house and get the pail for water flashed through my mind. It seemed so unnatural for me to be going to Miss Danford's house with her in this way. I didn't want this to be happening, but I was powerless to change the situation. I longed to be allowed to go home. She led me into the sitting room, and I sat dumbly in one of the overstuffed chairs as she busied herself in the kitchen making tea. I fiddled with the lace doily that covered the chair arm while she put a match to the fire that was laid with newspaper and kindling wood. It blazed up and she added a few small bits of coal. Its warmth soon permeated the small room.

I felt awkward and uncomfortable having Miss Danford bustle about doing the chores as I sat woodenly in the chair. She talked quietly as she brought in the tea tray and some biscuits on a plate. I didn't really know what my responsibility was to her. She had some chickens in the yard that would need feeding. Shouldn't I be making the tea and serving her? Was she expecting me to volunteer to help her in some way? What was I supposed to say? I tried to sip the tea, but quickly put the cup back in the saucer because my hands trembled slightly and I was deathly afraid I would spill some of it.

Miss Danford finished her puttering and came and sat in the chair opposite me. Until this moment, I had not been aware that she was a normal human being. I certainly had never pictured myself as sitting opposite her having tea in her comfortable sitting room. She had always been someone to avoid, someone with whom I should maintain a respectable distance. Now here I was, under this terrible cloud of uncertainty and fear, sitting in a chair opposite my mentor, who was attempting to draw me into rational conversation.

She spoke softly, but firmly. She was telling me that I must be brave and that I must think of others now. I tried to catch her words and make sense of what she was saying. As she continued to speak, the truth dawned slowly. Dadda was not ill. She was telling me he was dead. I could not take it in. I refused to believe that he was beyond the doctor's help. Something in me wanted to cry out, to tell her she was wrong, but the words wouldn't come out. Despite the warmth from the fire, I felt terribly cold and weak. My tea got cold in the cup and the biscuits remained untouched. Not only my hands, but my whole body shivered, and my throat was dry and uncooperative. I could neither speak nor cry. It was as though a strange paralysis had me in a vice-like grip.

How long we sat there I could not hazard a guess. As the room grew dark, Miss Danford pulled the heavy blackout curtains across the windows and the curtain across the outer door to keep out the draft. There was something surreal about watching her light her paraffin lamps. I remember wondering why she didn't use her electric lights, but l didn't dare to ask. She poked the fire, adding more coal to the hot embers. Her cat circled her chair, mewing piteously. She picked it up and carried it into the kitchen, talking to it gently. I could hear her preparing the cat's food. Just then there was a knock on the door.

I heard Lily's voice. She had come to fetch me. My relief almost overwhelmed me. In the lane, Lily shined the torch to lead us to the pump door. I could see by its light that the van was still parked against the house, but the doctor's car was gone.

"Dadda's not dead, is he Lily?" I said, hopefully. I longed to know that what I feared was not true. Lily stopped with her hand on the pump door.

"They'll be talk in the village, right enough," Lily said in the dark doorway, "and you may as well know straight out he killed hisself," she said it in a rush. "The police cum to the shop and made all on us answer questions; where we were and what we was doing, and yer Mum fainted and we didn't half have a fair bother."

The news stunned me. I didn't know how to feel or how to come to grips with what was happening. The overriding emotion that began to set in was dread. A coldness that had nothing to do with the north wind gripped my whole body. We hurried over the cold cobblestones to the back door. Just as we reached the door, Lily said,

"There's sumpin' else," we paused as she rushed on. "Fleet run off again and Mr. Broom's cum and took him for yer Mum. He's keeping him out to the farm out of the way, like." In some ways, that news was a relief. The dog was safe and probably happy to have space to run at will. We entered the kitchen door and I saw the table was set for supper. There was some sliced meat, boiled potatoes, a wedge of cheese, a loaf of bread and some jam laid out. Our two newest soldiers were already sitting at the table. They greeted us with effusive and somewhat false cheeriness.

Mummy was nowhere to be seen. Lily said the doctor had given her a sedative and she had gone to bed. I wondered who was in the Front room because I could hear noises and muffled voices coming through the tightly closed door. Lily had regained her "take charge" attitude and told me in no uncertain terms I was not to go in the Front room until I was told I could. After the grueling day I had endured, I was happy to be back in the house. I was not about to do anything that might set off a firestorm.

As I sat at the table I glanced up at the mantelpiece. The small packet of handkerchiefs with the piece of blue ribbon dangling loosely was still there. I wondered why Mummy hadn't taken it away, and if Dadda had thought about her birthday. What HAD gone on in this house today? It was too much to speculate.

Lily sliced the bread in lovely even slices, and passed the butter round. The soldiers exchanged some small talk, but otherwise we ate our small meal in almost total silence. Afterwards the chaps went down to the pub for a pint, and Lily and I cleared away the remaining food and did the washing up together. I was aching with curiosity and had sensed somehow that Lily was reluctant to say very much in front of the soldiers. Once they were gone she was very forthcoming. I learned I was to sleep with her that night because one of the morticians, whose voice I had heard from the Front room, was staying the night.

I was glad to be with Lily, and I think, actually, she was glad to have me too. I learned from her the horrific details of the day. She described how Mummy had taken Dadda's tea up to him with the morning post and how later Dadda came downstairs in his shirt-sleeves and talked with Mummy in the kitchen. Lily noticed that he must have been upset about something, because he never left his room without being fully clothed.

Lily related that Mummy had gone into the shop to wait on the morning customers, and she had gone upstairs to make the beds and empty the chambers. She heard a gunshot and when she came downstairs had told Mummy about it. Mummy had found Dadda slumped against the bird shed door with the back of his head blown off. Her screams brought not only Lily but also some of the customers running. Mummy fainted and had to be laid out on the kitchen floor.

Piece by awful piece I was able to put the puzzle together. It was as though I was outside all of the horror, somehow isolated from it. I seemed not to feel anything. It was as though I was looking in through a window at a horrible scene of a play being enacted, and I was in the audience. Lily and I huddled together under the covers with our hot water bottles.

Early in the morning Mummy came to wake me. Lily must have gone downstairs already. Mummy was fully dressed in her best dark grey dress with her hair freshly braided in its afternoon bun. Her face was ghastly white, and she had red splotches around her eyes and nose. She brought in clean school clothes for me and talked to me while I dressed in the ice-cold room. I could hear movement and men's voices coming from downstairs.

Questions poured out of me, but Mummy was not very forthcoming. She explained diffidently that a police inspector and some other men had come yesterday to hold an "inquest" about Dadda's death. It frightened me to think a policeman came to talk about Dadda's suicide, but I held my tongue. The Vicar, Mr. Hardingham, had also been to see her. I would have given a lot to know why, but suicide was another one of those shameful things that people couldn't talk about openly. I continued to question her, to ask what the Vicar had said. It was important to me to know if he'd said anything about Dadda going to heaven. If suicide was a sin, was Dadda forgiven for it? I needed to know. But it was like asking a brick wall to speak. Mummy gave out very little information.

I had to ask the big question, "Why? Why had he killed himself?" I had a gnawing feeling that I was to blame for his death. I felt it then, and carried the guilt with me for many years.

"Did he say anything about being upset with me?" I wanted to know. She looked at me as though I'd lost my mind. "He said nothing about you at all," she said indignantly. "The doctor said his mind snapped," she said with finality. "There's no use asking any more questions," she said, shaking her head as though to free herself from the thoughts that crossed her mind. At that moment I felt dreadfully sad for her.

I reached over to put my arms around her to comfort her and to be comforted, and for just a brief moment we were joined in mutual devastating grief. But Mummy was not one for outward shows of affection. She hastened to disengage herself from my embrace, straightened her dress and cleared her throat. I think she was struggling not to give in to the torrent of emotion that surely would have overwhelmed her if she had let it get the best of her. She rose quickly from the side of the bed.

"Come along, now," she said decisively, as she moved toward the bedroom door. She led me down to the Front room. It was very cold and the curtains were still drawn across the window. Black cloth was draped over the fireplace mirror and over the two portraits and the barometer. There was a sickly sweet smell that hung thickly in the air. The room had been completely changed around. One electric light, its shade draped in thin black cloth, stood on a small table casting an eerie glow.

By the dim light I could make out the bier with the coffin on it. Lucy's cage was gone. The corner chair in front of the bookcase had been taken out, and the coffin was pushed against the far wall. It stretched almost to the hearth in front of the empty fireplace. Other furniture had been moved out and there were several small chairs that had been brought in and set round the room. My eyes began to adjust to the gloom.

At Mummy's direction, I crossed the room to the coffin and looked over the side. Dadda was lying there with his eyes closed as though he were asleep. He looked very peaceful. His head was encased in a white satin pillow that showed only the front part of his face. He was dressed in his Sunday suit, the jacket unbuttoned to show his waistcoat. His watch chain and gold fob were missing. His good hand was clasped with his prosthesis across his chest in an uncharacteristic fashion, and I noticed that his signet ring was not on his finger. There was a slightly whiter band of skin where the ring had been. The skin on his hand and face had a strange, almost transparent look. The veins stood out in a way I had never noticed before. His cheeks were freshly shaven and what little I could see of his hair was combed nicely.

He looked so lifelike I found myself talking to him, telling him inane things and begging him to wake up. I babbled on and on. It must have unnerved Mummy because I could hear her muffled sobs behind me. I touched his hand and felt its coldness, and kissed his frozen cheek. I told him I loved him and was sorry for all the awful things I'd said to him. I began to cry and my tears washed over his face and down onto the satin pillow. Someone put a hand on my shoulder and pulled me away from the coffin. I didn't want to leave him there in the cold room. I struggled a bit with the unseen hand on my shoulder, but was soon led away.

There were other people moving about in the room. Everything became a blur. Most of the people in the room were strangers. All of them were solemn, speaking in whispers in the darkened room. I remember wondering where Uncle Aubrey was. Was he there somewhere? To this day I don't know. I was led into the kitchen. Lily was there with Lenny's Joyce and her mother Mrs. Borrott, and some other people. I don't remember anything at all about the rest of that day, only that I was not allowed to go to the funeral, and that I was told repeatedly not to make a fuss and upset Mummy.

Dadda was not buried in Wenhaston and no one ever told me where the funeral had been held. My guess was that his body was taken to Ipswich, but Mummy would not discuss it. There was such a stigma surrounding the circumstances of her husband's death, that part of her grief was surely the agony of knowing that the family was being whispered about in the village. When the funeral was over, the whole matter was washed into oblivion like waves lapping over sandcastles. I understood that I was not to speak of it, so I didn't. Mummy made it clear that life was to return to normal as quickly as possible.

By all accounts it seemed to do so. Outwardly, we went on with daily life. The added responsibility of keeping the books now fell to Mummy, and she in turn added more of the shop chores to Lily and me. More soldiers were pouring into our village and the surrounding countryside. Nearly every home had either evacuees or soldiers. Two additional soldiers were billeted with us, which filled our house to capacity. Now with seven to feed and care for on top of the shop chores, the days were hectic. Mummy seemed somehow to thrive on the increased responsibility. She put all of us into high gear. The house bustled from early morning until the blackout curtains were drawn and the supper dishes were cleared away. In the evenings, we women retired early. We no longer lingered in the kitchen as we had once done.

The back door was never locked, and the soldiers came and went on their own schedules. They kept their own evening hours. We saw them mostly at mealtimes. Sometimes in the late afternoons, they were in the back yard or the bicycle shed polishing their brass buttons and buckles or shining their boots. Occasionally one of the married soldier's wives would come for a few days visit, sometimes with a small child in tow. To accommodate them, Lily gave up her bedroom at the back of the house, and we both moved into the large front bedroom with Mummy.

The room accommodated the three of us easily. The room had quite a lot of furniture in addition to the two beds. Dadda's commode, a wooden chair with a chamber that slid underneath, was now unused, by unspoken consent. With the polished wood lid closed, it became a catchall for our bits and pieces. All three of us used the washstand with the two sets of toiletries and the towels that hung on the side. A good sized sliver of the transparent Pears soap that Dadda had used was still in its dish, and the green and gold bottle of his cologne stood neatly beside it.

As the days slipped by, we began to adjust to a new definition of normal. Mummy wore black dresses and hats for a full year, then eventually changed to dark grey. I wore a black armband on my winter coat until the following spring. We never spoke about Dadda, but I thought of him every day and in the night I dreamed about him. In the beginning I had been almost paralyzed by feelings of fear and dread. But as the days went on those feelings changed to ones of guilt and remorse. I sensed Dadda's presence with me; I felt that he was somehow able to see me and monitor everything I did. Far from feeling comforted by this, his imagined presence haunted me.

The thought that I had wished him dead, and had screamed it at him in white-hot anger, was all I could think about. In my heart I knew I could never be forgiven for my terrible sin. I had nightmares in which I saw him standing in the air raid shelter doorway with the gun in his hand, steadying it with his prosthesis. I saw myself crying hysterically and begging his forgiveness. But his eyes were closed as though he didn't want to hear me.

In my recurring dream I watched while he inserted the tip of the barrel between his lips and pulled the trigger. Vividly I saw the scene as though in slow motion. At the blast of the gun, his eyes opened wide. He looked at me for just a moment, his eyes grotesquely wild, and then his body slumped against the door frame. I saw his blood splattered everywhere. I envisioned myself screaming in horror, reaching forward in protest to stop him. But it was too late. He was forever gone.

Many nights I woke up crying. Some times during the daytime, I would break out in tears for no apparent reason. In an attempt to make me get hold of myself, Mummy would chide me with a hint of sarcasm.

"Your water lays fleet," she would say, meaning that crying came easy for me. She saw my emotional outbreaks as wallowing in self-pity, and "for my own good" she was trying to get me to stop giving in to it. So I couldn't let Mummy see me crying. I steeled myself to gain control in her presence. But often I would go to the heath or hide in the woods where I could be alone and cry to my heart's content.

I was often depressed and sometimes extremely lonely in the midst of people. There were times when I did not want to live. I began to plan my own suicide. But how complicated it all was. I didn't know how to go about it and I couldn't ask anyone. I thought I might be able to slash my wrists. There were several sharp knives in the pantry and Dadda's razor was still in the mug on the washstand. I'd heard that people did that, but I wasn't sure if it would work. I believed it would be painful to die, and I wasn't sure I could go through with it if the pain became unbearable.

What a horrible thing it would be if I only injured myself and didn't die completely. In actual fact, I didn't want to kill myself, but I didn't know any other way to end the constant misery that surrounded me. I was beginning to confuse my dreams with reality. It was getting difficult to sort it all out. I knew I was beginning to act strangely, and when my friends began to take notice, I distanced myself from them.

Lily went home on Saturday afternoons and didn't return until the following Monday morning. So on the weekends I had the whole bed to myself, a total luxury. Lily had complained a bit about my taking up most of the bed and the fact that I tossed and turned and often woke her up with my yelling. I hadn't told anyone that I was having realistic and terrible nightmares. I truly thought that others would think I had "gone peculiar" like Conkers Newby. The shame of that seemed harder to bear than the nightmares. But I was beginning to doubt my sanity.

The week before Christmas I was sleeping alone in Dadda's bed. I had felt headachy and ill all day. There was an ever-pervasive gloominess and a general air of lethargy that seemed to hover over me. I thought it might be a recurrence of the sleeping sickness. In any event, I slept fitfully and woke up in the morning with awful stomach pain. As I got out of bed I noticed a huge dark stain on the sheet. I pushed the cover back and realized there was a pool of blood in the middle of the bed.

I jumped away from the bed and caught a glimpse of myself in the wardrobe mirror. My nightdress was covered with blood. For one awful minute I couldn't decide whether I was having a nightmare or whether I had in fact killed myself. The ghastliness of it all hit me with full force. I began to scream hysterically. The grisly image of myself in the mirror, my hair askew, looking like a wild banshee, added madness to the horror.

Mummy had already gone downstairs. When she heard my

screams, she flew up the stairs and burst open the bedroom door. Somehow my hands were bloody and I'd put them up to my face. I was hysterical; Mummy took two strides across the room toward me. She took me by the shoulders and shook me, but I couldn't stop screaming. Mummy began scolding me, ordering me to stop screaming. When I didn't, she slapped my face. It brought me partially back to reality, but I was shaking and crying. She dragged me away from the mirror and sat me down on the side of the bed.

"Stop it, stop it" she was saying angrily. "You're waking up the whole household. Get hold of yourself. What's the matter with you?" She continued to shake me and berate me until I finally stopped screaming. But I was still quivering violently and gulping great noisy gasps of air. Mummy took in the scene almost at a glance: the bloody bed, my nightdress, my trembling body.

"What's wrong with you?" she said again. I was having difficulty breathing and couldn't talk very well, but I managed to blurt out something between sobs. I don't know what I said. But I must have said something about being dead because she looked at me with astonishment.

"You're not dead, and you're not dying," she said curtly. "Whatever gave you that idea?" She got the smelling salts from the washstand drawer, removed the stopper and held it briefly under my nose. In one whiff, the sharp fumes brought me to my senses, and I listened to what she was telling me with a new sense of trepidation.

"You've just come on queer, that's all," she said, matter-of-factly. "It happens to all women. You'll have it once a month from now on, and you don't need to be frightened of it." She asked me to sit quietly for a minute while she went down to the kitchen to fetch the kettle of hot water. After giving me instructions and showing me how to make a sanitary napkin out of a square of sheet lined with cotton wool, she took the bloody sheets and my nightdress and left me to bathe myself and get dressed. The soldiers were up. I could hear them moving about and going downstairs. I was sure Mummy was tending to them, boiling eggs and making toast. I wanted to go downstairs, but I didn't want to see anyone. Mummy let me stay in the bedroom for the rest of the morning.

I ventured downstairs in the early afternoon. I was feeling very weak partly from hunger, but also from emotional exhaustion.

Mummy was in the Front room with Joyce and her mother. They were frequent visitors, and it was a relief to see them. There was a Sunday fire going and they were having tea. Joyce flicked her cigarette ash into the fire and smiled at me. It was reassuring to know that she liked me, and I began to feel better. I was glad to have the tea that was offered and a sandwich from the pile on the tray.

"So you've got the curse, have you?" Mrs. Borrott said with a knowing smile. I looked at her with consternation. "The curse." What I had was a curse? I didn't know how to respond. I looked to Joyce for help, but she smiled broadly as if to say "Don't worry," and Mummy looked away. I knew this was something I shouldn't discuss, so I nodded my head and ate my sandwich in friendly silence. For once I was glad to sit quietly in their company, listening to them talk, while the afternoon crept into evening.

Chapter 14

Incendiary Bombs and Fiery Times

After the disaster in November, we were unprepared for Christmas. It was upon us before we'd had time to think about it. There was none of the usual scrambling to finish the knitted or embroidered gifts, or to gather decorations for the Front room. The house stood forlornly stolid against the North wind, and icicles formed along the edge of the roof. According to those who knew about such things, it was the coldest winter on record. Snow and ice storms were hampering transportation in many parts of the country.

This year Mummy had encountered much difficulty getting the necessary ingredients for the plum puddings, due to shortages and the rationing. With her usual forethought, she had managed to scrounge together enough to get two small puddings ready before Guy Fawkes Day. They sat in their bowls on the pantry shelf, covered with clean cloths tied round with string. Their presence this year seemed somehow out of place. The sight of them in other years had filled us with delightful anticipation; now, in light of recent events and because of food shortages, they seemed almost accusatory and somehow a bit indecent.

We were fortunate to have puddings this year. A lot of people didn't. Perhaps that accounted partly for the vague feeling of decadence. As shop owners, we had no special privileges. But with four soldiers besides ourselves requiring meals, we were permitted an extra allowance. We were supposed to adhere to the rules of rationing the same as everyone else, and to my knowledge we did follow them.

Early on in November, Mummy had begun to set aside a few Christmas luxuries as she was able, saving things for Christmas with fervour as she had always done. But after Dadda's death she went to the other extreme. Not only was she not collecting things, but she seemed almost bent on squelching anything that smacked of holiday spirit. She made it known that according to custom, it would be unseemly for her to take part in the season's festivities. This traditional moral code she saw not only as her own duty to obey strictly, but she made sure that I was suitably indoctrinated also.

A few days before Christmas, Mummy told me that Uncle Aubrey wasn't visiting us this year. I was terribly disappointed about that. I was looking forward to seeing him and hoping that he and Carly-luv would be able somehow to put our situation in balance. Perhaps they could give us a new perspective and set things right in our topsy-turvy world. Actually, I don't know how Mummy knew he wasn't coming. I'd been watching the post and hadn't seen a letter come from him. It was odd that he did not send a single present or even a greeting by post, which would have been typical of him. I found it all very strange.

I thought it might have something to do with the observance of a decent mourning period. Deep down I was afraid to speculate further. I knew that damage from the constant bombing in London was extensive. The Germans were keeping up a steady bombing of London and the surrounding areas. The news that we garnered from our sporadic listening to the radio, had been especially grim of late. Our live-in soldiers, who seemed well informed, said little, out of respect for our grieving household. We let the matter drop.

Doreen's parents invited Mummy and me to their home across the corner from us for Christmas dinner, and we were glad to go. Chocolate was now considered a luxury. Surprisingly Mummy scrounged up a few bars of Cadbury's, a tin of chocolate covered biscuits, and a few other things that she'd put by early on. We took them, along with one of the puddings.

Lily had gone home to be with her family, and one of our soldiers had gone on leave. The other three soldiers went with their unit to the Parish Hall where a festive dinner was being prepared for the troops. We had had no word from Lenny, so we were still anxious about him.

Doreen's house was delightfully warm and inviting. She and her mother had decorated their Lounge with paper chains and sprigs of holly, and the fire blazed warmly. Under ordinary circumstances, how wonderful it might have been. If there had been no dreadful cloud hanging over our heads or feelings of agonizing sorrow, we could have appreciated it more.

Doreen was an only child, and although she was three years younger than me, we often played together in her back garden. Sometimes other friends would join us there: her cousin Walter, Gladys, Peter Elmy, Clara Block and others. Mrs. Page, Doreen's mother, was always pleasant towards us children. Before rationing started she would often bring sweets to all of us. She'd count how many children there were, and then bring each of us a lollipop or half stick of licorice to chew on. Sometimes she'd make lemonade for us. It was always a special treat.

Paper products were beginning to be in short supply. Newspapers and magazines were being made with smaller dimensions and with fewer pages as the war progressed. The shop could no longer put groceries in strong paper bags. The ones we had to use now were thin and flimsy. Personal carrier bags, made of leather or other sturdy materials, had always been in vogue. Every home had one or two that were carried empty to the shops. Now people began a phase of making shopping bags with innovative materials such as oilcloth, linen, cotton, and even string. Customers brought empty jars and other containers from home to carry back a half-pound of sugar, rice or flour to help conserve the few bags we could get. We weighed out the loose goods on greaseproof paper on our contoured brass scale pan, then poured the contents into the customer's container. It was a challenge, but the shortage was intense and nobody minded.

We saved newspapers, magazines, and cardboard, and reused them many times. The fish and chips shop, the butcher, and other merchants looked to their customers to help provide the outer wrapping for their goods. There were demands from many sources for used paper. A busy industry sprang up to recycle paper. When it was processed, the paper often became rough and discoloured and a bit hard to read. But no matter how bumpy or how flecked the paper, newspapers, magazines, comic books and other reading material were still available. The used book market that had always been lively now came into its own.

Mummy didn't read much of anything, so I had never been exposed to the ladies weekly magazines or any of the paperback novels that Dadda called "the penny dreadfuls." But Doreen's mother read them avidly. Her home was a veritable mecca for this kind of literature. During my Christmas visit, I discovered a new type of reading material. The Women's Home magazines had articles on knitting, sewing, child care, cooking and a corner for Patience Strong, who was a poet of some note in that era. The part of the magazines that interested me the most were the romance novels, in serial format. Each new issue would bring another episode, and so we would read them and swap them round the neighbourhood. I believe poor old Conkers Newby was the last in line. By the time she got them, the magazines were usually in tatters.

I became immersed in reading the ongoing sagas. The trials and tribulations of the characters became very real to me, and I lost myself temporarily as I followed faithfully each successive episode. The plots usually moved with glacial slowness, yet leaving the reader hanging at a crucial point at the end of each episode. There were the inevitable love triangles, the miseries of those in love with the wrong person, the passion of secret love, and poignant stories of unrequited love. It was heady stuff and quite an education for me.

I also found Penguin paperback novels in the Halesworth *Newspaper and Book Shop* that covered a wide range of classics as well as current fiction. I mined the shelves with compulsion, finding fictional gems heretofore unknown to me. I particularly remember *Lady Chatterley's Lover,* as it raised the eyebrows of even the hardiest romance novel readers in the village. New paperback books cost sixpence, but used ones could be purchased for tuppence. With the pennies I earned running errands, I soon had my own well-used lending library to add to Doreen's mother's stock of "penny dreadfuls." I thought I was truly entering the adult world of high fiction.

It was a diversion for me that filled my mind with fantasy and nonsense. It helped me to run away emotionally, to avoid having to think about anything that was painful. It would take many years of wandering in a guilt-ridden wilderness before the pain was truly gone. But for the moment, I was released from the paralysis that had gripped me, and I could begin to find a new direction. In a few short weeks I had lost my childhood. It was a terrible loss. But I was growing up.

My forays to Halesworth became more frequent now, and nearly always included a stop in the little bookshop just up the street from Owen's house. Owen was three years older than me, and had left school and gone to work two years before. At sixteen he was six feet tall and aching to be sent into the army. His older brother and sister had already joined up, but he was needed at home for the time being. He was not very often about home in the daytime except on Saturdays.

On Saturday afternoons, we met outside the cinema along with our friends and waited for the theatre to open. We didn't really care what the film was about; we liked them all. We were beginning to learn the names of movie actors and actresses: Lon Chaney, Roy Rogers, George Formby, Deana Durbin and Joan Crawford were popular. We also saw the *Pathé News* and learned a lot about what was happening in the war. We got to see the King and Queen making the rounds in London, and saw the devastation of the bombed out buildings. After the news, the theatre played two cartoons, the coming attractions, and the feature film. It was an altogether marvelous outing.

Smoking was allowed in the theatres, and during intermission a vendor would come round selling cigarettes and little tubs of ice-cream that were well beyond our price range. Some of the older boys smoked during the picture show and the smoke would get so thick at times we could hardly see the screen. After the show we would gather in the lane that ran behind the theatre along the edge of a field. The lane ran past a bowling green to a stile in the hedge. We could meet there to rehash the film, to laugh and talk, but mostly to smoke a cigarette that someone would pass round. At that time few of us had the luxury of owning a whole packet.

For the first two years of the war, though we had ration cards issued to us, we seldom ran short of staple food in the village. But by 1941, we were beginning to feel the effects of food shortages, even in the country. Even though we had enough ration stamps, we began to be unable to find shops with enough food on hand. For this reason, my journeys to Halesworth became more frequent. Sometimes I would ride into Halesworth twice on Saturdays, once in the early morning alone and again in the afternoon with Gladys, Gonie and whoever else joined us that day for the matinee at the cinema.

Fish was becoming our main staple, as the meat supply to civilians was becoming more and more limited. The Wenhaston fish and chips shop by the Hut previously had plenty of fish on Friday evenings. Now the queues to get it were getting longer, and the shop would run out within a short time of opening. Fortunately for us, even if they ran out of fish, they always had potatoes to make chips. We had many Friday night meals that consisted of french-fried potatoes soaked in salt and vinegar. They were delicious.

So it was that on Saturday mornings, Mummy would ask me to ride into Halesworth early to go to the fish market, and also to the butcher shop on High Street. If we were lucky, there would be meat or fish to buy. It was always special when there was a fresh supply. Often they were sold out before I got there, but usually I could find something at the market. Once school was out for the summer, I rode in almost daily, taking orders for fish and ration books for meat from other families in the neighbourhood. It was always a bit of a challenge to see what I could bring home.

Mummy had been wrong about me getting "the curse" every month. It was the middle of April before I got it again. This time I recognized the warning signs, a horrible cramping pain in my stomach and a dull aching head. I was allowed to stay home from school for one day. The next day I went to school, but I was deathly afraid someone would know my horrible secret, so I stayed away from everyone. I didn't have it again until the following September. I hated the whole miserable mess, and wished fervently I'd been born a boy.

In the middle of summer, I got the notion that I was grown up enough to travel on my own to London to visit my family in Wembley. I had fairly regular correspondence with my mother, who discouraged visits because of the danger that existed with the blitz. However, a lot of the evacuees had begun to return to their homes, and I felt sure I would be safe. Besides, the thought of danger intrigued me; there was excitement in the idea of dodging bombs. I had saved enough from my errands for train fare, and wanted to strike out on my own. I prevailed on Mummy to let me go for a holiday. I knew she needed me, but I begged relentlessly. Toward the end of July, she reluctantly consented.

The train from Halesworth to Liverpool Street Station was packed with people, mostly men and women in uniform, but also children and older civilians. I was thrilled to be traveling with my small leather case and my tennis racquet in its wooden stretcher. It made me feel very grown up and important, even though I did have to stand in a crowded corridor a good part of the journey.

I remembered fairly well how to do the Underground from Liverpool Street. I could easily have asked for help, but wanted to do this on my own. I took the first train that said "Baker Street" on the front. I watched every stop carefully, so that I would be ready to jump off at the right stop. From Baker Street I had to switch to the Bakerloo line and look for the train that said "Watford." If I accidentally got on a train that said "Elephant and Castle," I would travel miles in the wrong direction. Fortunately, there was no extra charge for stupid errors. As long as I held my ticket and didn't go outside the station, I could ride the Tube all day long in any direction.

When I got off at Wembley, I had to find my way through a maze of stone steps and alleyways, and then cross a high steel bridge over the railway tracks. Later I learned several ways to get to our home in Wembley, by train and bus. I learned to take a different line that let me off at Alperton station. It was a shorter walk home from there. Traveling was adventurous to me. I never got tired of riding the trains, even when I got lost.

The rationing and food shortage situation was worse in Wembley than in Wenhaston. In the country we had meat shortages because the meat was being sent to the fighting men, but being near the sea, we usually were able to get fresh fish. In Wenhaston we hadn't really had a shortage of dairy products or vegetables. In London, the shortages were acute. Our ration books allowed two ounces of butter or four ounces of margarine and two eggs each, per week. Often we had to queue up outside the shops to buy them. We took turns doing that.

The differences in food shortages were not terribly noticeable to me. I found that the big differences were mainly in the strange complexities of city life versus the familiar simplicity of the country. In Wembley, we didn't have the comradeship of the close knit community as there was in the village. Nor did life revolve around the church in quite the same way as it had in Wenhaston. There were also different sounds, sights, smells, customs, and schedules, that required an adjustment to city living.

There were more air raids, too. Almost every night the sirens went and the searchlights filled the skies. We could hear the planes and the guns and the bombs as the enemy targeted the aerodromes surrounding London. The air field at Croydon got blasted on two consecutive nights during the first week of my visit.

On one occasion the second warning sounded, and we all had to get up in the middle of the night and troop down to the school shelter at the end of the road. Though we children didn't mind it much, my mother was extremely anxious, nervously herding us and sharply admonishing us to hurry. The wardens, including my stepfather, didn't sleep at all. They were in the streets, beating out the fires from the incendiary bombs that had fallen all over our neighborhood.

On another occasion, we came up from the shelter and bombs had landed all around our streets. The bridge over the railway tracks was damaged and the entrance from the street had a huge crater. The houses surrounding the station were severely damaged. One whole section of homes was completely gone. The few that were left standing were ruined beyond repair. Our own house and the others on our street were luckier. Though windows were shattered, the front door blown open, and plaster from the walls and ceiling covered the stairs and front hallway, the house was still standing and in fairly good condition. It took us several days to clear away the debris and board up the windows, but our homes were livable, and no one on our street was killed or injured. There were many new things to learn.

Getting to know my mother, my stepfather George Logan, and my brothers and sisters was the biggest and best new experience of all. I met and came to know everyone that summer. I gained a sense of each one's personality, and in the process learned a lot about myself. We were a large family and no mistake. Betty was the eldest of the five Sidey children and Phyllis was next. Then came Reg and Eric and then me, each of us eighteen months apart. The second family, my younger brothers and sisters, consisted of June, two years my junior, then Bob, and John. Lastly there was my baby sister Maureen. Her birthday was also in July, and she had turned three a few days before I arrived.

With such a large family to feed, it was imperative that we use our ration coupons wisely. My mother showed great initiative and planned well. I remember that she approached the Eaton family, a family of four who lived next door, to ask if they would like to trade four of our butter coupons, which constituted a half pound, for four of their margarine coupons which would get us a full pound of margarine. The Eatons were glad to do it. We all benefited.

Mother had been reared on a farm in Wales, and thought she needed to raise a few chickens for eggs and eventually for meat. We weren't supposed to raise chickens in the city, but Mother found a way to keep three or four in a coop just outside the kitchen door. When we peeled the potatoes for the evening meal, we saved the skins. She later boiled them and mashed them up as feed for the chickens. We had a marvelous supply of eggs, but not enough for everyone to have an egg each morning for breakfast. When one of the hens stopped laying, we had roast chicken for our Sunday dinner.

Mother was also astute with our meat coupons. Some days we were able to have a "fry-up" for our evening meal that might consist of sausage and onions or a thick rasher of bacon with beans. She pooled our meat coupons so that we could have a good-sized joint of beef or mutton on Sundays. It was a special treat, and the house smelled marvelous while it roasted.

Mother served the meat with thick brown gravy that we poured over everything: the meat, the Yorkshire pudding, roasted potatoes and even the brussels sprouts. She left the excess roast drippings to solidify in the pan. When the fat got cold, it formed a smooth white coating on top. There was a marvelous brown jelly substance underneath that we spread on bread to make a most delicious sandwich.

My stepfather George Logan worked long hours for one of the London newspapers. He was the first one up and in the kitchen in the mornings. On cold mornings, he got the fires going downstairs and made the tea. He always took my mother a cup of tea in bed before he left for work. In the evenings he helped my mother get the younger children ready for bed. He hardly ever called them by name. He referred to all the children as "Pet." Mother often used that term as well. George was a quiet sort, a "homebody" as Mother called him, who seldom raised his voice to us. Mother was frugal and stretched the budget in every way possible to provide meals and keep the bill collectors at bay. To this day I marvel at how she was able to manage the large family and keep her sanity.

We were all conscious that food was a major priority. Without question we were a hungry bunch. It was incumbent upon each of us to learn how to make the most of what we had, and to share with each other. My older brothers Eric and Reg were innovative short-order chefs. Both of them had jobs, so they contributed their fair share to the household. Whenever they came home, they brought something with them. They loved to make strange concoctions using powdered eggs, fried Spam, leftover vegetables and baked beans. Their simple menus, smothered with ketchup, tasted delicious.

Doug & Betty's Wedding 1940

My sister Betty was newly married to an RAF officer. Because of the housing shortage, she and Doug moved in with the family at 3 Vincent Road until they were able to find other accommodations. They also contributed their part toward the household expenses. It was wonderful to have them there. Next to Carly-luv, Betty was the most beautiful girl I had ever seen. Both Betty and Carly-luv had a very special elegance, a graciousness that set them apart from other women. But they were also different in many ways, certainly in looks. Carly-luv had wispy fair hair, very white skin and sparkling blue eyes. She was tiny in stature and always seemed rather fragile.

Betty's hair was raven's wing black, and her eyes were dark brown, darker than mine, with lovely long eyelashes. She was taller than Carly-luv and not in the least fragile; her body was curved in all the right places. Lenny would have said "Well-built," but nicely so. I hoped that someday I would be able to walk with the grace and self-assurance that Betty did. It was something to strive for.

A popular song of the day had lyrics that said: *"You ought to be in pictures..."* I thought Betty definitely should have been; her looks rivaled those of Deana Durbin, a film star in that era. Once when we walked down the street together, some men working in the street whistled at her. She flipped her head and smiled nicely to acknowledge the compliment. Then she told me sternly in a stage whisper not to pay any attention to them, and we walked on. At that stage in my life, that kind of attention embarrassed me no end. The men had whistled at her, but I was the one who blushed to the tip of my scalp. I admired the fact that she could stay so cool, and wished I could be like that.

Betty taught me new things that I would not have known otherwise. She showed me how to make a face mask out of powdered eggs, "to clean the pores," she said. She showed me how to make mouthwash from peroxide and salt, "to keep the teeth white and the gums healthy." It stung like crazy! Best of all she taught me to make my hair shine by adding vinegar or lemon juice to the final rinse water.

Betty's husband Doug was like another older brother. He looked smashingly handsome in his RAF uniform, and we all adored him. He could be stern with us if we got out of hand, but he was always pleasant. I was fascinated that he owned a car. The reality that it was old as the hills and required hours of tinkering escaped me at the time. We all begged to go for rides in it, and on rare occasions he took two or three of us round the corner and down the hill to the shops, a distance of about six city blocks.

My birthday on the thirtieth of July was also my younger brother Bob's birthday. He was eight the same day that I was thirteen. Betty and Mother made a delightful party for the two of us with all my brothers and sisters. After the party, Mother assembled us in bunches outside the front door to take our photographs. We took turns posing with each other. Later in the afternoon Mother took my youngest sister Maureen, who was then three years old, and John who was five, with her on some errand.

It was a lovely, warm summer afternoon. Eric suggested we could go to the swimming pool, and that sounded like a nice idea. He and Reg had taken some of us a few days before, and since swimming in a pool was a brand new experience for me, I was eager to go again. It was an indoor pool and there was a requirement that the girls wear bathing caps. I'd received a new bathing cap as one of my birthday gifts, so I thought it would be a nice chance to wear it.

For the moment, Reg, Eric, Bob, June and I were content to be out in the back garden, hitting a tennis ball over an imaginary net. Dennis Eaton, the boy next door, popped over to join us. Dennis was about fifteen or sixteen, close in age to Reg and Eric. He worked at a local cinema running the film projector. Whenever the film broke, Dennis had to splice it together hurriedly and get the film going again, while the audience stamped their feet and made rude noises. This was another new arena for me, so I moved over to listen. As we were chatting, Betty came out of the house to tell us she had to run to the shops. I expect she was going to queue up for something or other.

"Will you be all right for a little while? she asked us. "I'm just going to pop down the road." We said of course we would. "I shan't be long," she said to Reg, "You'll look after everybody, won't you?" At sixteen, Reg was the acknowledged "in charge" person. "And by the way," Betty said, "don't make too much noise. will you? Mrs. Piner gets very upset when there's a lot of noise." Mrs. Piner was the next door neighbour on the other side of us. The Piners had two children in their household, a boy and girl, whom we considered a bit spoiled. They were rather nice people, but were nevertheless a bit intolerant of our large family's occasional rowdiness. Their usual method of letting us know we were talking too loudly, was to knock on the kitchen wall with a broom handle. On occasion, Mrs. Piner had been known to threaten to call the authorities, so we had to be careful.

We promised to be good and with the best intentions went on chatting. Dennis ducked into his house and brought out some old used film that he'd brought from his workplace. It was no more good for anything, or so I thought. But Reg, Eric and Dennis decided to make stink bombs. They rolled the film up in tight wads, put a piece of paper around the wads and tried to light them. As the film caught, it smoldered and let off a most putrid stench. It filled the air and hung like a cloud over the whole back garden.

It was hard to get the stink bombs to burn properly. The darn things required a certain amount of air intake to get the correct effect. But the boys experimented diligently, and the rest of us stood around giving advice. After they had made enough of them to get it right, the boys began to compete with each other to see which could make the biggest bombs the fastest. Once the bombs were made, they tossed them out in the yard where they burned slowly, with thick smoldering acrid smoke pouring out of them.

At first it was really fun, but once the competition started, it got a bit too much. We were all yelling with excitement and holding our noses. The stench was terrible. Mrs. Piner came out of her back door and surveyed the situation. Bob saw her first and waved his arms at me. I, in turn, tried to get the attention of the others, but they were so engrossed they couldn't or wouldn't hear me. I picked up Reg's tennis racquet and whacked him, not meaning to hurt him, but I probably hit harder than I realized. Reg, however, didn't take kindly to my attention-getting method and turned round sharply, ready to do battle. I saw the warning signs and sprinted into the house, up the stairs and into the bathroom. The door had a lock, so I was safe. I was still clutching his tennis racquet.

The bathroom windows were open and the stench from the stink bombs filled the room. By climbing over the sink and leaning out I could talk to those below. I started giving orders that they'd better leave off making so much noise or they'd all get in trouble. I wanted to establish the fact that I was very grown up and could be in charge from the safety of the bathroom window. Reg, Eric, Dennis, June and Bob were all milling about in the yard and under the window. They paid no attention to my authoritative commands.

For sheer wickedness, I filled a bowl with water from the tap, sighted my targets carefully and then chucked the water out the window. Everybody but Reg saw it coming and scattered, laughing. But Reg was the lucky one. He got drenched. Oh, this was fun! I turned back to get more water. I was starting to enjoy this immensely. I threw the next batch as hard as I could to get everybody a little bit wet. They were yelling from below for me to stop throwing water, and Reg, who'd slipped in the house, was pounding on the bathroom door for me to "come out this minute," and give him back his tennis racquet.

I was not only stubborn, I was foolhardy. I kept the water going at a steady pace. Everyone who needed to go in or out of the house had to pass through the kitchen door, which was directly beneath the bathroom window. I had totally disrupted the stink bomb assembly line and now was threatening everyone who wanted to go in or out of the house. Reg found the opportune moment to duck back outside. I saw him standing just out of the water's reach in the middle of the yard. In his hands he was holding up my brand new bathing cap, threatening to tear it to bits. I was enraged at the sight, and ceased my merry water battle immediately. I picked up Reg's tennis racquet from the floor behind me and smashed the strings against the bottom edge of the window sash, twice. I was satisfied that the sharp edge cut through the strings; then I tossed it out the window to the ground below.

For weeks I had been looking for physical features in my brothers and sisters that I could claim as proof of genetic heritage. The idea that I had real live brothers and sisters was novel. I was trying to identify some physical evidence that we were indeed related by birth. Only Betty and I had brown eyes. Everyone else had blue eyes like Mother. But there were other things such as the shape of our faces, our noses and our hands that marked us as belonging to the same genealogical line on our father's side.

At this moment, looking out in the garden at Reg's face, I

discovered unequivocally that my brother and I had something that matched to a "T": our tempers. I recognized the flash point, and knew I was in trouble. I had seen the same flame of anger in Eric as well, though it had not been directed at me. I made a hasty decision to move out of the line of fire. I flung open the bathroom door, ran down the stairs, out the front door and down the street toward town.

As I ran I began to think of where to go. The only place I knew how to get to for sure was the Tube station. I thought I might go there and get on a train and ride around London. That would be fun. Unfortunately, I hadn't brought any money with me, so I couldn't do that. However, I could go down to the train station and watch the trains come and go. I got to the steel bridge that went over the train tracks, but the sides were too high for me to see over the top. I went across it and down the other side into the busy streets of Wembley. I decided to wander around and look the town over for a little while and then get back to the station when I was ready to go home.

I walked for ages along the streets of Wembley, sometimes stopping to look in the shop windows on the way. I thought I had my bearings, but I didn't. Eventually, I stopped someone to ask the way to the Underground. A nice lady gave me directions and off I went. I found the station all right, but it wasn't the same one that I was familiar with. It hadn't occurred to me that I might be directed to the wrong station. It didn't worry me though, because I was sure I could find the way back home.

I went down the steps and looked around the station. There was a bench, so I sat down pretending I was waiting for someone to get off the train. It was amusing for a little while, watching people coming and going, and it made me feel sophisticated sitting there alone in the train station. At last I decided to start for home. I must have turned the wrong way out of the station, because as I walked I didn't recognize anything. I stopped people to ask how to get to Vincent Road, but nobody knew. Finally I asked a policeman, thinking he would know, but he didn't. He made me go to the police station with him and handed me over to another policeman who sat at a desk.

"Whot's your name?" the officer asked in a cockney accent. I told him and he wrote it down on his note pad. "Where you from, then, duck?" he said. I gave him the address and explained to him that if he would give me directions to the "other" Wembley station,

I could find my own way home.

"Ow, I see," he said, looking at me as though I had a screw loose. He wanted to know how I'd got there in the first place, why I was wandering about getting lost, and on and on. I didn't want to tell him about the birthday party or the fracas I'd gotten into with my brother. In the end, I had to tell everything. He nodded knowingly and gave me a lecture about the curfew and about how I should get home before the sirens started. I'd forgotten about that. He called to another officer. They conferred for a few minutes, then the first one told me,

"Eddie'll see you get home, and don't go wanderin' about on your own again, you hear?" I felt properly chastised, and nodded my head. I went quietly with Eddie. So it was that I got home late in the evening with a policeman in tow. Doug answered the door and Betty was behind him. My mother and stepfather were behind them and the younger children were there too, but Reg and Eric had temporarily gone. All of the family were more than a little upset with me, and horrified to see the policeman. My new-found almost adulthood disappeared under their anxious questions and chidings. My attempted explanations sounded very childish, even to me.

Since I had come to no harm, there were stern warnings all round. When my mother got upset she had a habit of folding her hands together and making a clucking noise with her tongue while chucking her head back. "I don't know," she would say worriedly, "Blow me, I don't know," and she'd shake her head at you, anxiously, waiting for you to say something that would convince her everything was all right. When you did, she'd say with conviction, "Blessed children, I don't know." And then she'd smile at you. When she smiled at you, the anxiety was gone. It was good to clear the air.

All was well with Eric and Reg too. The next day, after we'd cleaned up the rubbish from the stink bombs in the back garden, they took June, Bob and me swimming. My bathing cap was not badly harmed. Reg complained that his racquet would always be wonky, but said he'd get new catgut and replace the strings. I don't know if he ever did.

The following week Mother took June, Bob, John, Maureen and me for a visit to see our grandmother in Wales. We went by train and

so had to walk with our cases to the station, and again over a maze of walkways when we changed trains. Bob, Mother and I took turns carrying Maureen, whose little three-year old legs could only walk short distances. The train journey was delightful and so was the week we spent visiting Wales. My grandmother's cottage was named "The Banal." It was an odd name, but perhaps was in the old French meaning: shared by tenants in a feudal jurisdiction. It was a cozy cottage set in the side of a hill, that overlooked a lush, green valley. The little lane that ran past the house was so narrow that we had to climb up the bank to let the occasional car through. Lorries didn't attempt to travel through it, and even bicycles didn't go more than two abreast.

My first impression of my maternal grandmother was that she was a strong person, both physically and mentally. She had outlived my grandfather by several years, and was able to run circles around me and my younger brothers and sisters. She must have been in her early sixties, and she was the most active and energetic "old" person I'd ever met. She raised chickens, guinea hens, geese, and an assortment of other creatures, including a couple of goats.

She awoke at dawn, got the fire going in the huge kitchen fireplace, fed and watered the chickens, and collected the eggs. Before breakfast, my grandmother took her fresh eggs to the market in Abergavenny, on foot. It was a distance of about four miles there and back, and hilly. Her day really started when she returned from the market.

I made many discoveries on that first visit, especially as I met relatives. I had delightful Aunts and Uncles galore and lots of cousins, all speaking with Welsh accents and willing to join in our daily adventures. It was in Wales that I first discovered castles, as there were many ruins scattered across the countryside. I'd read about castles, but had never actually seen one up close. My mother took all of us children to see Caerphilly castle. We walked into Abergavenny and then took the bus. What a wonderful adventure it was. We arrived back in Abergavenny in the late afternoon. Mother took us to the bakery, where for a few pennies, we purchased huge stacks of Welsh cakes to eat on the way home.

Sugarloaf mountain was within walking distance of the Banal, and we children could go there on our own and explore to our hearts' content. There was an old abandoned house on the way to the mountain, not far from my grandmother's cottage. We heard that it was haunted. We heard many tales of unusual happenings there. The local people avoided the place, but it presented a challenge to us children. We made sure that we frightened each other half to death by taking turns climbing and hiding among the rotting timbers, and making ghostly noises.

We returned to Wembley when the week was over. My holiday with my family lasted nearly a month. I returned to Wenhaston just before school began. I still had not seen Trafalgar Square or Buckingham Palace, but my world had expanded a good deal nonetheless.

Mummy was glad to see me and welcomed me back. Lily was leaving us soon and Mummy would be without help in the shop. I wished I didn't have one more year of school. What a strange turn my life had taken. Only a few short years before, I had loved school and higher education had been a cherished goal. I had begged to be part of the Saunders family and to have Dadda's name. I had nourished dreams of going to a better school, of making him proud of me. Now I wanted nothing better than to be able to leave school and strike out on my own, to "make something of myself" by the skills I already believed I possessed. I was no longer a nobody without identity. I had found my family and I was beginning to find my footing.

There was something else working through all of this that I was unable to see at the time. Looking back over the years, I can see how God has guided my life, how He has led me in the way He wanted me to go. I'm convinced that though I wasn't aware of it at the time, God had His hand on my life. He led me through the maze and intricacies of childhood so that His higher purpose could be worked out. While I was crying and begging to be adopted into a human family, my Heavenly Father was leading me into adoption into His own special family. He well knew that my biological, earthly family would someday be precious to me. But more than that, that His desire for them, as for me, was to bring them to that place of awareness of His everlasting love; to draw all of us into His Heavenly family.

It would take me a lifetime to learn His ways and to accept His leadership. For this moment I was blind and dumb, struggling with worldly emotions and ambitions. I continued to look for a permanent home on earth, searching for the place that would offer me the best security, love, and peace.

In Wenhaston as in the country places of Wales, the world moved at a slower pace than in the cities. But because of the war, the pace had stepped up considerably. In the most remote corners of our island country, people understood the meaning of wailing sirens and the need to carry their gas masks. The country was united against a common enemy, and no matter the sacrifices, the majority of the people were prepared to see it through to the end. The changes in our world came subtly, but most noticeably in our quiet village.

One of the most prominent changes in Wenhaston was the increase in population that came with the evacuees and the troops of soldiers who moved in and out of our village. The more subtle changes were in the ways our lives became geared to stay alert, and how attuned we became to accepting our new situation.

On my way home from school one day, I saw workmen installing a telephone kiosk at the place where Back Road met Front Street. Though it was a long time before telephones were commonplace in private homes in Wenhaston or Wembley, it was now possible to telephone certain places of business. It was thought to be a step forward, particularly for emergencies, but it was soon adapted for every use imaginable. The kiosk seemed always to be occupied, and sometimes a line formed outside, while villages waited their turn. How quickly we moved into the new telephone era, and we wondered how we had ever done without it.

Despite the telephone, our best means of communication was still the reliable postman. He delivered mail to Majuba house twice each day, and always we were anxious to get news from far away. We had never understood about Lenny's letters coming to us after he was reported missing. Always we hoped there had been a mix-up and that we would hear from him again. To our delight, we did hear from him. Because of the censoring, we were not able to make out exactly were he was, but we knew beyond a doubt that he was alive by the dates on the letters.

Lenny said that he had been incapacitated by a leg wound. He claimed it was nothing to worry about and said the leg was healing nicely. A severe case of malaria had hospitalized him for a long time. He told us that no sooner had he partially recovered from one bout, than he was struck down again. It had taken weeks for him to recover his strength enough to sit up and write letters. Fortunately, he was now on the mend and hoped to be out of hospital soon. He did not mention coming home on leave, but the fact that he was alive and recovering from his infirmities was wonderful news indeed.

School was a bore for that last year, and I became a bit of a rebel. One day when I was poking about in the bicycle shed, I found my old catapult and some of the lead pellets Dadda had helped me make. We originally made them for target practice or to shoot at the occasional rat that showed itself around the dustbin. I know Dadda would have been horrified to learn I was now using them to break the school windows. It was pure devilment, and no mistake. I was disgruntled with school and dissatisfied with my own seemingly endless failures.

Enduring Sangster's daily tirades was hard to bear. Besides, like most of my peers, I did not have clear direction for the future. How could we really plan beyond the end of the war? Did it really matter whether we planned a career or not? With all the bombs that the Germans were dropping on us, would we even survive until the end of the war? No one could hazard a guess. It was better not to think too long and hard about it.

At thirteen and a half, I was too old to play the games I'd once enjoyed, and too young to join up for military service. I took out my frustration on the school building, methodically putting holes in most of the windows that were reachable from the playing fields behind the school. The pellets went in cleanly and left little round holes, so I had to go back several times to make any noticeable amount of damage to them. It was an exhilarating challenge.

I had to be especially cautious and resourceful after my first forays. I knew Mr. Donald Crisp, the village policeman, would be watching the building to catch the perpetrator. He lived only a few doors down from the school. The Tibbenhams lived in the first house, hard by the school. I suspected that they had a good view from their kitchen window of anyone going down the path to the playing field behind the school. Actually, I was nearly caught once. Primrose and her mother were out in the front garden as I rode my bicycle out of the lane. They didn't look up as I rode by them, so I didn't think they'd seen me. It was a close call, and I decided to branch out away from the school. It was then that I became the village terror, making targets of windows up and down Front Street.

It became a nasty game for me. The mysterious window breaker became the talk of the town. At school, we were alerted to be on the lookout for the culprit. I was gaining fame without anyone knowing about it. I wanted to stop, but it was like a disease that had control of my mind. I started to regret I'd ever got involved with it. It was a crazy thing to do. My downfall came in an unexpected way.

Two of our resident soldiers had moved out and another had gone on leave. The remaining one had Lenny's room all to himself, and I was able to go back to my old room for a short while. It was lovely to have my own room again, even briefly. I had my catapult and some pellets in a little bag in the top drawer of my chest of drawers. One morning I got up and looked out of the window at the heap of ground over the air-raid shelter. It was now beginning to get weeds all over it, but it was still an ugly mound.

Something moved in the grass. I thought it might be a rat, so I got my catapult out, put a pellet in and sighted it. Whatever creature it was must have dug in because it didn't run away. I shot a few more pellets but didn't hit it or even seem to scare it. I kept looking intently, but saw nothing moving. What I did see as I scanned the scene was a bag of something that looked like rocks. I was curious about it because it didn't seem to belong there. At least, I'd never seen it before.

I hastily put on my clothes and ran down to have a closer look. I had not been anywhere near the shelter since Dadda's death. It felt strange to go so close to it now. I avoided looking at the steps and the bird shed door. My nightmares had lessened somewhat, and I could almost force the images from my mind. I wanted to avoid having the scene in my mind's eye, so I skirted the steps without looking at them. I found the bag and pulled it up out of the dirt.

To my consternation, it was full of hand grenades. I threw them back on the ground as though they were snakes, and ran in the house to tell Mummy. Our soldier was already downstairs at the breakfast table. Mummy was serving him porridge. Both of them quickly came out to see the bag of hand grenades, and without touching them, our soldier verified that they were live grenades.

I was called in for questioning because I'd found them. There were two police officers besides Mr. Crisp: an army officer and Mr. Ellis from next door, in his warden's uniform. I couldn't answer any of their questions. I kept repeating that I had nothing to do with putting them there and didn't know anyone who could have. They also questioned Mummy and Lily and our resident soldier, but they couldn't shed any light on the matter either. It was a big mystery.

Later in the day, men came to dig around the shelter looking for other weapons. As they dug, they unearthed the pellets I'd shot in the ground that very morning. Of course they matched the ones found inside the school and the various homes where I'd shot them during my rampage. I don't know how I lied my way out of that kettle of fish, but I managed to escape punishment by the skin of my teeth. Mummy thought she recognized the pellets, and asked me about them privately. However, she didn't say anything to Mr. Crisp, and the matter was dropped.

I was glad in a way to be nearly caught. Though it added another layer to my full guilt pool, I had escaped no telling what punishment, probably life in gaol. I hated my own rottenness, first for the devastation and then for the lies I told to cover up my misdeeds. I buried the catapult in the woods and vowed never to make another one.

Chapter 15

Tidings of Comfort and Joy

O tidings of comfort and joy, comfort and joy
O tidings of comfort and joy.

Traditional English Carol

As Christmas drew near, I began to think of going to Wembley to be with my family. Mummy was going to stay with the Borrotts as she hoped that Lenny might be coming home some time soon. We still had not heard from Uncle Aubrey, and I knew in my heart that he must be dead. I couldn't believe he would have left us without a word. It just wasn't like him. Mummy said she didn't know what had happened to him. In any case she would not speak about it to me. I missed him almost as much as I missed Dadda, but I was beginning to develop a protective shell around myself. I would not dwell on the past or on anything painful. I was managing to get beyond all that, or so I thought.

I left for Wembley the week before Christmas. My sister Phyllis was home on leave from the ATS for a few days. She looked smart in her uniform and I was thrilled to hear the stories she told about her adventures. She was a member of the "First Mixed Battery" to be formed at Bristol-Portis Head. Her ack-ack gun crew worked together to shoot down enemy planes that were caught in the searchlights at night.

She reluctantly told me the horrific story about how the Germans bombed Leeding Hill in Bristol and how she helped dig out survivors. I listened open-mouthed as she told me about finding arms and legs and digging further to find the mangled bodies that went with them. The war, she said, changed her perspective; it gave her a sense of living only in the moment, that nothing was permanent. She did not want to speculate on tomorrow or the future. She had been engaged to a local Wembley chap, but when she was home on leave she broke their engagement and gave him back his ring.

Doug and Betty had moved into new quarters on Scarle Road, just a few blocks away. The Lounge in Mother's home had become an extra bedroom. While she was there, Phyllis and I shared the bed in the downstairs room. Phyllis liked to read, so we were able to swap books and magazines and bone up on all the "penny dreadfuls." Reg and Eric had factory jobs that required them to work in shifts at odd hours, so sometimes they had to sleep in the daytime. My older brothers and sister were talking about the news of the Japanese attack at Pearl Harbor, and what it meant to have America enter the war.

My mother loved to take the younger children out to the theatre. The afternoon pantomimes were very reasonable priced, but still an enormous cost for five of us. It was a wonderful treat for Christmas. That year we went to see *"Peter and the Wolf."* It was my first time to see a real live play in a theatre, and I was completely fascinated by it. On the way home in the Underground the siren must have gone. When we got to our station at Alperton, the wardens wouldn't allow us to get out on the street to walk home.

"Not 'til we get the all-clear, Ducky," the warden said to my mother's protests. My mother said a few "Oh, blows," and "I don't know's." She fretted about George being at home with Maureen, but then got us marshaled into a bunch, and we sat huddled together so we wouldn't get lost. The station was crowded. As each new lot of passengers got off at the station, we became more tightly packed. We could hear the thud of bombs and the roar of the guns. I wondered where Phyllis was, and if her crew had caught a Jerry plane in their searchlight. Every so often the wardens would come down to where we were and give us an update on what was happening. Some of the bombs were very close, but there were no direct hits. Someone started singing *"There's a land of begin again,"* and soon the crowded underground shelter was ringing with the popular tunes of the day. The younger children grew weary and finally slept. The singing faded and soon the rest also fell asleep.

Sometime early in the morning, the wardens came to tell us it was all clear and we could go home. The concrete floor had been a hard bed, and some of the older people and even the children had stiff necks and sore backs. It was good to get out in the fresh air.

George had been worried sick about us. He was genuinely relieved to see us. He soon had some tea and toast for all of us to eat, and we were ravenously hungry.

George and Mother decided that we should not stay in Wembley for the holidays. She told us we were going to Gran's for Christmas. That same afternoon, Mother supervised while we packed some clothes, tidied the house, and set off with our gas masks strapped around us for Alperton station. My stepfather had to work and couldn't go with us, but he was to come along the next day. So the five of us, June, Bob, John, Maureen and I set off with Mother for Abergavenny.

It was a lovely Christmas. My grandmother killed two fat hens, chopping off their heads in one swift stroke. We watched in awe as they ran around the yard spurting blood. When they dropped, my grandmother picked them up and hung them up with string around their feet, to bleed and get cool. Later we helped pluck the feathers into a big sack that was already half full. She said she would have to wash the feathers and pick them over; then she'd use them in heavy ticking to make feather mattresses. I learned that as in Wenhaston, so in Wales. Nothing was wasted or thrown away.

My stepfather arrived on Christmas Eve in the middle of the afternoon. Gran had set us all busy doing something. Snow had fallen and she was out putting some fresh straw in the chicken house. My mother was cooking something delicious smelling in a pot hanging over the huge kitchen fire. June and the boys and I had gathered some holly branches, armloads of them. Gran said that we should put the ones with bunches of red berries on the mantelpiece, and hook some over the curtain rods. We should pile up the rest of them in a heap outside where they would dry. Eventually she'd be able to use them for faggots to start the fire.

After supper, George and the boys left to join a group that was going round to houses singing carols. The rest of us were sitting cozily round the fire. We sat up straighter when they came outside the kitchen door and began to sing for us. I had been feeling sorry for myself, missing the wonderful closeness of Dadda and my wonderful Uncle Aubrey on other Christmas Eve nights. I was foundering again on a dark shoal until I heard those beautiful male voices outside in the cold night air. Their voices brought me out of my depths. Suddenly the realization that this holiday represented the birth of Jesus reawakened a spark in me that I thought was forever gone.

I could hear the sound of my brother Bob's voice above all the rest. He had a way of pronouncing words in his little boy voice that was instantly recognizable and charming. He changed all the "r's" into "w's" and sang at the top of his lungs. I can hear him to this day singing,

> "God west ye mewwee genkalmen, let nothing ye dismay. Weemember Cwyist our Savieor was born on Cwismmas day..."

It was a jolly group. My uncles Tom and Joe and their sons had done the rounds along with my stepfather and my two young brothers. Now as they sipped Gran's home-made brew, told stories and sang rollicking songs, I had fleeting thoughts of the *Compass*, the stained piano, Lenny's accordion, and the friendly talk around the dart board. It all melded together somehow. I dared not think about Dadda nor attempt to make comparisons. I buried my memories a little deeper and covered them over with the pleasure of the moment. The Welsh voices joined with the cockney accents, and Bob's unique style was something to remember. I was surrounded by boisterous, laughing, happy family members.

It was good! Gran's cottage was not large, having only two bedrooms under the sloping eaves. Mother, George, John and Maureen shared one of the bedrooms, while the rest of us shared the other with Gran. Bob had a small mattress with blankets on the floor, while June and I were to share the bed with our grandmother. We children retired early, earlier than we wanted to. Our bedroom was over the kitchen and the floorboards had wide gaps between them, so the room was toasty from the rising warmth of the kitchen fire. We could hear the men's laughter floating up to us. By stretching flat out on the floor we could see through the cracks in the floorboards to the activities below. Soon my uncles said their goodnights and left to go home. We knew the others would soon wend their way up the stairs.

We scampered into bed and pulled the covers around our heads, pretending to be asleep. Gran brought her oil lamp up the stairs with her and began to undress. June and I peeked through the covers to watch. Gran removed her long, almost floor length apron first, then her homemade cotton dress. Under her dress, she wore a long white petticoat that she pulled over her head, and laid ceremoniously over a small chair. Under the petticoat, Gran wore a "combination," knitted woolen underwear made like a boiler suit, that was buttoned from the neck all the way to the bottom. Underneath the "coms," as they were commonly called, she had a vest and other garments, most of which remained on her body. She removed her boots and lisle stockings, one at a time, then she put her long, flannel gown over her head.

By this time, June and I were shaking with laughter, wondering what she'd do next. Gran sat in a small chair by the bed and pulled on bed socks over her bare feet. Lastly she took a flannel cap and put it over her head and tied it under her chin, turned out the lamp and slid into bed with us. Hardly had her head touched the pillow, when she began to snore. June and I laughed cautiously as we, too, drifted off to sleep.

Christmas day dawned beautifully. There was a fresh layer of snow over the ground, that turned the world into a fairy land. Gran was already up, dressed, and feeding the chickens by the time the rest of us awoke. Our window overlooked the valley, so the three of us pressed our noses to the glass to get a better look. My stepfather was outside bringing in coal for the fire. We could hear him talking to Gran and see the little puffs of smoke from his morning cigarette curling over his head in the cold air.

Mother and Gran began preparations for dinner before we'd finished our breakfast eggs and toast. The smell of the feast reached us outside as we frolicked in the snow, pelting each other with snowballs first, then gathering up the snow in strange looking shapes to make an unwieldly snowman.

Dinner was festive with the two roasted hens, lots of vegetables, and homemade bread. We had plum pudding for afters that was loaded with little trinkets and one thrup'ney bit. We all got something in our piece of pudding, but John was the lucky one who discovered the thrup'ney bit in his piece. There were Christmas crackers all around after the pudding, so we pulled them with delight and scrambled through the contents inside. There were the usual paper hats and miniature games and funny toys. We donned our hats and took turns reading the riddles that came rolled up along with them. The adults brought out their presents and passed them round.

We children had no gifts to give, either to each other or to the adults. My stepfather had brought a bottle of port for Gran to serve with the Christmas pudding, and Mother had hidden some things in her suitcase under Maureen's clothes. She had some cigarettes for George and some sweets for Gran. We children watched in surprise as Mother brought out several small packets wrapped in tissue paper. My sister Betty had managed to get gifts for everyone: Mother, George, Gran, and each of us children.

It's hard to remember exactly who got what, but I remember some of the children's gifts. I know there was a painting book, the kind that had the paint already in the page. When the picture was brushed with water, the colours appeared like magic. There was also a paint box and a wooden top with a small stick and string tied to it. I clearly remember my own gift because it was the first grown-up present I ever received. It was nice-smelling talcum powder in a pretty round box and a blue powder puff that went with it. I don't think I ever used it. I kept it for ages, carefully tucked away among my prized possessions.

Our journey back to Wembley on Boxing Day was uneventful. The trains were packed with servicemen and civilians like ourselves who were returning home after the holidays. Two days later, I left Wembley and returned to Wenhaston. I now had only six months to go before leaving Wenhaston school forever. Though I chafed at the thought of enduring that length of time under Mr. Sangster's tutelage, in actual fact the last months were not nearly so bad as I had anticipated. I was busy with many things and the weeks seemed to fly by. I left the school and the final vestiges of my childhood the first week of June, 1942.

My first real job outside of the shop, was as a nurses aide in training at Halesworth hospital. I was assigned to a ward on an upper floor. I reported to the head nurse each day when I came in at seven o'clock, and before I left at three o'clock in the afternoon. I never saw the head nurse during the day, but I was at the beck and call of all the nurses who worked under her. The job should rightly have been called "ward cleaner" because that's mostly what I and the other aide did.

The ward seemed huge, and the floor had to be swept, scrubbed and waxed every morning. Besides the ward, we also had to clean another large room that was considered the nurses station, and a smaller room that was their "common room". We gave the ward a second sweeping after the noon meal, and then went over it with the "buffer." It was a heavy bottomed object, covered with rags, that we had to swing vigorously from side to side and under each bed in order to get the linoleum shiny.

The nurses gave the cleaning duties to the youngest and newest aides that came to work at the hospital. For several months a girl named Marjorie and I were the cleaning staff for Ward A. We also had bed-pan duty. We fetched clean ones from the cavernous bathroom for the nurses when they rang a bell. Then we collected them again from beside the patient's beds, emptied and cleaned them, and sterilized them in a special sink that had a boiling water spigot.

There were other jobs that weren't quite as strenuous or distasteful, and were somewhat more enjoyable. Rolling out the meal cart while the nurses distributed the food was one of these, and so was collecting the dirty dishes afterwards. We sometimes exchanged a word or two with the patients while we cleaned. It seemed to brighten the day for some of the patients. When a patient in pain smiled at us, the job seemed not quite so difficult. The most enjoyable job that Marjorie and I shared was preparing beds for new patients.

Learning the art of making beds was the only part of the job that I ever felt was training me for nursing. In the beginning, the nurses showed us how to do the job properly, how to layer the rubber sheet in the correct position, how to stretch the sheets tight enough to bounce a penny on them, and how to fold the corners swiftly and neatly. When the nurses were satisfied that we were capable, they allowed us to do them on our own. It seemed like a great accomplishment.

I worked at the hospital for nearly a year, not earning much money, but I was supposedly getting nurse's aide training, which was worth a lot. I gave Mummy a small amount of my earnings each week, which was the accepted practice of that era, and saved most of the rest to buy a new bicycle. I helped in another way also. By being in Halesworth every weekday, I was able to do any shopping that needed to be done. It saved Mummy and Lily from making so many trips.

Sometimes I stopped in at Owen's house before I left for home. I would just call in for a moment and briefly exchange pleasantries with his mother. Owen was never at home on weekdays, but we saw each other on Saturday afternoons at the picture show. I was now able to buy my own ticket, and occasionally afford my own cigarettes. Most of us smoked liked chimneys, girls as well as boys. It was the thing to do. I never learned the art of holding a cigarette between my lips while riding a bicycle. That was mainly a boy's skill, and I was beginning to become aware of more feminine traits.

Cigarettes were scarce. Loose tobacco was easier to come by. We began to roll our own cigarettes in a simple hand held device that had two rollers covered with a bit of grey rubber. We inserted small squares of thin cigarette paper between the rollers, put in a smidge of tobacco, licked the edge of the paper and clamped the contraption shut, rolling the cigarette with our fingers until we had an acceptable facsimile of the real thing.

Though we sometimes behaved as if there was no war going on, freely living our daily lives, we were always conscious of lurking danger and of the tightening restrictions the war brought. We heard our bombers with their Spitfire escorts flying out on their nightly missions, and heard them roaring home again in the early morning hours, some of them limping badly and some not returning at all. Nightly, the sirens sounded and searchlights lit up the skies over our heads. The skies were dotted with barrage balloons, but occasionally an enemy plane slipped through. Then dogfights and the angry rat-tat-tat of machine gun bullets shattered our countryside peace. We carried our gas masks faithfully, sniffing the air for anything that smelled out of the ordinary.

The call of duty was strong. Owen, like all the young men, was eager to join up, and was thrilled when the army sent him an invitation. I went to see him off at the station early one morning. We stood on the platform chatting until the train roared into the station. We promised to write to each other, and though we didn't say it in so many words, we made unspoken vows of commitment to each other. There seemed to be so many urgent things we needed to say that we had never said to each other before, and now didn't know how to put them into words.

At the last minute, Owen boarded the train, put his luggage in the first carriage he came to, and let down the carriage window. He leaned his tall frame way out, and smiling broadly, swooped his arms down to encircle my waist. He picked me up from the platform and kissed me resoundingly on the lips. I was shocked silly, but in a wonderful way, not caring that we were surrounded by dozens of people who would probably think our behaviour bizarre. I returned his embrace, loving the moment. As the doors down the line slammed and his father's whistle sounded the signal for the train to leave, Owen lowered me to the platform. It was just in the nick of time. I blushed furiously and he laughed at my confusion. He leaned out the window, grinning and waving and throwing kisses to me until the train left the station.

I waved for just a minute, then I ran across the bridge, grabbed my bicycle and raced to the top of the hill where I could catch another glimpse of him as the train went round the curve. The train picked up speed and chugged out of sight. My last glimpse was of his blonde head and long arm, still smiling and waving and blowing kisses.

After the train was really gone, I stood in the same spot for ages, holding on to my bike, tears streaming down my face. How strange it is that the source that sparks the greatest fire also produces the deepest sadness. I stood alone, overcome with muddled new feelings of love, joy, and happiness, mixed with a terrible sense of loss and loneliness. His last words, shouted over the roar of the train with a wide grin, had been a promise: "I'll write every day." I knew he meant it. It was something to hold on to.

Owen was true to his word. He did write to me every day for the first few weeks he was away, and for the next two years there continued to be a steady flow of letters that went back and forth between us. I answered them all. We never seemed to run out of things to write to each other. I looked for the early morning and afternoon post with religious fervour. I couldn't always be at home when the postman came, but the letters gave me a reason to hurry back from wherever I'd been.

In the beginning, Mummy didn't particularly like the idea of my total involvement in this letter-writing campaign. She frowned on the acronym SWALK (sealed with a loving kiss) that we wrote boldly across the back of each envelope. Her main concern was that it seemed rather vulgar. It was the same old "What will people think?" syndrome that had been a part of her upbringing and still haunted her strait-laced generation. She eventually accepted Owen as being special to me, and allowed me to have him in for tea when he was home on leave.

In other ways, too, Mummy was beginning to bend a little. The events called "socials" at the Hut on Friday and Saturday nights were now crowded with service men and women, as well as with half the village, young and old. Some American servicemen were now part of the crowd as well, adding a new dimension to village life. The socials were a marvelous diversion, and the fish and chips shop next door to the Hut did a lively business. When the fish ran out, they served double portions of chips. Potatoes were still plentiful. The *Compass* and all the surrounding pubs were filled to overflowing.

New bands including American players were appearing in rotation with other areas, and they played new tunes. Dances like the tango and the jitterbug were getting popular, and we were challenged to learn all the new steps, while we continued to polish our skills on the old, familiar foxtrots and waltzes.

Lenny's Joyce and her mother often came to our house on their way to the "social" evenings. They finally persuaded Mummy to go with them. Of course Mummy wouldn't dance. Most of the older people wouldn't, but it was the beginning of a new era for some of them. They watched us younger ones and kept an eye on us. When we didn't have male partners, Gonie, Joy, Primrose, Gladys, Barbara, Clara, and I would dance with each other. Nothing escaped our chaperones' attention. Whenever a boy from school asked us to dance, they nudged each other and snickered. When a soldier asked one of us to dance, the older women raised their eyebrows and watched intently from their chairs along the wall.

Joyce was a good friend and frequent visitor to our house. She shared Lenny's letters with us, and helped us prepare parcels of homemade cake and other special treats to send to him. We only knew he was well, and was with his unit somewhere in the world. We still couldn't guess where. Every time we thought he might come home on leave, his unit would move and he would go with them. He was an excellent mechanic and I'm sure his skills were much needed. The fact that he was alive and well, with only occasional bouts of malaria, was all that mattered. We wrote to him faithfully. Sometimes Mummy would ask me to write to him for her. It was a special duty that I enjoyed immensely. Between all of us, our letters kept our postman hopping.

Joyce bought a new bicycle and sold her Raleigh Sport model to me. It was in great condition with fairly new equipment that included a three speed gear shift, a dynamo and a complete tool kit in its black leather saddle bag. It was the first bicycle that I totally paid for with my own money, and I treasured it.

In the summer of 1943, I left the Patrick Stead hospital at Halesworth and transferred to Bulcamp Union, the place where Joyce worked as a nurse. They needed certain employees, and I was ready to make a change. The hours were different: eight to five, with an hour for lunch. I was suited for the job and the pay was about the same. The work was not quite as demanding and it was closer to home, being only a mile and a half instead of three miles.

The Bulcamp residents who were able did much of the hard work, scrubbing and waxing floors in the wards and in their own quarters. The men kept the grounds and cleaned windows outside. Though Joyce lived at home, some of the nurses boarded on the premises, having private rooms with shared bathrooms and kitchens. One whole section of the second floor was off-limits to the residents. I was hired to clean the nurses' quarters, their common room, the paid workers' common room and bathrooms. It was a large area, but the cleaning was done to a set daily schedule, so it was not overwhelming.

The rest of the paid workers including the resident's kitchen supervisor, the seamstress, the supervisor of ward cleaners and various others met in our common room at lunch time. They were a nice group, and we soon became good friends. Often if I was not too busy, one of them would ask me to help them with this or that. If I needed a hand with something, one of them was sure to help. It broke the monotony of humdrum routine to visit with each other now and then.

Dora Self was Bulcamp's seamstress. She mended everything

imaginable: sheets, shirts, underwear and mattress covers. She was also one of the newer employees. Her job had been vacant for about six months before she arrived, and there was a backlog of repairs to be done. Dora was a whiz on the sewing machine, and in a short time had begun to make a dent in the stacks of torn clothes and bedding that had almost filled the little room where she worked. She was from Wenhaston too, and lived with her mother in one of the Council Houses by the school, next to Ruth Napthine.

Dora liked to laugh and sing. Often after we'd eaten our lunch and still had some time, Dora would tell us funny stories, or she'd start us off singing a song and we'd all join in. We began to meet in the mornings and ride to work together. We'd wait for each other for the ride back in the evenings, usually chatting and singing all the way.

Dora was married, and her army husband was overseas. Her mother kept Dora's two small children, Gillian and Allen, during the daytime while Dora worked. On Saturday nights Dora crossed the road from her house and joined the rest of us at the social. She was a terrific dancer and I learned all the new steps from her.

I'd been at Bulcamp almost a year when I had an awful accident that put me out of commission for three weeks. I was helping to clean the windows in the women's ward. They were very tall windows and the top ones were almost impossible to reach without a ladder. By standing on a chair and using a rag on a broom handle, I could almost reach the top. The chair I was using was a ladder back type, and I attempted to use it as a ladder. When it slipped, I fell full force, head over tin cup and landed astraddle the chair, injuring my pelvis as well as cracking my head on the hard floor.

The nurses came rushing, checking me over for broken bones. Unfortunately, Joyce was working the night shift and was not on duty at the time. I would probably have confided in her and she would have understood that I didn't want to be put in one of the hospital ward's beds overnight, which is what I thought might happen. So I said nothing to the nurses that came to tend to me. They were nice, sterilizing and bandaging the gash in my forehead. They didn't realize that I'd damaged my pelvis and I was too embarrassed to tell them.

They gave me permission to leave work early. Dora took the

liberty of leaving early with me. She hadn't asked permission, but she was her own person and most often didn't wait for others to make decisions for her.

I don't know how I managed to ride my bike home. It was a painful ordeal. Dora took me to her house and put me to bed. Then went to fetch the doctor and went to the shop to tell Mummy I'd had an accident. The doctor couldn't come that evening, but the District Nurse came. She said I needed compresses and scolded me for not staying at Bulcamp where the nurses could have seen to me. Joyce came in the morning when her shift ended. She scolded me, too, but brought me some magazines to read.

I couldn't read them though or concentrate on anything for a while. For several days I stayed in bed in terrible agony. Dora and her mother took turns caring for me. It was awful. Mummy came to see me and brought a big saucepan of good soup. She wanted me to come home, but the doctor said I shouldn't try to walk until the swelling went down. By the end of the second week, I began to hobble around and by the third week I was able to walk up and down the stairs. I was anxious about going back to work because the matron had sent word by Dora that she would have to fill my position soon. The nurses who had attended me had reported no broken bones or major injuries. Since no one had told her my injuries were internal, it was no wonder she couldn't understand the situation.

Dora went to talk to the Matron for me, explaining my problem and offering to do certain of my jobs while I was recuperating. I don't know what transpired between them, but apparently Dora lost her temper and said things to the Matron that she shouldn't have. The Matron threatened to sack her, and Dora then burnt her bridges by telling her what she could do with her job. We were now both out of work, for there was no way I could go back to Bulcamp under the circumstances. The Matron refused to give either of us letters of recommendation. It was going to be more difficult for us to find creditable employment.

When I was fully recovered and able to ride my bicycle again with only occasional discomfort, I helped in the shop while I looked for another job. Walter's sister Kathleen was now working at the shop, and though my help was appreciated it was not really needed. During this time of rationing and shortages, certain things had been cut out of the shop's inventory. Paraffin was one of these and cheese was another. Sugar, flour, rice, tea, Camp Coffee and chocolate were severely limited, but shipments came in sporadically.

Mummy had also sold off the entire stock of drapery and dress materials, along with lace and trims. Just a few cards of pins and needles, some buttonhooks that hardly anyone used anymore, and a few packets of coloured embroidery thread were left. Cigarettes were in short supply, and old-fashioned matches were beginning to be hard to get. "Zippo" lighters that used a thimbleful of fluid, a tiny bit of flint, and a wick that needed constant trimming were the latest thing.

I had been going back and forth to Wembley for short visits. Now as my sixteenth birthday approached, I went for a longer stay. My older brothers Reg and Eric would soon be leaving home to join up. While I was at home they took me to film shows and dances that I could never have gone to alone. I was just beginning to wear makeup, mostly a little Yardley powder and Tangee lipstick, which was all I could afford and literally all that was available. The Tangee lipstick changed colour after it was applied. It never changed much for me, but always seemed to remain a rather sickly orange. Betty gave me a tube from her precious store that was a brilliant lush red. I was delighted to have it and painted it on with an extra heavy hand, thinking that more was better. However, Eric and Reg didn't agree.

They took me with them one afternoon to see the American film, *"Gone With The Wind."* As we stood in a long queue outside the Majestic, they both began to chafe with me to rub some of the lipstick off. I didn't want to. I thought I looked nice with lots of lipstick. They told me in no uncertain terms that the lipstick made me look like a "proper tart" and threatened they wouldn't take me in to see the picture unless I wiped it off. Reluctantly, I complied.

The Cinema had graduated seats and graduated price levels. The further back you went, the cheaper the tickets. We went nearly to the back row, a mile from the screen. Fortunately we were young and had good eyesight. Reg flirted with all the usherettes and sat apart from me to make sure none of them thought I was with him. Eric, the good soul, sat beside me and at intermission bought me a packet of sweets. Several times they took me with them to the

Wembley school dances, which were similar to the socials we had in Wenhaston. Both my brothers were handsome and were excellent dancers. They danced with me sometimes, but I didn't lack for partners either.

Our neighbours Dennis Eaton and Darrell Scofield were both fairly good dancers. Dennis' older brother Ernie and his girl friend were champions. When they got up to do the jitterbug, the rest of us would clear the floor to watch them go through a fantastic routine. Ernie was a husky chap who was lighter on his feet than he looked. His girl friend wore short, full skirts that belled out and showed her underwear when he threw her over his shoulder and twirled her in time to the music. I wondered what the matrons in Wenhaston would have said about that!

In August, my mother was able to find a service job for me in Wimbledon, a town not far from Wembley. It was as a junior maid for a Doctor and Mrs. Gordon. Their baby boy was nearly a year old, a good natured child who stayed in his nursery a good deal of the time. Mrs. Gordon was a trained nurse and helped her husband with his surgery every weekday morning, sometimes beyond the noon hour. Mrs. Mullen, an older women, was the housekeeper. She cooked the meals and saw to the needs of the baby while the parents tended to patients. She was also the overseer for the young maids who came and went, apparently at a rapid rate. When I first arrived, Mrs. Mullen complained that I was the third girl she'd had to train that year.

It was my job to make the beds, clean the bathroom and Hoover the floors each morning. On certain days, Mrs. Mullen helped me change the sheets and clean the brass on the two outside doors. They were side by side, one for the house and the other for the surgery. Delivery people came to the kitchen door at the back of the house. Laundry, which included all the linens and the baby's nappies, was picked up twice a week. A man who drove a three-wheeled van and wore a striped apron delivered groceries, meat and vegetables. Their air-raid shelter was a dismal metal "dog house," as Uncle Aubrey had called them, in the back garden.

In the afternoons I took the little boy out in his pram for an airing if it wasn't raining. On my one afternoon off each week, I went to Wembley to visit my family. On my second visit home, I said goodbye to my brother Reg who had joined the Navy and was leaving the next day. The following month, I said goodbye to my brother Eric who also joined the Navy. I saw them a few more times before they were sent overseas. They wrote home and sent pictures, and we answered them. Letters were our only means of communication.

I spent most of my free time in Wimbledon in my room writing letters. I had no friends my own age close by. All my friends and family were miles away, either in Wembley, Wenhaston or in the Army. Even if I had known where the Cinema was, I couldn't go alone. While I worked at the Gordons' house, my spare time was not truly my own. In the evenings I sat with the baby, while the Gordons went to see a play or to other functions. I began to feel hemmed in by the circumstances and cut off from the outside world. I only stayed three months and then returned to Wenhaston.

Chapter 16

New Beginnings

For God so loved the world, that he gave his only begotten Son,
that whosoever believeth in him should not perish,
but have everlasting life.

John 3:16

I returned to Wenhaston in a way that seems humorous now. At the time it seemed rather sophisticated and dramatic, but it proved costly. I worked for the Gordon family in Wimbledon, and they had a private telephone. In fact they had two lines: one for Doctor Gordon's surgery and one for their residence. This seemed an unbelievable luxury to me. They instructed me how to answer the telephone, and to write messages on the pad beside it. I enjoyed answering the telephone more than any other job they asked me to do. I made a point, perhaps a bit overdone, of speaking clearly in the most posh voice I could muster. I hardly ever got to answer the telephone, though. When it rang, Mrs. Mullen usually beat me to it. I got to answer the telephone when she was out of the house, which wasn't very often.

I had given Mrs. Gordon my two-week's required notice, and she had promised to give me a letter of recommendation on my last day. I had only two more days left to work when I began to worry about what I should do next. I didn't especially want to stay in the city, and going to another strange home as a maid did not appeal to me either. I truly wanted to go back to familiar territory, to Wenhaston.

If I'd thought about it a week ahead, I could have easily posted a letter and received an answer, but I hadn't. Now there wasn't time for that. I thought about it and got the splendid idea of telephoning Mummy in Wenhaston from the Gordons' telephone. I had no idea of the cost or even whether my call would go through. There were some private telephones in the village, but the Saunders shop did not have one yet. Wenhaston did, however, have the telephone kiosk at the junction between Back Road and Front Street.

In those days, the telephone was a novelty in the village. Anyone passing by answered it when it rang. I planned to ask the person who answered the telephone to please take a message to the shop for me. I thought if I gave Mummy the Doctor's telephone number, she might be suitably impressed. She might also return the call, which would make me feel quite important. The kiosk telephone rang twice, and Mr. Ellis who lived right next door to the shop picked it up. I identified myself, and he was ever so surprised and pleased to hear from me.

"Hello Joyce," he said brightly, "How 'yer keepin 'yerself? Awright, are yer?" When I told him I was in London, he raised his voice a few decibels. It was as though he thought by shouting into the telephone, the sound would travel further. He went on for a bit, shouting in my ear and wanting to chat, while I tried to get a word in edgewise. I was finally able to break in and say that I wanted to get a message to Mrs. Saunders.

"Oh, yes," he said quickly. "She'll be in th' shop, likely, this time a' day. I'll go right away, down the road, and get her for you. I shan't be a mo." With that he banged the handpiece on the little shelf in the booth and rushed off. I could hear the kiosk door squeak as it opened for him.

I tried desperately to call to him, shouting into the telephone as loud as I could, asking him to stop. I didn't want to talk to her necessarily. I simply wanted him to take a message to her for me. There was nothing I could do but hold on to the telephone and wait, hoping desperately that Mummy could leave the shop. If I hung up I would lose the connection. If I tried to redial, since the receiver was off the hook, all I would get would be a busy signal. She would come to the phone box for nothing. I was in a quandary as to what I ought to do. It was possibly ten minutes before Mummy picked up the receiver; it had seemed to be at least an hour.

She was out of breath. She thought I must be in terrible trouble to have used the telephone to contact her. She had run all the way from the shop. While she gasped and panted, I hastily related that I had been working for a Doctor's family in Wimbledon, and that I was leaving in two days. I asked if it would be all right to come back to Wenhaston and perhaps work in the shop. When she caught her breath and realized I was not in serious danger, she relaxed somewhat. She told me that Walter's sister Kathleen was still working in the shop, but that she wouldn't mind me coming back to live at the house. She said Gladys was working for Clark's Shoe Shop in Halesworth, and that there might be other jobs available there. She promised to ask around.

Telephone Kiosk

When I hung up the receiver, I imagined Mummy walking home up Back Road, past the Newby's house to the shop. Possibly she would tell the customers in the shop where she had been. It was not an everyday occurrence for her to talk to someone in London by telephone. I felt sure it would make a nice tidbit of news over afternoon tea.

Unfortunately for me, the talk was not cheap. Mrs. Gordon was furious that I had used the telephone in the first place. When she found out what it had cost, she docked my pay, leaving me with hardly enough to pay for train fare. She also withheld my letter of recommendation, saying that my actions proved me untrustworthy. I was ashamed of myself and mortified that I was now leaving in disgrace. My employment record was beginning to look pretty dismal.

It was cold and rainy when I stepped off the train at Halesworth and caught the last bus to Wenhaston. The red double-decker buses had been replaced with the more comfortable, less noisy, but to my taste less daring, single deck green coaches. Knowing I would most likely be on the eight o'clock bus, Mummy had saved supper for me. It was a warm welcome, and I wondered briefly at the change in her attitude. It was good to be back in Wenhaston.

I visited some of my friends in the next few days. I stopped in at the shoe shop in Halesworth to see Gladys. It was easy to see that she was enjoying her job, and felt lucky to have it. Gonie was walking out with Norman Siberry, an American soldier stationed at Holton Air Base. Her brother Pat was now in the service, and her little sister Crenia would be leaving school soon. Gonie had "bobbed" her hair since I'd last seen her. Her beautiful chestnut hair that had been long enough to sit on, was now a more stylish shoulder length. It suited her lovely, oval face, but I missed seeing the braids.

Barbara English was courting a chap from Wrentham and both Clara and Joy were spoken for. Kathleen was engaged to marry an Irishman she'd met at a Saturday night social. All in all, things seemed to be changing rapidly. Dora's husband was still overseas, and letters were few and far between. She was doing sewing for people at home, so she was bringing in a little money, but not nearly enough to cover her family's needs. She had heard that the Americans had finished building Holton Air Base near Halesworth, and that they were hiring civilians for certain jobs. Dora and I got ourselves dressed up nicely and went to see if we qualified for anything.

It was a scary thing for us to do. We knew nothing at all about the "Yanks" as we called them, and had no idea whether we had the kind of skills they required. Dora was not the shrinking violet type, and with her in the lead I was ready to follow. We applied together. We discovered we met the qualifications to be waitresses, so after filling out masses of papers, we were sent to the base hospital unit for blood tests and a general physical. We were told to report back in a few days.

When we returned we were hired as waitresses. They gave us

light green cotton uniforms with white detachable collars and cuffs and white aprons. They also gave us a list of instructions about wearing our hair in a net, "snoods" we called them, and about wearing shoes and stockings. They gave us name tags to pin to our uniform dresses, and issued identification passes so that we could get on and off the Base. We were told where to pick up our paychecks at the end of each month, and when we learned the amount, it staggered us. In order to pick up our paychecks, we first had to report to the base hospital and get a blood test. We found it a strange arrangement, but since the pay was three times what our pay had been at Bulcamp, we didn't argue. We were pleased to have good jobs.

The base buildings were mostly Quonset huts, half round with tin roofing. There were also several oblong wooden buildings scattered about. Some of these housed the base exchange, the hospital, the canteen and the Officer's mess. We worked in these last two buildings. We would be alternating between the two with several other girls. The sergeant in charge made out the schedule and posted it on the bulletin board. Dora and I asked for, and usually got, hours that coincided so we could come and go together.

We were happy about that. Some mornings we started at seven and served breakfast at the canteen, and then switched to the Officer's Mess through lunchtime until three o'clock. Other days we worked in the canteen through lunchtime and then switched to the Officer's Mess for the evening meal, leaving the base at nine o'clock. The scheduling was such that we only had to stay late one Saturday night each month.

The base was quite noisy. Planes were going out and coming in most of the time. It was also an enemy target, and there were times when things got quite lively. Stray enemy planes found the Air Base on occasion. Though they never managed to hit it with bombs, there were several dogfights in the air above us. I was walking between the Canteen and the Officer's Mess one day when an enemy plane fired at us. It was a surprise attack, and people shouted and ducked for cover. The machine gun bullets rattled against the Quonset huts as the siren sounded. No one was hurt, but it was scary nonetheless.

On the days I finished early, I helped Mummy in the shop. Kathleen and I were good friends, and now that I was sixteen the three year age difference didn't seem so wide a span. We liked to style each other's hair. I was learning to use a "rat," a roll of soft brown material that you swept your hair around. I practiced on Kathleen. She in turn liked to put her hair up in rag curlers to make her naturally curly hair wave in a certain way. We spent a lot of time getting our hair just right.

Kathleen's fiancé Bob called in often to see her. Mummy referred to him as "Kathleen's nice young man." Everybody liked him. He was a round faced, good natured chap, who always had a cheery word for everyone. He was an accountant by trade and was a civilian employee working at Holton Air Base. He and Kathleen had met at the Hut at one of the Saturday night socials, under the watchful eyes of her mother Florrie and several aunts, cousins and other relatives who lived in Wenhaston.

Kathleen knew that the love of my life was Owen. She had seen me writing to him often, and had picked up letters from him on the doormat inside the front door. But she was a born matchmaker. She and Bob were always plotting ways for me to meet this friend or that whom they thought was just right for me. I did meet some of them, but no one I really cared for. It didn't stop them from trying, though.

My jobs at the Base threw me into constant contact with young American servicemen. We were not supposed to fraternize with the soldiers, which meant that we were not supposed to go out with them. It was all right to be friendly, to laugh and joke with them, which we did. Dora made no bones about the fact that she was married, so though she flirted somewhat, everyone knew she was not serious. With Owen as the absent love of my life, I too was spoken for. But a lot of the guys tried to start conversations with us, particularly over the counter in the Canteen. Mostly they were lonely and homesick and just wanted, as they put it, to hear our British accents. They told us it was "cute" the way we talked. They imitated the way we talked and we picked up some new words and phrases from them.

While we served them coffee, soup and sandwiches, we exchanged pleasantries. They would often pull out their wallets and show us photographs of their parents, their girl friends, and especially their cars. These were the things they missed. Most of them could ride American style bicycles, but found British bikes difficult to manoeuvre. They were astonished at the distances we traveled on our bicycles and at our dependency upon them.

I learned a lot of new things about food. One of these concerned ice cream. The Americans ate huge quantities of ice cream both winter and summer. This was a brand new concept for me. I associated ice cream with summer and particularly summer at the seaside, not as an everyday dessert. I found it to be delicious, but entirely too cold. It hurt my head to eat it, so I warmed mine in a saucepan and drank it. Thus I caused consternation among the American kitchen crew, who had never seen that done before.

Owen's letters and mine continued to travel fast and furious between us. They were still the main focus of my home life. When he was home on leave, he came to Wenhaston. Mummy invited him to stay for tea and to go with us to the Saturday night social. He let me know that he didn't like the idea of my working at the American Air Base. Owen, like many of his peers, was beginning to resent the competition the American soldier's represented. I tried to reassure him that I didn't "walk out" with any of the Americans, even though I often saw and danced with some of the same guys from the base at the socials. I had picked up some of the "Yank" words and phases, and that also became a source of contention between us.

I didn't think the rift between us was anything to worry about, but I did notice a certain coolness creeping into Owen's letters. He began to tell me about places he was going and the people he was seeing when he was off-duty. I could sense he was trying to make me jealous, and he succeeded. One girl's name in particular kept cropping up. He referred to her as being "built like a brick you-know-what." In return I began to call her the girl with the "large lumps." Not to be outdone, I described some of the handsome Americans who were begging me for "dates," a new term in my vocabulary. It was aimed at making him jealous, and I believe he was.

We supposed that we were good-naturedly teasing each other, but we both began to realize that something was going wrong with our relationship. When he was promoted to Sergeant, Owen sent me a picture of himself with his new chevrons on his sleeve, sitting on a low wall. He had a few days leave coming, but had decided to spend it in Colchester where "large lumps" lived. His unit would be moving soon, and he said he would be coming home for a few days before he was transferred. I was disappointed to say the least, and wrote back to tell him about an American fellow who'd been paying some attention to me at the dance hall in Southwold. Our letters were becoming more like weapons of war than endearing missives. I was beginning to hear the death knell to my future with Owen.

The good bands at the socials became legendary. Because of the scarcity of qualified British musicians, only a few good bands were native. The American bands had the edge in our corner of the world, and we knew it. It was an odd turn of events that our own single men were mostly out of the country fighting, while the American forces were on our doorstep in great numbers. We welcomed them and were glad they had come to help us fight the war. Our embattled country embraced them, but it was ironic nonetheless.

The band that became a huge favourite in the area seldom came to Wenhaston or to Halesworth. It played more frequently at the dance hall in Southwold. Dora and I liked to go there when Dora's mother would agree to put the children to bed for her. We could only go when we didn't have the dinner shift at the Officer's Club, because we had to be at Southwold by seven o'clock in order to get in. Going to Southwold also meant we would be much later getting home than when we went to the socials in Wenhaston or Halesworth, because of the distance.

We liked the Southwold socials for the superior band that played there and for other reasons too. For one thing the building was brick and the dance hall was nicely appointed with a proper bandstand and a spacious, smooth floor. There was a refreshment centre at one end of the hall where we could buy sandwiches and non-alcoholic drinks. Small tables were set up all around the edges of the dance floor where we could sit during intermission and have refreshments. The Ladies' room was spacious and clean, a real bonus that was hard to find in most places. Traveling by bicycle as we did, we always had to carry a change of clothes and shoes. Creature comforts were scarce; we suffered the long ride and inconvenience in exchange for small luxuries.

We depended on our bicycles to get us home. We could not afford to lose them. As bicycles and spare parts became scarce, bicycle thefts had become a growing problem. Some of the social halls we visited had no good place to store bikes, but at Southwold we could park our bikes safely in a sheltered area behind the hall for a few pennies. We only had to be sure not to lose our tickets for them.

Dora and I met many Americans at the socials in Southwold. The socials were popular with all the service men and women as well as civilians. We learned to recognize the country and branch of service each represented by their uniform style, colour and insignia. There were some Irish, some Canadian, some British, but the majority around our area were Americans. In Southwold the doors opened at seven; fifteen minutes later the place would be packed out and those in charge would be turning people away. There was a rule about how many the building should hold. When the limit of tickets was sold, they were not supposed to let anyone else in.

There were always those who hung around outside until intermission to see whether anyone would leave to go to a nearby pub. Then there were those who passed tickets to friends somehow, and with all the comings and goings, it was difficult for the headcounters to keep track. Dora and I danced and had lots of fun, and at the end of the evenings we rode the eight miles home together, usually singing and chatting all the way. The Americans liked to flirt with us, and sometimes asked us if they could see us home, which was laughable. Hardly any of them would have ridden the eight miles home with us and then the extra miles back to their bases. But we were flattered by the offers.

We never went with any of them because we both were "spoken for." Dora was already married, and by unspoken agreement, I knew I was going to marry Owen some day. But we did enjoy the camaraderie and the attention we got at the dances. One young man, Neal Hart, an American who played the piano with our favourite band, was especially friendly. During the long intermissions, when the band rested and they put Glen Miller records on the turntable, Neal sought us out. He was a delightful conversationalist, articulate as well as funny. More than anything he liked to play on words that might have nonsensical meanings. I liked playing word games with him and laughed at his corny jokes.

For instance, he said he played the piano "by ear," and waggled his head over the keys to show us how that was done. When he didn't pull out his wallet to show us a picture of his car, we asked him about it. He said he didn't have a car or a girl friend back home or a wife, either. He pulled out photographs of his parents and of his fourteen-year-old sister Mary Sue, and told us about his older brother Fletcher and sister-in-law Gwen, and their two small sons, Pat and Mike. In turn, I showed him a photo Owen had sent me early on, during his army training days. It showed him standing tall on a three-legged stool, naked from the waist up, holding his rifle over his head and smiling broadly.

Neal was different from most of the other fellows we met, quiet spoken and easy to talk to. He hated wearing glasses, but they were necessary to correct his shortsightedness. His eyesight prevented him from doing some of the more heroic jobs that he would have liked to do, such as flying planes. Whenever he could, he would take his glasses off. He would kid around and sometimes walk into things on purpose, making fun of himself.

For all his foolishness, he seemed more mature than most of the young Americans we had met. Neal was the studious type and his conversations showed him to be a deep thinker. He was the first person, outside of the long ago caravan missionaries, who talked about Jesus as though he knew Him personally. I was intrigued by his knowledge of scripture, and by the way he wove it into every conversation. Though some of the others in the group found this a bit offensive, I did not. I genuinely wanted to hear what he had to say about the Bible. We talked and sometimes muddled our way through differing views of what the church and Christianity meant to each of us.

Neal told us about his father's conversion from a hard drinking, brawling braggart to a gentle giant of a man. Neal told us that he himself had been well on his way to being an alcoholic, until his father led him to the Lord. Dora and I looked at each other when he told us that. Neither of us had ever heard that expression before. We didn't quite know what to make of it. Neal said that his father, who had been a hard drinking man in his early days, had been converted, "born again," and was now a Christian. Neal said that the change in his father's life had been a powerful witness to him, that their whole family's lives had been drastically changed. Dora and I had never had a conversation like this with anyone before.

Sometimes, over our cigarettes and sandwiches, Neal made us

laugh with funny stories. He could be such a clown. But sometimes his conversations turned serious. One evening there was a crowd around our table, and at intermission we had to make room for him to join us. I don't know how the conversation got started, but at some point Neal asked one of the men a startling question.

"If you were to die tonight, where would your soul go?" Everybody laughed, thinking it was a joke, but Neal persisted. "There are two possibilities," he said, "you'll either wake up in heaven or in hell. "Do you know where you're going after death?" he persisted. It was a hard question to answer because none of us at that table knew for sure. None of us thought it was even possible to know where we went after death.

"Do you know where you're going?" someone asked Neal, goading him. When he answered that his soul was going to heaven, someone else asked him how he could be sure of that. Neal answered with a question, "Do you believe the Bible is true?" he asked. We all more-or-less agreed that it was, but in actual fact none of us had given it much thought.

"Then, look up John 3:16," Neal said. "It says: For God so loved the world, that He gave His only begotten Son, that whosoever believeth in Him should not perish, but have everlasting life. This is the whole gospel in a nutshell. God has made us a promise to save us, if we trust Him."

Neal went on to explain that because of Adam's sin, we all are born in sin. That is to say, we are separated from God who cannot look on our sin. But he said God created man in His own image and He loves the man He has made. He wants man to come to Him and be reconciled. Neal went on, the Bible says "God is not willing that any should perish, but that all should be saved."

"If God loves us so much, why would He allow any of us to go to hell?" someone asked.

"Ah," said Neal, "that's because He's given us a choice. We have the freedom to choose whether we want to be His children or not. God doesn't want to force us; He simply invites us to come to Him of our own free will." "It's all in the Bible," Neal continued. "The whole story of how God has communicated the message of salvation down through the ages and how we can be reconciled to Him. In the Old Testament for hundreds of years a blood sacrifice had to be made as a sin offering. The blood of animals was given as the price for sin, and as a precursor for the ultimate sacrifice that would one day be given. The penalty for sin had to be paid, so man could be reconciled to God. In the new covenant, that perfect sacrifice is Jesus. He has paid the price for our sin."

Neal's eyes were bright with enthusiasm. He was leaning across the table, speaking quietly but earnestly. A few of the people at our table began moving away. The rest of us sat silently trying to digest what we were hearing, until one of the women in an army uniform piped up boldly:

"Well, I don't think I'm a sinner. I'm a good person and I'd never hurt a fly. I've never stolen anything or killed anyone." She hesitated momentarily and then said with a wide grin, "That is, except for a few Jerries." We all laughed and turned to see what Neal would say to that.

"God says we are ALL sinners," he said. "In Romans 3:23 it says, 'All have sinned and fallen short of His glory.' But God has provided a way for us to be forgiven. If we confess our sin, and ask Him to forgive us, He will be faithful to do just that."

There was no time for more. The band was tuning up and Neal went back to the piano bench to play for the second half of the evening. On the way home that night Dora and I talked about the evening and particularly about the question of dying and whether we would go to heaven or hell. Some of the old questions I'd asked Dadda came back to me. I remembered that he hadn't given me any clear answers then. Could this young American possibly know more than Dadda about such things? I didn't know the answer to that, and the more I thought about it, the more confused I became. I couldn't take it all in. Dora and I weren't going to die tonight, we reasoned. We were alive, young, and happy. It was too difficult to worry about such things. We began to sing *"Under the spreading chestnut tree."*

We didn't see Neal again for several weeks. Kathleen had asked me to be a bridesmaid for her, and her wedding plans were in full swing. We went to the dressmaker to be fitted for our gowns and to Jenkins Photographer's in Southwold to have our photographs taken. It was all very exciting. Kathleen's cousins Doreen Page and Mary Cullingford were also going to be bridesmaids, and Mollie

Huron was to be maid of honour. Mollie and Kathleen were about the same age and were good friends. Mollie was engaged to marry Peter Wright who was serving overseas in the Coldstream Guards. After the war, we learned of Peter's heroism at Salerno, and that he had been awarded the Victoria Cross for his bravery. He became Wenhaston's hero, and a source of great pride to the village.

At this time, though, all our attention was on hair styles, new shoes, flower arrangements and headpieces. Mr. Ennis, the Red Cross Director for Holton Air Base, who was to be Bob's best man, had promised to get the girls in the wedding party new stockings. Stockings of any kind were hard to get. We were thrilled to get our very first "nylons." The Vicar had read the Banns of Marriage at three Sunday morning services before the great day, so everyone in the village knew the date and time of the wedding. The church would no doubt be packed, and there would be a celebration at the *Compass* in the evening.

The day dawned bright and clear, though slightly chilly. It had rained the day before, and there were still a few puddles about, so we carried our good shoes in bags. I don't know how he managed it, but Bob arranged for the bridesmaids to be picked up by car and taken to the church in fine style. We assembled in the back of the church, shed our coats, changed our shoes and sorted through the bouquets while the car returned to fetch the bride.

Despite the fact that the bells were silent, it was a joyous occasion. Everyone was in high spirits. The men wore boutonnieres on their coats and the girls carried pretty bouquets. Kathleen was a beautiful bride and very nervous. She held on to her father's arm tightly as he walked her down the aisle. The groom was handsome and smiled reassuringly at Kathleen as she came to meet him at the altar.

Reverend Hardingham began the familiar passage, "Dearly beloved..." I giggled inwardly as I remembered the many times we had acted out the ceremony in our back yards. Now here we were, assembled at the altar, actually going through the wedding ceremony. In the blink of an eye, it seemed, we had made the transition from childish play-acting to adult reality. Walter was somewhere in the crowd that moved outside to throw confetti at the bride and groom. I imagined he was giggling too.

The photographs of the wedding took ages to be completed, but they finally arrived. In addition to the group picture taken outside

Bob & Kathleen's Wedding
1944

the church, we had gone to the studio in Southwold to have other photographs taken. At the photographer's insistence, each of the bridesmaids had posed alone for a keepsake shot. When I next wrote to Owen, I described every detail of the wedding and enclosed the photograph of myself in my bridesmaid's dress.

We had alluded to the subject of marriage many times in our letters to each other. We had talked about the kind of house we hoped to live in, and how many children we wanted. Both of us had agreed, since we were from big families, that we, too, wanted lots of children. We had taken for granted that we would someday be married to each other, although Owen had never actually asked me. Of late, we seemed to be on rocky ground. I was beginning to be unsure of my standing with him, but had been reluctant to initiate definitive questions. Now as I wrote shortly after Kathleen's wedding, while the air of romance was strong, I swallowed some pride and boldly asked him if we were considered to be engaged. I told him that I loved him with my whole heart, and wanted to know that I belonged to him.

It was agony for me to wait for Owen's reply. In a few days I received a letter from him telling me his unit was shipping out. He said by the time the letter reached me, he would be gone. All leave had been cancelled at the last minute, so he hadn't been able to get home to say goodbye. He said that he had visited with "large lumps" in Colchester, and that he had met her family. He said she was the one who had taken the photo of him that he had recently sent me.

A horrible pain formed in the pit of my stomach. It was obvious he hadn't received my letter with the photograph. The thought that it was too late for me to stop it added embarrassment to injury. I could read between the lines that this new interest was more than just a passing acquaintance. He said that he couldn't tell me where his unit was going, but he wanted me to continue to write to him. He ended the letter by telling me he would always love me as a special friend.

I was crushed. I was hurt. I was humiliated and undone. By turns I was angry, sad, miserable and devastated. I confided in Dora and poured out all my pitiful woe to her. She was a good listener and allowed me to rattle on and on, but had few suggestions on how to cope with a broken heart. She told me it would eventually mend, but that it would take time to "get over" Owen. In fact it did take a long time to get over Owen. My social outlook changed. I felt insecure without the protection of knowing he was in my life. I was no longer tied to anyone or "spoken for," but it was a freedom I did not feel comfortable with.

Kathleen and Bob moved into a lovely cottage on Narrow Way in Wenhaston. It was a large two story home, well suited for entertaining guests. Bob had many friends from Holton Air Base, and invited me when they had a gathering. They entertained many servicemen, and were constantly trying to introduce me to nice young men. One of these was George Merino. George, whose nickname was "Turk," was a lieutenant stationed at Holton Air Base. He was rather tall and broad shouldered and had an affable smile. He drove a jeep back and forth from the Base to Bob and Kathleen's house. Sometimes Bob rode with him, but Turk was not allowed to have any other civilians ride with him.

Turk was probably twenty six or seven, which made him ten years my senior. At that time in my life, though I preferred men a few years older, Turk seemed ancient. He flirted with me and seemed very nice, inviting me to go with the three of them when they were going on special outings. On one of the days when I was not working, I went on the train with them to Bungay, a town a little larger than Halesworth. Kathleen had been there before, but I had not. Most of my train travel had been going in the other direction, toward London. This was a new experience.

I enjoyed the day and went on several other outings with them. One Sunday Bob drove us to Felixstowe, a lovely seaside resort. Another time he took us shopping in Ipswich. Turk always went with us, and over meals in tea shops and pubs, we talked about life in the United States, how certain things were the same and what differences he saw. He made it known that he was interested in me, and asked me to wear a friendship ring. I liked him, but I didn't like him that much. At a social one night, one of Turk's acquaintances told me Turk was married. When I confronted Turk, he told me that he and his wife weren't getting along and that they intended to get a divorce as soon as he returned home. That was the end of the friendship for me.

After a prolonged absence over the summer months, Dora and I went back to the Southwold dance hall one evening in August. Neal was overjoyed to see us and didn't wait for intermission to talk to us. He left the band to struggle along without the piano. When we got over the initial greetings, he asked me to dance with him. I was a bit surprised because I didn't think he liked to dance. The band played a slow number called *"Won't You Change Partners?"*

As we danced, we talked. He told me he had wanted to get in touch with me, but didn't know how. He said he had talked the band into playing in Wenhaston twice, but we weren't there. I was touched by his genuine warmth and by his obvious interest in me. He asked me about Owen, wanting to know if I was engaged to him. I told him I was not sure of my standing with him because his unit had been transferred and I thought he had found someone else. It was the first time I had admitted to anyone outside of Dora what I feared to be the truth. We danced nearly every slow dance together. During intermission we sat near Dora but apart from the others at the table.

Neal asked me for my address so he could get in touch with me. He said that he wasn't sure when his unit would ship out, and said he wanted to be able to write to me. We joked about the address. In our small village in those days, merely the name of the person and the name of the village was address enough. Up until then, he said he didn't know my last name. He wrote them down in a small notebook he kept in his jacket pocket.

"He's keen on you," Dora said as we rode home that night. And although I protested, I had to agree with her and to admit that I liked him, too.

In the next few weeks, I saw Neal often. He was not stationed at Holton, but he was able to catch a ride over, and came to the Air Base to see me several times. At Holton, there was a USO building where they held live shows. He came to the canteen and drank gallons of coffee while he waited for my shift to end. There was a cinema that showed the latest American "movies." Though employees weren't supposed to fraternize, Neal took me to see the shows.

There were many other civilians there as well, and no one ever questioned our being there. I thoroughly enjoyed the live shows even though some of the American humour escaped me. I liked being with Neal. He was such a gentleman, serious and funny all at the same time. He asked me one night if I would "go steady" with him, which he said meant that neither of us would go out with anyone else. I told him I would like to do that.

For the next six months I went steady with Neal. I met him at the dances in Southwold whenever Dora and I could go. Sometimes his band came to Wenhaston. When it did, I introduced him to Joyce and her mother and to Mummy Saunders and lots of my friends who came to the socials. They invited him to the *Compass* to have a pint with them, but he was reluctant to go because he didn't want to be tempted to have a drink. It was hard for my friends to understand him. To most of them going to the pub for a pint was as natural as riding a bike or eating fish and chips. Some of them pondered whether his aversion to alcohol had something to do with his religion.

I wondered about that as well. When I asked him about it, he told me that where he came from, our pubs would be equated with bars, which were places of sin. He said Christians wouldn't think of going to them. I told him that even the Reverend Hardingham came down to the *Compass* occasionally for a pint. Surely Neal didn't see him as sinful. He said it was just a different way of looking at things, that in fact America had nothing to compare with the British pubs. We dropped the subject, but I continued to wonder about it.

I stayed in Wenhaston that Christmas. Neal had been reassigned to a Base near London and could not get off for the Christmas Holiday. He wrote to me though, a very sweet Christmas card that depicted the Christ child in the manger with angels hovering overhead. Since I had left school, my church attendance had become sporadic. Neal's card reminded me of what the season was really all about. I needed the reminder.

The Base at Holton let every one go early on Christmas Eve, and as Dora and I bicycled home a light snow began to fall. It was a beautiful sight. Mummy was cooking the evening meal when I came in. Later in the evening Joyce came for a visit. We had both begun to knit jumpers by a new pattern that was complicated. I had only a small portion of the back of mine finished. Joyce, who was a fast knitter, was well ahead of me.

It was a memorable Christmas Eve in that it was totally different from any I had ever known before. The fire burned brightly, but I felt a draft that brought a chill into the house. The house itself creaked and complained, as though it understood and sympathized with our lonely longings. We spent a quiet evening, knitting and talking. There were no decorations, no tree, and no carolers came to serenade us.

The Borrotts had invited us to have Christmas dinner with them, and we were pleased to go. I wracked my brain to try to think of something we could take to them that would be a special gift. Mummy had made sausage rolls and a Christmas cake that was decorated with all the old decorations saved from past Christmases. We needed some music to liven the day. I had a great idea and I believed it would work.

Mummy was doubtful, but she let me rummage through the box room. Uncle Aubrey's gramophone was almost buried under cardboard boxes that we had thrown in on top of it. It was heavy as the dickens and awkward to carry. With Mummy's help, a piece of board and yards of heavy string, we managed to get it situated on the handlebars of my bicycle to take it to the Borrott's house. The horn was easy because it was in a bag that we strapped to the rear carrier. Mummy had her hands full with the food she was carrying, some in her front basket and some strapped to her rear carrier. I'll never understand how we managed to get that lot down the hill to the Borrott's house without any of it falling off, especially since the snow had stuck and there were patches of ice. We walked our bikes most of the way, hanging on for dear life. Mummy fretted anxiously the whole way.

We got there without mishap. Joyce's brother Derek helped us untie the gramophone, laughing as he lugged it in the house. There was a lovely warm fire going in the heath and the room was cheery with paper chains across the mantel. There was much laughter as we wound it up. We blew on the needle to get the dust off. In another moment there was a hissy scratching and then the music boomed out: *"Miss Otis regrets she's unable to lunch today..."* Everyone laughed at the silly old song. What a joyful noise it was. Soon we were all singing to the music, and when we ran out of steam, we ate the wonderful, delicious food.

We left the gramophone at the Borrott house. For one thing we didn't think we could haul it back up the hill, but for another it seemed the right thing to leave it for Joyce and Lenny for a future time when they would have a home of their own.

Chapter 17

A House Not Made With Hands

...we have a building of God, an house not made with hands, eternal in the heavens.

2 Corinthians 5:1b

The street in Wembley was packed with cheering people, running, waving their arms, shouting. My mother and I were finishing our shopping when we heard the news that the war was over. It was the seventh of May, 1945. We had been standing in queues nearly the whole morning, mother waiting at the butcher's and I at the greengrocer's. We had done very well between the two of us, and as we met we had congratulated each other on our successful shopping.

As Mother approached, she opened her mouth to speak to me when the sirens went, not one, not two, but sirens coming from everywhere—not the warning sirens, but the ALL CLEAR! She was mouthing the words, trying to make me understand, happiness bursting over her face. People came pouring out into the street joyfully proclaiming the news: "IT'S OVER, IT'S OVER, THE BLOODY WAR IS OVER!" We heard loud shouts and screams of joy over the wailing of the sirens. It was full daylight, but the searchlights were turned on and the ack-ack guns began to roar. Above the din, the church bells began to ring, first from one church, then from another and another, until the clanging was deafening.

I stood amazed at the noisy scene, trying to take in all of it. I wanted to remember exactly where I was and what I was doing on this momentous occasion. I turned to look at my mother standing beside me on the pavement. A moment ago her face was uplifted, glowing, eagerly straining to speak happy, smiling words. Now her head was bowed down in her hands, her shoulders shaking violently. She was sobbing uncontrollably, venting all the pent-up anxiety in a rush of release. Tears of joy, unbridled, unashamed, ran down my mother's face and the faces of countless others up and down the noisy street.

We held each other tightly, squashing our parcels between us. The mob was getting thicker, and people were running helter-skelter, hugging and kissing tearfully, exuberantly, anyone and everyone. Mother mopped her eyes, calling to anyone who would listen:

"Isn't it wonderful?" my mother said, laughing and crying all at once. "THANK GOD, IT'S OVER, IT'S REALLY, REALLY OVER."

They were dancing now and singing. Men and woman spontaneously caught strangers as partners and swung them in the street. Someone started the silly gestures to *"Hands, knees and boomps-a-daisy,"* and we joined in clapping our hands, first together then onto our knees and then turning our backsides, bouncing our bums together, whooping and yelling at the top of our lungs. A man nearby yelled: "Three cheers everybody" and the familiar cheer reverberated, gleefully: "Hip Hip Hooray, Hip Hip Hooray, Hip Hip Hooray." We were getting a bit hoarse, but still we shouted and cheered. The gaiety knew no bounds, and more people joined the noisy crowd with each moment. The bells were deafening and the guns roared on. Mother and I wanted to move, but the crowd was milling around us, blocking the way. We were caught up in the swirling joy, and we were loving it.

I don't know how long we stayed, milling with the rest of the joyous group, before we finally inched our way down the street toward the steps that would lead us home. All across the bridge and up the wide avenue, past the remains of the bomb damage, the crowds were celebrating victory. It was the same at our street. Front doors were flung open and the occupants of the houses were out on the street. We could hear the church bells near and far joyfully pealing. Guns from surrounding areas were booming the glad tidings. A wonderful madness had gripped us all. There was singing and dancing in the streets throughout the night.

The next morning we stripped the windows of the heavy blackout curtains and cleaned the tape from the window panes. It was hard to believe that we would no longer be enslaved by our enemies. But old habits die hard. We continued to carry our gas masks, forgetting we no longer were obliged to do so. We were attuned to listening for the siren, and we caught ourselves still trying to hear it.

For the next few months we relearned the art of living freely. The fear of attack began to leave us, and we turned our thoughts to the future. Rationing stayed in place for about two years after peace was declared, and shortages of goods and services remained critical. Britain had suffered through six long years of deprivation. We were lean and weary, tired of the bloodshed, and now we were faced with more years of struggle to rebuild the nation. It would take time and energy, but as in war, so in peace, we would muster our courage.

We were grateful to our Allies who stayed to help. The Americans could have packed up and gone home, but thankfully they didn't. It took nearly two years for the Holton Air Base to close down to a skeleton crew. At Bovingdon, the Base where Neal was assigned, it took even longer.

I had recently returned to Wembley from Wenhaston. I had continued to work at Holton for a few weeks after the Christmas with the Borrotts, but I began to struggle with bouts of depression while I lived at Majuba House. Dark thoughts of suicide began to plague me again. I could not explain nor justify my strange moods. At Christmas the house had seemed to be shrouded in a dark cloud. There was a coldness, a forbidding clamminess, that seemed to settle over it and me. It seeped into my very heart and soul. I spent my days working and my nights sitting with Mummy in the gloomy house. It was more than I could bear.

Dora tried to shake me out of the "doldrums" as she called it. I was glad to have her as my friend, but nothing seemed to help. I'd lost interest in going to Southwold since Neal had been transferred to Bovington. He wanted me to come were he was, telling me there were jobs on the Base, but I didn't want to go. I wasn't sure what I wanted or where I wanted to be. Dora and I went to the Halesworth socials a few times, but the town had so many memories of Owen, I couldn't enjoy being there.

My mother wrote to me and asked me to come to Wembley with her. She said the Zepp Dry Cleaners, where she worked part time, was looking for office help. She thought I ought to apply. I had put my application in and was waiting for word from them on the day the war ended. A few days later, when mother went to work, the manager told her he would like me to come in for an interview. I was glad of the chance. Though I was nervous, I must have said the right things because the manager hired me.

I went to work in the office with several women who quickly showed me how to compare and add ticket totals and do filing. It was a good job, and there was the possibility of advancement. In a matter of months I transferred to the front office as receptionist. I learned to use the switchboard and sat with the headphones on. I took incoming calls and routed them to the correct offices, and placed outgoing calls for the busy executives. It was good to be at home with the family in the evenings. Neal came to visit whenever he could get a pass, and we wrote to each other on a regular basis.

My life revolved around the two daily posts, work and family. My sister Betty lived a short distance away and now had a brand new baby, my first nephew, Christopher. He was the sweetest baby I'd ever seen. He had lovely, blonde curly hair, a beautiful smile, and a lovable, cuddly disposition. Occasionally, when Doug's duty kept him away, I went down the road to spend the night with them. It was always such a treat to spend time with Betty and the baby. She in turn visited Mother and the rest of us frequently.

Both my older brothers and my sister Phyllis were serving too far away to make many visits home. Reggie's letters came from various ports of call, from Clyde Bank in Scotland, from Rangoon, and then Ceylon. His letters were infrequent, but always full of good cheer and amusing incidents. All the photographs we got from him included nice looking girls, a different one in every port. Eric's letters were a bit more regular and his photographs were of him alone or with his shipmates. Before he left England, Eric had pledged himself to a girl named Anne from Uxbridge. She came to our home for an extended visit while Eric was serving in Malta. After a few weeks she returned to stay with her mother to wait out the war.

Phyllis sent us letters too, to give us news of her whereabouts. When the war was over, the armed forces personnel were still in demand for a variety of duties. Phyllis and the majority of service men and women stayed with their units, helping to dismantle

weapons long after the fighting stopped.

My four younger brothers and sisters were all in school during the week. I enjoyed taking them on outings. As often as I could, I went with them to their favourite playground at Alperton park. It was a massive playground full of swings and slides and other equipment. I liked the chain of rings that hung from steel supports and allowed you to swing with your body from one to the other across a wide expanse. They were in graduated heights that challenged our ability. Naturally, we loved the competition. June was agile and was a strong competitor. The boys, Bob and John, were no slouchers. Maureen was content to find the swing she liked and stay on it until we had to leave for home.

There was a constant stream of letters from several friends in Wenhaston, but Dora was the most faithful. She had left Holton Air Base and was doing sewing at home again. Her children, now both in school, needed her attention during the day. She was waiting for her husband to be "demobbed" and was hoping that they would be able to move into a home of their own when he returned.

Neal wrote to me regularly and came to Wembley on many

weekend passes to see me. It was no secret to me or my family that he was seriously in love with me. He was most attentive in his own shy way. I liked his kind, thoughtful ways, his wit, and his wonderful sense of humour. It was no surprise to any of us when he asked me to marry him. It was no surprise to any one either that I was thrilled to accept his proposal.

Before he asked me to marry him, he made a point of taking my mother and stepfather aside to ask their permission. My mother thought that Neal was a fine gentleman for observing this ancient custom. Neal said he definitely wanted a church wedding, and I agreed. Mother explained to him that until I was eighteen, we couldn't get married in the Church of England without her consent and the Church's. It was settled that Mother would go with me to see the Rector of our Parish in Wembley. As it was nearly Christmas, we set a tentative date for March of the following year. We thought it would give us time to get organized for a nice church wedding.

Our plans nearly went awry, for no sooner had we set a tentative wedding date for March, than Neal had word that his unit was moving out for Germany in two weeks. He said he had put in a request to be allowed to stay until March when his normal enlistment period ended, but was not sure his request would be granted. He wanted us to try to speed up the process so that we could be married in case he was forced to leave. Meanwhile, he had re-enlisted for one year. That time would begin in April after his current enlistment ended.

Our Christmas that year was a mad rush of planning and preparations. Neal got a three-day pass for the holidays and arrived on Christmas Eve, loaded down with parcels. He brought us some special gifts of food from the Base. There were some tins of ham, fruit, and boxes of chocolates and sweets for the children that were practically impossible to get in our shops. He brought cigarettes, including a whole carton of Lucky Strikes for George, who was a fairly heavy smoker.

He brought me two pairs of nylons and a very special box containing an engagement ring. It had a thin gold band with a tiny solitaire diamond. He had bought it at Marks and Spencer's, and apologized for its small size. It was the best he could afford on his Army pay. It fit my finger perfectly and I thought it was beautiful.

Neal brought out his Bible on Christmas morning and read to us from Luke chapter two, verses one through twenty, the story of Christ's birth. Though we all knew the story by heart, we had never thought to read it as a family. Afterwards he prayed out loud, thanking God for the many blessings we had, and asking His guidance for our future. Praying like this was a new concept for me and my family. Neal told us that his family read the Bible and prayed together every day. He told us that they were including all of us in their daily prayers. It was a lot to take in.

Neal went back to Bovington on Boxing Day and my mother and I began to tackle the many tasks needed to get ready for the wedding. First, we had to get a copy of my birth certificate. I had to go into London to the Records Office for this document, and search through the tomes that were filed by year and in alphabetical order. In that era, hardly anyone kept birth certificates at home. It was common practice to locate one's own in the official records when needed. For all I know, that practice may still be the same today.

I was fascinated as well as intimidated by the spacious and gloomy building with its massive long tables and musty books. The large doorways with their shiny knobs and the dark paneled walls stirred a memory of the buildings at Dr. Barnado's Home. There was a formidable looking gentleman sitting at the reception desk. He looked up as I approached. I had the distinct feeling from his expression that he was annoyed by my intrusion.

"Can I help you, Madame?" he asked officiously as I neared.

When I told him my mission, he sighed faintly, attached his pince-nez across his nose, and opened a large volume from the stack in front of him. After several questions about the year and place of my birth, he found a page and ran his finger down it. Finally he looked up, and removing his glasses, pointed me toward the correct room. He gave me some brief instructions before turning back to his desk.

It was like a treasure hunt going through volumes of handwritten entries before locating the record of my own birth. It took me ages, but there was something delightful about finding the information recorded there. I found my father's and mother's full names and the home address where I was born, 35 Richmond Road, Dalston. Finding this information gave me a sense of belonging that was extremely gratifying.

After I took the information to the clerk, I had to wait my turn to get the certificate made out. There was a charge of two shillings, which I gladly paid to take this precious document home with me. I wrote to Neal and told him all about my experience. I also told him that once again I had been to London and still hadn't seen Nelson's Column.

The next thing on the agenda was a visit to the church. I took a day off from work to go with my mother to see the Rector. We found the Church office, and my mother did the talking for both of us. The Rector was pleasant. He told us that on short notice we couldn't post the Banns, but if my mother was agreeable, he would waive that formality. Neal had to send papers from the Base confirming his bachelor status, and there were a few other details that needed working out. The Rector set the wedding date for the tenth of January 1946. I believe Neal and I must have had the shortest engagement on record.

It was a rush to get ready. I had no time to prepare properly. Betty helped pull it all together. She gave me a pale blue dress that was the smartest one she owned. It was slightly big for me across the shoulders, but fitted everywhere else. I went to a shop on High Street in Wembley and found a pair of leather shoes with unusual looking wedge heels. I thought they looked American, and I bought them despite the fact that they cost a whole week's wages.

My mother and sister Betty made all the preparations at top speed. Flowers and silver horseshoes appeared and Mother lent me her prayer book to carry in my hand. Betty hired a car to take us to the church, an unthinkable luxury. It was a beautiful Bentley and was adorned with white ribbon stretching from the high bonnet ornament to each side of the front doors.

Neal arrived the evening before the wedding and stayed with Doug and Betty. They met the rest of us at the church at the appointed time. My sister Phyllis was able to get a few days leave to come to the wedding. My mother gave me away, Betty was Matron of Honour, Maureen was bridesmaid, and Doug was Neal's best man. My two younger brothers Bob and John put on their best clothes so they too could be part of the festivities.

June stayed at home to take care of Christopher. She and my

two older brothers were the only ones missing from the family gathering. It was not possible for Mummy Saunders or any of my Wenhaston friends to travel to London to attend the wedding. Instead they inundated us with congratulatory cards and letters.

Surprisingly it all worked like clockwork, but not because of any organization on my part. I was so nervous I could barely remember my own name. The words that I had learned by heart were now said over me as I stood trembling at the altar.

"Dearly Beloved, we are gathered together in the sight of God...," the Rector intoned. My brain repeated the phrase, "In the sight of God." My heart skipped a beat. Up until now, these words and their meaning had been play acting for me. I had taken them lightly, because they hadn't seemed real. At this moment I realized how serious the words were and the fact that I was committing myself for life, "until death" to this man beside me. I found myself crying. Neal gripped my arm anxiously. He'd taken his glasses off and had to peer closely to see why I was shaking so much. Betty handed me a handkerchief so I could blow my nose. On the way back down the aisle, Neal asked what the matter was. I told him I was nervous. I was, too.

Neal & Joyce's Wedding
10 January 1946

When we stepped outside the church, an amateur photographer who happened by took our picture. I hadn't noticed him until Betty told us all to assemble ourselves for the photographer. We shuffled around a bit. Someone told him to hurry up, that we were freezing to death. We all laughed and at that moment the camera clicked.

Mother had prepared a meal for us at home that she called a Wedding Breakfast, even though it was now lunchtime. Neal and I left soon afterwards. He had booked a hotel in London for three days for our honeymoon. He was lucky to have found a room for us because the hotels were packed to overflowing. He was luckier still to have been able to afford a hotel in the heart of the city. The desk clerk asked Neal for proof that we were married, so Neal produced our marriage certificate showing that we had been married at St. John's Church in Wembley earlier in the day.

We most wanted to see the Houses of Parliament, Big Ben, St. Paul's Cathedral and Westminster Abbey. They had all sustained damage from the Blitz. We were able to go inside some of them, but not all. Fortunately, though we had little money, we were able to get around London for a few pennies by bus and visit many of the most important places. One day we were able to hear the boys choir at St. Paul's. They were practicing singing, *"I Know That My Redeemer Liveth."* I thought it was the most beautiful singing I had ever heard. Neal loved music, and was as thrilled as I was. We both stood transfixed as the sound of their singing soared around us.

We did see a good bit of London. We walked through Hyde Park and visited the London Museum and I finally got to see Nelson's Column. It gave me a pang to realize that one of the reasons I wanted to see it had been to relate that experience to Dadda, who could not travel to see it himself. I thought about Uncle Aubrey and Carly-luv, wondering what they would have thought about my being all grown up and married to an American soldier. How much my life had changed since they had helped me make my girlish plans to visit London.

The irony of my youthful years mixed with my grown-up status was brought home to me more strongly on the last day of our stay. Not having very much money between us, we had been careful to visit only places that either didn't charge admission or that only cost a few pennies. We were down to our last few shillings and had to save some of it for our fare back home. Neal had to get back to the Base the next day and I had to get back to my job at Zepp's.

We discovered that in London there were theatres that showed Disney cartoons all day long, something we both loved. Once we'd paid for the tickets, we were able to sit through the cartoons several times. Our money being in short supply, we hunted for ways to stretch it. For instance, we couldn't afford to eat dinner at the fine restaurant at our hotel, but breakfast was included in the price of the room. We had one good meal each day.

In the afternoons we hunted for tea shops and small cafes to have our afternoon and evening meal. On this, our last day in London, we had a breakfast of boiled eggs and toast at the hotel. Neal had tried the kippers, which were saltier than he could endure. Now in the late afternoon, we were hungry again. We found the theatre and before we went in looked around for something to take in with us to eat. As it happened there was a greengrocer's shop a short distance from the theatre. With my identification card, showing I was under eighteen, we were allowed to buy a bunch of bananas. What an ironic twist it seemed to be. Here I was sitting with my new husband in a cartoon theatre in war torn London, eating bananas for supper, laughing my head off at the antics of Donald Duck.

For the next two months while Neal searched for a place for us to stay in Bovington, I stayed in Wembley. I was still working at Zepp's, and because we were so short of money, I wanted to keep my job as long as possible. Neal had been granted an extension to stay in Bovington as he had requested until his normal enlistment ran out. His one year reenlistment would officially begin in April. We hoped he'd be able to spend the year in England, but it was not to be.

Neal got passes and came up to see me almost every weekend. He loved London and wanted to see as much of it as he could. It was too expensive to stay in London, so we made day trips into London from my mother's house in Wembley. We went to see everything, and to save money, we walked from place to place rather than take taxis or buses. It was fun and we both enjoyed exploring London.

In March I started to have sharp pain in my side whenever I walked very far. I wondered briefly what appendicitis felt like. I had heard that it was painful. One weekend that Neal was home on a pass, we had walked the streets of London 'til I could walk no more. Usually the pain stopped as soon as I sat for a while, but this time it didn't. By the time I got home, I could not stand up. The pain was unbearable, and I had started to hemorrhage. Mother got the doctor for me, and he immediately sent for an ambulance to take me to hospital.

I should have talked things over with my mother or sister when I first felt the pains, but I didn't understand enough to realize what was happening. I hadn't known I was pregnant. I wished with all my heart I had talked with them, and perhaps I could have prevented the miscarriage. Upon my arrival at the hospital, I was taken into the operating theatre and knew little of what went on after that. Neal had to report back to the Base, but my mother came to see me each day while I was in hospital. She talked with the doctor and then explained to me that the excruciating pain was caused because the foetus was caught in the Fallopian tube and the tube had burst. The doctor said that had we not got to hospital when we did, I would likely have bled to death. He also told mother that they had repaired the tube as best they could, but it was impossible to save the baby. It was a hard blow for Neal and for me.

Soon after I came out of hospital, Neal was able to find a room in a private home a stone's throw from the Base. The landlords, Mr. and Mrs. Covington, were a middle-aged couple who took in boarders. They included two meals a day for me in the price of the room. Neal ate at the mess hall on the Base. It was a nice arrangement.

For entertainment, we went to see American films at the Base theatre. Neal also took me to the Base chapel to the Christian service on Sunday mornings. I enjoyed the services, particularly the singing. Neal was sometimes asked to play the piano, which was something he loved to do. I was surprised to find that a lot of the hymns that were sung in the American Church service were the same as those that were sung in England. I couldn't get over the informality of the religious services and the familiarity of calling the Chaplain by his first name, which was Ron.

There were other differences, too. When Ron finished each sermon, he gave an invitation. He would always invite anyone who didn't know Christ as Saviour to come forward. He said salvation was a free gift from God and it was up to each of us to either take it or reject it. Very often one or two would go to the altar, and Ron would pray with them while we sang a final hymn.

We gathered again with Ron and a large group each Sunday evening for an informal Bible study. We met in the "Rec. Center," a Quonset hut that was sparsely furnished with a few tables and chairs. There was a pool table at one end of the large room, and there were two tables for table tennis down the centre. There was a snack bar down across the room from the entrance. Every Sunday evening there would be a lot of shuffling, moving things to make space for everyone. There were never enough chairs, so we sat on the floor. Afterwards the group stayed to chat, and to have coffee and doughnuts.

The Bible study was totally different from anything I had done before. This was not just memory verses or reciting psalms. Each of us took our Bible with us and followed along in ours as Ron read from his. Neal and I shared his Bible. I was horrified to find that he had underlined and marked passages, writing little notes beside some of them.

Ron told our group that the only way to get to truly know the Lord was to study His word. He said that God had preserved His word through the ages for our enlightenment and instruction. The study was in Second Corinthians. The group had already gone through the first book of Paul's letter to the Corinthians, but I didn't have that as a background. However, Ron was aware that his students were working on different levels of Bible knowledge, and made his lessons understandable for all of us. I liked the way he verified and expanded the text by leading us to look at other parts of the Scriptures.

I had never heard the story of St. Paul's conversion. In fact I didn't realize it was in the Bible. Ron showed us in the New Testament, in the book of Acts, chapter nine, the whole account of Saul of Tarsus. What an amazing story it was. Saul was a religious leader of his day who dedicated his considerable talent and energy to persecuting Christians. When he met the Lord Jesus Christ on the road to Damascus, he was forever changed. Though his name change from Saul to Paul was significant, the most incredible change in him was his change of heart. Ron likened Paul's prior personality to that of a tyrant, one who was intelligent, powerfully placed and well respected by the rulers of Rome.

Ron said that the remarkable thing about Paul was that once he accepted the Lord, he became as passionate a teacher of the gospel of Jesus Christ as he had once been a tyrant persecutor of Christians. Paul's background, his early life as a student of Old Testament law, should have made him a prime candidate to look for and receive Jesus the Messiah. Paul was a respected member of the religious community, the Sanhedrin, and had studied under the most revered scholars of his day. But he was totally and blindly ignorant of the true message of salvation until Jesus met him in the road.

Knowing the story of Paul made it easier to study his letter to the young church that he had founded at Corinth. It was obvious that he was dedicated to Christ and to building the Christian faith. His message to them conveyed a depth of concern and understanding that struck a chord with me.

Each time I attended the study I learned new things. And each time I learned something new, I had a dozen questions about how the Bible related to me in the day and age in which I lived. I had always thought that the message, the instructions, and the reproofs of the Bible were for a day and an age that was gone. I came to learn slowly that the Bible is the "living word," that though the world changes; customs, styles and worldly governments pass into oblivion, God's word is timeless and unchanging. It was a wonderful dawning of truth for me.

One question haunted me above all others: "How can I know beyond a doubt that salvation is for me?" I wondered about it and asked Neal. Neal pointed out a scripture in Romans, chapter ten, verse thirteen: "For whosoever shall call upon the name of the Lord shall be saved." Neal said that this was God's promise to us and that God never broke His promises. How then, I wanted to know, could I gain the ability, the faith, to believe God's promises are true. He pointed me to another scripture in the same chapter, verse seventeen which says: "Faith cometh by hearing, and hearing by the Word of God."

He said, in other words that God would give me the faith to believe, and my faith would grow as I listened, read, and studied the

Bible. It was a beginning. Ron's study in second Corinthians lead the group through the concept that when we give ourselves to Christ, our bodies become God's dwelling place. This idea was totally new to me and I was fascinated by it. In the fourth chapter, starting at verse four the Bible says (in a modern, understandable translation):

> "The god of this age has blinded the minds of unbelievers, so that they cannot see the light of the gospel of the glory of Christ. ... For God...made his light shine in our hearts to give us the light of the knowledge of the glory of God in the face of Christ." (NIV)

Our teacher explained that before we come to Christ, we are so blind that we are unable to take in spiritual truth. Once we accept Christ, the scripture tells us, "We have this treasure in earthen vessels" (our earthly bodies). In other words, God takes up residency in our bodies. He comes to live in us, when we invite Him in. What an awesome concept. I began to imagine God not "out there" somewhere, but actually living within me. It seemed incredible that my body could become God's home. I couldn't wait to know more about this.

Now that I had begun to learn a little of how God works, I was hungry to know more. One of my childhood questions had been: "What is Heaven like?", and more importantly, "How do I get there?" No one had ever answered those questions to my satisfaction. Dadda had mainly avoided my questions, but had indicated that if we were "good" all our lives, God would take us to heaven when we died. My own notion had been that if I didn't quite measure up, but at death had a Rector who said the right prayers over me, God might accept me.

I was beginning to discover that I could never be good enough on my own to warrant a place in heaven. If I never told a lie, if I never swore, if I never stole a penny nor hurt another human being, I still couldn't be good enough. No person, no priest or Bishop could open the door to heaven for me. Christ, I was discovering, is the door to heaven and only through trusting in Him would I be able to enter.

I found out that salvation can't be purchased by good works. It is a gift from God that can only be granted through the blood of Jesus and taken by faith. In Ephesians chapter two, verse 8, I found these words: "For by grace are ye saved through faith; and not of yourselves: it is the gift of God; not of works, lest any man should boast." How could I learn to lean on these words? Ron had been leading us through chapter four in second Corinthians, teaching us to look for God's guidance and trusting Him by faith to lead us. At the end of the chapter were these words:

> "While we look not at the things which are seen, but at the things which are not seen; for the things which are seen are temporal; but the things which are not seen are eternal."

"But how can we believe things that we are not able to see?" someone asked. "Only by faith," Ron replied. "And," he continued, "Jesus told doubting Thomas that there's a special blessing to those who have not seen Him and yet believe." (John 20:29)

The imagery of Jesus as the "door" providing entrance to God's house intrigued me. I had heard of the "house of the Lord." In school I had recited the twenty-third Psalm many times. It ends with, "...and I shall dwell in the house of the Lord, forever." David believed that God would allow him to go to that heavenly home. I recalled the stories of David and remembered the terrible sins of adultery and murder he committed. Yet David was sure of his standing with God. I still had a long way to go before I could make certain connections in the scriptures.

I struggled to relate my earthly situation with things beyond. The door to my mother's and stepfather's home in Wembley was always open to me. I was welcome there and I knew it. I liked the house, but it was not a permanent home for me. It was always temporary.

As a child I had given my heart to Majuba House. It had absorbed and enchanted me. There had been boundless human love in that house, and I thought mistakenly it would always stay the same. Lately though, I was beginning to see the house with new eyes. It seemed to have grown cold and unfriendly. I had outgrown its security, and there was a forbidding air about it. I wanted to cling to the ideal of childhood, but God was moving me from the temporal and turning my eyes toward a more permanent home with Him.

I was beginning to grasp the germ of an understanding, when I came across the beginning verses of Second Corinthians, chapter five:

> "For we know that if our earthly house of this tabernacle were dissolved," (speaking of physical death) "we have a building of God, an house NOT MADE WITH HANDS, eternal in the heavens. For in this we groan, earnestly desiring to be clothed upon with our house which is from heaven."

My heart leaped with joy at the promise of a new home in heaven. I was learning, as so many others before me had, that God Himself has prepared a home in heaven for His children, for those who want to be with Him. I couldn't then, and I cannot now, image how beautiful it will be. I began to look at the earth and see the beauty of God's creation with new eyes. I saw the perfection with which He has made the smallest flower and the highest mountain, and I was awestruck. To think that the majesty and symmetry on earth is merely a foretaste of God's design for my heavenly home filled me with a hunger to know more of His love and power.

That first Bible study was the beginning of a long quest into scripture that has continued over the years. I constantly rediscover that there is always much more to learn. The Bible is truly a "fountain that never runs dry."

In April Neal was sent to join his unit in Germany. Before he left, he made arrangements and signed the necessary papers for me to immigrate to America. I was scheduled to leave for America the following month. I stayed with the Covingtons for a short while after his departure and then went home to Wembley to spend the final few weeks with my family.

After Neal left, there was much to do and not much time in which to do it. I had to find my way to places in London where I had never been before. First, I had to go to the Foreign Office to apply for a passport. Next, I had to find a studio to have photographs taken, small ones for the passport and larger ones to leave behind. Then I had to gather clothes and treasures to take with me. I was concerned that I wouldn't remember recipes for my favourite dishes, so mother gave me a "Good Housekeeping" cookbook to pack in my suitcase. Time was short. I would be leaving the country in a few weeks.

I needed to take one last look at Majuba house, and to say goodbye to Mummy and all my friends in Wenhaston. The house looked strangely unfamiliar to me as I walked toward it from the *Compass*. As I started past the Newby's house, I hesitated a moment and then knocked politely. For the first time in my life I had a legitimate excuse to visit this house. Mrs. Newby opened the door and invited me in. The house was messier than I remembered and smelled rancid. Conkers talked excitedly, rambling on to me for several minutes before I got a chance to say anything. I was not sure she recognized me or understood what I was telling her. Before I left, I dug into my purse and found a lipstick to give to her. She took it gleefully and offered me a cup of tea. I made my excuses and left, being careful to close the door quietly behind me.

Mummy was serving Mrs. Ethridge when I entered the shop. They both greeted me brightly, wanting to hear about my plans for going to America. I stayed for two days in my old room, feeling very awkward and strangely out of place. In the evening Mummy came with me to gather with the villagers at the *Compass*. There were not many of my school chums still in the village. Those that could join us made a lively crowd. Gonie had left for America, but her mother and sister Crenia were there with Joyce and Mrs. Borrott, Gladys, Kathleen, Bob, Walter, his mother and father and Dora. It was a pleasant evening.

After making many promises to write, I said goodbye to my friends. In the morning, Mummy and I talked of many inconsequential things. I got my bicycle out of the shed and she helped me load my case and all the bits and pieces I was taking with me. I was taking my beloved bicycle to my sister June, who was eagerly awaiting its arrival. Mummy said she was in a hurry to open the shop, and I had to catch the train in Halesworth. We stood outside the shop and she kissed me quickly.

Jean & Walter Wilson's Wedding

"Let me know how you get on," she said. "Lenny'll be home soon, and he'll be sorry he missed seeing you." We said "Cheerio" to each other. Both of us were afraid to linger. Neither of us wanted to think of or say anything that might be painful. I knew how she would hate it if I started to cry, so I prayed I wouldn't.

I took just a minute to sprint up the lane and say goodbye to Miss Danford. She was pleased that I had come to see her, and asked me to write to her when I was settled in America. On the way back down the lane, I saw Mr. Ellis outside and waved to him. He smiled at me, raised his hand in greeting and called over the fence to me,

"Mind 'ow you go then, girl. Mind 'ow you go."

My mother went with me to Southampton where I was to board the ship. I was glad to have her company. We talked a lot on the train, speculating about what America would be like and how I would fit in with my new family. She knew, as I did, that I would have to make many adjustments. She encouraged me to try my best, to make concessions if necessary in order to adjust. If I was truly unhappy, she told me, I could always come back home.

"The welcome mat will always be out for you, Pet," she said. I was glad to hear her say that, but somehow I didn't see that as a

June on Bicycle

possibility. Mother said she hoped some day "when she won the pools," to come to see me in America. I liked that idea. Ten years later, without winning the pools, she came for a visit and brought my youngest sister Maureen with her. The three of us toured Washington D.C. together.

I did not board the ship immediately at Southhampton. In fact, I did not know which day we would set sail. I'd been given directions to a place near the port where the Americans had set up a temporary housing area for the hundreds of G.I. brides who were waiting to be shipped to the States. I showed my identification at the gate and was allowed in. Mother and I said our goodbyes outside the gate. She smiled for me as I took her photograph with my Brownie camera. Then she took my face in both her hands and kissed me.

"God be with you, Pet," she said and then added, " 'til we meet again, God be with you." She looked at me fondly before she turned to go. I watched her walk away toward the train station. She was wearing her jaunty black hat with the white trim round the brim. It bobbed up and down as she walked. When she reached the corner she looked back, smiling and waving. We blew kisses over the short distance to each other and waved again before we each turned away.

We sailed from Southampton in May, 1946. It was a ten-day voyage on the Edmund B. Alexander, a converted troop ship. Up

Mother in Washington, DC

close, the ship seemed immense. I had only seen ships from a distance before, from the promenade at Southwold. There were nearly a thousand brides who sailed that day, all novice sailors. The ship was outfitted to carry troops, so while the quarters were adequate, there were no luxuries. We were assigned quarters and were given a diagram showing the layout of the ship which included six decks, the "mess deck," recreation lounges, and a ship's store. There were four lower decks and two above. The upper decks were for the girls who were pregnant or who had small children with them. The rest of us were packed in like sardines in the "below decks." We slept in hammocks that swung to the swaying of the ship and we shared community showers and toilets.

We had been told in our many briefings to stay on deck as much as possible, so we did. We were drilled in the use of life-jackets, and taught the meaning of the ship's bells and how to respond to the loud speakers that squawked and sputtered a good deal of the time. We could see land for a long distance after we left the dock. We saw the chalky white cliffs as we passed Dover. Most of us who had so often sung about them had never actually seen them. It was quite a thrill.

The second and third days out were stormy and the sea was rough. It was impossible to go up on deck and nearly everyone was seasick. But by the fifth day, the weather was pleasant and we spent the time on deck wrapped in our coats writing letters, reading, and sitting in deck chairs talking to each other. Two days before we arrived in New York, the weather changed dramatically. The sun was hot on deck and we came out of our woolen coats and jumpers to bask in the sun.

It was a thrill to see the Statue of Liberty as our ship pulled into New York harbour. Some of the girls were met by their new relatives in New York. The rest of us were organized to travel to other destinations by train or bus. The group of us going to Baltimore was almost the last to leave the ship. We were taken by bus to the train station, and guided by Red Cross workers to our proper destinations.

Neal and his sister-in-law Gwen met me at the train station in Baltimore. I was surprised and pleased to see Neal. When I left England he was not sure that he would be able to get leave for my arrival in America. Neal introduced me to his family. His mother had written to me several times, so I felt I already knew her. She hugged me warmly. His father hugged me too. His younger sister Mary Sue was fifteen. She told me we'd be sharing her room when Neal returned to Germany. Neal's older brother Fletcher, his wife Gwen and their two boys Pat and Mike, completed the family. They welcomed me warmly. It was a great beginning.

Neal gave me a whirlwind tour of Baltimore while he was at home, introducing me to all sorts of new places and things. He took me for a trolley ride into downtown Baltimore and showed me the school he had attended. He took me to a park where we had a picnic, and to the brand new multi-story Sears and Roebuck Department store. He took me to the corner drug store for an ice-cream soda and to the A. and P. Grocery Store where I first saw cantaloupes and watermelons. He took me to his church and introduced me to Pastor Otis B. Read, who prayed with us and asked God to watch over Neal as he traveled back to Germany.

Neal told Pastor Read that he hoped to be a missionary and that we would be looking for a posting when his year was up with the army. Pastor Read said that we should come to see him when Neal returned. Meanwhile, he told us he would join with us in prayer to seek God's guidance for us. I thought being a missionary was a noble calling, but I still had doubts about my standing with God. I didn't see how I could be much help to other people when my own heart was so filled with fear that I could not live up to God's standard of excellence. I had questions about whether I could be forgiven for my hateful behavior toward Dadda. Though I tried hard to bury the past, it haunted me that I was somehow responsible for his death. I worried whether suicide was a sin, and if so, would I be held responsible for causing his death? I agonized silently about whether I could be forgiven.

I know I was trying to resolve these issues intellectually, and at times, as in Ron's Bible study class, I came close to grasping the truth. Though I didn't know it then, God was leading me through a maze of experiences. In His own time, step by step, God would reveal Himself to me. For the moment I struggled to find my footing, contenting myself with small glimmers of light. I didn't yet know the true joy that awaited me.

Neal's leave was soon over. It was difficult to see him go. He would be gone for nearly a year before I saw him again. Meanwhile we wrote to each other faithfully and there was much to tell each other in our letters. I soon got into the household routine. Mary Sue was a good roommate and we became inseparable friends. We lived in a small community known as Hamilton, a suburb of Baltimore. Neal's mom drove me to the Social Security Office in her big black Packard car. I needed to get a card with a number that would allow me to work. I was fortunate in being able to get a job a few weeks after my arrival.

My first job was serving behind the counter in a drug store a few blocks from home. This shop resembled the chemist's shops I had known in England. It had no soda fountain or tables and chairs as did the other drug stores in Hamilton. I could identify with the paneled walls and the neat display cases and the sterile looking glassed-in prescription counter across one end. It even smelled the same. It was a pleasant place to work.

Mary Sue was out of school for the summer. It seemed incredible that at fifteen she still had three years to go before graduating. She had her own radio and book shelves in our shared room, which I thought was total luxury. The Baltimore summer weather was hot and humid, sometimes unbearably so. We spent a lot of time in the evenings sitting on the porch in the swing, listening to the radio and sucking on ice cubes. Sometimes we walked down the street to the corner shop to get a cold drink. We bought chocolate bars, Almond Joy and Mounds, and Mary Sue taught me to put salty peanuts in our bottled Coca-Cola.

I attended the Baptist church with the family on Sunday mornings. The services were similar to the ones Ron had conducted in Bovington, with Pastor Read giving the invitation at the end of each sermon. There were times when I would like to have gone to the altar, but something always seemed to be holding me back. It almost seemed as though I was in a tug of war.

The congregation was getting ready to move out of the Baptist church at the time I arrived in Baltimore. There was a lot of excitement about the new building that was soon to be built a short distance away. The new church was to be non-denominational and would be called "The Church of The Open Bible." By way of preparation, the church erected a massive tent on the new building site in which to hold Revival services during the summer. They invited a number of different preachers to speak, and special musicians came to lead the singing.

The huge tent was packed every night and many people went forward when the invitation was given. It was a totally new experience for me. The singing captivated me. There were new tunes that were joyful and lively, with words that were easy to learn and sing. The night air, even after sundown, was stifling. The ushers had put paper fans on each of our folding chairs, along with the song sheets. The congregation fanned while they were seated, and when they stood to sing, they shouted "Hallelujah," and "Praise the Lord." It was a whole new, wonderful world.

The preachers that came to speak were terrific speakers, knowledgeable and well-versed in the Scriptures. Each illustrated different aspects of scripture, and while some were more eloquent than others, all gave invitations at the end of their sermons. On one of these nights Pastor Read preached the sermon. He took his text from John, chapter three. It had to do with a man named Nicodemus, who came to talk to Jesus about how he could be saved. Pastor Read explained that this man was a learned man: a Pharisee, a ruler of the Jews.

He came to Jesus by night, possibly because he was afraid or ashamed to come to Him in the daylight. He came to Jesus because he was curious. He wanted to know something about God that he couldn't find out from the learned scholars of Israel. Nicodemus recognized that Jesus was no ordinary man because of the miracles he was performing daily. When he approached Jesus, Nicodemus immediately called Him "Rabbi" or teacher, which was a term of respect and honour. Nicodemus came to Jesus as one intellectual to another, wanting to understand the supernatural power Jesus possessed.

Jesus told Nicodemus, "Except a man be born again, he cannot see the Kingdom of God." Pastor Read paused and emphasized this point. He said that until we commit ourselves to God, we are blind and unable to see or understand spiritual things. Nicodemus continued to question Jesus, mystified as to how he could be "born again." Obviously Nicodemus could not comprehend the rebirth Jesus was talking about. Jesus explained to him that it was a spiritual, not physical, birth. When Nicodemus continued to be puzzled, Jesus said to him: "Art thou a master of Israel, and knowest not these things?"

It was to Nicodemus that Jesus explained the incredible love of God that brought Him to earth to give us the gift of eternal life. Jesus said: "Whosoever believeth in Him should not perish, but (shall) have everlasting life. For God sent not his Son into the world to condemn the world; but that the world through him might be saved." He went on to say "He that believeth on Him is not condemned; but he that believeth not is condemned already." Pastor Read explained that every person has a choice to make while he is alive, that to hear the truth and ignore the invitation is to choose condemnation.

"Think of salvation as a gift, because that's what it is," he said. "Think about the gift God wants to give you that is the most precious treasure on earth: FORGIVENESS FOR SIN. God holds this gift out to you. In order to possess His forgiveness, you must reach out and take the free gift God offers you." To know "about" the gospel will not save you, he said. God has promised us that as far as the East is from the West, so far will He remove our transgressions from us, if we ask Him."

He quoted scripture from Isaiah 1:18: "Though your sins be as scarlet, they will be as white as snow."

"There is no sin so bad," Pastor Read continued, "that God can't forgive it. Come to Jesus. Trust in the power of His blood to cleanse you of all unrighteousness."

I wanted God's forgiveness more than anything I'd ever wanted in all my life. I'd been carrying my load of guilt for a long time. I saw the possibility, and I wanted to take the free gift of salvation while it was being offered. Pastor Read went on to talk about the security of God's salvation.

"When you come to Jesus, His love will never let you go. Nothing on earth will ever be able to separate you from the love of Christ." He asked us to turn in our Bibles to the eighth chapter of Romans and begin reading at the thirty-eighth verse:

> "For I am persuaded, that neither death, nor life, nor angels, nor principalities, nor powers, nor things present, nor things to come, nor height, nor depth, nor any other creature, shall be able to separate us from the love of God, which is in Christ Jesus our Lord."

The Holy Spirit touched me. When the invitation was given, I went forward to give my heart to the Lord Jesus Christ. It was the most precious moment of my life. Neal's Mom said that the angels rejoice in the heavens over each sinner who comes home. Through tears of joy, praise, and thanksgiving, our family rejoiced on earth for the new life that had been born.

That memorable tent meeting was held on the twenty-fifth of July, 1946. It was a Thursday. The following Tuesday I celebrated my eighteenth Birthday. I had indeed come a long way, but still had far to go.

I began a new life that night. I did not know then what was in store for me or how God would steer my footsteps. As a new Christian, I was like a baby learning to walk, teetering and stumbling often. It would take many years of study to learn His ways and to walk where He would guide. For this night, though, I was sure of His saving grace. I now had a new name and it was written down in glory, a new home not made with hands where I would dwell eternally, and the assurance that He would never leave me or forsake me.

Through the years I have learned to trust God's promises, each day a little more than the day before. As I allow Him to, He leads me onward. Though I constantly waver, He never does. His faithfulness constantly delights and amazes me. When I stumble, He picks me up, dusts me off and sets my feet back on the pathway. I'm thankful He is with me on my life's journey. My heart rejoices at the sure knowledge that He is in control of my destination. I can now say with confidence the words of David:

> "...and I shall dwell in the house of the Lord forever."

Printed in the United Kingdom
by Lightning Source UK Ltd.
116158UKS00001BC/7

9 781591 604730